Praise for *Angels in Vietnam*

One of the best books to come out of the Vietnam War. Dr. Fisher tells a story as only a combat veteran can tell it. The mud, heat, fear, frustration, sorrow, anger, detachment and anguish surrounding a young "grunt" draftee and his comrades will grab your heart and wring out your emotions. While many Vietnam veterans continue to deal with why they were chosen to fight, what they did while they were there and their personal chaotic road to recovery, he makes a convincing case for the fact that "there are no accidents."—Bob Resling. Lt. Col., (Ret) U.S.A.F. Pilot, Vietnam-Laos-Cambodia 1969-1972

"A harrowing evocation of the Vietnam War that portrays its haunting emotional legacy with—believe it or not— love and purpose."

"This is a compelling and triumphant story of one young man's life and destiny with the consequences of the Vietnam War."

Angels In Vietnam *is a must read for all Veterans of the American War in Vietnam. John's ability to "let it all hang out" in truth through words is remarkable. His story has given me the courage to move forward with my truth in my heart and hands.*—Daniel martin Vietnam Veteran, U.S.M.C.

"A completely different approach to the horrifying experience of the U.S. soldiers in Vietnam. It leaves you with purpose and meaning."

"A spiritual perspective of surfing and Vietnam—who would have thought that the two could combine for survival in a tragic wartime experience?"

For Samantha;

We don't always understand,
but "there are no accidents."

Angels
in
Vietnam

Please accept this gift
and love from . . .

JW Fisher

JOHN WESLEY FISHER

www.pronghornpress.org

Every blade of grass has its Angel
that bends over and whispers, Grow, Grow.

—The Talmud

Part I

The Quest

1

Charlie and Gage straddled their surfboards for nearly thirty minutes outside of the breaker line, waiting for the sea to move. It was late afternoon at Sunset Beach. They had been out in the water most of the day, riding the huge swell that had hit the Pacific Ocean islands. Though their bodies were exhausted, they sat poised to catch their last wave into the beach.

Gage looked over at Charlie with eyes bloodshot from the excessive exposure to the salt water. "Something ought to be coming, don't you think?" he asked, his voice impatient.

"Take it easy, man," Charlie said, slapping water at his friend. "You know how long it takes sometimes. Remember that time out at Newbreak? Shit! We must have waited twenty-five minutes to catch that last wave."

"I know, Charlie. That's what I'm worried about. It'll be dark soon and these waves are too big to be messing around with when you can't see what you're doing. Everybody else has gone in already. Maybe we should just paddle in."

"Not me, man. There's one more set out there and it's got a wave with my name on it," Charlie said. He looked out toward the horizon and saw a massive wall of liquid heading their way.

"Whoa, Baby! Look at that!" He turned to grin at his friend, but Gage was ahead of him, paddling out toward the oncoming waves.

"Get a move on it, Charlie!" Gage shouted.

The two California surfers had been riding the north shores of Oahu for three weeks. Charlie Armfield had come to the Islands to improve his surfing skills so he could compete with the top surfers on the competitive circuit. Gage Saltman had come because Charlie was his best friend, and Charlie could talk him into almost anything. This was by far the best day yet. The approaching swells promised to be the biggest challenge of their trip.

They lay on their stomachs stroking their arms into the water to propel the boards as fast as they could.

"Don't let it get you, Charlie!" Gage yelled. "Come on! We've got to get out there," he continued, struggling to catch his breath.

"I'm coming, I'm coming!" Charlie panted.

The approaching set appeared to have at least five waves to it, but getting over the first one before it broke was top priority. Usually, if a wave broke while they were paddling out, they were experienced enough to confront the white water. But with a swell this big, it would be a tough job, not only to make it through, but to hang on to their surfboards. If they got caught inside, the turbulence would whip them like socks in a clothes dryer.

They paddled as fast as they could, their hearts pounding a frantic beat. The wave was bearing down and it wasn't until the last moment they knew they could make it up and over. The next wave appeared to be even bigger and scarier.

"Damn it, Charlie. It's going to get us for sure."

"Don't think about it, man. Paddle your ass off."

As they ascended its huge face, the wave started to feather at the top like it was ready to break.

"Dig!" Charlie yelled. He inhaled a big breath and ducked through the lip of the wave breaking through to the other side. As he came out, he looked around to find his friend. Then he saw Gage being sucked backward by the pull of the passing wave.

"Stroke it, man, stroke it! You can make it," Charlie shouted.

Gage paddled, pulling at the water as hard as he could and finally broke free from the drag. But the next wave was just as big and Gage dropped behind. He started a double arm stroke to catch up. Charlie leaned back and gestured frantically to encourage his friend, until they were side by side again.

"Come on, Buddy! We better get going," Charlie said.

With strength they didn't know they had, they paddled with their hardest, most powerful strokes toward the next wave.

As he came up and over that one, Charlie decided to catch the one behind it. He continued to paddle out. At the last moment, he prepared for take off. He sat up, whipped his board around, and stroked into the biggest wave of his life.

He pushed up and sprang to his feet. His left foot was forward and his right foot was back, supporting his weight to keep the nose of the board from pearling into the water. He held his breath. His board screamed down the mass of water to the bottom of the breaker. Then, shifting his weight onto his left foot, he leaned into a turn that brought him into position facing the wave. Up ahead, a monstrous, roaring wall, more than twice his height, bore down on him. As it moved in toward the beach, it began to break behind him.

This is why you're here big guy, Charlie thought. *Let it all hang out.*

He manipulated his surfboard, using short, sharp turns on the face of the wave to increase his speed and to keep him out ahead of the breaking section. He shivered with exhilaration. Why not, man? Go for it!

With a deliberate turn, he cut his board back toward the crashing white water. Just before he hit the turbulence, he spun his board around to avoid disaster. He leaned back on his right leg to stall his forward progression. If he could slow down enough, he'd get inside of the breaking wave.

The water curled over him, creating a tunnel of pure speed. His mind raced, zigzagging back and forth from the sheer exhilaration of his accomplishment to the anxiety of possibly being overpowered. Three seconds in the tube seemed like minutes, but he kept his head up and drove his stick toward the illuminated opening at the end. He felt different—euphoric—was he even alive?

Just when he thought he could make it back out, the curl sucked him into itself. Charlie was ripped from his board into the white water. It held him under for nearly a minute before releasing him to the surface.

He gasped for air. Then, knowing the next wave was about to crash on top of him, he sucked in a breath and dove down to get out of the way. The wave caught him halfway and churned his body like a pebble in a cement mixer. He went limp, trying not to fight, to conserve energy. When the turbulence subsided, he swam toward what he thought was the surface, but he hit his head on the ocean bottom instead. That's when his breath gave out.

With no air left, he grabbed his nose and clamped his jaw shut to fight the urge to inhale. He kicked his way up to the surface and found a quiet sea. Inhaling deeply, he eased onto his back, and floated. Exhaustion dragged at his body.

Charlie knew his board had washed in with the wave. He faced a long swim to shore, but it had been an unbelievable tube ride, even if it ended in a wipeout. He bobbed along, trying to regain his strength, and let out a hoot, "Aaaaahhhhhooooo!" to signal Gage that he was all right.

When he finally reached the shore, he looked up and down the beach. His board was nowhere in sight. Two kids ran up, pointing toward the horizon. "Your board's been sucked out, *Haole*."

His surfboard, captured by a rip tide, was floating out to sea.

Charlie ran and dove into the current. He swam as hard as he could. The board was barely visible. Even though his arms felt like heavy rubber, he would not stop swimming. It was the only board he had. Stroke after stroke, fighting fatigue, he pulled himself through the water. When he thought that he couldn't force his arms to reach out again, he heard a voice.

"Hey, Charlie," Gage called. "Relax. I'm on my way."

When Gage paddled along side, Charlie grabbed onto the rail of his board like a lost whale calf finding its mother.

Charlie grinned, "What took you so long?"

"Come on, Charlie. We better get out there and find your board."

It was hard to paddle two on a surfboard, but Charlie knew it was a lot better than trying to survive alone. When they reached the drifting board, they were nearly a mile out to sea. The sun had dropped below the horizon. When they finally dragged themselves and their boards onto the beach, the full moon lit their way, charting their bedraggled steps across the sand.

Later that night, Gage turned to Charlie, who was already half asleep. "Hey, man, what was that wave like?"

"Incredible." Charlie yawned. "I was inside of a pipe and going so fast I can hardly explain it. At first I thought I had it made, but then the wave just overpowered me. I could hardly believe how much force there was."

Charlie propped himself on one elbow. "Before I wiped out, it felt really weird—like I was traveling to the center of the earth or something." He hesitated, then looked directly at his friend. "Gage, I know this is going to sound strange, but it almost felt as if I left my body for a moment. Like I became part of something else, part of a whole." He shrugged and dropped back on the pillow. "I don't know how else to say it."

Gage didn't answer. Worn out from their day, Charlie, too, fell asleep.

Later that week, Charlie and Gage were up early to enjoy the sunrise. With their sun-bleached hair and strong bodies nearly matching in physique, they often passed for brothers. Gage was ten days older than Charlie was— both of them nineteen. They had been inseparable since they were twelve, when they'd taught themselves how to surf.

With the Vietnam War in progress, both of them had registered for the draft, as required by law, when they turned eighteen. More introspective than Charlie, Gage worried that he might get drafted into the army.

Charlie remained oblivious to the draft. His dad, a Methodist minister, was mindful that Charlie could be drafted unless he was attending college. He persuaded Charlie to give it a try. After a semester of bad grades—the result of his preferring the beach to the classroom—Charlie quit school. His parents tried to convince him to stay in school to avoid being selected, but Charlie ignored their pleas. His only interest was the surf.

Despite his parents' objections, he pursued his sport's goal of becoming a champion surfer. Charlie intended to be good enough to be chosen for next summer's American Surf Team. He hoped to surf in the World Surf Contest, which would be held in San Diego, his hometown.

While Gage loved to surf, he worked at becoming a chef. He took a culinary arts course and intended to seek an apprenticeship. Now that he was out of school, he, too, was available for the draft.

Charlie had persuaded Gage to come to Hawaii to surf by agreeing to visit some of Honolulu's finer restaurants, not to eat, but to check out their menus. When one manager asked if they wanted to be seated, Charlie explained that they couldn't afford to eat there, but his friend was curious about the restaurant because he wanted to be a chef. The manager had taken them to the kitchen to give Gage a chance observe.

As they sat watching the sunrise, the air was peaceful, the water as smooth as glass. Suddenly, two dolphins cut through the water's surface, flew straight up in the air, bumped noses, and splashed down again on their bellies.

"Wow! Did you see that?" Gage asked.

"I sure did. Unbelievable!" Charlie exclaimed.

They sat for a moment, filled with awe.

"You know what, Gage?"

"What?"

"I think those dolphins know something we don't," Charlie said. "Have you ever noticed that they have a permanent smile on their faces?"

Before Gage could comment, an elderly Hawaiian man walked up to them. "Did you see the dolphins jumping?" he asked.

"Yes," Charlie said.

Gage nodded.

The old man nodded at Gage, and then at Charlie.

"You know, those dolphins are special," the old man said. "They used to live on the land like us, but they thought better of it. They even had legs, but they got rid of them. They still breathe air like we do, and they have pretty big brains like us, too. But they're civilized. They don't have wars or fight with each other like we do. No, sir. Dolphins are peaceful."

He nodded again, as if to emphasize the truth of what he'd said. "And you know what? They mate for life. I think they're the happiest creatures on earth." Smiling, the old man nodded again and started walking up the beach.

"Hey, man, thanks for all the information," Charlie called after him.

The old man stopped and looked back at Charlie and Gage. "You guys surfers?"

"Yes," they said in unison.

"Then you know some of those secrets of the sea...what those dolphins left land for. We can all learn something from the sea, if we just pay attention. You surfers ought to know about all of this." He turned and trudged up the beach.

Gage frowned. "What did he mean by that?"

"I'm not sure, but I've thought about it before. There's something about the water out there, something I haven't been able to put my finger on. When I paddle out for a session of waves, it's like something in me changes. When I take off on a wave, there's a whole different thing that happens. It's like the sea is trying to talk to me, Gage."

Gage lowered his head, continuing to frown, and ran his fingers through the sand.

"I tried to explain this to my Dad one time," Charlie continued. "He said it sounded like I was in another dimension. Like an ethereal space. Something that few clergy have even known. I don't know about that, but it's something different, something special. I want to understand it. But when I get wrapped up trying to figure it out, I seem to get lost."

Gage looked up, "Hey, it sounds good to me. Just go with it, man."

"I don't know. Maybe that is what's behind my wanting—no, *needing* to surf on the American team. If I get good enough to do that, maybe I will understand what's going on. What do you think, Gage?"

"Never gave it much thought. I love surfing as much as you do, Charlie. I just don't care that much for competition."

"You know, you really rip out there, Gage. You could compete if you wanted to. It's cool if you just love to surf. But for me, it's about learning something, too. Like what that old man was talking about."

Gage jumped up, pointing at the surf. "Look! I think it's starting to pick up. Hey, man, are we going to sit around and talk about it or get it on with the real stuff?"

They ran to get their boards and were immediately into another day of surf.

On the day they were scheduled to fly back home, they got up early for their last surf session. The waves were head high; the swell was smooth and glassy. The outside wave line was an easy paddle that day, only a few hundred yards with the smaller swell, and they were well conditioned after a few months of surfing in the challenging Hawaiian breakers.

Gage caught the first wave and rode it all the way into the beach. As he made his way back out, Charlie took off on a beauty. He began with a series of quick turns and then cut back into the curl line. After another big turn, the wave began to curl over and Charlie was inside of the tube for a few seconds.

When he popped back out, he cut back, turned hard and stalled by leaning back onto the tail of his board. When the nose of the board began to rise into the air, he leaned forward and walked up to the nose, put his left heel on the tip, and hung five toes over.

"Aaaaahhhhhooooo!" Gage hooted in admiration.

Charlie finished the wave by trimming his board right through a fast section and kicked out just before reaching the shoreline.

The day was a perfect example of how the whole trip had gone. They rode waves every day, and when they boarded the plane, they were a couple of stoked surf rats. Charlie felt that he was ready to show the world what he had learned in the Islands.

"I'm ready, Gage. Really ready."

"What's your first step?

"I'm going to enter as many contests as I can. You know what it was like for me before. Never could quite get over the top. Now I think I'm ready to rip."

"If you surf like you did today, Charlie, you'll be on the team by the end of the summer. Just in time for the World Contest."

"That's what I want Gage. That's exactly what I want."

"Only one thing I can see that might hold you back."

"What? I'm going to surf in that World Contest if it's the last thing that I do. I'm ready. I can taste it."

"What happens if you get drafted?" Gage had a grave look on his face.

Charlie looked at Gage in disbelief. How could he even think of such a thing? What would the army want with him? *I don't even know what in the hell they're trying to do in Vietnam. I'm a surfer, not a soldier. Nothing is going to stop me from surfing in that contest.*

2

The stage was set for the announcements of the early spring Redondo Beach Surfing Classic. Hoppy Swartz, president of the United States Surfing Association, walked up to the platform. A pioneer in California surfing, he was a tall, balding man who carried himself with dignity. The crowd quieted as he picked up the microphone.

He began with the junior winners, starting with the last place finisher and moving toward the first. Then he announced the men's division, again beginning with last place. The crowd applauded and hooted as the president read each name.

The crowd's reaction continued, until the second place finisher's name was called. A hush came over the crowd. Usually, when second place is announced, the crowd knows who the winner of the contest is because there is only one person remaining who it could possibly be. But this year's winner was relatively unknown to the winner's circle. Low murmurs ran through the crowd.

"And the winner of the Redondo Beach Classic is—Charlie Armfield."

A respectful, but reserved ovation began as Charlie made his way up to the stage. Respectful and reserved that is, except for a small contingent at the back of the crowd made up of Gage and other members and friends of the Las Olas Surf Club, including Charlie's girlfriend Cher Crowley. Charlie and Gage had been members of the Las Olas Club since eleventh grade.

"Aaaaahhhhhooooo!" cheered the group.

"Way to go, Charlie," Cher shouted.

"All right, Charlie!" Gage shouted so loudly that Charlie turned and grinned at his friend.

As Charlie received his trophy from President Swartz, the newly crowned Miss Redondo Beach stepped up to Charlie and planted a big kiss on his cheek.

"Aaaaahhhhhooooo! Aaaaahhhhhooooo!" Charlie's club chanted, jumping up and down at the back of the crowd. They continued to chant as Charlie came down from the stage and made his way toward them. All except for beautiful, blond Cher. She flipped her long hair over her shoulders and stood, hands on her hips, glaring at Miss Redondo Beach. Charlie noted Cher's reaction, but shrugged his shoulders and grinned at his friends, holding up the trophy for all to see.

The crowd broke up quickly, except for the Charlie Armfield supporters. They remained, crowding around Charlie, hooting and patting him on the back. This was a huge accomplishment for a member of their group, and they were in no hurry to leave.

Cher was silent on the beach and on the drive home in Charlie's van. He had purchased the 1960 VW van with his earnings from washing dishes at the A&W Drive In, shortly before he and Gage went to Hawaii. Still pleased with his purchase, he chose to enjoy the drive south on U.S. Highway 101, despite the chill from the passenger seat.

Charlie and Cher had been dating since their senior year in high school. Together they had enrolled at San Diego State College, where she continued as an art major after Charlie dropped out.

Finally Charlie said, "You're still mad about that smooch from the queen, aren't you?"

"Of course not," Cher snapped. "And she was certainly no queen."

"Right. Then what's the deal with your weird attitude? Aren't you happy for me?"

"Of course I'm happy for you. I'm just worried about what's going to happen next, that's all." Her voice softened. "I'm afraid, Babe."

"Afraid of what?"

"I'm afraid that now you're going to be so busy with surfing contests, you'll forget all about me," she said. "Besides, what if you get drafted and the army takes you away from me? Oh, Charlie." A tear ran down her cheek. "I'm so worried about you." She put her head into her hands and began to sob.

Little was said until Charlie pulled up in front of her house and turned off the engine. He put his arm around Cher. "First of all, I'm not going to forget about you just because I'm surfing more contests. Look at you. You're the most gorgeous creature on earth. How could I forget about you?"

Cher wiped her tear-stained cheeks and smiled up at Charlie.

"And second," he continued, "what would the damn army want with me anyway? I'm just a lazy, good-for-nothing surfer and they probably don't even know I'm alive. Hey Babe, can you imagine me marching around some jungle with a rifle, trying to kill somebody?"

She shook her head and put her arms around him.

"Of course not," Charlie said. "Now, put this crap out of your mind."

Just then they heard a noise and looked up to see Cher's father standing in the doorway, watching the van.

"Uh oh, I better get going. Give me a call tonight," she said, climbing out of the van.

Later that week, Charlie pulled his car into the driveway at his parents' house. He still lived at home, but he and Gage were talking about getting a place of their own. They had been short of cash since they returned from Hawaii, but Charlie had some news that just might change all of that.

"Well I did it!" Charlie yelled, banging the door open.

Charlie's parents, John and Louise, were sitting at the kitchen table, and looked up at their son with anticipation. Neither of them said anything, waiting for Charlie to continue.

"Well, don't you want to know what I did?" Charlie asked, annoyed by his parents' lack of response.

Louise held up her hand. "Hold on a second, Charlie. Before you tell us your news, I have to tell you something before I forget. The phone has been ringing off the hook for you lately, and you're never around for me to give you messages."

Charlie smiled, thinking he already knew what the calls were about. "Oh really. So who's trying to call?"

"The calls are from surfboard companies." She reached for the message pad by the phone. "Gordon and Smith phoned on Monday and yesterday Hobie, Con, and Hansen called. They want to know if you would be interested in riding on their team."

"Yes, I know. Isn't it exciting? Paul got the same phone calls."

Paul Macon was the advisor of the Las Olas Surf Club. He and his wife, Carol, lived alone down by the beach. They had no children of their own and had befriended some of the surfers. Paul actually helped a group of them form the Las Olas Surf Club before Charlie was a member.

"Paul got the calls, too?" John asked, with amazement.

"He sure did. I guess they really wanted to get in touch with me."

"So, did you call them all back?" Louise asked.

"Yes, I did. That's what I want to tell you. They all gave me a proposal to ride their surfboards. Hobie, and Gordon and Smith gave me the best deals, and I chose Gordon and Smith. I like the fact that they're locally owned here in San Diego. So I am now officially employed."

John and Louise had puzzled looks on their faces. "What do you mean, you are now employed?"

"I mean I will be getting paid just to ride surfboards. They put me on the payroll as a consultant so I won't cancel out my amateur status for the World Contest," Charlie grinned. "And not only that. Now I get free surfboards anytime I want. They're making me a new one as we speak."

"Charlie, what makes them think you will make the American Team?" Louise asked.

"Hey, man, they said that if I continue to surf the way I did last weekend, I'm a lock," Charlie said, feeling insulted.

John frowned. "I don't think that 'hey, man' is an appropriate way to address your mother."

"I'm sorry, Mom. I'm just so excited! This is the first positive indication that someone besides me believes I can make it. And, Mom, Dad, I am going to make it," Charlie said. "I know I am. And when I do, Gordon and Smith is going to add the 'Charlie Armfield Model' to their line of surfboards. I'm going to be famous."

"That sounds pretty good, Son. But listen, Charlie, would it hurt to enroll in school at the same time that you work on your goal?" John asked.

"Hey, you guys don't understand. Expert surfing isn't like some other kind of sport that you can do while you're studying in school. I'm going to have to put all of my attention into this deal. I need to hit it every day and concentrate on what I want to accomplish on each wave so I can be the best that I can possibly be. School work would bog me down. I'd be going nowhere fast that way."

"But what if you get...," Mike, Charlie's older brother, said, entering the room.

Charlie held up his hand to interrupt his brother. "Wait a minute. If you're going to try and put the fear of the draft in me, I'm not buying it. When I'm representing the Americans in the World Contest, why in God's name would they want me for the army? The way I look at it, I'm serving my country in something that's even bigger than the Olympics. Would they draft someone about to be in the Olympics?" Charlie asked.

"I don't know," Mike said.

"The answer is 'no.' You're sounding just like Gage and Cher. I need everybody to back me now. I'd appreciate your cooperation. Please?" Charlie pleaded. "Besides, Mike, what are you going to do when you graduate from college next year? Answer me that, smart man."

"I'm going to join the Peace Corps, Charlie. Maybe you should do the same."

"Well, maybe I would if I wasn't so damn busy with something as important as this," Charlie said. "Sorry about the language, Dad."

Louise reached over to grab onto her husband's hand. There was a tear in his eye, and it was not because of his son's language. John Armfield had been selected for the World War II draft more than twenty years ago. He'd opted to take a ministerial deferment, much like his eldest son would do, with the Peace Corps.

"What's the matter, Dad?" Charlie asked.

Louise spoke for her husband. "We're just worried about you, Son. Wartime is something we've lived through before."

"You don't have to worry about me. Vietnam isn't like that other war. We're not fighting to protect ourselves these days. They'll make exceptions when they find out I'm representing my country in another way. I just know they will." With that, he left the room, but hesitated outside the door to overhear the exchange between his parents.

"You know, Louise, I never could have imagined taking up arms against another man. We were being threatened, and I knew it was important that our country defend itself. But I thought it would be better to serve by helping people understand the strife, rather than being a part of it myself," John said.

"I know, Dear, but your son has a mission in his young life, and he can't see the bigger picture right now. All we can do is pray that he's successful in his endeavors, and pray even harder that the Vietnam War comes to an end soon."

During the early part of the summer, Charlie performed in a spectacular fashion on the competitive circuit. At Pacific Beach he received a first place award. He received second place awards at both Santa Monica and Oceanside, and won another first place at Huntington Beach. He felt that he was well on his way to getting the recognition he needed.

Gage stayed right by Charlie's side through the competition, until late June, when he received a letter from the board of directors of his Culinary Arts College. He called Charlie with the news.

"Charlie, you're not going to believe this. I finally got accepted into the apprenticeship program I've been wanting. I now have a job at Lubach's Restaurant down by the wharf."

"All right, Gage! I'm really happy for you, man. Hey, that's a pretty fancy restaurant, isn't it?"

"It sure is, Charlie. I'll be working from three in the afternoon until eleven at night, Wednesday through Sunday."

Charlie was silent on the other end of the phone.

"Charlie, are you still there?"

"I'm here, man. That means you won't be able to come to the contests with me anymore, doesn't it?"

"Sorry about that, man. But this is a really cool job, Charlie. You should see some of the stuff I get to make at this place. I've got to tell you, I've never been so happy in all of my life."

Charlie heard the excitement in Gage's voice. He had to be happy for him, even though Gage was his main man—his only support team. Gage talked to him about the wave conditions and, together, they planned Charlie's strategy. Gage knew how to pump him up and sometimes, literally, pushed him toward the water when it was time for his heat. As disappointed as he was that Gage wouldn't be with him, as uneasy as he was about being alone at contests, Charlie was happy for Gage.

Charlie's next contest was to be held at Hermosa Beach in the Los Angeles area. Usually it was just Charlie and Gage going to the contests. Sometimes Cher would show up for the finals, but his parents could never attend because of their involvement with the church on the weekends. Mike was always busy with school. This time Cher invited herself along. They drove up the coast to the Hermosa contest in Charlie's van.

It was the first contest without Gage, and Charlie was nervous. He wasn't talking much in the van, and he felt a twitch in his forehead.

"What's the matter, Babe?" Cher asked.

"Just a little apprehensive I guess. I can't believe Gage isn't here."

"Hey, I'm with you now, Charlie. Everything's going to be all right," she said.

Charlie managed to smile at her. He hoped she was right. While he enjoyed Cher's company, she didn't surf, and she certainly was no substitute for Gage at the contest. How would he do without his main man?

As it turned out, Charlie failed to make the finals. The intensity that made him successful in previous contests was missing at Hermosa Beach. He surfed well, but was beat out in the quarter-final heat.

Early the next morning, Charlie went to Gage's house to pick him up to go surfing. Since Gage didn't have to work until three in the afternoon, they went surfing every morning, except on the weekends when Charlie was away at contests.

Charlie pulled his van into the Saltmans' driveway. He climbed out and walked around to Gage's bedroom window, being careful not to wake anyone else. Gage always left his window open so Charlie could wake him in the mornings. He stuck his hand in the window, lifted the covers at the foot of the bed, and started pulling at the hairs on Gage's leg.

"Okay! Okay! I'm up! Damn, that's a rude awakening."

Charlie laughed. "Hey, man, I believe you started this tradition the day you got your driver's license and picked me up in the morning."

"Yeah, I know, but I still hate it. Be out in a minute."

When Gage got out to the van, Charlie was sitting in the driver's seat with a despondent look on his face.

"I didn't even get to the damn semis at Hermosa."

"So what the hell happened?" Gage asked.

"I don't know. It just seemed like I didn't have the drive or something,

Gage. It wasn't the same without you there, man.'"

"Hey, you had Blondie there to give you support. I'm surprised you didn't surf your brains out, just to impress her."

Charlie laughed and shook his head.

The next two contests went much like Hermosa Beach. He failed to make the finals at Carlsbad, and couldn't even get out of his preliminary heat at Manhattan Beach. The next contest would be at Ocean Beach where Charlie and Gage had learned how to surf.

Charlie gave Gage a call that Sunday night after driving home from Manhattan Beach. "I humiliated myself this time, man. Maybe I should just give up. That's three in a row, and I feel like I'm sinking fast."

"Don't worry about it, man. You're going to kick butt at O.B."

Charlie groaned. "Not the way I've been surfing lately."

"Listen, Charlie, all you have to do is come up with a new scheme, that's all. You need to figure out how to get in tune without me being around. I'm no damn lucky charm or anything. I was just able to help you get focused, that's all. You can do this by yourself, man. Get your head out of your ass, and I'll meet you at the beach in the morning," Gage said.

The next morning Charlie was down at the beach at dawn, waiting for Gage. Could he focus himself as Gage suggested? He had to do something. As he sat watching the waves, he started visualizing himself on his surfboard, paddling into a set wave. He saw himself ripping a big turn, walking to the nose and hanging ten. *Wow,* he thought, *this is really cool.*

He tried it again, seeing himself on the board. Over and over, he repeated the image. Mentally he'd caught fifteen waves before Gage arrived. When the two finally hit the surf, Charlie literally tore the surf apart.

"Hey, man, what the hell got into you?" Gage asked, when they came in out of the water. "I've never seen you surf like that."

Charlie shrugged his shoulders and grinned. Had what he had tried— repeatedly seeing himself ripping in the waves—had it really affected his performance? He couldn't be certain and he wasn't ready to talk about it. But one thing he knew, he was going to try it again. Maybe this was what Gage wanted Charlie to figure out for himself, so he could get himself in tune when Gage wasn't around.

Heck, Charlie thought, if this is all I have to do, I'm going to show the judges at Ocean Beach how to surf!

Before dawn on the morning of the contest, Charlie was up early, sitting on the beach visualizing his performance on the waves. He had practiced the technique every day that week, and had even started it at home in the evenings before he went to sleep. He had it down pat. First, he would get a sharp picture in his mind of the surf and how it was breaking. Then he inserted himself into the scene. If that was what it would take, he was well prepared.

By the time of the first heat, all of Charlie's surf club friends were there, including Gage, who could come in the morning because the contest was held at Ocean Beach. Cher was there, and his parents, too. With the contest being held at Charlie's home beach, he felt like he had a home field advantage. Not only was he familiar with the surf, he had familiar faces cheering him on, too.

He tried to keep mostly to himself. He wanted to visualize as much as he could, and didn't want to let Gage in on it, until he had proven that his system worked.

"What the hell are you doing, man?" Gage asked as he plopped down in the sand next to Charlie.

"Trust me on this one, Gage. I'm trying out a new focusing technique. If it works, I'll tell you all about it. Don't be offended, man, but I need some space before my heat."

Gage put his hand up over his head. Charlie grabbed it.

"You've got it, Buddy. Talk to you later."

Before Charlie began his first competition, there was the customary pre-heat conference. The six surfers in the heat gathered around the contest coordinator who distributed different colored jerseys and gave instructions.

"Most of you guys know what the rules are. For those who don't, the heat will be fifteen minutes long. There are three judges. They will score your waves from one to ten. You will be judged on your top four waves, so it's important to get at least four waves. They will be judging the length of your ride, the maneuvers you complete, your style, and overall performance. That's about it. Paddle out and wait for the horn blast that signals the start of the heat."

Charlie caught the first wave. He stood up quickly and faded back toward the white water before carving a big turn. He guided his board up the swell, bounced it off of the lip of the wave and came straight back down to the bottom. He turned quickly and walked up to the nose. He put his left foot over the tip of his board and then, casually, slid his right foot up next to it, hanging ten toes over.

The wave started to speed up. He crouched down and slid his right leg back, leaving his left on the nose, hanging five. The wave curled over him and he was in the tube for a second before coming out. He stood up, still standing on the nose, back peddled off the nose, and kicked out of the wave.

Charlie surfed so well that the crowd gave him a standing ovation when he came out of the water. He placed first in the heat, and was scheduled to surf in the quarter-finals later that day.

Afterward, Charlie walked up the beach carrying his surfboard under his arm.

"Charlie, can we take you out to lunch?" his dad asked. Charlie looked around to see his parents and Cher following behind him.

"Sure, I guess so, but I have to be back early to get ready for my next heat," Charlie said.

At lunch, Charlie's parents couldn't stop talking about how great Charlie had performed that morning.

"Charlie, I can't believe how you surf those waves. Nobody out there was even close to you," his mother said.

"Thanks, Mom. Guess you haven't seen me surf in a long time. You probably thought I was just a silly kid with an out-of-reach dream. But I'm for real, Mom, if I can stay focused."

After lunch, Cher wanted to take a walk down the beach.

"Sounds great, Babe, but I need to get back to get ready for my next heat."

"Oh, Charlie, the heat is over an hour from now. Can't you just take some time for me?"

"Sorry Babe. As much as I'd like to, I need to get back. I'm not trying to avoid you, honest."

The rest of the contest went without a hitch. Charlie breezed through the quarter and semi-finals. The finals were held on Sunday afternoon, and he continued to dominate the Ocean Beach surf for all the judges to see.

When the last wave had been surfed, Charlie was the overwhelming champ, winning first place. He was the hometown hero. His new system worked. It would be in his bag of tricks forever. With this win he hoped he would make the American Team.

After the contest, he saw Hoppy Swartz walking to his car. Charlie hurried to catch up to him.

"Excuse me, Mr. Swartz. I am pretty interested in trying out for the team to represent our country in the World Contest this year. What do you think my chances are?"

"Son, today you surfed like you belong on the team," Hoppy said. "But the committee choosing the team is not having tryouts, so it's your reputation that gets you on. I would imagine that at least four out of the five who will represent America are a dead lock. There's only room for one more."

"Do you think I have a chance?"

"Of course you have a chance. But you're pretty new on the scene, so they will go by your contest results. Charlie, you've had a rough time of it lately. I would say that to have any chance at all of making the team, you need to have a strong showing at the U.S. Championships in San Clemente. It's going to be tough, Charlie. This contest is by invitation only, so all of the top surfers will be competing, and several of them want the chance to be on the team, too."

Charlie lowered his head.

"Good luck, Son," Hoppy said, as he got into his car, shut the door, and rolled down the window.

"Thanks for your help, Mr. Swartz."

Oh my God, Charlie thought as he walked back to get his board. He shook his head and stared at the sand. *I worked so hard to get recognized and those other guys are automatically in because they're older and have been competing longer? Why not have a surf-out? Now Hoppy tells me I need to have a good showing at the U.S. Championships. What the hell is a good showing with all that competition? I'll have to win the damn thing hands down. Oh, man!*

3

On Monday evening, the day after the Ocean Beach contest, the Las Olas Surf Club held its monthly meeting. Usually the meeting was held at the Ocean Beach Methodist Church, where Charlie's father was the minister. This time Paul and Carol Macon offered their house so the club could have a party afterward out on the beach. Charlie was so depressed about the upcoming U.S. Championships that he forgot about the meeting.

"Hello?" Charlie said when his phone rang.

"Hey, man. Where the hell are you?" Gage asked.

"What do you mean?" Charlie said.

"We just had a club meeting over here at Paul's, and the damn hero didn't even show up. What's up with that, man?"

"Oh shit, Gage. I forgot all about it."

"Well, it's not too late. We just built a bonfire out on the beach. Get your ass down here," Gage said, sounding annoyed.

When Charlie arrived he received a warm welcome with handshakes and hoots from his friends and hugs from Paul and Carol. Charlie was gracious, but guarded with his emotion. When everyone finished greeting him, he eased his way to the back of the crowd and was looking for an opportunity to slip away, when Gage tapped him on the shoulder.

"What's going on, Buddy? This beach party was planned in your honor and you look like you're at a funeral or something. Is everything all right?"

"I'm sorry, man," Charlie said as the two friends sat down in the sand away from the rest of the group. "I talked with Hoppy Swartz after the contest and I don't think he gives me much of a chance to get on the team."

"What the hell are you talking about, man?" Gage said. "Yesterday you were crowned the O.B. champ, and today you sound like you're all washed up. I think you need a serious butt whooping or something."

"If that would help, I'd let you do it, man," Charlie said as he picked up a handful of sand and threw it to the side. "But Hoppy wasn't very encouraging about my chances. Gage, I've wanted this for a long time now and it seems that it's almost out of reach."

He picked up another handful of sand and was about to throw it, when Gage grabbed his arm and put it down.

"All right, let's back up here now," Gage said. "What the hell was that new technique you were talking about? It apparently was pretty damn successful, if you ask me. You know I had to work, but what I heard from the guys was that you surfed so well those judges didn't even know anyone else was out there. So what gives?"

"One morning last week, while I was waiting for you to show up, I started visualizing myself ripping the waves. And then when we went out it really seemed to work pretty well. So I kept it up. I even started visualizing myself surfing before I went to bed at night. That's what I was doing when you showed up before my heat at O.B. You told me that I needed to find a new way to focus," Charlie said. "I think that's what I've done."

"I'd certainly agree with that, man. In fact, I think you've figured out something really big here. From what I've seen, you're surfing even better than when I was trying to help you."

"I don't know about that..."

"Well I do, man, and if you ask me, all you have to do now is practice this technique as much as you can, and you'll be ready as ever to secure a spot on that damn team. When is the San Clemente contest?"

"It's in two weeks."

"I'll tell you what. Tomorrow is my day off. At the crack of dawn, we're heading up the coast," Gage said, slapping his friend on the back.

"Where the hell are we going?"

"We're going to San Clemente, you idiot. We're going to work on your new technique at the place where it's all going to hang out at those championships. You're going to make it so that committee has no choice but to include you on that team, man," Gage said, grinning from ear to ear.

The following day, Charlie spent the whole day just watching the surf at San Clemente beach. Gage asked several times if he wanted to go out, but Charlie said he just wanted to visualize for awhile.

The next time Gage asked, Charlie said, "No, but if you want to, go on ahead without me."

Gage did just that, and Charlie ended up not even getting wet that day.

"I think I've seen enough of this place now," Charlie said when Gage came in. "In fact, not only do I have a good mental picture for my homework tonight, I'm going to be dreaming it as well."

"I bet you will, man," Gage said, bumping Charlie on the ass with his surfboard. "If this works you'll become an instant genius."

"What do you mean, 'if this works'? So now you're the skeptic? Let me tell you something, man, I'm feeling hot now. I don't think there's anything that's going to keep me from doing what I want. You got me going again, you little sonofabitch. If you back me a hundred percent, I really will do it," Charlie exclaimed, raising his voice.

"I'm with you, Buddy! You're going to blow some minds," Gage said, turning serious.

Three days before the contest, Charlie called Cher and told her he was going camping.

"What?" Cher said. "You're pulling my leg. You wouldn't do that just before the biggest contest of the year."

"Yeah, I would, Babe, because I'm going up to San Clemente State Park. I'm going to camp out on the beach and listen to those waves break," Charlie said with conviction.

"You're a lunatic, Charles Armfield. What good is that going to do?"

"Beats me, but something tells me to go do it. So that's what I'm going to do. I think I need to be alone for a few days to really get focused."

"Charlie, sometimes I wonder if I'm really your girlfriend or not."

"Of course you are, Babe. You're just going to have to trust me on this one."

"But Charlie, you know I have an art show at the college this weekend and won't be able to come up to the contest. That means we won't get to see each other until next week."

Charlie had forgotten about the art show, but being reminded filled him with a sense of relief. It meant there wouldn't even be girlfriend distractions at the contest.

"This is pretty important to me, Babe. I think I'm just going to go for it. Don't be mad, okay?" There was silence, and Charlie heard a sniffle on the other end of the line. "Are you okay, Cher?"

"Yes, I'm fine. I guess this contest is pretty important to you."

"Thanks, Babe. I'll see you next week."

"Hey Charlie?"

"What?"

"Good luck, Babe. I hope you win it all," Cher said quietly.

The remaining portion of Charlie's pre-contest preparation—three days and nights—was spent in campsite number five. Instead of surfing, he watched the waves during the day and listened to them at night while he slept. The only time he went out to surf the break was when the sun rose on the morning of the contest. Two hours later, the contest coordinator announced over the loud speaker that it was time for all surfers to clear the water, because the contest was about to begin. Charlie went in and sat alone on the beach and visualized until it was time for his heat.

Charlie hadn't talked to anyone for three days, and he continued his silence when he collected his jersey and hit the surf for his first heat. The waves were average size that day, three to four feet high, and the water was glassy with a slight wind starting to pick up.

After paddling out, he sat for a moment before maneuvering into position to catch a wave. He thought to himself, well, big guy, here goes. Just have fun out here.

Charlie surfed the first heat with such poise and concentration that he breezed into the quarter-finals. When he came out of the water Paul and Carol Macon were standing on the beach waiting for him.

"Hey, I didn't know you guys were coming up," Charlie said, smiling. "How do you think I did?"

"Charlie, you were magnificent," Carol said.

Paul put his arm around Charlie and said, "If you surf like that in the rest of the contest, you can't lose, my friend. By the way, where have you been the last couple of days? We rented several rooms at the Holiday Inn for club members. We tried to get in touch with you to let you know."

"I've been camping in the park up the beach."

"Well, you don't have to do that anymore," Carol said. "The club took some money out of the treasury and paid for the whole weekend. Come stay with us tonight."

"No offense, but I was thinking I'd keep my campsite tonight. I'm kind of in a groove right now with my surfing. I know the guys will want to party and I really think…"

Paul interrupted, "You don't have to explain, Charlie. The way you surfed out there just now tells the whole story. I'll explain it to everyone, and we'll see you tomorrow."

"Thanks, man. I need to get back to work now, so I'll see you later."

Charlie walked down the beach with his surfboard under his arm. He sat down next to the contest area and started visualizing for the quarter-finals.

That night Charlie built a fire at his campsite and sat listening to the waves. He thought about the quarter-final heat that had gone as planned. If he could only keep the pace, he knew he would have a good chance to win it all.

He was now one of twelve surfers in the semi-finals. Two of the semi-finalists were already on the American Team.

Billy Foxx, five years older than Charlie, was also from San Diego. He was in the Wind'n Sea Surf Club and rode for Hobie Surfboards. The thought of Billy—one of Charlie's idols when he'd first learned how to surf—competing against him, was nerve-racking.

The other surfer on the team in the semis was Mick Norris. Mick was from Long Beach, California, was a member of the Long Beach Surf Club, and rode for Harbour Surfboards. He was only two years older than Charlie, but had been competing since he was in the junior division, which was for seventeen years of age and under. Charlie had only surfed in the men's division, and this was only his second year.

"Oh, man," he thought, mumbling out loud. "Why are those guys in this contest anyway? They've made the American team already. Now I have to show my stuff against two of the top surfers in the country. If they beat me out in the semis, my chances of making the team are shot."

Charlie didn't know which surfers would be in his semi-final heat so he decided not to worry about anybody, except himself. *Hey big guy, the only thing you have control over is your own performance, so just do what you've been doing and let the powers-that-be take over.*

Charlie wondered if those powers-that-be already knew who was going to win the contest. His father, being a Methodist Minister, always spoke as if God knew everything before it happened. Charlie didn't even know what he thought about God, let alone His powers. But as he continued to listen to the waves, he decided to offer a prayer to his cause.

"Dear Lord, I guess if you know everything already, you know I'm still trying to figure you out. My dad has been trying to pound Christianity into me since I was born, but I don't know about all of that. I do feel that there is some kind of power out there, and sometimes I think my visualization is pulling it into me. Anyway, I guess all I want is to be ready for the challenge I have ahead of me. And if I'm supposed to win, I will. Amen."

At the first pre-heat conference of the day, Charlie met Billy Foxx for the first time. Mick Norris was in the next semi-final heat.

"Hi Billy. My name's Charlie Armfield. I've been admiring your surfing for a long time."

"Yeah sure. Nice to meet you," Billy said without making eye contact with Charlie.

Then the contest coordinator spoke. "You guys know the rules. You still catch as many waves as possible, and the best four count. The only thing different is that you get twenty minutes instead of the usual fifteen. Just paddle out and wait for the horn blast to signal the start of the heat. Good luck, men."

At the start of the heat, Charlie whipped his board around on the first wave and paddled to take off. He was just about to stand up when Billy moved right in behind him and paddled into the wave.

"Hey, man, if you take off in front of me you'll be disqualified," Billy shouted.

Charlie stood up and immediately kicked out of the wave. Then he thought to himself, *wait a minute. I took off first and he intentionally stole that wave from me. What an asshole!*

Charlie decided to stay clear of Billy Foxx. From that point on, if Billy was in the line-up at the same time, Charlie backed off until Billy had already taken off. With the extra time, Charlie didn't worry about catching enough waves.

As it turned out, Charlie only caught four waves, but they all scored high points. The winner of the heat, by one point, however, was Billy Foxx. Charlie was second. When he first learned of the results, Charlie was furious.

Paul and Carol walked up to Charlie.

"Did you see what he did to me? He took off behind me!" Charlie fumed.

"It's okay, Charlie. The top two from each of the semi-final heats go to the finals," Paul said, trying to calm him down.

"Don't let him rile you up, Charlie," Carol said. "I thought you had the best rides."

"Thanks, you guys. I'll be all right. I think I'll just go over here and sit for awhile. I need some time to cool off," Charlie said as he trudged away.

He went over into the contest area and sat in the warm sand to watch the second semi-final. Mick Norris was ripping the place apart. When he paddled into a wave, however, Charlie noticed the rest of the surfers would stay clear, much the way it happened with him and Billy Foxx. But then Charlie noticed something else.

All of the surfers were hanging out in the middle of the designated contest area. The waves were breaking from left to right, which meant the best place to take off—away from the crowd—would be to the north.

He stopped watching the surfers and started checking out the northern part of the contest area to see if he could find a good take-off spot. With the next set, he saw a peak that popped up quickly, but then faded out. He watched several more waves and the same thing happened. *They peter out before I could ride very far*, he thought. *Shoot! Must be a sand bar that makes that happen.*

But he kept watching, and he noticed that the wave built back up again when it got inside. *Maybe if I caught that wave*, he thought, *I could hit the bottom of the peak on my take-off, come up and bounce off of the lip, and then go straight. I might even have to get on my knees to paddle for a bit to stay into the swell. Then when it builds back up again I can ride it all the way into the middle and beyond.*

He started to visualize his strategy. *Yes*, he thought, *it just might work.*

He watched it over and over. The second heat came to an end, and it was announced that the finals would be held in an hour. Charlie didn't budge. He kept watching and putting himself on that peak.

He thought about going out in the water to give it a try. But no, maybe one of the other finalists would notice and figure out his plan. Besides, visualization had worked before, and if he had this north peak figured out right, it would work again.

An hour later the announcement was made for the finalists to meet with the contest coordinator.

"There are four surfers who have earned the privilege to participate in this year's United States Surfing Championships," the announcer said over the intercom. "All of the contestants are from California this year. Mick Norris from Long Beach, David Woodley from Santa Cruz and Billy Foxx and Charlie Armfield from San Diego. Good luck, men."

The coordinator spoke privately with the contestants. "Okay, guys, this is the final. First of all, congratulations on getting this far. This heat will last twenty-five minutes and your best six waves will be counted for your score. I hope you all have a good session. Now paddle out and wait for the horn blast."

Charlie made an attempt to shake hands with the other contestants. Mick and David obliged, but Billy started walking to the water before Charlie got to him.

All of the surfers paddled out. Charlie decided to stay with the group for the first ten minutes to avoid suspicion. He caught a couple of good waves in that time, but Billy and Mick were battling hard and taking most of the good ones. Then Charlie slipped away from the group and paddled north.

None of the other finalists noticed when Charlie caught his first peak. He paddled in and pulled off a beautiful bottom turn, bounced off the lip, and pointed his board straight in toward the beach. He had so much momentum that he stayed right with the swell while standing up. When the wave built back up he made a quick turn and flew into the section. At first it looked like he wouldn't make it, so he crouched down near the nose to increase his speed.

Meanwhile, Billy was paddling into the same wave. He apparently didn't see Charlie coming, and before Billy knew it, he was riding in front of Charlie, which was a violation. That meant that one of his counted waves would be a zero.

When they both kicked out of the wave, Billy looked back at Charlie. "Where in the hell did you come from?"

Charlie just shrugged his shoulders and paddled back to the peak.

On his next wave, he noticed the group was watching him as he took off. This time when the wave built back up, Charlie stalled and then crouched down to get completely tubed in the section. On the third wave he turned quickly into the re-built section and walked to the nose, hanging five toes over, clear across the beach. It was after the third wave that Billy and Mick decided to give the northern peak a try.

Mick took off first, but he turned too quickly and lost the wave when it faded. Billy was next. He hit the bottom turn all right, but neglected the lip and lost the wave. They each tried again with similar results and paddled back to the middle.

Charlie surfed the rest of the heat by himself, using the north peak.

In the afternoon, ninety minutes after the final heat, the crowd hung around waiting for the final tabulations. It was the first time in five days that Charlie had allowed himself to socialize.

"Hey, anyone want to go out and catch a few waves?" he said, clowning around.

"Very funny, Charlie. Nobody is going anywhere until we find out the results," one of the other members of the Las Olas Surf Club said.

"What's taking so long, anyway?" Carol Macon said as she shuffled nervously in the sand.

"Oh, I don't know, maybe they forgot who was out there so they just have to make up a winner or something," Charlie said, chuckling. He seemed relaxed, but his forehead began to twitch nervously.

Finally, Hoppy Swartz made his way up to the platform. The only sound that could be heard until he reached the steps was that of the distant waves. Then his sand covered sandals scraped each stair as he climbed up and grabbed the microphone.

"Because there is so much at stake with this contest, I am going to make a change in the usual procedure," Hoppy said. "Instead of starting with the last place first, I'm going to start by announcing the winner. I am doing this because the committee has also decided that this year's winner will represent the United States in the World Surfing Contest to be held in San Diego, two months from now."

Charlie stood barefoot in the warm sand, wearing a Gordon and Smith T-shirt and the surf trunks he'd worn in the final heat. Perspiration coursed down his face.

Hoppy cleared his throat. "This year's winner of the United States Surfing Championships," Hoppy paused, "and member of the American Surf Team…," he trailed off, then raised his voice, "is Charlie Armfield!"

Charlie just stood there for a moment, feeling stunned. He fell to his knees, hands together, and pointed them up toward the sky in thanks. He felt like he was going to cry, but restrained himself.

People crowded close. "Congratulations," they said, thumping him on the back.

"You really deserve it, Charlie," he heard over and over.

"All right, everybody," Hoppy said, "give the man some room so he can get up here to collect this hardware." Hoppy was holding up a three-and-a-half foot trophy in his hand.

"Char-lie, Char-lie, Char-lie!" chanted the crowd.

He stood up and walked toward the stage.

When he reached the top step, he waved to the crowd and turned to accept his award. Hoppy shook his hand and handed him the silver-plated trophy with a surfer on top.

"Congratulations, indeed, young man," Hoppy said, "and good luck in San Diego. It certainly will be nice to have a local San Diegan represent our country in the World Contest."

He held the microphone out to Charlie. Charlie stepped back and shook his head no. The crowd applauded, chanting his name. Hoppy looked stern. "Here young man. They want to hear from you, too."

Charlie put his award on the stage floor and took the microphone with both hands. He looked into the crowd. If only Gage were here to share this— the most important moment in his life.

"You wouldn't believe how hard I worked…" Charlie paused. "How hard I worked to represent my country in the World Contest. And with that hard work, I feel like the waves in that ocean back there," he pointed behind his back, "have given me something special. I don't know exactly what I mean by that, or for that matter even what the hell I'm saying."

Laughter erupted from the crowd.

"But I feel touched by some kind of energy out there. I want to know more about it, and maybe if I do, I will win for the Americans. Thanks."

On Tuesday evening of that same week, a congratulatory party was held at the Armfield residence. Charlie wasn't sure he wanted it, but his parents insisted. Since it was Gage's night off, he offered to organize it and make sure every one of the surf club members was there.

"Can I have everybody's attention please?" shouted Gage. "I want to take this opportunity to congratulate the Las Olas Surf Club for having a member who is on the United States Surf Team."

Cheers erupted from the crowd. Gage put up his hand for quiet. "You all know there are only five on that team, and we have one of them among us!"

The noise exploded again, and this time the windows shook. Charlie's parents stood at the back of the room with their older son, Mike; all of them awed by the reception. Gage picked up Charlie's newest trophy and held it high up over his head, and the group became even louder.

"And we also have the American Champion here with us as well," shouted Gage. Gage held up his hand again and looked at Charlie. "We are so very proud of you, man. First, because you're in our club, and second, for your accomplishments in the world of surfing. Charlie, none of us quite understands what goes on between you and the waves when you're out there, man, but we respect it—and you. You are incredible, my friend. We wish you luck against the rest of the world."

"Way to go, Charlie," someone yelled, and the rest of the crowd exploded with chants of, "Charlie! Charlie! Charlie!"

Paul Macon whistled for attention. "Hey, guys. Let's quiet down some before the Reverend and Mrs. Armfield have the police knocking at the door."

Everyone laughed, and then Louise Armfield spoke up. "There are refreshments on the dining room table. Have at it, everybody."

Charlie enjoyed seeing his friends from the surf club again. He liked to hang out with them, but had kept to himself most of the summer with the competition.

But then he had a conversation that was not very pleasant. He and Gage were talking to Nate Jamison. The expression on Nate's face was solemn.

Cher walked up and touched Charlie's arm.

"Charlie, can I talk to you a moment?"

"Sure, in just a minute, Babe. Just let me finish talking to Nate, here."

Cher looked quizzically from Charlie to Nate and back. She nodded and dejectedly returned to the group gathered around the refreshments.

"So when did Will leave?" Gage asked.

"Last Wednesday," Nate said. "He's been over there for almost a week now, and we haven't heard anything from him. I guess they have some in-country training or something for awhile, and then they're placed into a unit."

"Shit!" Charlie said. "I didn't even know he got drafted."

"Yeah, that was about five months ago. I'm surprised you didn't see him when he was home on leave before he left for Vietnam. I know he wanted to go to one of your contests, Charlie. Maybe he didn't make it," Nate said.

"Well, keep us in touch, will you?" Charlie said.

Charlie looked at Gage. "What a bunch of crap that is," he said, shaking his head.

Gage studied Charlie for a moment. "And you know what, man? That could be us someday."

"Get off it, will you? They can't be taking every Tom, Dick, and Harry, and not the ones who are doing something important. You've got a great apprenticeship program going for you, Gage, and I'm already doing something for my country. We're going to be all right, man. Just keep cool and don't worry about it."

"You knew that Will was working as an apprentice down at the shipyard, didn't you?" Gage said.

"No, I didn't. Well, I still think they can't take everybody," Charlie said, as he turned away from Gage to find Cher.

He found her in the kitchen talking to his parents. He walked up and put his arms around his mother and Cher. His father did the same. His brother Mike walked in and saw the group hug going on.

"Hey, how about me, too?" he said, smiling

His dad pulled him in between him and his wife.

"You know, Charlie," Mike said, "we didn't give you much of a chance to get this thing done, but you went on without our help and pulled it off. Pretty darn incredible, if you ask me. I'm proud of you, little brother."

"Thanks, Mike, but you guys were there for me, even if you didn't know it. The Armfield clan is always together, whether you were there watching me or not.

Gage walked in and squeezed in between Cher and Charlie's dad.

"And this guy," Charlie said, "even though he copped out on me and worked on contest days, he saved my life."

"I did? How?"

"You know what I'm talking about, man, with the new scheme, and I can't thank you enough," Charlie grinned. "Hey, I just remembered. Gage really did save my life once. One time, when we were surfing the North Shore in Oahu."

"No way, man. You would have made it by yourself."

"I don't know. I was sucking air pretty hard by the time you came to my rescue."

His parents looked at each other, wide-eyed.

"Enough, Charlie," Cher said. "I don't think we want to hear any more of this, do we Mrs. Armfield?"

"Hey, I do," Mike interrupted. "What happened, Gage?"

"Never mind," Charlie's father said as he broke the circle and took Charlie aside. "Charlie, we know you are involved with a dangerous sport. But it looks to me like it has provided quite a spiritual connection for you as well. You've accomplished feats now that few men have. We're all proud of you, Son."

"Thanks, Dad, I want to learn more about that so-called spiritual connection you keep talking about. You seem to understand more about what I know than I do, and one day I hope to get it, too."

"Hey, I've got to get home, Charlie," Cher interrupted. "That's why I came to get you twenty minutes ago when you were talking to Nate. What was that all about anyway?"

Charlie looked over at Gage. Their eyes locked for a moment. Then Charlie shook his head. "Oh, it was nothing, Cher. Come on, I'll take you home."

Two weeks later, a surf club invitational was scheduled at Malibu. For the first time ever, the Las Olas Surf Club was invited to participate, because now they had a member of the American Team on board. Gage asked for the weekend off, and surfed in the contest with Charlie. The two friends had a great time, as did the entire Las Olas Surf Club.

While the Wind'n Sea Surf Club scored the most team points and won the event, Charlie won the Men's Division using the same techniques he'd utilized at San Clemente. At the end of the invitational, the host team, the Malibu Surf Club, staged a barbecue on the beach. During the awards, Hoppy Swartz made an unexpected announcement.

"Before the World Contest next month, Greg Bond, one of the top surf filmmakers, has agreed to produce a publicity series of our team. He has a seaplane and has invited the five members of the American Team to join him next week on a trip down into the Baja of Mexico," Hoppy said. "How about it? Will you guys go?"

Randy Patton from Malibu, nodded as did Mark Tanner from Oahu, Hawaii. Billy Foxx and Mick Norris also accepted.

When Charlie was asked he said, "Are you kidding? I wouldn't miss it for the world."

Everybody laughed.

The trip lasted for three days and, for Charlie, it was an incredible experience. He met and surfed with some of his surf heroes. By the end of the trip they were pretty close friends. Even Billy, after snubbing Charlie at San Clemente, opened up.

Greg Bond's pilot made a series of passes along the coastline until they spotted a good break. He then circled back and landed—on the beach if there was one—or on the water if there wasn't. They had two surf sessions per day. Sometimes they surfed well-known spots. Other times they surfed places that probably had never before been ridden. At night they landed in coastal towns to bed down in a hotel.

Greg Bond got some great footage and promised a private showing sometime before the World Contest. He wanted to put together a piece that could be shown on network television so the American sports fans would know more about the World Surfing Contest. It would show it was the surfing community's equivalent of the Olympics. His efforts were sponsored by the United States Surfing Association to help promote the image of the sport.

When they returned, the plane landed at a small airport in Los Angeles. Charlie had left his van parked at the airport, so he still had a two-hour drive to get home before he could call Gage. He had so many stories to tell about surfing with the best surfers in the world. *Hey,* he thought, *now* I'm *one of the best surfers in the world, too.*

And the surf had been good, about four to six feet high, perfect for everyone to show his best stuff in the waves. His excitement grew as he sped down Highway 101.

He remembered the feeling of the plane landing on the water the first time. The whole group had hooted with joy. Then they'd opened the door and dove into the water, where they treaded until their surfboards were handed down to them. The temperature was warm in and out of the water. It reminded Charlie of Hawaii.

Randy Patton, Mark Tanner and Billy Foxx were the senior members of the team, and Charlie guessed they were in their mid-twenties. Mick was twenty-one, and Charlie knew he, himself, was the youngest at nineteen. But in the water, everybody was the same on the trip.

"Wow!" Charlie said out loud. "I went surfing with the best."

He smiled in anticipation as he rounded the corner and pulled into the driveway at his parents' home, parked, and hurried up the walk to the front door. Then he stopped short, sensing something was wrong. He glanced at the front window and saw his mother watching him, hands on her face.

Oh my God, he thought. *What's happened?* He ran up the steps and banged the door open.

"What is it, Mom? What's wrong?"

She shook her head, unable to talk.

"Mom, are you all right?"

His father entered the room. "She's all right. Well...I guess she's all right. We're all pretty upset. Come over here with me, Charlie, and have a seat."

"What the hell's going on?"

"Son, this letter came in the mail for you today." He held it out to Charlie.

He took it and read the return address—United States Government, Selective Service Department. It was addressed to Charles W. Armfield. He stared in disbelief, unwilling to open it.

"Come on, Son. We all need to get this over with," his dad said.

Charlie forced his fingers under the flap, tore it open, pulled out the letter.

"Attention Charles W. Armfield:
You have been selected to serve in the United States Army."

He dropped it in his lap and looked at his dad. "They wouldn't do this to me, would they? After all that I've worked for, they wouldn't. Would they, Dad?"

"When do you have to report, Son?"

Charlie scanned the rest of the notice. "In two weeks," he said, his voice barely a whisper.

Two weeks! The World Contest is scheduled to begin in just less than a month. Horrified, he stared blankly at the sheet of paper in his hands.

His parents sat close beside him. His father put his arm around his shoulder. His mother held his hand, tears running down her cheeks. They sat in silence for several minutes.

Suddenly, Charlie sprang to his feet. "Hey, wait a minute. I'm going to call Hoppy and see if they can do this or not."

John and Louise shook their heads as Charlie went over to the phone table to find the directory.

As he thumbed through to find Hoppy's phone number he mumbled, "They can't do this to me." When he found the listing, his fingers hurriedly worked in the rotary dial.

"Hello, Mr. Swartz. This is Charlie Armfield. Excuse me for bothering you at home and all, but I wanted..."

"Oh, Charlie. How was the trip? Did you get some good surf for the film?" Hoppy asked.

"The trip was great, Mr. Swartz. The surf was unreal and I think the film should be just what you expected. But what I'm calling for was to ask you about something pretty important."

"What is it, Charlie?"

"I was drafted today, Mr. Swartz." He paused to take a deep breath. "I was wondering, since I'm on the American Team, am I able to get out of the service?"

The conversation went on for nearly fifteen minutes. When Charlie hung up the phone, he ran out the door into the backyard.

Charlie's father waited awhile before approaching him. "I'm sorry, Son. Not what you were hoping he would say?"

"Hoppy said there was nothing that could be done. Not even Cassius

Clay was able to avoid the draft." He picked up a rock and threw it at a tree in the back corner of the yard, but missed. "Shit!"

Charlie looked at his father. "He said he already checked into the situation, just in case it might affect his team before the contest. They laughed at him, Dad." He swallowed hard, trying to steady his voice. "I have to go into the army unless I can prove I'm unfit to serve. I'm a damn surfing champion, Dad. I'm going to be the fittest fool in the damn ranks!"

Charlie spent the rest of the evening by himself. He didn't even want to call Gage or Cher. He needed time to think, to figure out what to do. It was too late to join the Peace Corps or try for any other conscientious objector program. He was certainly going to be fit. Even if he could fake it, how could he then justify surfing in the contest? He could try to test mentally incompetent, but he would be ashamed to tell his parents about it. He'd heard about others defecting to Canada, but was there rideable surf in that country? No matter what he thought he could try, it still wasn't going to get him into the contest.

Later that night, he decided to call Gage to see if he had any ideas.

Gage's mother answered. "Hello?"

"Hello, Mrs. Saltman, this is Charlie. I'm sorry to call so late. Can I speak to Gage, please?"

"Oh hi, Charlie. Gage has been wanting to talk to you all afternoon," Mrs. Saltman said.

"I know, but I just didn't get around to calling. I'm sorry I waited so long."

"Oh it's not your fault, Charlie. He could have called you, but he's been kind of afraid to call, I guess," Mrs. Saltman said.

"Afraid to call? Why?"

"Gage was drafted today, Charlie. He was afraid that maybe you were, too."

Charlie was silent for a moment.

"Oh, my God! I was so busy freaking out about my own problems I never even thought that it could be happening to my best friend, too."

"So he was right," Mrs. Saltman said. There was sadness in her voice. "Charlie, can I have Gage call you in the morning?"

"Sure Mrs. S. How is Gage doing?"

"He's pretty shook up, Charlie. He was doing so well with his apprenticeship. He sort of feels like his world is coming to an end."

"I understand," Charlie said. "I feel the same way."

Shit, he thought as he hung up. *How could I be such a damn fool? Gage has been afraid he might be drafted because he finished his school course. He warned me that it might happen to me, too. Hell, everybody warned me, and I just ignored them like I was some special guy in this world. I'm nothing but a damn fool. Then, I sat around moping about my own problems, and ignored the fact that my best friend just might be in the exact same situation. He wants to be a chef, not a soldier. Now we're both being taken away from our goals.*

He stayed up all night, feeling helpless with nowhere to turn. At one point, he lay back on his bed and tried to let everything on his mind go. He thought about his technique when a huge wave wipes him out. He just let his body go limp and let the turbulence take him where it willed. But no matter how hard he tried, his mind still returned to his upcoming induction into the army, and eventual participation in Vietnam.

At dawn, his parents came into his room to check on him. Charlie was an angry young man. His eyes were sore from being up all night.

"This is a crock of shit, you know that?" he said, his voice vibrating across the room. "I don't know the slightest thing about that war in Vietnam, and now I have to go fight in it." He smashed his fist into his pillow. "Damn it all," he said, starting to cry. "Who the hell are those people, anyway? Why can't the Vietnamese fight their own damn war? Now I'll never be able to know…"

"Never be able to know what, Son?" his father asked softly.

"I'll never be able to know what it would be like to surf in the World Contest. I still needed to get better. I wanted to know what it would be like to get that good, to know the ocean that well. Instead, I'll know about war. I'm going to lose everything I've worked for."

Part II

The Crusade

4

The air felt brisk on Charlie's face as he and Gage dropped onto the granular silica of Ocean Beach. Hair shaved close, clad in wetsuits, and weary from a long afternoon of surfing, neither spoke as they watched the crimson sun. Its fiery glow belied the late March chill that hung in the air as it sank slowly below the horizon until only a thin streak of light remained.

The usual crowd that gathered at the beach to observe the sun's daily ritual quietly dispersed. Charlie glared at Gage.

"You know, Gage, I'm sure going to miss these ocean sunsets. Surfing, too, of course."

Gage nodded in agreement, and then tried to cheer Charlie up. "I have to tell you, man, you haven't lost a step out there."

"It doesn't feel the same though. When I took off it seemed like I was a stranger or something. Like the waves were mad at me for leaving like I did."

"Maybe it's you, Charlie."

"What do you mean by that?"

"Maybe it's you that's mad. I don't think I've seen you smile once since we were drafted," Gage said.

"What's there to smile about?" Charlie turned his head and spit as far as he could into the sand. "We both had things to do and our damn country decided it had to revamp our plans for its own use. The day after tomorrow we're going to Vietnam. Is that what you had in mind?"

"Of course not. Come on, man. Let's walk over to Paul and Carol's and shower," Gage said.

Paul and Carol were used to having unannounced guests from the surf club. They had built an outdoor shower for their friends, and it was a place where the surfers often congregated. As Charlie and Gage shuffled through the cool sand toward their house, Charlie started thinking about their army experience the past six months.

First they had gone to Fort Ord to complete their basic training. *How fortunate,* he thought, *to be in the same platoon with Gage.* Their heads were shaved, their civilian clothing was exchanged for olive drab, and they were treated as less than second class citizens. But they had each other and that part made the whole experience tolerable.

"Hey, Gage?"

Gage looked over at Charlie.

"I'm really sorry you got drafted, man, but I don't know if I would have made it through basic without you," Charlie said.

"I think you might have been in the stockade," Gage said.

"What do you mean?"

"What do I mean? Damn! You weren't exactly cooperative with the sergeants. If I hadn't been there to calm you down, I'm sure you would have jumped one of them."

"Come on. I wasn't that bad."

"Maybe not, but there were times I was worried. You did blow some minds though. They never saw anyone train as hard as you did."

"That's the only way I could blow off steam, man. Every time I looked at one of those lifers, I blamed him for me missing the World Contest. And then there was that 'Charlie' bullshit they pinned on me."

Gage shook his head in disgust. "Hey, man, when I heard them calling the enemy in Vietnam 'Charlie,' I knew you were going to catch some shit. Why in the hell didn't you tell them your name was Chuck or something?"

"Because I needed some way to defy them. To hell with them, anyway."

"Yeah, but I thought you were going to bite the dust with all of those push-ups and sit-ups they made you do. But in the end I guess you showed them. Shit! They never saw anyone get a perfect score on the fitness test before."

"Hey, man, you almost did it, too."

"That's because I was just trying to keep up with you, Charlie. I never would have worked so hard if it wasn't for you."

"Sorry about that, man," Charlie said. "Hey, it was great having you there for my birthday, too. Turning twenty in basic would have slipped right on by if you hadn't been there with me."

"You started it, man—getting everybody in the barracks to sing Happy Birthday on mine. It was my duty to get even with you."

Charlie and Gage laughed together. Their birthdays were ten days apart, and were probably the only fun memory from basic training.

Then Charlie remembered when their orders came down and they were separated. He had to go to Fort Sill, Oklahoma, for artillery training on 105 howitzers. Gage remained at Fort Ord to train as an army cook.

"I'm sure glad you got to be a cook, Gage."

"Hey, Charlie, did they treat you like shit at Fort Sill, too?"

"Yeah, pretty much. Not quite as bad maybe, but being in Oklahoma was the pits. At least at Fort Ord we had the ocean close by. How about you, did they treat you good or bad?"

"It was a piece of cake, man. The worst part of all for me was learning how to make the crap they feed you in the army. It's a real insult to my culinary expertise. You know what I mean?" Gage said, laughing.

"I know what it tastes like. Hey, what's in that shit-on-a-shingle stuff, anyway?"

"You don't want to know, man." They both laughed. "So what do you do on those big guns?"

"Hey, you don't want to know about that, either. I can't believe I was learning how to kill people, Gage. It was the worst feeling knowing that the howitzer round has a destiny for destruction. I don't know how I'm going to act when they're headed for real people."

They arrived at Paul and Carol's and there was already someone rinsing off in the shower.

"Hey Charlie, look who's in the shower," Gage said. "Hey, Nate, what's happening, man?"

Nate turned and saw his friends standing in front of him with their surfboards under their arms. "Whoa, what's with the new look? You guys trying to start a fad with the shave jobs?"

"Real funny, man. You know what happened to us," Charlie said.

"Yeah, I know. You guys home on leave or something?"

"Something like that. Hey, what do you hear from your brother?" Charlie asked.

"Will's in the Central Highlands near the town of Pleiku. At least that's where his basecamp is located. Who knows where the hell he is? Got a letter from him last week, but he's not telling much about what's going on. He's infantry, so I guess it's not much fun. I sure wish he were home."

"Yeah, me, too," Charlie said. "So what's it like where he is?"

"It's pretty mountainous with thick jungles. I guess the monsoon season is going on now and it's wet all the time. He has to sleep in the rain and everything. It gets kind of cold there at night, but in the day it's hot and muggy, with lots of bugs."

Charlie looked over at Gage. Then he kicked at the sand and slammed his board down. "Shit! What's the damn sense in all of this anyway?"

Nate looked apologetically over at Charlie. "Hey, you guys going to the surf flick over at the Strand Theater tonight? Charlie, you're going to be in it, man. Just before the main event they're playing the promotional that you were in for the World Contest. I've seen it before and it's really cool. You got the best waves in the whole thing. Have you seen it yet?"

"No," Charlie said angrily. He walked over to the shower and traded places with Nate, and directed the stream of water onto his head.

"So I heard that Colin Robins won the World Contest," Gage said.

"Oh, you guys know about that?" Nate said.

Charlie stuck his head out of the shower. "Of course we know. The captain made an announcement on the rifle range."

"Sorry about that, Nate," Gage said, apologizing for Charlie's behavior. "He's still pretty sore about missing the contest."

"That's okay, Gage."

Nate walked over to Charlie. "Hey, man, everybody who saw the contest agrees that you would have kicked ass, Charlie. I'm not trying to make you mad, but it's true. This was the first time a local didn't win. That Aussie wouldn't have had a chance with you out there, man. Have you ever seen him surf?"

"I think we saw him surfing in Hawaii one time," Charlie said.

"Well then you know he's pretty good, but you still would have taken him.

"Hey, Nate, how did you manage to keep from getting drafted?" Gage asked.

"You know that intelligence test you had to take? Well, I deliberately flunked it. I made them think I was mentally retarded."

"And they bought it?" Charlie said.

"They sure did. Now I'm out of the draft for good. Hey, I better get going. Maybe I'll see you guys at the movie, okay?" Nate said.

Charlie finished rinsing off and stepped out of the shower.

"Hey, Gage, could you have done that? You know, act goofy to get out of the service?"

"I don't think so."

"Is Nate ever going to feel guilty about doing that? He sounded like he was proud of his accomplishment. I don't want to go to Nam, but I couldn't live with myself if I got out of it that way," Charlie said.

"I don't think I could either. Some people just don't have much of a conscience when it comes to stuff like that. I guess Nate could do it, but we couldn't, and his brother Will couldn't do it either," Gage said, passing a towel over to Charlie.

"Can you get into college if you're a retard?" Charlie took the towel. "And how about getting a job? Who in the hell would hire you with a record like that?"

"I don't know, man," Gage said, stepping into the shower. "So Charlie, are we going to the surf flick tonight?" He stuck his dripping head out of the shower and smiled as if he knew what the answer would be.

"Hell no! I couldn't care less about seeing that stupid thing. Wonder why they didn't remake it when I copped out like I did."

"First of all, man, you didn't cop out. Like you made the choice to leave or something? And second of all, maybe they left it the same out of respect for you. You would have won that damn contest, Charlie. I think everybody knew you were surfing better than any of the other team members. And besides, man, they held the finals right here at your home beach. You would have killed them all out there in your own surf."

"Don't remind me, man. It's over now, and I didn't do shit except learn how to fire weapons at human beings." Charlie lowered his head. "I didn't kill anybody in that damn contest, but where I'm going now, I just might have to."

Gage turned the water off and retrieved the towel from Charlie. "Come on, Charlie. Let's get the hell out of here."

Charlie's van was parked down the street and as they started walking toward it Gage said, "I don't give a shit what you say, Charlie. We're going to that surf movie even if I have to drag you there."

The Strand Theater was located two and a half blocks east of the Pacific Ocean on Newport Street in Ocean Beach. Ever since the doors opened at 7:30 for its 8:00 showing of *Surf Fever*, there had been a continuous line of people wanting to buy tickets. Excitement filled the air.

Charlie, Gage, and Cher arrived five minutes before the film began. Charlie and Gage wore sweaters, shorts and sandals. Cher was wearing a short flowered sundress and a light white cardigan. Those standing outside the theater immediately recognized Charlie, despite the ball cap he wore to cover his short hair.

"Hey, look," one of the bystanders said in a voice that easily reached Charlie. "There's the guy who would have won the World Contest. You know, that Charlie guy, the one on the team who got drafted."

"Wow, he must feel pretty bad about having to miss the contest," his friend said.

Inside the theater, Charlie and his friends sat in the back, to keep from being conspicuous. But Charlie was recognized, and the word spread before lights were dimmed and the curtains opened.

The first film shown was the clip taken of the American Team surfing along the Baja coast. The first scene showed the Team—Randy Patton, Mark Tanner, Billy Foxx, Mick Norris, and Charlie—getting onto the filmmaker's plane, while the surfboards were being loaded underneath in the baggage compartment.

Aerial shots of the coastline were interspersed with close-up shots of the passengers. When they located rideable waves there was a lot of scrambling in the plane, and the crowd in the theater started to hoot as the plane landed. Then the surfing began.

On one wave, Charlie took off fading in toward the white water and pulled off a huge turn just in time to disappear within the tube. When he popped out again he was on the nose of his surfboard. The whole house started cheering. The wave continued as Charlie backpedaled from the nose and cut back. Then with a smooth half turn and a stall, he walked up to the nose again and hung ten toes over clear into the shore break. Again he backpedaled and bounced his board off the top lip of the wave and straightened out into the white water.

The entire team demonstrated top form for everyone in the Strand Theater to see that night, but the crowd reacted most to the waves Charlie rode. Gage would elbow Charlie from time to time with a big grin on his face. Cher squeezed Charlie's hand every time he took off on another wave, and wouldn't let go until another surfer was in the eye of the camera.

"Cher," Gage whispered in front of Charlie, "can you believe this guy? He stole the show from the rest of the team."

"Bullshit," Charlie interrupted. "The other guys ripped, too."

When the clip was over the lights went up so the operator could change movie reels. Some of the people in the audience stood up, turned toward the back of the theater and chanted, "Charlie! Charlie! Charlie!" Soon everybody was standing, and the chorus became louder. They continued, unwilling to stop.

Finally Gage nudged Charlie. "Stand up, man."

Charlie stood up and tipped his hat. The crowd gave out a huge cheer. Charlie sat down and looked at his friend. Gage, still standing, continued to clap. For one brief moment, Charlie actually forgot he would soon be going to Vietnam.

"Sit down, man," Charlie said, grabbing Gage's sweater and pulling him into his seat. "Did you know this was going to happen?"

"I had a good idea," Gage said grinning. "So are you pissed at me, or what?"

"I'll let you know later."

Gage laughed.

Cher put her arm through Charlie's, grabbed his hand, and smiled. They sat back and watched the surf movie.

When it was nearly over, Charlie leaned and whispered into Gage's ear.

"Hey man, thanks for bringing me here, but do you mind if we leave a little early? You know, before everyone starts walking back here."

"No problem, man."

After Charlie dropped Gage off at his house, he drove to his secret parking spot out at Sunset Cliffs.

"Do you want to go for a walk?" he asked Cher.

"Where would we go?"

Charlie got out of the van and walked around to open Cher's door. He smiled and took her hand. "I know a way to get down that cliff over there. We can walk along the beach at the bottom. It's all right, the tide is low. Come on, it'll be fun."

The cliff cut downward sharply, but Charlie had negotiated the path many times, usually with a surfboard under his arm. A master guide, he led Cher down with little trouble. Clouds splotched the sky, but the full moon poked out occasionally to shine on the tide pools between the exposed rocks.

As they walked along the sandy edge in silence, Charlie reveled in the feelings stirred by the audience's response to the Baja film. Although thrilled about their ovation, he could not forget that his immediate future was far away from surfing. The fact of his inevitable departure for Vietnam crept, panther-like, out of the night and back into his mind.

Without warning, it started to rain.

Charlie grabbed onto Cher's hand. "Come with me, Babe."

They ran over to the side of the cliff and ducked into an opening.

"Charlie, what's this?"

"It's an old cave. I used to play in here when I was a kid. Come on. It's safe in here and we can keep dry until the rain stops."

They felt their way along the cave wall for nearly twenty feet before Charlie sat down on a rock and pulled Cher down next to him. He put his arm around her, drew her close, and began kissing her. She was very receptive to the affection, yielding to his advances. They made love in the coolness of the cave as the rains continued to beat down.

Instead of letting up, the sky opened up with pelting water droplets. Charlie, after kissing Cher on the forehead, got up and walked out to check on the weather.

He called back with his report. "Guess I was wrong, Babe. The rain's not going to stop anytime soon. I'm sorry about that."

"Charlie?" Cher said softly. "Are we going to be able to make it up the cliff now?"

"Sure, why not?"

"Won't it be muddy?"

Charlie had climbed the cliffs many times when it was muddy. But maybe, he thought, they could use the secret passageway at the back of the cave.

"Hey, we can climb up the cliff from in here. There is a hole up at the top to get out, and then we can run to the van. Let's go."

"But, Charlie, is it safe? I'm frightened."

"It's a piece of cake. Just take my hand and don't let go."

It was pitch black inside that hole in the earth, but Charlie knew the way. As they started up the rocky incline, Charlie was determined to lead the way to safety.

"In a minute, I'll have to let go for just a second to climb up a steep part. Then I'll reach down and pull you up. Don't worry, it's not that hard."

"Damn you, Charlie," Cher started to cry. "I'm scared. Let's go back."

"Come on, Babe, this is an adventure. Just relax and we'll be out of here in no time. Now, hold still and don't move until I tell you."

Charlie climbed up the five-foot wall and bent over to grab onto her hand.

"Now hold on tight while I pull you up."

As he pulled she started to struggle. Her hand was slipping and she started kicking at the wall to get a foothold.

"Stop trying to help. I can't hold on if you're moving around like that."

"Charlie, I'm going to fall."

"No you're not, damn it! Stop wiggling!"

He braced himself and, with one big tug, hauled her up next to him. She threw her arms around him and wept.

"Listen, Babe. Just trust me to get us out of here. Calm down now and everything will be all right."

He clasped her hand and they started off again. Three steps later, there was a shrieking noise with the flapping sound of bird wings. Cher screamed and stepped into a hole, twisting her right ankle.

"It's just a damn gull. Nothing to be afraid of. Come on, let's get out of here."

"Charlie, I can't move."

"What is it now?"

"I sprained my ankle!"

"Oh, man. Are you okay?"

Not waiting for her reply, he pulled her toward him and reached down and put his right arm under her legs, his left arm behind her back, and picked her up. She put her arms around his neck, and he proceeded to carry her the rest of the way up. From that point on, the incline was gradual, although he did have to put her down a few times so they could crawl under a ridge.

When he finally reached the hole it was smaller than he remembered. *Damn*, he thought. *I guess I was half this size the last time I climbed through here.*

He set Cher down, and then maneuvered his right arm up the hole in order to make his shoulder width as narrow as possible. Then, digging at the dirt wall with his feet, he pushed upward until his left arm was free. Then he braced his hands on either side of the hole and pushed up so his feet would clear.

He peered down into the blackness. "Now grab on," he instructed Cher. "And no wiggling this time. I'm going to pull you straight up."

He thrust his right hand down and circled her wrists. With one swift pull from Charlie's strong arm, she popped out of the hole. Both of her knees were bruised, her right ankle was swollen, her white sweater was dirty, and her sundress was torn. She sat down and held onto her ankle.

Charlie sat down next to her. The rain drenched their bodies. "You okay?" Charlie asked again.

"Yeah, I guess so."

"Sorry about that, Babe. I thought it would be an easier way up and we could stay dry."

She looked over at him; his hair was soaking wet, water dripped off of his nose.

"Well, we didn't exactly do that, did we?"

They both smiled. Charlie picked her up and hurried to the van. He put her down, opened the door, and helped her in. Then he ran around to the driver's side and climbed in. They sat there for a moment, staring through the window at the sheets of rain. Charlie's mood turned sour, matching the black, stormy sky.

"Guess I'll be sleeping in this stuff pretty soon," he said quietly.

"Oh, Charlie, I'm so scared for you," Cher said.

5

When Charlie and Gage arrived at the airport for their 10 a.m. flight, their families awaited them. The two had figured there was plenty of time to go surfing before heading to the airport. Now, dressed in their army khakis, they joined their families for the few minutes remaining before they departed for their unknown destiny.

"Hey Bro," Charlie's brother, Mike, said. "I was hoping that you paddled out to some boat and it took you away."

"That would be nice, but I don't know where to go, Mike."

John and Louise Armfield stood quietly, listening to their sons' conversation. Mike was scheduled to leave in a few weeks for the Peace Corps, and they would soon be alone. They stepped closer and put their arms around them.

"I never dreamed that any of my sons would have to go to war," his father said to Charlie. "I'm sorry you're caught in the middle, Son." His father's voice trembled, "Your mother and I will pray for you everyday."

"For you and for Gage, as well," his mother said. "It will be a long year for all of us, but we'll be with both of you in spirit every single moment you're away." She turned so Charlie could see who was standing behind her. "Your grandparents are here, too, Charlie."

Charlie walked over to greet his grandparents, Walter and Rebekah Armfield, who were well into their seventies.

"Thanks for coming Grandpa and Grandma."

Walter, a decorated World War I veteran, stood at attention in front of Charlie. "You are doing a great thing for your country, Son. I am proud of you."

"Stop it, Grandpa!" interrupted Mike. "Things are different now. This war is a bunch of crap and Charlie shouldn't have to be doing this like you did. This isn't our war."

"Michael Armfield!" Charlie's mother scolded. "This is your grandfather you're speaking to."

"I'm sorry, Grandpa, but…" Mike said.

Gage and his parents were standing quietly, listening to the Armfields' conversation.

"Hey listen, all of you," Charlie interrupted. "Everything's cool. It's true that I don't want to go, and neither does Gage here. But we're here now, whether we like it or not. We all need to be as strong as we can. Gage and I will be fine. If you all just envision the very best for us, then I believe that's what will happen."

Had he really said that? Charlie could hardly believe himself, talking about being strong and envisioning the best. He wished he felt as strong as his words. Was this something like his surfing scheme? It almost seemed like someone or something had put those words into his mouth. Whatever it was, everyone seemed to understand and they all settled down. He turned back toward his grandfather.

"I want you to take this with you, Charlie." Walter held out his hand.

"What is it, Grandpa?"

Walter opened his hand to reveal an old, World War I vintage knife. The sheath was a tarnished metal and there was rust in the hinge.

"My father gave this knife to me before I shipped out to France. Read what it says on the side."

Charlie looked at the knife, and saw the word "believe" inscribed in cursive.

"It's just like what you said to us, Charlie. Believe and everything will be all right."

There was a sincere look in his grandfather's eyes. Charlie grabbed his hand and shook it with a firm grip.

"Thanks, Grandpa. This will bring me good luck."

"Where is the beautiful Cher today?" Mike asked.

"Oh, I think she sprained her ankle or something," Charlie said.

"Why don't you give her a call before you have to board?" his mother suggested. "She needs to hear what you just told us, too."

"She does?"

"Of course she does, Son. I don't think you realize just how much that girl cares for you."

"All right, I'll give her a call."

Charlie walked over to the phone booth, deposited a dime, and dialed Cher's number.

"Hello?" Cher answered.

"Hi, Babe. How's the ankle doing?"

"It's better, but I can't walk on it very well."

"I'm at the airport, just about ready to go, so I thought I'd call and say goodbye."

"Charlie, please don't say goodbye. You'll be home soon, I just know you will. Don't ever say goodbye, okay?"

"Hey, that was supposed to be my speech."

"I don't know what you're talking about, but I love you, Charles Armfield, and nothing is going to keep me from doing that."

"I love you, too, Cher. I'll see you soon, okay?"

When the kisses and hugs were finished, Charlie and Gage walked outside toward the the plane. They were going to Seattle, and on to report at Fort Lewis for processing to Vietnam.

Charlie and Gage had been at Fort Lewis for only two hours when the Sergeant shouted, "I need two soldiers right now to fill empty seats. You and you, get over here!"

They were processed in the next two hours, and ordered into a military transporter bus headed for McCord Air Force Base, twenty miles north of Fort Lewis, where the plane for Vietnam was waiting for them.

"Shit, man, I thought this was supposed to take a couple of days," Charlie said.

"Yeah, me, too," Gage said. "This is really freaky, man."

"Not only that, but can you feel the energy on this bus? Damn, Gage, everybody is scared shitless in here."

They looked around at all of the strange faces. A group of black guys sitting in the back started chanting to the bus driver.

"No, Mr. Busman, please. Take us away from here. Please Mr. Busman, please, we don't want to go."

"That's making me nervous, man. I wish they'd shut-up." Charlie was irritated.

The driver turned around, a concerned look in his eye.

"Even the driver's eyes make me nervous," Gage said.

Charlie nodded. "Hey Gage, ever wish you were able to keep that school deferment?"

"You better believe I do!"

"Me too! You know, if this bus gets a flat tire, I'm out of here."

Gage looked at his friend in amazement.

"How about you, Gage?"

"I'm...I'm...right behind you, Charlie."

But the bus stopped right in front of the gangway to the plane. Orders were given to get off the bus, and march up into the plane. A light rain dampened their clothing as they got off the bus. There was only room for one footstep on the ground before the next was onto the steps going up into the plane.

They sat down and Charlie, swiping at the rainwater on his shirt, turned toward Gage. "You think they figured we might run for it if they parked too far away?"

"Would we have, Charlie?"

"I don't know, man." Charlie bared his teeth. "You know what?"

"What?"

"My last step on American soil was with my right foot. When I get back, I'm stepping off that plane with my left."

"What's the point in doing that?"

"The point is, Gage, that the next step after a right is always a left. I feel like my country has sold me out. Right now we're on our way to some obscure place in Southeast Asia to help some strangers fight some stupid civil war. Did anybody help us fight our civil war?"

Gage shook his head.

"Hell no! Then what's the deal here? All of the guys on this plane have been donated, man. This should be none of our business. The American government has sent us up the river for no damn reason. When I survive this war I'm stepping off with my left, just like the damn thing never happened."

"I hope it's that easy, Charlie."

The plane landed in Cam Ranh Bay, Vietnam with the sun shining down from the midday sky. The soldiers were herded off the plane and onto a bus headed for the processing center. A sergeant barked out orders saying they would be staying in barracks for the next few days, until more orders came down determining their destination.

"Man," Gage said, mopping his forehead on his sleeve. "This is more humid than Hawaii ever was."

"I wonder if the whole damn country is like this," Charlie said.

The wooden barracks had a three-foot wall of sandbags around the perimeter. Inside, bunks were staked in twos with mosquito netting surrounding each one. Charlie and Gage took two top bunks side by side, stripped down to their underwear, and stretched out. The rest of the men sat around as if they were waiting for something to happen.

"Hey, might as well get comfortable, right, Gage?"

"Right. Hey, Charlie," Gage said, looking around the room. "Do any of these guys look like they could kill somebody?"

"No, I don't think so, man. Well maybe that guy over in the corner. He looks like he maybe escaped from prison or something," Charlie said, laughing quietly.

"No, man, I'm serious. Most of these guys don't look old enough to be away from home, let alone fight in a war."

"Hey, Gage, when was the last time you were allowed to vote in an election or have a drink in a bar?"

"I'm not old enough to do either."

"Exactly, man. All of us are too damn young to be fighting in this stupid war. We can't even vote, and they told us we have to be here. There's no justice at all when it comes to our country and this war, Gage."

Just then a sergeant walked into the barracks to check on the new arrivals.

"Well, you guys look right at home. What would happen if this place got hit?" he asked.

"What do you mean by 'got hit'?" Charlie asked.

"That means a raid by the gooks, Private."

"I guess we would be up a shit creek. Does that happen around here?"

"No, not here at the Bay. I'm just giving you guys a hard time. You go ahead and relax, but I'll bet that where you're headed it will be the last time you get to lay around in your skivvies like this."

"Hey, Sarge, where do you think the worst place is to go right now?" Gage asked.

"Probably up at Pleiku in the Central Highlands."

Charlie looked at Gage, his thoughts on their friend Will.

"They've been getting hit pretty hard, ever since the Tet Offensive started at the end of January," the sergeant said.

"What's Tet Offensive?" Charlie asked.

"I don't really know. I think Tet is a holiday celebrating the Chinese New Year or something. All I know is that the gooks really step up the fighting, and this year has been the worst yet. I sure hope you guys don't have to go there."

"I sure hope that Will's all right," Charlie said.

After three days of waiting, the men were assembled in the road outside the barracks for their orders. Charlie and Gage were anxious to learn what destination the U.S. army had chosen for them. They had heard a few names mentioned, but most of the areas in Vietnam were unfamiliar.

"Private Saltman, front and center," shouted the sergeant.

Gage and Charlie exchanged a curious glance when the sergeant called Gage's name. He shrugged his shoulders and marched up to the front.

"Private," the sergeant said.

"Yes, Sergeant."

"You have been selected to remain here in Cam Rahn Bay as a cook, you lucky sonofabitch. You're never going to see any action around here."

Gage was dismissed to the mess hall, but he wasn't about to go very far until he learned Charlie's destiny. Then a long list of names was called all together, and Private Armfield was one of them.

"Front and center soldiers."

Thirty-five men filed out of the ranks and headed up to the front. Their army fatigues were soaked under the arms from perspiration, not only from the heat, but also due to their anxiety. Charlie's forehead began to twitch.

"You men have been selected to serve in the Central Highlands. You will be home based at Camp Enari near Pleiku."

Charlie looked around and spotted Gage standing in the back of the formation; his mouth was wide open. They made eye contact and Charlie mouthed the word "SHIT!" *I have to get the worst place,* he thought.

"Front ranks, attention! Right face! Forward march!"

A C-130 Military Aircraft stood ready, and the Pleiku-bound men were on their way to the war without explanation or farewell. Gage ran after them, trying to catch up with Charlie.

"Charlie, Charlie!"

Charlie looked around when he heard his name, and saw Gage chasing after the group.

When he caught up, he protested, "This is bullshit, Charlie. Why you and not me?"

"Hey, don't worry about me. Before you know it, we'll both be back on the beach, you hear me? Just keep cool, man," Charlie said.

Gage, a horrified look on his face, continued his pace alongside of his friend. "Oh, Charlie. I don't want you to go alone, man."

Charlie jumped out of the ranks and hugged his friend. "I'll be all right, damn it. Besides, I'm not alone. Look at all these guys. You're going to be a cook right here where it's safe. You always wanted to be a cook anyway, so really nothing is changed. I'm happy for you, man, but now I have to go to where they want me and…" Charlie swallowed hard, trying to be brave; but he knew his fear must show in his eyes and Gage couldn't help but see. "I'm going to be all right, that's all. See you later, Gage."

Charlie turned, leaving his best friend behind, and ran to catch up with the others boarding the C-130 for Pleiku.

Will I ever see Gage again? he wondered. *Wait a minute. What the hell are you doing to yourself? Don't even think about what you don't want to happen. Isn't that what you've been telling everyone else?* Charlie looked down at his GI-issue jungle boots and sighed.

6

The large, wide body C-130 military plane landed at an air force base outside of Pleiku. Charlie and the other replacements from Cam Ranh Bay disembarked. They wore jungle fatigues and carried duffel bags, and immediately boarded a bus to Camp Enari.

The air, hot and muggy from a recent rain, added to their feelings of apprehension. Scraggly dogs and scantily clad children played in the road, pretending to challenge the passing vehicles that sloshed through murky potholes, spraying muddy water in all directions. Older people, seemingly oblivious to the dirt or any danger to the children, sat alongside the road making trinkets out of wood and cloth. There was a smell of putrid meat cooking, and a vendor walking along selling over-ripe fruit stuck on a skewer shish-kebab style.

Most of the Americans had never seen a Vietnamese person before, let alone a third world scene, one choked with poverty worse than the slums of Watts or Harlem. They stared out the windows, disbelieving what they were seeing. Charlie seemed to be the only one aboard who was not shocked.

"Holy shi-it!" drawled Bill MaGuire, Charlie's seatmate. "Look at that filth. Have you ever seen anything like that?"

Charlie nodded. It reminded him of the Mexican villages he had visited while surfing. He stared out the window, wishing he were in his VW van cruising down a coastal dirt road in Baja California, rather than here, on an army bus bound for Camp Enari.

"You know," he said finally, "the country just to the south of ours is very much like this. There are dark-skinned people there, too, but they speak Spanish. Have you ever been down there?"

"I sure haven't. And if it looks like this, I'm glad I haven't," Bill said. "This is the worst place I've ever seen. How can they live like this?"

"Because they don't know any other way. Our country lived like this at one time, too, but we developed technology that carried us onward with civilization while these people have stayed the same. Hey, what's so bad about it? They don't look like they're as stressed out as we get back home," Charlie said.

"Yeah, but they have to live such a hard life. I'll bet they don't even have bathrooms in their homes," Bill said.

"No, I'm sure they don't," Charlie said as he waved to a group of kids next to the bus. "But I'll bet they don't worry about it because they don't even know what indoor plumbing is like."

Actually, Charlie thought, *those people look so peaceful and innocent. I'll bet they don't even know what this Vietnam War is all about. Here I am, completely uprooted from my life, taken away from my hard earned surfing opportunities, and they probably don't know why I'm here, any more than I do.*

When they arrived at the camp, they stood in ranks at the outdoor reception area as the resident lieutenant shouted out the orders.

"This is the Fourth Infantry Division of the United States Army, and you will be in training and quartered here for the next seven days. There will be classroom and rifle range work. It will behoove each and every one of you to pay close attention. As a matter of fact, what you learn here just might save your ass from extinction."

Charlie put his head down. *Oh shit,* he said to himself. *There's no way I'm letting this asshole scare me.*

"That goes for you, too, Private!" the Lieutenant said.

Bill MaGuire, standing next to Charlie, gave him a quick nudge on the hip with the back of his hand.

Startled, Charlie looked up.

"Do you think this isn't worth listening to?" demanded the lieutenant, looking directly at Charlie.

"Yes, Sir. I…I…mean no, Sir," Charlie stammered.

As the rest of the new men started to chuckle, the lieutenant spoke up again. "What exactly do you mean, Private?"

"I think the training is important, Sir. I am just thinking that perhaps it is also important not to get freaked out here. I think we all need to stay focused on survival, as well as being well prepared."

The lieutenant stared at him for a moment without saying a word. Then he shook his head and continued.

"At the end of the training, each of you will be assigned to a battalion within this Division. The first order of business is to issue you a weapon for your tour here in Vietnam. Queue up at the supply room to your right. After you receive your weapon, proceed to the large classroom on your left, for cleaning and firing instructions. That will be all."

Charlie, shaken by the confrontation, lined up behind Bill, waiting to receive his weapon.

"Shit, why can't they just treat you like a regular person? I thought when basic training was over, things would be different."

"I don't think it's ever going to be different in this man's army," Bill said.

"I guess not. Hey, by the way, where are you from, Bill?"

"I'm from Atlanta. How about yourself?"

"San Diego," Charlie said.

"That's California, right?" Bill said.

"Right. Georgia, right?" Charlie said, smiling.

Bill looked surprised, as if to say everybody knows where Atlanta is.

"Hey, I know where it is, man," Charlie said. "Just kidding around."

He shook Bill's hand, and when he let go noticed a beautiful green ring on Bill's fourth finger.

"Hey, that's a beauty," he said pointing to the ring.

"Thanks. That's a jade stone. My uncle gave it to me before I left. He wore it during World War II, and thought it would give me good luck."

"No shit?" Charlie reached into his pocket and pulled out his grandfather's knife. "This was my grandpa's during World War I."

They laughed together and continued exchanging small talk while they waited in line.

After Bill received his weapon, Charlie stepped up and was greeted by the supply sergeant holding a shiny black rifle.

"You think we'll be needing this any time soon?" Charlie said in a jesting manner, to see what the sergeant would say.

"I wouldn't be a bit surprised," was the reply from the sergeant. There was a smirk on his face.

Charlie looked up at him, frowning.

"Just kidding, Private. Hey, don't worry about anything around here. This is a base camp, and we haven't been hit the whole time I've been here. And I'm getting pretty short now."

"What do you mean, 'short'?"

"That means I'm a short timer for this toilet of a country."

"Oh, I see. Man, this is lethal hardware. What the heck is it?" Charlie had trained on a heavy M-14 rifle made of wood and metal. This piece was mostly plastic with a metal barrel.

"It's an M-16 semi-automatic. You two will be getting acquainted this week, and it's going to become your best friend over here."

Charlie took the rifle and turned to walk away.

"Hey," the sergeant said, waving another M-16 in the air and pointing to it, "I hope you both make it back here about this time next year."

"Yeah, me, too."

Charlie ran to catch up with Bill. *This time next year? Holy shit! I'm going to be here for a whole damn year? What in the world will become of me?*

Charlie knew how long he was supposed to be stationed in Vietnam, but hearing the sergeant say it hit him like an oncoming wave in a giant set. He slowed down and started scuffing his feet along the dirt pathway. *Oh, man,* he thought. *Why did I ever let this shit happen to me? I must be the stupidest guy in the world.*

Three days later Charlie and Bill sat at a long table with a half dozen other soldiers, inside a large tent that was being used for a classroom. There had been quite a bit of classroom work and, even though he thought it was important information, it was boring to Charlie. Apparently some others considered it boring as well, evidenced by the number of carvings in the tabletop.

As Charlie's eyes wandered over the markings, a fresh one jumped out at him. For a second he couldn't believe what he saw. Could it be? Yes! Clear and freshly chiseled, "O.B. RULES," was etched into the surface of the table. Could it be his O.B.? Yes! It had to be. All of a sudden he started to snicker.

"Hey," Bill said, throwing an elbow into Charlie's side. "Shut up before you get us all in trouble."

"Can't help it, man," Charlie whispered. "Look at this." He pointed to the fresh carving on the table.

"So what's that supposed to mean?"

"That's where I'm from, man. I'm from Ocean Beach in San Diego. We're always going around saying that O.B. rules. You know, kind of like a cheer or something."

Charlie stared at the message. "Maybe Will did it."

"Who?"

"Oh, never mind," Charlie said, unable to control a big smile.

At two o'clock in the morning, on the last day at the training center, the men in the barracks woke suddenly to the sound of sirens.

"What the hell is that?" Bill said as he sat up quickly in his bunk.

"Beats me. You've been here as long as I have," Charlie said.

The door slammed open. A sergeant ran into the barracks and yelled, "Grab your weapons and get into the bunker outside!"

The men in the barracks jumped out of their bunks, slipped on their boots without tying them, and ran outside wearing only their skivvies and carrying their rifles. Then they climbed down into a big hole in the ground, using the steps that had been carved into the dirt. The hole was covered with steel sheets with sandbags piled on top.

"Anybody know what's going on?" Charlie asked.

"The base is getting hit!" the resident lieutenant said as he climbed into the bunker.

Just then Charlie saw the supply sergeant sitting across from him. "Hey, Sarge. I thought this place was safe."

"Me, too, Private. I'm too short for this shit."

"Hey, listen up, Greenback," the lieutenant growled at Charlie. "No place is safe in Nam. There's Cong all around here. They might even be working right here at Camp Enari. When they go home at night, they get their buddies and come back for us. Don't ever trust a gook. No matter how friendly they seem."

Oh shit, Charlie thought. *No place is safe? So what are the odds of surviving a year without a safe place anywhere?*

Okay, big guy, Charlie told himself, *better figure out how to handle this. You can freak out, or you can stand up to this crap over here. Why not look at this like another contest? Just picture the outcome of this ordeal the way you want it to be. If you get freaked out about dying, that's exactly what might happen.*

From a distance, Charlie could hear machine gun fire and mortar explosions. The bunker was dark; nearly forty men were crammed into the hole. There were benches to sit on, but leaning back he found a dirt wall. Everyone was perspiring and the adrenaline was high. But Charlie decided it wouldn't do any good to panic. *It's going to be all right,* he thought.

Soon the siren went off again, this time to signal that all was well.

At the break of dawn, the troops assembled at the reception area to learn their assignments within the Fourth Infantry Division. As usual, the resident lieutenant stood in front of the men with the orders in his hand. He was shifting from side to side as if he were trying to decide how to begin.

"Before I read off your assignments, I want to inform you men of the activity that occurred last night. The camp alert began when three Viet Cong soldiers infiltrated the base camp perimeter. As you learned in class, these Cong are locally recruited South Vietnamese, and they always live near the area they fight in. The three last night were on a suicide mission. They didn't get past the wire on the perimeter, but the whole camp was alerted in case there was a bigger attack to follow."

He paused and looked over the men and, for the first time, Charlie felt a kind of compassion from the lieutenant. I*t sort of looks like he is sorry that he has to turn us loose into this mess,* he thought.

After the orders were read off, the men were told how to find their new units, and were dismissed. Before leaving, Charlie went up to the lieutenant.

"I want to thank you, Sir, for providing the training. I'm sure it'll help us while were here."

The lieutenant appeared to be stunned. "Nobody ever thanked me before."

"Well, I didn't want you to think I didn't appreciate what you were offering, that's all," Charlie said.

The lieutenant appeared embarrassed, not knowing what to say. Then finally he said, "You were right, Private."

"About what, Sir?

"Stay focused, Private, and good luck."

Charlie, Bill, and thirteen other men were assigned to the 402nd Artillery Battalion. Most of the battalions in the Fourth Infantry Division were hit hard by the effects of the Tet Offensive. Apparently, the 402nd and the infantry battalion, the 125th, that the artillery supported, had been hit the hardest. Many of the new recruits were being assigned to these battalions to replace the casualties.

The men walked down the road three quarters of a mile, and were met in front of the 402nd headquarters by First Sergeant Payne. He was a short, bulky man in his early fifties. He took off his hat to scratch his balding head before addressing the new arrivals.

"Welcome, men. You will have a short orientation by the battalion commander in a few moments, but first I need to ask if anyone here has attended college."

Charlie looked around and saw that nobody raised a hand. *What the heck,* he thought. *Maybe this is for a soft job around here.*

"I have, First Sergeant."

"Around here you call a first sergeant 'Top,' Private. The rest of you men proceed into the headquarters tent to your right. Private, you come along with me."

Charlie followed the man into another tent, where he was ordered to have a seat.

"What is your name, Private?"

"Charlie Armfield."

Top glared at Charlie for a few moments, and then continued.

"Captain Williams and I are looking for a replacement to work with the Intelligence Squad of this Battalion. We need someone who knows how to type. Do you have that qualification, Private."

"Yes."

"Good, then you will be accompanying me to the forward basecamp in the morning. Meet me here at 0500 sharp. We catch a chopper out of here at the crack of dawn. Give me your orders, and I'll get you assigned to me."

"May I ask what the Intelligence Squad does, Top?"

"We're the team that plans the activity for the three batteries of this battalion. Each battery has six 105 howitzer guns and they support the companies of the 125th Infantry Battalion. We're stationed at a forward base camp near Kontum. You'll soon learn that this will be a great job compared to the front, Private."

"Thank you, Top."

"Don't thank me. You just happened to come along when I needed someone. Your typing will come in handy. By the way, you're going to learn a hell of a lot about maps, too. Do you think you can handle that?"

"I'll try, Top."

"Yeah, okay then. You're dismissed. Remember, 0500 sharp."

"Dismissed, Top? What should I do until tomorrow morning?"

"Two tents south from here is the transient quarters. You can bunk out there for the night. You do know which way is south, don't you?"

Charlie pointed to his left.

"Okay, that will be all, Private."

Top had never introduced himself to Charlie. *Wow, what a weird deal this is,* Charlie thought. *He didn't even ask how much college I had, only if I could type. Thank goodness for the ninth grade typing class is all I have to say. Or maybe I shouldn't be so quick to be grateful. Working with this guy might be worse than battle.* He thought about that for a moment, and decided he was probably wrong.

Captain Williams met Charlie and Top at the chopper pad of the forward base camp.

"Looks like you found us a replacement, Top."

"Yes, Sir," Top said, as he saluted the captain. "This is Private Armfield. He just got in country and has some college experience."

Charlie stood still with his bag draped over his shoulder, as the captain looked him over.

"Put your bag down, Private, and salute the captain," ordered Top.

"No need for that, Private," the captain said as he stuck out his hand, showing Charlie that a handshake was sufficient. "Glad to meet you, Private. I'm Captain Williams. What's your first name?"

"Charlie."

Top cleared his throat to get Charlie's attention.

Charlie looked over at Top who was scowling at him. Top made a gesture toward the captain. Charlie turned back toward the captain and shrugged his shoulders.

Top spoke up. "It's Charlie, *Sir.*"

Charlie was embarrassed. "Charlie, Sir."

The captain laughed and addressed Top. "I think we can be a little more informal out here, Top." He turned toward Charlie again. "Where're you from, Charlie?"

Charlie could feel Top fuming next to him but decided the captain was cool, so he relaxed as he answered, "I'm from San Diego, Sir."

The captain stared at Charlie for a moment with his mouth open.

"That's in California. Is everything all right, Sir?" Charlie asked, wondering if he had said something wrong.

"Yes, of course. I know where San Diego is, Private. I was just surprised because I'm from San Diego, too."

"No shit?" Charlie spoke so fast he didn't realize what he'd just said. With his face feeling flush, he looked over at Top.

"I mean," turning back to the captain.

"Hey, don't worry about it. I was about to say the same thing," the captain said, laughing. "What part?"

"I'm from Ocean Beach."

"You're from O.B? That means we went to the same high school, Charlie," exclaimed the Captain. "I'm from Tunaville."

Top spoke up with a curious tone, "Tunaville, Sir?"

Charlie started laughing and the Captain joined in.

"That's by San Diego Harbor," the Captain said. "The slang for that area where we lived is called Tunaville because a lot of the people there are tuna fishermen. Right, Charlie?"

"Yes, Sir. Do you surf, Sir?"

"No, I never did get around to trying that. Always wanted to, though. How about you?"

"Yes, Sir! That was my whole life," Charlie said, lowering his head.

"That is, until I got drafted."

The captain looked Charlie over again, this time with admiring eyes. "I think we're going to get along just fine, Charlie." He leaned over and whispered into Charlie's ear. "My name is Joe Williams, class of '60."

Charlie smiled. "Shit, that's the year I learned how to surf. I was in eighth grade."

As the three men started walking toward the camp, Charlie realized that he had alienated himself from Top. He never did think Top liked him, but now he knew he was in trouble for making friends with the captain.

After a month of serving with the Intelligence Squad, Top called on Charlie for a special assignment.

"Private!" Top yelled. Sergeant Payne always spoke as if he were mad at Charlie.

"Yes, Top?"

"You will be going to Camp Enari today. Bravo Battery was hit hard, and we need someone to investigate the casualties and write a report. I can't leave here right now, so I'm sending you in to do it."

"What do you mean, investigate? What do I do?"

"Just go catch a chopper back to Camp Enari and when you get there walk to our headquarters and check out a jeep. They know you're coming and a map of the camp is waiting. Then drive to the infirmary. You'll be told what to do."

When Charlie arrived at the infirmary he was nervous. *Investigate?* he thought *How do you investigate casualties?*

He walked into the tent and was greeted by Lieutenant Murphy, a medic with the Fourth Infantry Division Headquarters.

"Can I help you, Private?"

"Yes, Sir. I'm Private Armfield with the 402nd Artillery."

"Oh yes, I've been expecting you. 'Ever done this before, Private?"

"No, Sir."

"Come with me." The lieutenant gestured for Charlie to follow him, lifted a large flap in the tent, and walked into the next room. There were body bags lying on floor. Beside the bags were backpacks.

"You need to go through the belongings of these casualties and write down everything you find, even personal items found in their wallets." He paused a moment and handed Charlie a tablet of paper and a pencil.

"Then look at the dog tags on the body so you know whose stuff you inventoried. When you're finished, you can use a typewriter in the other room to write a report. If you need any help, I'll be on the other side of the flap."

Charlie swallowed hard and looked into the lieutenant's eyes. *You've got to be kidding,* he thought to himself. Then he looked at the bodies and began to count how many were there.

"There're twelve, Private. It shouldn't take that long if you get busy." He put his hand on Charlie's shoulder and said, "It's a routine procedure, Private. Somebody has to do it and it looks like you're the man today. Good luck."

The lieutenant left the room, and Charlie walked over to the first body. "Well, here goes nothing," he said out loud.

He opened the backpack and found an army shirt, underwear and socks, a small transistor radio, a shaving bag, a perfume soaked silk scarf, a paper tablet with a letter started, and a wallet. Before he opened the wallet he read the soldier's unfinished letter.

5/10/68

Dear Mom;

The shit has been flying around here pretty heavy lately. The battery has been getting contact for the past three days, and I don't know how many fire missions we've had, but it's a lot. I think my ears are going to fall off from all of the explosions. I think we're pretty safe though, being up here on the hill and all, with the infantry surrounding our guns. Don't tell any of this to Jill, okay? You know how she worries about me being over here.

That was all that had been written in the dead soldier's letter so far. *Shit,* Charlie thought, *why does anybody even write home? How can you tell people what's happening over here?* Charlie had only written home once since being assigned to the Intelligence Squad, and he didn't say anything about the war. Actually he found it so hard to think of small talk to write about that he hadn't written again.

He picked up the wallet and started going through it. He found a military identification card, a verse from the Bible, a letter from his mom, and a high school picture of a pretty girl. On the back of the picture it was signed, "With love from Jill."

He jotted all of his findings down on the tablet, and then took a breath before opening the body bag. He grabbed the tab to the zipper and began to pull it open; stench escaped from the deteriorating body.

"Oh my God!" He grabbed his nose and finished opening the bag. Then he dropped his hand when he saw the face of a young man. His chest was open and blood had drenched that entire area. Around his neck Charlie found the dog tags with the inscription, Joseph F. Spaniel, U.S. 69782501, Blood Type B +. He looked at the face of the dead man. *Damn it, Joe. You died for what, man? You look so innocent.*

He turned back and found the Bible verse tucked into Joe's wallet, and read what Joseph had carried.

Psalm 91:1-2, 7, 11

> *He who dwells in the shelter of the Most High,*
> *Who abides in the shadow of the Almighty,*
> *Will say to the Lord, "My refuge and my fortress;*
> *My God, in whom I trust."*
> *A thousand may fall at your side,*
> *Ten thousand at your right hand;*
> *But it will not come near you...*
> *For he will give his angels charge of you,*
> *To guard you in all your ways.*

Charlie set the verse down and looked at the dead soldier's face. *I think God forgot the angels, man. Maybe there aren't any angels in Vietnam.*

Charlie continued his work. When he was going through the belongings next to the fifth bag, he found an unopened letter addressed to Private William MaGuire. He looked at the left-hand corner and saw the return address from Atlanta, Georgia.

"Oh no!" He quickly opened the bag, and there was a body without a face. The facial features had been destroyed beyond recognition, but around the neck the dog tags revealed the name of the body. Charlie slowly grabbed a tag and read William MaGuire.

"No, it can't be!" He reached down into the bag and pulled on the right hand of the body. There he saw the green jade stone ring on his fourth finger. "Oh my God!"

Charlie looked up and saw the lieutenant standing over him. "Do you know this guy, Private?"

"Yes, Sir. We came into country together. We've only been here a month," Charlie said, shaking his head. "He's already dead!"

"You know what, Son?" Lieutenant Murphy said as he knelt down and placed his right hand onto Charlie's right shoulder. "This body is dead, but the person isn't. The person is the 'being' part of a human being. The human will go home now and rot in the ground somewhere, but the 'being' part is still alive and will always be around in spirit, and in the memories of all who knew him. That's what the real person is—not this body."

He lifted his hand off of Charlie's shoulder and stood up.

Charlie stood up and looked into the lieutenant's eyes. "I think I understood that, Sir. But what I can't understand is, why? Why did the person and body have to come to Vietnam to get separated?"

The lieutenant shrugged. "I don't understand that part either, Son."

There were no choppers flying back to Kontum that day, so Charlie had to take a convoy. When he got to the convoy checkpoint, trucks, jeeps, and tankers were lined up for nearly a mile. He hopped into the back of a big two and a half-ton truck and laid back for the trip.

As the vehicles started to move, he tried to relax, but his body was jouncing up and down with every rut in the road. He tried to visualize a five-foot glassy swell, but it was no use.

As he was getting slammed in the back of the truck, the thought of the bodies back at the infirmary wrenched back into his mind. *Okay,* he thought, *so they're just bodies. But how in the hell can their deaths be justified? How can a country send soldiers off to a war that nobody knows the reason for?* Charlie stared blankly off into the jungle, confused about the ethics of the United States.

Then he thought about his friend Bill. *Shit! Bill's parents probably don't even know what happened to him yet. Damn! This could have been me.* His eyes closed and he saw his mother opening the front door of his house to greet a stranger dressed in a military uniform.

"Hello, my name is Lt. Bad News. Are you Mrs. Armfield?"

"Yes I am. Oh my God! You're not here to tell me about my Charlie, are you?"

"Well, Ma'am, as a matter of fact, I am. I am sorry to report…"

"No! Please don't say it, please," shouted Charlie's mom.

The loud report of shots snapped Charlie out of his daydream. He quickly rose and peered over the cab of the truck. He saw smoke up ahead. One of the tanks was on fire, and a jeep had driven off of the road and was lying on its side in the ditch.

"What's going on?" Charlie yelled into the cab of the truck.

A captain sitting next to the driver shouted back, "We're getting hit, Private! Lock and load and stay low."

Then a hailstorm of bullets ricocheted off the side of the vehicle.

"Open fire!" the captain yelled.

Charlie saw no targets—only flashes in the bushes off to the left of the truck. "Open fire at what?" he yelled back.

"Open fire!" the order came again.

Charlie put his M-16 rifle on automatic, and pulled the trigger until all twenty rounds had been dispensed into the jungles. There was a grassy division between the bush and the road, and his bullets traveled about thirty yards before they disappeared. He reloaded and continued to fire until they were out of the contact area.

Finally, when it appeared it was all over, he sat back, still clutching his weapon in the ready position. What in the world had just happened? Although bullets were flying everywhere, he didn't seem to be hurt. But, had he hurt someone else? Did he just kill someone? *Oh, my God, what have I done?*

Pictures flashed through his mind, ghastly snatches of dead bodies lying back in those jungles, torn and mangled bodies like the ones he had seen in the infirmary. *Oh, my God. Did I just kill somebody? Oh shit! What if they didn't want to be here either? What if I just killed someone who didn't want to be here either?*

When the convoy reached the Kontum checkpoint, Charlie gathered his weapon and dragged himself toward the forward basecamp. A jeep drove by.

Charlie, with his head down, didn't see who was driving until it turned around and pulled up beside him.

"Get in, Private," Top said. "Heard you got a taste of a little action."

"It was pretty heavy, Top."

"Oh, yeah," Top said laughing. "Well, it won't be the last time you get into heavy shit around here, so you just better get used to it."

Charlie stared at Top. How could anyone become so callused about killing?

"By the way, Private, how much college do you have anyway?"

"About a semester, I guess," Charlie said.

"You guess?"

"Yeah, I think I have that many credits. Why?"

"Well, we just got a new recruit in who has a bachelor's degree. The captain has decided to keep him here with us, so you'll be reassigned."

"Wasn't I doing a satisfactory job, Top?"

"I suppose you were, but we're going to take a chance that this guy is more qualified. By the way, the Captain liked you enough to put you in for a promotion. You'll be heading out into the field with a little rank."

"A little rank?"

"Yes, you are now a corporal. It's pretty unusual to be promoted this fast, but it was Captain Williams' idea—not mine."

"Will I get a chance to say goodbye to him, Top?"

Top hesitated, "No, I…I…don't think so. He's pretty busy right now. Besides, you need to collect your belongings and get to the chopper pad. I'll stop by your tent so you can pack, and then I'll take you to the pad."

By that afternoon, Corporal Armfield was on a helicopter with a group of new recruits. They were all heading out to "C" Battery, also known in the military alphabet as "Charlie" Battery, of the 402nd Artillery.

"Are you new in country, too?" one of the new recruits yelled, so as to be heard over the slapping sounds of the helicopter blades.

"Almost," Charlie said. "I've just been hanging around camp for awhile."

"My name is Al Strangemeir. What's yours?"

"I'm Charlie Armfield."

The new recruit shot him a surprised look. "Wow, your name is Charlie and you're heading out to Charlie Battery to fight Charlie?"

Charlie shrugged his shoulders, nodding, his mouth forming into a smirk at the irony.

When the chopper landed, the battery captain was on the chopper pad to meet them. Once the noise and turbulence from the chopper had decreased with its departure, the captain addressed the group.

"I understand that one of you troops has been in country for awhile working with the intelligence."

"That would be me, Sir," Charlie said.

"And is it true you've been working with maps and have a top-secret clearance?"

Everyone who worked in the Intelligence Squad had to be cleared with a top-secret clearance. Charlie had gone through the process shortly after arriving at the forward basecamp.

"Yes, Sir."

"Good. We have a need for you out at a different location, Corporal. You will be going farther forward to be on a communication team."

"Communication, Sir? What exactly does that mean?"

Charlie could see a concerned look on the captains face.

"Son, that means you will be with our liaison officer with Delta Company of the 125th Infantry. You will be a forward observer, operating a radio for Lieutenant Alvarez."

Charlie stared at the Captain. "A forward observer, Sir?"

"Sorry, Corporal. Somebody has to do it, and it just so happens we need to fill the position at the time you came along. I'm glad to get someone with some map experience out there."

Charlie boarded another chopper thinking how ironic his whole experience in the military had become. Because he quit college, he was drafted. That little college was enough to get a so-called soft job with the Intelligence Squad, but not enough to keep him there. So he was sent to the guns. Now it appeared, however, that the Intelligence Squad knowledge over-qualified him for the guns, so he must become a forward observer. He must now go out as far to the front as one can possibly go.

7

The slap, slap sounds of the helicopter blasted Charlie's ears as it hovered over the jungle valley. He didn't recognize the fumes in the air. They were definitely from smoke, but he knew they were not from a forest fire. There weren't any doors on the chopper, so he stuck his head out to have a look.

The soldier sitting in the doorway with a machine gun mounted next to his seat said, "Don't get out there too far, Corporal. Some gook may take a potshot at you."

Charlie pulled back in, even though he wanted to see where he was going. He felt awkward leaning out of the door anyway, with his heavy pack on his back and his weapon clutched in his hands. But it was nerve racking to sit and watch the sky go by without being able to look down.

"Where are we going?" Charlie asked, trying to control the muscles of his forehead that twitched nervously.

"You're going to find out soon enough, Corporal."

Frowning, Charlie studied the chopper gunner.

"Hey, I don't even know where we're going," said the gunner. "Out to some jungle wasteland is all I know. It all looks the same to me."

When the aircraft began to descend, Charlie again looked out cautiously. It was then that he saw the soldiers, maybe a hundred of them, spread out in a large circle. *So, who are those guys,* he wondered? They were all lying on their stomachs and it was obvious they weren't resting when he heard the gunfire.

Shit! Are those guys Americans, or gooks? His eyes widened as he looked over at the gunner, searching for an explanation.

"Sorry, Corporal. Looks like we have to drop you into the middle of a firefight. Get ready to unload."

Charlie scooted over and sat in the open doorway, his legs hanging out over the edge. The pilot took the chopper down about eight feet off the ground and yelled, "Jump!"

"What?" Charlie couldn't believe what he heard.

The gunner put his hand on Charlie's back, giving him a shove. "Get the hell out of here!"

He dropped out of the chopper, landed awkwardly on his heels, and fell backward due to the weight of his pack. He rolled quickly, still clutching his rifle, and studied his options. A group of men, crouched and holding rifles, were off to his right. *Shit, I sure hope those guys are Americans,* he thought. He started a cautious, low crawl toward them.

One of the men looked over at him. Charlie saw his face, dirty and partially covered by his helmet—he had slanted eyes. Charlie froze.

The soldier looked Charlie over, then grinned and spoke English. "Don't worry, Buddy. I may look like a gook, but I'm from Chinatown in Frisco. Hey guys, look at this. That chopper just shit us a new grunt."

Charlie took in a deep breath and blew it out hard. Red-faced and speechless, he looked at the soldier.

"Don't worry about it, man," one of the other grunts said. "Sam here has to keep reminding us, too. Hell, I woke up the other night and almost strangled the poor bastard."

"You picked a hell of a time to join the company," Sam said.

"Actually, I'm with the Artillery looking for Lieutenant. Alvarez. You guys know where he is?"

"He's around here somewhere, but I wouldn't go looking for him yet. This shit's not over."

The artillery rounds started blasting the ground fifty feet out from their position. Everybody hit the dirt.

"It's going to be over soon though," Sam said. "Just stay low 'til it gets quiet."

Huge explosions blasted all around them. Charlie heard whistles before each, and then the ground shook. *Damn, those things are getting pretty close,* he thought. *What did Sam mean it would be over soon? How does he know that? Are those our artillery rounds coming in?*

Five minutes later, silence fell across the land. Nobody said a word, so Charlie continued to lie still. After another five minutes, he heard movement from the men around him, but he still wasn't sure it was okay to look up. Then he felt a tapping on his shoulder.

Startled, Charlie turned around quickly to look into the dark eyes of another soldier. He flinched backward and raised his weapon.

"Holy shit, don't shoot, Corporal," the stranger said.

Sam laughed. "Looks like Lieutenant Alvarez found you first, Buddy."

"Sorry to scare you, Corporal," Lieutenant Alvarez said. "Come on over here with me so we can get better acquainted."

Charlie stood up, his legs wobbly. He wiped the sweat off of his forehead and followed the lieutenant.

"Have a seat in my office, Corporal," Lieutenant Alvarez said as he pointed to a mound of dirt half covered with tall grass.

Charlie sat down, still jumpy from the firefight. Meanwhile, the soldiers got up, formed a large rank in a single line, and walked out into the jungle.

"What are they doing?" Charlie asked.

"We do a sweep after every firefight to look for and count the dead enemy. Have to be careful, of course, that there are no live ones still around. Sweeping is the worst part of this fucking war."

Charlie started to speak but the sounds of a helicopter drowned out his voice. The big bird landed on the ground where there wasn't any bush. There were five bodies lying on stretchers, accompanied by two medics, at the landing zone. The medics quickly loaded the stretchers and the helicopter lifted into the air and sped away.

"Are they dead, Lieutenant?"

"Either that or injured pretty badly. Hey listen; I want you to call me Robby around here. I don't want the gooks to hear you calling me lieutenant, and by no means will we be saluting. I'm a big target if they know my rank.

Besides, we're all pretty casual out here. Your name is Charlie, right?"

"Right. How did you know?"

"I radioed to call in the artillery, and they told me you were on your way. That was about the time I saw you jumping out of the bird. Sorry I couldn't welcome you to the bush."

Charlie laughed, remembering the fright of his introduction to the front, still shaking from the thought of it all. They sat for nearly ten minutes, not saying much, trying to relax, when Charlie saw another soldier staring at him. The soldier started toward him.

Robby followed Charlie's eyes and glanced up. "Do you know that guy?" Robby asked.

"I don't think so."

He was a grunt with the infantry—dirty clothes, unshaven face with a blond shaggy mustache, wearing a backpack and holding an M-16 in his right hand.

"Charlie? Is that you?"

Charlie sat for a moment, amazed that someone would recognize him.

"Yeah, I'm Charlie all right."

He stood up to get a closer look, and the guy threw his arms around him. Robby, curious about the confrontation, stood up, too.

"How do you know this guy?" Robby said, addressing the grunt.

"I ought to know him. I've been in the water with him a hundred times."

Charlie pushed himself away and looked into the grunt's blue eyes.

"Will? Goddamn it! Is that you, Will?"

"Who in the hell do you think it is?"

Charlie threw his arms around his friend. As they embraced, Robby watched, speechless. Will started laughing and lost his balance, pulling Charlie with him onto the ground. They rolled in the dirt, laughing hysterically.

"Hey, I guess you guys really do know each other. Damn, nobody around here runs into someone they knew back in the real world. I can't believe it," Robby said.

They stood up again, still laughing. "I don't believe it either," Will said. "Two surf rats from O.B., in the middle of this hellhole. Shit, man! Nate wrote me that you got drafted."

"Yeah." Charlie felt like he was going to cry.

Will looked over at Robby. "Is he working with you?"

Robby nodded affirmatively.

"Oh, man! This is a crock of shit! Would you believe that this guy is just about the best surfer in the whole world?"

"Really, Charlie? Where in the hell are you guys from?" Robby asked.

"San Diego," Will said, pride in his voice.

"Hey, Will, I knew you were around here somewhere, but I never expected to see you, man," Charlie said.

"What do you mean?"

"Your brother told me you were in the Central Highlands. Then I saw the 'O.B. RULES' on a desk at basecamp."

"No shit! I was hoping somebody important would see that."

Charlie stared at Will, feeling confused. "I don't know if I'm important, man, especially if I'm out here."

"Let me tell you something, man. Seeing you right now is the most important thing that has happened to me in my entire life." Will clutched Charlie's arm, shook his head and smiled.

"Hey, Will," Robby interrupted. "You're out on LP tonight, aren't you?"

"Yes, Sir."

"Why don't you take this new corporal out with you?"

"Oh, man! This is his first night. Don't make him go out there on his first night. Don't you have some briefing to do with him or something?"

"We've got plenty of time for that. Besides, I think he would rather be with you than anybody else on his first night."

Will looked at Charlie. "Do you know what LP is, man?"

"Not a clue."

"LP stands for listening post. We're going to be out there in the bush tonight, my friend, and we can't make a sound. We take turns listening for gooks."

"So what if we hear something? What the hell do we do?"

"We click out a code on a radio. We can't move, but we signal the rest of the company, and they take over from there."

Charlie's eyes widened. "Holy shit!"

Robby walked up to Charlie and handed him a box that was twelve inches high, twelve inches wide, and four inches thick. It had a four-foot retractable antenna and a coiled cord with a phone receiver on the end of it.

"You can use this tonight, Corporal," Robby said. "It's going to be yours anyway until you're out of here, I'm afraid. You are now officially an

RTO. That means radio telephone operator. Tomorrow we'll be doing the FO—forward observer—stuff and you'll be getting acquainted with it. For now, just hang out with Will."

At nightfall the two California surfers headed out into the central highland jungle with only their weapons and Charlie's radio. They hiked out a hundred yards from the perimeter of Delta Infantry Company's camp, and sat down to make themselves disappear in the bushy wasteland. Will, a Vietnam grunt for nearly seven months, had lots of experience with listening post duty. For Charlie, however, this was his first assignment, and he felt nervous.

The thick bush, alive with mosquitoes and the noises of other insects, all contributed to Charlie's anxiety. The waxing half moon shed enough light so they could see each other's faces. Will smiled to try and comfort his old surf buddy, but Charlie only nodded to acknowledge the gesture. Then Will put his hand out. Charlie grasped it quickly, grateful for his friend's strong squeeze of reassurance.

Charlie looked into Will's eyes and felt an instant connection. He thought Gage would always be his best friend, but Will clearly had become a comrade sharing an equally unknown destiny. Will told him he was somebody important, and now he knew what he had meant. He had never felt such a bond with another human being.

Before they left for their LP position, Will instructed Charlie on what would happen. They would take turns sleeping at one-hour intervals. There would be ten hours of darkness, so potentially they would get five hours of sleep, each. Charlie was supposed to nap first, but when he closed his eyes, he was too anxious to sleep.

When it was Charlie's turn to listen, Will closed his eyes and was instantly asleep. *How can he do that,* Charlie wondered? *Can I get so conditioned that I can just sleep when I'm supposed to?*

It was Charlie's third shift when he heard a noise. It sounded like men walking toward them, about thirty yards out. He shook Will, who sat up, instantly alert.

He looked at Charlie and appeared to read the message of the danger in his eyes. Will listened until he heard the noise, grabbed the radio, and started clicking.

The stepping noise continued. It sounded to Charlie like five or six men walking directly toward the LP position. Will grabbed Charlie and shoved him to the ground, just as the infantry opened fire.

Shit, Charlie thought, *what if that noise wasn't from the enemy? What if it was innocent civilians out there?* But when the return fire began, there was no longer any doubt.

Charlie hugged the ground, trying to disappear into the foliage. Bullets zinged overhead. The shooting continued for several minutes, which seemed like hours to Charlie. When it stopped, there wasn't a sound to be heard, not even footsteps. Will waited twenty minutes before he gave Charlie the "all's well" sign, making a circle with his thumb and first finger, and lay back down to go to sleep.

Five minutes later, Charlie saw the bush, less than ten feet away, move. Then a shot whistled by his left ear. Will sat up and reached for the radio, but Charlie's M-16 shot out before he could signal a distress call. He heard a thud and a moan, and Charlie knew for sure, this time, that he had just shot his first enemy soldier. He stared blankly at Will, his eyes watering.

Early the next morning, as the bright orange sun rose in the east, the grunts were already flanked side-by-side for the sweep. They found five North Vietnamese army soldiers huddled together twenty yards out from the LP, their bodies ripped to shreds from the infantry attack. Charlie had suspected there were six men. He and Will found the last one as soon as they stepped out from the listening post.

Charlie stood over the NVA soldier, looking at the blood on his face. There was a bullet hole above his right eye, and his mouth was wide open as if he was crying out with pain. He looked young, maybe younger than himself. The dead man wore green fatigue clothing, his pantlegs rolled up to just below his knees. He had leather thong sandals on his feet and a small backpack. A fatigue hat lay next to his head.

A small bag was tied around his waist. Charlie knelt down on one knee to touch it, and discovered it was full of rice. Will watched as Charlie put his head in his hand and started mumbling to himself.

"Oh my God. I killed you, and I don't know why. I didn't want you to die, man. This isn't my fault. I don't even know why I'm here."

Will helped his friend up. He put his arm around Charlie's shoulder as they walked back to camp.

"I remember my first one, man. I was shook up for over a week. But you know what? After awhile over here, you start to get numb to this shit. I don't know how many I've killed by now, but it's like I've become a hard ass or something, because it doesn't faze me much anymore."

"I don't know if I want to get like that or not. I just killed somebody. Took him away from his family. Damn it, man, his parents are going to be devastated."

Will led Charlie over to a bush away from the rest of the men. He sat down and motioned for Charlie to do the same. Then he reached into his pocket and pulled out a small bag.

"What's that, man? You carry rice, too?" Charlie asked.

Will laughed. "No, man. This isn't gook food, but sometimes you find a bag like this on them, too. This is marijuana. We find it growing all over the place around here. I think God put it here so we could mellow out during combat."

He reached into his pack, grabbed a box of C-rations, and pulled out a small pack of cigarettes. He pulled one cigarette out and started carefully rolling it between his fingers until the tobacco started to fall out. When the paper was empty he held it up and started to refill it with the green weed.

"Hey, Will, is this a good idea?"

Will looked at Charlie as he put the re-made joint into his mouth, struck a match, and inhaled as he lit the end.

"Brother, I think I would be half crazy by now if it weren't for this stuff. It's like having your girlfriend around to give you some comfort. In fact, we even call it Mary Jane."

Charlie stared at Will, confused by his words and by what he was doing.

"Listen, man," Will said. "Almost everybody out here is smoking. It allows us to see this bullshit with a different point of view."

"So, is it legal?" Charlie asked.

"Not really. The lifers know we're doing it, but they don't say much. Even some of them smoke."

"But how do you stay focused when you're drunk?"

"This isn't like drinking, man. When you're drunk you're out of it and it's all over. When you smoke you get high. You still know everything that's going on. You just take on kind of a euphoric view, that's all. It's saved my life out here more than a few times."

Will passed the joint over to Charlie.

Charlie hesitantly took it and sucked in a puff of smoke. It didn't hit him all at once, but slowly his mind began to ease. They each took a couple of hits before Will put it out.

"We don't need much, man. Once you get turned on you just stop, because more doesn't do very much. When you keep drinking you just get drunker, right? But when you smoke you seem to come down with more. At least that's the way it works with me," Will said.

Charlie felt eased—smoothed. He didn't seem to be as nervous as before, and he felt alert—not groggy like he thought he might.

When Robby came over, he stood up and greeted him. "Good morning, Robby."

"Well, good morning, Charlie." Robby looked at the two soldiers and smiled, as if he knew they had smoked.

"Hey, Charlie. You did a great job out there last night and I want to commend you. That last gook could have caused a lot of trouble."

"You're damn right," Will interrupted. "Charlie here saved my life for sure."

"I saved your life?"

"Damn right you did," Will said. "You saved both of our lives, man."

Charlie looked at Robby, shrugging his shoulders.

"You sure did, Charlie," Robby said, nodding his head up and down. "And probably some of the rest of us as well."

Charlie looked up at the sky. The blue color looked brighter than usual. There was sweat starting to bead up on his forehead from the rising temperature of the morning, but it didn't seem to matter. He looked around at the terrain. It was green and beautiful—so lush in the jungle.

How can such a beautiful place be filled with so much horror, he wondered. *We kill here to keep from being killed. We take precious lives, families are ruined forever, and then we smoke to cover our feelings. We smoke to try to make everything all right. But it isn't. Worst of all, we don't even know why we're here, in a foreign land, fighting someone else's war.*

8

Charlie could hardly catch a breath, the air felt so thick and soggy. He and Robby were accompanying an eleven-man squad that had been in the bush for over a week without contact. That meant they needed to keep moving. Their packs, loaded with rations and ammunition, weighed close to seventy-five pounds.

The forward observer lieutenant had explained to Charlie that their mission was surveillance of the immediate area. The squad preceded the large company of infantry soldiers by nearly a mile, making sure the way was clear. If they received contact, it was their job to alert the company and try to retreat. If that was not possible, they were to counterattack until they could be rescued.

The forward observers were along to protect both the squad and the company from being outnumbered. Calling for artillery fire missions from the 105 howitzer batteries in the area would accomplish this. The 402nd Artillery Battalion was their back up. It fell to Charlie Armfield, as the radio-telephone operator, to alert Charlie Battery when help was needed.

They stopped just short of dusk to prepare for the night. Robby, the highest ranked soldier in the squad, established the LP positions and gave the orders. There were also a staff sergeant, three spec fours (a rank similar to a corporal), and five privates first class besides Robby and Charlie.

As darkness settled in, the men spread out and took turns standing watch. Robby and Charlie took turns, also, staying close in case they needed to work together. Talking out loud was forbidden within the ranks at night. Because they stayed together, the FO and RTO were the only ones who could have a whispered conversation. Usually they were so exhausted they just went to sleep.

This night, however, Charlie was curious and wanted to ask some questions. "Robby, I don't even know where you're from," he whispered.

"I'm from San Antonio. You know—the home of the Alamo. My ancestors were the ones rushing the fort." He put his hand to his mouth to keep from laughing out loud.

"Shit, Robby. I don't even know your real name."

Robby grinned, stuck out his right hand and said, "Roberto Luis Mendoza Alvarez. Glad to meet you."

Charlie grabbed his hand and shook it. "Why did you join the army?"

"I wanted to be somebody. This was the only way I knew how. I'm the youngest of six. One sister and I are the only ones who graduated from high school. I wanted to go to college, but there wasn't any money. I knew I'd get drafted, so I joined. I got lucky and was shuffled to OCS. So here I am, a second louie in Vietnam. Like you, I don't know why in hell I'm here, except this is a way for me to be successful at something."

Charlie looked away, stunned by Robby's answer. *Oh my God,* he thought. *I'm pissed because the army brought me here and kept me from being successful. He asked the army to bring him here so he could be.* He shook his head and looked back into Robby's eyes.

"How long have you been out here, Robby?"

"Three months. In another three I hope to be promoted to first lieutenant and get stationed back at Camp Enari."

"Camp Enari? Shit, that means you'll be leaving me?"

"Yep, unless I don't get promoted. The captain has sent in a good report on me, though. Even recommended me for a medal."

"A medal? What in the hell did you do to get that?"

"I led a squad, just like this one, through an enemy battalion position, without us hardly being noticed."

"What do you mean, 'without us hardly being noticed'?"

"I lost two men when we bumped into one of their reconnaissance squads. We took care of them pretty quickly, but ended up with two casualties."

"Wow, man. That must have been heavy. Did you know those guys very well?"

Robby hesitated, then peered into Charlie's eyes. "One of them was my RTO. You replaced him three days after he was killed."

Charlie returned Robby's gaze. "I'm sorry, man," he said, shaking his head. Then he looked away not knowing what else to say.

Robby was going to take the first watch, so Charlie lay down, trying to sleep. But all he could think about was the former RTO. *Shit,* he thought. *I replaced a dead soldier just three days after he was killed. Now I'm out here doing the exact same thing. If that guy hadn't been killed, I would have been placed on the guns.*

Charlie didn't get much sleep that night. When Robby assembled the men at dawn, he was not eager to get on the march. The morning moved slowly, and finally Robby signaled everyone to halt for a break. They scattered in a circle, took off their packs and dug out C-rations for a meal. Charlie found he had beans and wieners when he opened the box. The staff sergeant immediately bargained for a trade.

"Hey, Corporal, how about some ham and lima beans for your beans and wieners?"

"There is no way in hell I'm trading for lima beans, Sarge. Those things make me gag."

Everybody started laughing.

"All right, then. Be that way. I was going to throw in my dessert with the deal, but you can kiss my ass, now."

"Sure you were, Sarge," Private Wallace said. "You never give up dessert. In fact you're usually begging for ours."

"Shut up, Private. Hey, do we have an extra claymore? If I'm going to have to eat limas, I got to have them heated."

One of the new privates spoke up. "Hey, Sarge, how are you going to heat your food with a claymore mine?"

The sergeant smiled. "I set the can out in the jungle and face the claymore right next to it. Then from back here, I detonate the mine. That way I don't have to open the can, either. I just take my fork and scrape the food from the land."

There was laughter again, from everyone except Charlie. Sarge had pulled the same joke on him when he first arrived in the bush.

"Hey, Sarge, don't you get tired of that one?"

"What I get tired of is stupid questions."

"They're not stupid if they're trying to learn how things work around here," Charlie said.

"All right, then, you tell him," the staff sergeant said.

Charlie addressed the new recruit. "Inside of the claymore is a substance called C-4. If you take a hunk and burn it under a can, you've got yourself a hot meal."

"That's right," Robby interrupted, "but we're down to our last four claymores, so there won't be any hot meals for awhile. Let's finish up now and prepare to move out."

Charlie took the four-pack ration of cigarettes out of the C-ration box, and stashed them in his right shirt pocket. He never smoked them, but he always kept a few handy for making joints. Earlier that morning, he'd stumbled across a very healthy plant. He'd picked a few branches and positioned them around his helmet to dry in the heat of the day—a trick Will had taught him. When the staff sergeant had asked him about it, Charlie explained it was camouflage.

Late that afternoon, they encountered deadly contact. Private Wallace, the point man, dropped with a blistering volley of fire from the jungle up ahead. Everybody hit the ground as enemy small arms began snapping in the air above them.

Clutching a map, Robby crawled over to Charlie, who went into action. He ripped the radio receiver off of his pack strap and called for the battery. By the time he made a connection, Robby had the location charted on the map, and Charlie read out the quadrants. The battery rogered the report, but before a fire mission could be called in, an air-control chopper in the area intercepted the call.

"I have you spotted," the pilot reported. "Your element is encircled by an estimated reinforced enemy company."

"Roger that," Charlie said. "Looks like we're not going anywhere."

"Spread out, stay low and circle," Robby yelled. "We need a heavy volume of fire to keep from being overrun, so let's get with it."

M-16 rifle fire began. Then the staff sergeant, who was carrying an

M-60 machine gun, started to flare rounds out in every direction. The enemy pulled back, and the squad breathed a short-lived sigh of relief, until the 60-millimeter mortar rounds began to drop among them.

"Now we're in for it," yelled the staff sergeant. "They're going to shred us into a million pieces."

Robby quickly estimated the enemy position and had Charlie call in a fire mission. Charlie had been in a few skirmishes before, but this was a big one.

Okay, big guy, he thought. *You know exactly what to do—keep your head clear—we need action now. Just like a damn surf contest—see it all coming together just like you want it.*

Between the two of them, Robby and Charlie skillfully directed the artillery. 105 millimeter rounds came bombing down at about three hundred yards out to their left flank, where the majority of the activity was coming from. Then they delicately edged the rounds to within sixty yards of their position. But the enemy fire continued, this time from their right flank.

"Shit!" Robby said. "I was afraid that was going to happen." He directed artillery defense in that direction. But the enemy fire then began from the rear and the forward positions.

"Holy shit, man. We're going to need more help," Charlie exclaimed.

"Right! Ask them if there's another battery within range."

"We need more help!" Charlie yelled into the receiver.

"Roger that. Alpha Battery has already been called in on the mission."

From that point on, Charlie began to communicate with both batteries, carefully guiding twelve 105 howitzer rounds to their right, moving forward, and to their left, moving backward, providing a protective wall of steel for the surveillance squad.

"Charlie, direct Alpha Battery to move fifty yards to the right." Robby was yelling to be heard above the explosions.

"Sergeant! Move the men to the right when the rounds start pulling out on that side."

They moved out, still enclosed in their now mobile wall of steel. Then they filled in the hundred yard gap left behind by directing Charlie Battery fifty yards to the right. With this technique, the patrol was able to move more than a thousand yards, to an area where two choppers could have a landing zone to remove the patrol.

The choppers skillfully landed, quickly evacuated the men—ten of them still alive (three of whom had shrapnel wounds in their arms and legs), and one casualty. Wallace was dead, but the staff sergeant made sure that when the patrol moved out, he was dragged along with them.

Ten minutes later they were dropped off at the company site, and were free from the enemy. The grunts, who had been following the action by listening in on another radio, began to congregate to see how many survivors there were. Will was in that group as the surveillance patrol unloaded from the choppers. Charlie jumped out and immediately made eye contact with his friend.

Will ran up and put both of his hands on Charlie's shoulders. "Am I glad to see you! I thought there was no way you were going to make it out of there, man. Did you know you were outnumbered, twenty to one?"

"We were?" Charlie said. "Damn!"

"Damn is right. But somehow you have an estimated enemy casualty of around 150. How did you do it?"

"Beats me. All I did was follow Robby's orders. He was incredible! He had me talking to twelve howitzers at the same time. We made this protective wall for ourselves and moved out to a clearing where we could be evacuated. It was unreal, man."

"How many casualties?"

"One. Wallace," Charlie said, shaking his head.

"Wow! You guys just pulled off the impossible," Will slapped Charlie on the back.

"Whatever, man. All I know is that I don't ever want to go back there again."

Will looked Charlie in the eye and shook his head. "I don't think you're going to get your wish. I heard we're pulling out in the morning to go clean up that place."

Charlie stared at his friend. "No, Will. I don't want to see what happened."

"I'm sorry, man. You don't happen to have any stash, do you?"

Charlie reached into his pocket and pulled out some dried leaves and the cigarettes. "Found it this morning."

"Wow! How did you get it dried so fast?"

"I just did what you told me to do—put it on my helmet."

"Didn't anybody say anything to you?"

"Sarge asked about it, but I told him it was camouflage."

"And he bought it?"

"I don't know, man, and I really don't give a shit. What's he going to do, bust me? After killing all those people, I think maybe that would be the best thing for me anyway. The stockade has got to be better than this shit."

Charlie lowered his head and kicked at a rock—and missed. "Goddammit, Will."

"All right, calm down, man. Let's make a joint with that stuff of yours."

The next morning, at the crack of dawn, the company commander ordered the men into five platoons. Then he selected one small point squad to proceed the main group. Charlie and Robby were part of the point, and so was Will, who stayed close to his friend.

"I don't know about you, Robby, but the thought of going back there gives me the creeps," Charlie said.

"I'm with you, but we can't leave this situation unfinished. By tomorrow there'll be a couple of more companies joining us. Intelligence must think there's a lot more involved than just what we bumped in to."

"Shit, *that* makes me feel a lot better. How about you, Will?"

Will shook his head. "Nothing surprises me anymore. To survive a tour in hell, you have to take on the attitude that everything just happens. There's nothing you can do about it. Just let it be. Keep calm and take it a day at a time."

"You know, Will, that was my approach when I was surfing in contests. I figured I couldn't control the conditions, or the guys I was surfing against. What I had was myself and my ability to do what was within me."

"Cool, man. And it must have worked. Nate said you were doing so well you were a cinch to win the World Contest."

Charlie trudged along in silence, mulling over Will's words. A heavy sadness infiltrated his thoughts, shrouding his memories of his contest successes.

"Hey, Charlie…"

"What?"

"You okay, man?"

"I guess so. I'm so goddamned pissed that I missed that World Contest." He cleared his throat and spit off to the side.

"I'll bet. Hey, I want to know something, man. You were so much younger than the other top surfers were. Shit, I watched Billy Foxx ripping when I was just learning. How did you manage to get yourself competing on that level?"

"Gage and I went to Hawaii the winter before last. My goal was to ride the most powerful waves possible so I could get better. I figured that was the best place to go. Later on, I'd sit on the beach and visualize riding waves before I went out into the water. It made me surf better. Before long, I tried visualizing at home, too. It really worked, man."

"Wow!" Will said.

Charlie lapsed into silence. *I won all of those contests and still had to win the championships to make the team. But damn it, I did it. I won and made the team. Was that my goal? I earned the right to surf for the U.S., but did I expect to win the world contest?* He took a deep breath and shook his head. *No, that wasn't it. Damn it, big guy, don't you remember? What you wanted was to know what it would take to win. It was learning about the energy of the sea that spurred you on. Dad called it the spiritual connection.*

"Hey, Will?"

"Yeah?"

"What if we take that scheme of mine and make it work for us here in Nam?"

"What are you talking about, man? Like we're going to start visualizing perfect battles or something? I'd much rather visualize being in no battles at all."

"Well, that's kind of what I had in mind."

"How, man?"

"What I mean is, we can't control the battles we're going to be in, right? You already said we need to take one day at a time. But how about if we visualize ourselves surviving every battle and going home."

"Hey, man, I never see myself getting killed, but sometimes I do wonder if today's the day I die. A year's a long time, man. Sometimes I wake up wondering."

"Well, what if you changed that, and woke up seeing yourself living through all of it?"

"I never thought about doing that."

"Well, maybe you should think about it," Charlie said. "Maybe we both should think about it. Every day."

They walked in silence.

"You know," Will said, "I think it's like praying."

"What's like praying?"

"What you said about seeing us surviving. Is that what you meant, like praying? You ought to know about that, with your father being a minister."

"My dad taught me how to pray, but I don't think I ever thought about that, or even understood what I was doing. But when I practiced visualizing before surfing contests, it was like pulling this energy into me from outside my body. I think it helped me to achieve my potential. I don't know if it was from God, or what. All I'm saying is, if we visualize that and we're supposed to go home, we will."

"What? What do you mean, 'supposed to go home?'"

"Wow. I don't know, man. I can't believe I said that. Hey, Will? Do you think God already knows what's going to happen to us?"

"Whoa! You're getting way over my head, man."

Charlie didn't continue to pursue the topic. He wasn't even sure about the question, himself. He remembered the dead soldier, Joseph Spaniel and his Bible verse. Something about trusting in God and he will send angels to protect you.

I don't know, he thought. *Was the Psalm verse like visualization? If it was, it didn't work for Joseph.*

He put his head down and grabbed onto his pack straps to hoist the pack up higher onto his back. It was a tough march through the bush that day, and the weight seemed to increase with each step. His fatigue shirt was sweat soaked under the load, and the pack slipped back down almost as soon as he adjusted it. The perspiration dripped from his forehead, and he started to become mesmerized, watching the moisture fall onto the ground.

When he looked up again, it was like he was somewhere else. He looked around and saw the green wasteland of the jungles of Vietnam, and for a moment he could have been anywhere. *Actually, Hawaii was a lot like this,* he thought. *In fact, the islands were* just *like this.*

He began to visualize the surf off the north shores of Oahu. He saw himself stroking into a large wave, and held his breath while his board screamed down the mass of water to the bottom of the breaker. He cut a hard turn so he was facing the wave. Up ahead a monstrous, roaring wall of liquid was his challenge. He began to guide his surfboard using short, sharp turns on the face of the wave to increase his speed and keep him out ahead of the breaking section. Then he cut his board back and set up a tube ride by stalling his forward progression.

Then it happened. The water curled over him, creating a tunnel of pure speed. He was inside of a pipe and going as fast as he could, when a large hand reached down from the sky and pulled him out of his body. Instantly he felt as if he was no longer a separate being. He felt as if he was part of a whole being. He *was* the whole being. Everything was one—like the waves in the ocean. They seem separate, but they are only part of the vastness of the sea.

He looked down and saw the soldiers hauling their heavy packs, watching intently for signs of the enemy. Even his body was seemingly alert, ready for whatever was ahead. All of the men were involved with the elements of the war, but he sensed they were all part of the whole being. They were all there as individuals, but they were not separate. There was only one consciousness.

Robby stopped and raised his hand, signaling everybody to stop. "We must be getting close—smells like burned gun powder around here."

Charlie snapped out of his vision.

Robby dropped to one knee and looked at his map. "We're in the area, all right. Charlie, get me the company commander."

"You got it," Charlie said.

After they made their report, they stayed at ease until the rest of the company arrived. Then the captain organized a sweep with all of the men in a linear formation. They found piles of weaponry, including 263 brand new AK 47 rifles, 106 rockets, 195 mortar rounds, and signal equipment, including thirteen field telephones and nine radios. They found no live enemy, and very few dead ones.

Charlie and Will stayed close together.

"Hey, Will, how many do you think there were in that company?"

"Around 200. Why?"

"If the estimated body count was 150, how did the survivors get all of those bodies out of here?"

"Beats me, man. Maybe that's why they had to leave all their shit behind. They probably had a body under each arm. At least your body isn't here."

"Yeah," Charlie said. Then he suddenly stopped and pointed fifty feet to his right, at a body hanging out of a rocky pile.

"Whoa, look at that." It appeared an NVA soldier had been crushed by a rock slide, probably caused by the 105 barrage that Charlie called in the day before. His left arm and head were visible, the rest of his body pinned by the debris.

"Goddammit, Will. This is a bunch of shit."

Charlie walked over and worked to free the body. Then he laid it down on the ground and, one by one, piled the rocks over it.

Will sat down and watched his friend carry out the burial. When Charlie finished, Will stood up and put his arm around him.

"I've never seen anybody do that before, man. Most of the guys around here just spit on them, or cut an ear off or something."

Charlie looked at Will in horror. "You mean to keep? Like a trophy?"

"Yeah, I guess that's what you would call it. This place has a tendency to make an animal out of you," Will said.

Charlie shook his head. "Oh, man. We can't ever let ourselves get like that. You've got to promise me, Will. Don't ever get like that."

They found another body toward the end of the sweep. Will looked at Charlie, as if to ask if he was going to bury it. Charlie nodded affirmatively, and they walked over and rolled the dead soldier into a ditch. Then Charlie used the sole of his boot and kicked dirt all over him.

"It's the least we can do, man," Charlie said. "I'll bet he didn't want to be here either."

Later, Charlie overheard the captain tell Robby that this was the biggest treasure chest he'd ever found in the jungle.

"Looks like your surveillance squad is lucky to be alive, Lieutenant. I've never seen so much gook armament."

Charlie looked at the two officers as they shook hands. He put his head down, sickened. *Oh, man,* he thought. *What in the world is going to happen next?*

9

Two months later, Charlie sat alone in the middle of the company camp, weary and exhausted. It was just past noon, only moments after Charlie and Robby had returned from an overnight surveillance mission. His fatigues were dripping wet from the long hike he'd just completed in the heat of the day. He'd never before felt that dirty.

Bathing in the bush was difficult. Occasionally while out on patrol, they had an opportunity to clean up in a river, but this past mission was all on dry land. When it rained, there was another chance for washing, but the monsoon season was over for this year, and that just made matters worse because the dust turned to mud when it mixed with sweat.

In the distance, Charlie heard the slapping sounds of an approaching helicopter. Will had been gone for over a week on R&R—the army's idea of vacation for a soldier in Vietnam. Will had gone to Hong Kong; Charlie missed his friend. For the past week, he'd watched all the choppers land to see if Will was on board.

From the ground he could see a figure sitting next to the gunner. *Come on Will,* he said to himself. *Let that be you, man. Wait a minute, what the hell am I saying? Maybe I should be wishing that he never had to come back to this pit.*

Charlie stood up to see who was getting out, then took off running for the pad with rejuvenated energy. Will jumped out, carrying a large red bag with a black U.S. insignia stamped on the side. When the rest of the men saw the red bag, they also started heading for the pad. Charlie got there first.

"You expecting a letter from Cher or something," Will said, smiling.

"What are you talking about, man?"

"I thought you were running to see what I had in this mail bag."

"Shit, I hardly noticed the bag. How come you have it, anyway?"

"It's been sitting back at basecamp for nearly a week. When the postal clerk heard I was coming out, he asked if I'd bring it."

One of the sergeants relieved Will of the bag, and began a mail call.

Charlie took Will aside, eager to know all about his R&R.

"Hey, man. That 'stache is coming along pretty good. Bleached blonde already, too," Will said, pulling at the ends of Charlie's mustache.

Charlie pushed Will's hand away. "Thanks, man. Hey, come on; tell me about the R&R."

"It was pretty cool, man. For awhile I just roamed the streets of that huge city. Then I met this hippie dude from the states."

"What?"

"Yeah, an American living in Hong Kong, if you can believe that. I don't know what he was doing there. For all I know he could have been a drug dealer or something. I kind of hung with him for awhile, because it was just neat to be with somebody who wasn't in the army. But then he wanted to do some weird shit, so I bugged out."

"Like what kind of weird shit?"

"One night we went to this strip bar. That was all right, I guess, but at the end of the show he took me back stage. That's when I found out all of those so-called girls were really men."

"No way."

"I'm telling you, man, you could hardly tell. If one of them wanted to go out with me, I probably would have—until I found out, of course. It was really freaky."

Just then the sergeant called out Charlie's name. "Where the hell are you, Corporal?"

"Right here, Sarge. What do you have for me?"

"It's a package."

"Well all right," Charlie said, following with a surfer's hoot. "Aaaaahhhhhooooo!"

One of the other grunts yelled out, "Hey everybody, Charlie's got cookies."

Whenever somebody received a parcel from home, it was usually cookies, and immediately a crowd formed around the lucky soldier. The common courtesy of the jungle was that the addressee got the first and last sample of the goodies, and whatever he could grab in between.

"All right, stand back you guys," Charlie yelled, trying to get some elbow room to open the package.

He tore the brown wrapper off to find a box. There was scotch tape sealing it. Before he pierced the seal, he shook it.

"Hey, not so hard," Will said. "All you're going to have is crumbs if you keep that up."

"I don't think this is food," Charlie said. "It feels like clothes or something."

"Clothes?" one of the other soldiers said, disappointed. "Why in the hell would somebody send you clothes out here? Do they think you need to get dressed up to kill gooks?"

Charlie looked up, offended.

Will gave the guy a shove.

"All right, all right. I was just kidding. Open up the Goddamn thing before we all pass out from anticipation."

Charlie cut into the tape with his World War I knife, and opened the box. There was tissue paper on top. He pulled it away and just stared. What the hell is it, he wondered. Nobody said a word as Charlie picked it up. It was made of terry cloth, but it wasn't a towel—it was too small, and besides, it had a button.

Somebody spoke up. "I know what that is. It's a wrap-around thing for when you get out of the shower."

Everybody laughed hysterically, all except Charlie.

"Who's it from?" Will asked.

"It's from Cher. I never told her I wasn't at basecamp anymore. Shit, I wouldn't be caught dead in this contraption, even there."

Robby walked up and joined in on the chortling. "I think a fashion show is in order here. What do you think men?"

Charlie looked at Robby, pleading for mercy. "No way!"

Before long, the entire camp had circled around, chanting for a show. Finally Charlie stood up and started to put it on over his clothes, but the group was not going to let him get away with that.

"Strip," someone shouted.

The men started howling and chanted "Striptease, Striptease, Striptease."

Charlie looked around, but nobody was offering a pardon. Slowly, he started to unbutton his shirt. Will let out a hoot and Charlie started to get into it, dancing around inside the circle. When his shirt was off he unbuttoned his pants and dropped them down to his ankles. He didn't try taking them off because he wouldn't be able to get them over his boots; he hadn't had his boots off for quite some time, due to all of the action. He'd quit wearing underwear more than a month earlier because of the lack of supply, so he was completely exposed. He quickly wrapped the garment around his waist and continued to dance, almost tripping on his pants.

The laughter was unbelievable; even the lifers were wailing at the spectacle.

"Hey, Will," Charlie said, looking his friend right in the eye. "Does this remind you of Hong Kong?"

Will laughed and shook his head.

Then—just twenty feet out from the group—a mortar round landed. Three men went down. Everyone scattered and hit the ground. Charlie rolled around in the dirt, trying to rip the wrap off and pull up his pants. When he finally succeeded, he low-crawled over to Robby, and discovered that the lieutenant had been hit.

"Oh shit, Robby. Are you okay?"

Blood spurted out of Robby's right arm just above the elbow; he was trying to stop it with his hand. Charlie looked back at the wrap, lying in the dirt where he had thrown it. He crawled back to get it and used it to wrap around Robby's arm.

Robby, already weak from blood loss, stared into Charlie's eyes as if to say thanks.

A firefight began with small weapon fire off to the west flank. Charlie knew he had to take over as the forward observer. He looked over at Robby who, barely conscious, was holding a map out to his RTO. Charlie grabbed it. Quickly he surveyed the terrain and then concentrated on the map.

Okay now, Charlie thought, *we're in a valley, and fire is coming from the hillside to the west.* He quickly located the enemy position on the map, and put his finger on it to show Robby.

Robby looked at Charlie with blurry eyes. Barely able to shrug his shoulders, he indicated that he didn't know.

Oh shit, Charlie thought. *Well, here goes nothing.*

He called the artillery battery and gave them what he hoped was his location and where he wanted the rounds. He took a deep breath and looked over at Robby, who was now unconscious.

"Hang on, man, please. We're going to get you out of here. That is, if I did everything right."

It would be only minutes until the artillery would come, but it felt like hours to Charlie. Would it come where he wanted it?

He lay down next to his FO and made sure both of their helmets were secure. Then, just as he heard the whistles of the incoming rounds, he rolled Robby over so he was face down. Charlie took a deep breath, held it, then rolled over next to Robby.

The explosions shook the earth. Charlie looked up as he exhaled. The enemy hillside was filled with smoke.

"Oh my God, Robby. I did it, man. A damn bull's eye on my first try."

Robby didn't move. More rounds followed. Twenty minutes later it was over.

"We're clear," Charlie shouted into his radio. "We need medevacs in a hurry."

Charlie turned Robby over, unbuckled his helmet, and wiped the dirt from his face. He lifted his head up and held it.

"Come on, Robby. Everything's going to be all right now."

Robby open his eyes. "What happened?"

Charlie let out a sigh of relief. "Oh, nothing much. You got hit during a God damn fashion show, and now you're going to get a free ride out of here, that's all."

The medevacs started arriving. Charlie picked up Lieutenant Alvarez and carried him in his arms over to the landing zone. The medic waited with a stretcher, and Charlie laid Robby down on it. Charlie grabbed one end of the stretcher and the medic grabbed the other. Together they hoisted it up into the chopper and shoved it in.

Robby looked up at Charlie. "You did it without me, didn't you?"

"Hell no, man. You were right there with me the whole time. You take care. Maybe I'll see you in the real world sometime."

After all of the wounded were evacuated, the company commander ordered a sweep, and started looking for his FO.

"Hey Corporal, where is Lieutenant Alvarez?"

"He's on one of those choppers heading out of here, Sir."

Wide-eyed, the captain looked at Charlie. "Was he hurt bad?"

"I don't think so. Lost a lot of blood though. He got hit; main artery in his arm is all that I saw."

"So who called in the guns?"

"I did, Sir."

The captain snapped to attention, and nodded his head, approving.

"Well done, Corporal. You couldn't have hit the target any better than that. It's a good thing, too. It may be awhile before we can get another lieutenant out here. Looks like you're my new man on FO."

Charlie looked at the captain. All of a sudden, he felt a wave of confidence flow through his body. He didn't say it, but could have told the captain that he was ready for the task. Why, he didn't know. He stood up tall as if to say, yes Sir.

"You'll need an RTO, Corporal. Pick one out and let me know who he is. Make sure he is competent."

"I have somebody in mind already, Sir. Specialist Jamison."

The captain looked Charlie in the eye. "He's from your hometown, isn't he?"

Charlie nodded his head affirmatively.

"You've got him, Corporal. By the way, I'm putting you in for a promotion. You should be a buck sergeant by the end of the month."

Later that week, Charlie and Will were sent out on a dangerous mission. It was exciting for Charlie to have Will with him, but this assignment worried him. As the leader, Charlie walked point in a small squad of six men. Flanked out a quarter of a mile, one to the right and one to the left, were two other squads made up of twenty-two men each.

"Hey, Sergeant," Will said, smiling at his friend.

"What's with this sergeant shit? Besides, I'm not a sergeant until the orders come down."

"I'm just proud of you, man. I've been here for almost a year now and all I'm ever going to make is spec four. They didn't even let me be a corporal."

"So what's the difference, anyway?"

"Hey, a corporal has more clout in the army. We get paid the same, but that's about all. Corporals get way more privileges."

"Well, you don't have to be proud of me, man. I don't know how I deserve these damn promotions, and I don't care either. All I want to do is get my ass out of here."

All of a sudden, Charlie sensed danger up ahead. He slowed down the pace and listened attentively. Then, without warning, the sharp stutter of enemy machine gun fire echoed loudly through the jungle.

"Hit it!" Charlie yelled.

The men dropped for cover and positioned themselves for return fire.

"They're up on that hill. Open fire while I call for help."

Will crawled over to Charlie's position and held out the receiver. Charlie grabbed it and radioed the company commander.

"We're getting hit at twelve o'clock." Charlie shouted to be heard over the popping of the weapons.

"Spread out and make your way up to the base of the hill. I'll have the others over there in five minutes. Then surround the hill and take it," was the response from the infantry camp.

"Take it? No fire power?"

"It's too dangerous. We think there's a large cache of weapons up there. Artillery could blow you all to smithereens."

Charlie took a deep breath and sighed, shaking his head. "Roger that." *Okay big guy—like the biggest wave of your life.*

The hill was 100 yards ahead and about the same distance up to the top. When the other patrols arrived, Charlie repeated the orders.

"Circle around and start moving up," he snapped. "Stay low and spread out!"

Okay! Charlie said to himself. *We're on our own now. Just keep your ass low and concentrate on what you want. You're going to make it, big guy. You're going to make it.*

Up front there was a flash from the bush. Charlie raised his weapon and squeezed until a half a dozen rounds were fired. An enemy soldier dropped to the ground and rolled down the hill toward him. Charlie pulled aside at the last second, and the body rolled on by. There goes number eight, he thought.

Will was off to his right, firing intermittently. He heard the cries of wounded men up ahead, and then one off to his left. *Shit! It's one of my men.* He crawled over to Private Robinson, a newcomer in country. His right hip was covered with blood.

"Oh my God! Oh my God! I'm going to die!" cried Robinson.

"Settle down, Private. It's just a leg wound. Everything's going to be all right."

Charlie looked around to see if there was help available. Half way down the base of the hill, Spec Four Hawkins was busy doctoring another wounded soldier who was shot in the stomach.

"Got a bad one here, Charlie," he yelled.

Charlie looked Robinson in the eye. "You're okay, man. Just sit tight and I'll be right back. Don't move, do you hear me?"

He crawled down the hill; the medic reached up and handed him a pressure bandage.

"Make it tight."

"You got it, Doc."

When he returned, Robinson was in tears. "What's going to happen to me?"

Instead of answering, Charlie went to work on his leg. He reached into his pocket and pulled out his grandpa's knife and guided the blade to make a slit in Robinson's pant leg. Then he stuck the knife in the ground and ripped at the slit, pulling it up to the top of the garment. After exposing the bloodied tissue, he tried to wipe it clean with the sleeve of his own shirt, then applied the bandage. *Make it tight,* he said to himself. *Make it tight.*

After he finished, he looked his wounded charge in the eye. "Listen up, man. I'm going to have to leave you for awhile, but I'll be right back. Just sit tight, protect yourself, and start seeing the outcome of this the way you want it to be. What's your first name, anyway?"

"R...Richard."

"Okay, Richard, soon you're going to be going to a nice comfortable hospital bed. See yourself doing that, okay? Can you imagine that?"

Richard nodded his head.

Charlie grabbed his knife, wiped the blade clean on his pant leg, folded it in, and reached to slip it into his pocket. He looked around just in time to see a body blown to bits.

Charlie gasped. Specialist Hawkins had just left a wounded soldier, had taken two steps forward, and had stepped on what appeared to be a land mine. A head went flying into the air—arms off to the sides—blood burst out of the body like a water balloon exploding in midair. Charlie stared in disbelief.

Robinson cried to Charlie. "What? What happened?"

Charlie couldn't say anything until he took a deep breath. He shook his head, and then looked Robinson in the eye.

"Nothing, Richard. Keep thinking what I told you."

From a distance he saw Will moving cautiously along, bullets missing him by inches. Charlie stood and ran up the hill. When he was within twenty feet, he dove to the ground, grabbed a hand grenade from the front strap of his pack, pulled the pin, and hurled it into the bush above Will.

"Fire in the hole!" he yelled to warn his friend.

Will put his head down and hugged the ground. Debris from the explosion flew on top of him.

Charlie hustled up the hill and hit the ground next to Will. "You okay?"

"Yeah, I think so. Sounds pretty quiet up there now, thanks to you, man."

Together they crawled upward to find the remains of NVA soldiers. Intestines hung out of one headless body. Another had a head but no arms or legs. Other pieces were scattered around. Charlie figured there must have been three soldiers because he saw two intact AK 47 rifles and parts of another.

"Nine, ten and eleven," Charlie said softly.

"Nine, ten and eleven what?" Will asked.

"That's how many I've killed."

"Oh no, man. Don't be doing that." He put his arm around Charlie.

"I know there's more, but that's how many I've seen. I know what happened to each and every one of them, too. I'll never forget what those bodies looked like, Will."

"At least they're not standing here looking at you."

"Yeah, I guess." He turned and led the way up.

They conquered the hill within the hour as Charlie counted numbers twelve and thirteen. The sweep counted thirty-six killed in action, including both U.S. and NVA soldiers. Nine of the fifty Americans climbing the hill were dead. Thirteen others were wounded and would be medevaced. There were no surviving NVA. And no cache of weapons was found.

Charlie went back down the hill and found Private Robinson, who was lying on the ground trembling from fright.

"It's all over now, Richard. Now you get to go for a ride."

The young man lifted his head to look at Charlie. His eyes were blood shot, his face muddied.

"Really?" he burst into tears.

"Yeah, really." Charlie slowly turned his head toward the remains of Specialist Hawkins. "Your body gets to go home early, with your being still inside of you."

When the rest of the Infantry Company met the forty-one survivors later that day, the commanding officer walked up to Charlie with a big grin on his face, as if he were proud of his new FO. Charlie stood in silence, looking down at the ground.

"Well done, Sergeant."

"Well done, Sir?"

"I understand twenty-seven gooks are no longer participating in this war, and that you led the troops to the victory. That NVA vantage point has been known as 'Hill 595.' It's been a hideout and sniper location for quite awhile. We thought there might be an ammo cache up there; sorry I couldn't let you have the guns. You'll be joining Lieutenant Alvarez with a medal, young man."

Charlie kept his head down. *Yeah*, he thought. *I led the troops to victory, all right. I also led nine of them to their death.* He felt sickened to be the leader of such mayhem.

"What's the matter?"

Charlie looked up. "Nothing, Sir."

"By the way, we have a new lieutenant coming out sometime later this week, so you'll be back to your old duties as RTO soon."

"But, what about Will, Sir?"

"The company is going to be split up for awhile. Half of Delta Company will be heading south and west toward the Cambodian border on a separate mission. Since he's now an experienced RTO, Specialist Jamison will be participating. We'll all be joining them before long. The whole Division is moving south. The forward basecamp is even relocating to Ban Me Thuot."

Will passed a joint over to Charlie on the eve of his departure for the Cambodian border.

"It's not your fault, man," Will said, blowing smoke out of his mouth. "I always wanted to be an RTO anyway. Hey, look at it this way: instead of surfing ocean waves, we're both going to be heard over the airwaves. We're going to be in the waves at the same time, man."

Charlie chuckled without smiling. "Yeah, but I feel responsible for your having to go on this mission."

"Shit! Just cool it with the responsibility crap. The army does what it wants. Nobody has any control. Besides, it was fun being with you on that hill, man."

"Fun?"

"Yeah! Hey, I probably would have been there anyway. Might as well have been there with you by my side. By the way, thanks for saving my life again. If you hadn't thrown that grenade when you did, I would've been a goner for sure."

Charlie was at a loss for words. The vision of Specialist Hawkins popped into his head. He looked at his friend, glad he was alive. Tomorrow they would be separated, and he would be getting a new lieutenant. It seemed like there were so many different experiences in Vietnam and nothing remained the same for very long. Now, Will was leaving.

He reached into his pocket and pulled out his grandfather's knife. "I want you to have this."

"What for?"

"It's a lucky charm. You take it, man, because I want you to make it back home so we can do more than just hang together in those airwaves. You and I are going to get tubed in the real stuff, you hear me?"

"But you'll be needing this lucky charm as much as I will, Charlie."

"Just take it, man. It'll make me feel better."

From his experience working with the Intelligence Squad, Charlie knew where Will was going. The "Ho Chi Minh Trail" was on the Cambodian border, and dangerous because the NVA used it to get their supplies down from North Vietnam. Charlie was worried that Will's mission would involve intercepting the enemy on the trail.

10

Charlie and Lieutenant Harvey balanced on the rice paddy dikes as they made their way toward the Montagnard village. They were accompanying a ten-man reconnaissance squad whose mission was to investigate Viet Cong activity. Included in the group was an interpreter from the Allied Army of the Republic of Vietnam.

Charlie didn't like having to cross rice paddies, situated as they were out in open spaces with no trees around. He felt like a sitting duck. On this particular journey across the fields, the dike stopped before they were across, forcing them to jump in and slosh through the flooded crop.

"Uh, oh! Looks like we're at the end of the road, Sir. Hope it's not too deep, because we're going in." Charlie jumped in.

The rice paddies were so muddy it was impossible to tell the depth. This time the water nearly reached his waist. His feet sank into the sludge on the bottom, but he continued walking as if nothing was unusual.

For the lieutenant—newly arrived in country—the rice paddy presented a formidable challenge.

"Lift your feet all the way out of the mud before you step forward,"

Charlie said. "Otherwise you might…"

Charlie paused when he heard a splashing sound behind him. He turned around and saw the lieutenant floating face down, his heavy pack preventing him from righting himself.

Charlie back-peddled to help. He grabbed onto the lieutenant's pack and stood him upright.

"Are you all right, Sir?"

Coughing and spitting the lieutenant replied, "Y…yes, I think so." He paused to catch his breath. "What were you saying?"

"I was saying, if you don't lift your foot all the way out of the mud before you try to step, you might fall in. Sorry I talk so slow," Charlie said with a smirk.

Noting the lieutenant's frustration, Charlie tried to reassure him. "It's okay, Sir. That happened to me once, too. There's a lot to learn out here, but after awhile you'll get the hang of it."

On the other side of the paddy, Charlie gave the orders. "Spread out and light 'em if you got 'em. We're going up the hill into that village in twenty."

He took Lieutenant Harvey aside.

"Thanks for taking charge, Sergeant. The captain told me you've been doing a great job out here," the lieutenant drawled, pulling off his pack. It slipped out of his hands and fell to the ground.

It seemed strange to Charlie to see an officer in the field who looked so much like a rookie. Robby had always seemed to be in control, but this new guy's nervousness was obvious.

"How long have you been in country, Sir? Hey, before you answer that, I have to quit calling you 'sir' out here. It could be dangerous for you. You got a first name?"

"My name's Tim. I arrived a couple of weeks ago."

"Great. Call me Charlie. Where're you from, Tim?"

"New Orleans. How about you?"

"San Diego."

The lieutenant took off his drenched shirt. He started to ring it out and let out a shriek. "Aaahhh!"

"What's the matter?"

"There's a worm on my chest."

Charlie crawled over to the lieutenant to have a look. "Oh, I see you've met Louie the Leech," Charlie chuckled. "At least that's what I call it."

"What do I do with it?"

"Hey, Anderson," Charlie called to one of the other men. "You got a grit lit?"

"Sure do. Why?"

"Got a leech over here. Come over, will you?"

Private Anderson brought his cigarette over to where Charlie and the lieutenant were sitting.

"Thanks, man," Charlie said.

He took the cigarette and moved toward the lieutenant.

"What are you going to do?" the lieutenant asked, moving backward.

"Hold still, Tim. Louie burrows into the flesh and this is the only way to safely remove him. If you pull him out there's a chance of breaking the head off, and then you've got a buddy inside of you for a long time. It can make you sick if that happens. I'm going to burn his ass and hope he comes out on his own."

Charlie carefully placed the end of the cigarette on the tail end of the leach, trying not to burn the lieutenant.

"Whoa!" Charlie said, thrilled that the leach was backing out. "You're not even going to get a scar out of this one, man. Shit! Last month I had to burn into my arm to get old Louie out."

"I'm sure glad you didn't tell me that before you started."

Charlie started laughing as he handed the cigarette back to Anderson.

"How long have you been in the army, Tim?"

"I joined up last October."

"October! That's when I got drafted."

"It seems like I've been in the army all of my life. My father is a full bird colonel. He wanted me to go to the academy, but I couldn't get in. I went to Louisiana Tech instead, and he made me join the ROTC. The army actually paid my tuition, but after graduation I had a hundred and twenty days to enlist, or pay up. I wanted to get a job and pay them back, but my Dad convinced me I would get drafted anyway."

"What have you been doing all this time?"

"Artillery training."

"Wow, Tim. We've been in the army about the same amount of time, but while you were stateside learning how to do this shit, I was over here getting on-the-job-training. Do you know much about being an FO?"

"Sort of, but I feel awkward out here." He lowered his head.

Charlie studied his new lieutenant for a moment. *Look at the poor bastard. He's going to cry any minute now. And this guy is going to be my superior over here? No way! I'm going to get killed if I follow him.*

"Hey, Tim?" The lieutenant looked up, frightened.

A wave of compassion overcame Charlie. "Don't worry, man. You just stay close and everything will be all right. I'll show you how it works over here."

"Thanks, Charlie. I'm sure I'll get the hang of it."

"Right." Charlie picked up his pack thinking, *oh, man. I sure hope you do. It's going to be a long year for you if you don't.*

Charlie stood up and called the men together. "I'll walk point, and I want a left and a right flank formation spread out behind. Let's move out slowly and make our way up."

Charlie was used to leading the men, and it didn't seem strange to be taking over for the lieutenant. Nobody seemed to be suspicious. Last thing he wanted was for anybody to know the lieutenant wasn't under control.

"What do you think, Tim? Should we move in from the left or right side of the village?" Charlie held out his left hand, giving him an unspoken recommendation.

"The left looks best, Charlie."

"Then, on the left is where we'll go."

Charlie started trudging up the face of the hill. It was nearly five hundred yards to the village. There were no trails and he wove in and out of thick brush. He glanced around when they reached the top and saw that everyone was breathing hard.

"What do you say we catch our breath before we start walking through? That okay with you, Tim?"

"Great idea, Charlie. Are we going to run into any trouble here?" Tim asked, apprehension in his voice.

"Beats me."

Charlie walked forward to have a look into the village. He saw children playing, heard dogs barking. He rejoined Tim.

"I don't think we're in for any problems, but keep your guard up, just in case."

He turned to address the rest of the men. "Listen, there are families in here and I don't want anybody to do anything stupid. Go in with the attitude that they are people just like us, probably scared like we are, too."

Charlie looked over at the lieutenant and then back to the group. "Leave the women alone, too. The lieutenant and I don't condone that kind of shit, and you know what I mean. Now let's be careful in there."

Sergeant Thom, the interpreter from the ARVN army, came up to the front of the rank to be with Charlie and Tim as the squad proceeded to inspect the village. There were seventeen structures. Charlie knew their presence would not be a surprise because someone more than likely would have noticed them crossing the rice paddies.

The children looked up and ran into the grass huts as the soldiers proceeded into the middle of the community. The dogs, however, stood their ground, barking and growling as the soldiers approached.

"It's okay, boy," Charlie said, addressing a mutt. "We're not here to cause any trouble. Just looking around, that's all."

Charlie didn't like this kind of duty. He felt like he was intruding on private lives, but he also understood the mission was important. There had been a lot of VC activity in the villages lately. Every village was a potential enemy hangout.

The NVA went into the villages to recruit individuals, persuading them with communist propaganda. The villagers, also known as *Montagnards*, were told that men were needed to help liberate the South Vietnamese people from U.S. aggression. Their military structure might only consist of three men, but could be as many as twelve to make up a squad. Sometimes they organized into platoons with four squads, but for the most part they acted individually in the war effort.

Charlie ordered the men to split up and look around. He took the lieutenant and Sergeant Thom with him, and approached the grass huts directly, to meet the people.

"Tell them we're just looking around, Thom. We don't want to hurt anyone."

As the interpreter talked with the people, Charlie and Tim looked into the huts, scanning for weapons. Charlie often made eye contact with the people, and talked to them in English.

"I know you can't understand me, but I want to tell you what a nice family you have here. We're just here to check things out and we don't want you to be afraid."

The *Montagnards* looked at him curiously. Charlie wished he could have been there on different terms. *None of these people look like enemy,* he thought. *But then again, that's the problem. The VC are just ordinary people who act unexpectedly.*

When all of the homes had been checked and nothing was spotted, the men regrouped and made their way out of the village. As far as Charlie was concerned, it was time to get the hell out of there.

Sergeant Thom stopped them and pointed to the graveyard.

"What about it?" Charlie said.

"Too many fresh graves," Thom said.

Charlie looked and counted seven graves that appeared to be freshly covered. "Hey, maybe they had an epidemic. I say we get the hell out of here."

Thom looked at the lieutenant.

"Charlie," the lieutenant said, nervously. "I learned in training that the VC often hide things for the NVA in graves."

"So, Tim, are you suggesting that we dig up these graves?"

"Maybe we should."

"Hey, man. If that's what you want to do, you'll have to make the order. You know what I want to do."

"Charlie, I think we better do it," the lieutenant said, uncertainly. "There might be supplies and arms down there."

As the lieutenant turned to address the men, Charlie spoke quietly behind his back.

"There might be bodies down there."

The lieutenant looked back at Charlie. There was fright on his face, and Charlie could see the man didn't really know what to do.

"Okay, Tim. I guess we better do this one by the book."

The lieutenant gave a sigh of relief and turned back to the men. "Those who have entrenching tools, break them out."

Most of the men were carrying an army-issue entrenching tool that had a wooden handle, eighteen inches long, with a folding, six inch shovel spade on the end. The spade could be opened up and locked into place with a threaded sleeve.

"We're going to dig up these graves," the lieutenant said. "Proceed with care."

Charlie looked on with horror as the seven graves were being uncovered. *This is bullshit, he thought. All they're going to find are bodies in these holes.*

One of the Montagnard women walked by, carrying a large basket on her head. When she saw what was happening she screamed and ran into the village, dropping her load.

"Oh shit," Charlie said. "This is a Goddamn insult to these people."

Just then, Private Anderson, who had been digging frantically, shrieked, "Oh my God." He stood there with a head balanced on his tool. "Oh my God," he said again, shaking so hard the head rolled off.

Charlie ran over and saw the face of a Montagnard man staring up at him. There wasn't much flesh left, but there was still hair growth on the chin.

"Just put it back on, man. Put it back on real gentle like." His voice was quivering and he thought he was going to cry. "We're so sorry," he said, addressing the corpse. "This is not right!"

A group of nine villagers were running toward the graveyard, crying and screaming. Sergeant Thom ran out to intercept them, with his rifle in hand, yelling in Vietnamese, and holding his arms out to keep them from passing.

Charlie looked at the crowd, abashed. "Cover this grave back up." He had turned around to look for the lieutenant when Private Stavis yelled out.

"Charlie, I think I found something."

Charlie ran over to Stavis who was kneeling in a hole nearly four feet deep. Charlie jumped in and brushed the dirt away from a burlap bag. He grabbed Stavis's entrenching tool and sliced the bag. Rice came pouring out. He glanced up and saw the lieutenant looking down on him.

Charlie jumped out of the hole. "Get this bag out of here, Stavis, and see what else is in this hole."

He turned to the lieutenant. "I guess you were right."

He looked around at the rest of the men to see if anyone else had found anything. "Dig carefully men. Some of these are for real."

When Stavis pulled out the bag of rice, the villagers fell silent. Charlie looked over and saw a stunned group. *I wonder if they knew about this. They look more confused than I do.*

Sergeant Thom began interrogating the villagers. They shook their heads from side to side. All Charlie could understand was, "No, no, no."

"I think we better hustle up and get out of here, Tim," Charlie said, frantically. "My gut feeling is that these people don't know what's happening, but there may be others in the village who do."

Charlie and Tim hurried the men. All in all, they uncovered twelve bags of rice, which they cut up and poured back in the holes, mixing the rice with dirt. They found three more bodies that were buried close to five feet down. That's when Charlie realized that the first body found—the one Anderson had decapitated—was only a couple feet down when exposed.

"Tim, as much as I hate this shit, we better go and see if there's anything under that first body. I think it was too shallow when we found it."

Charlie looked at Anderson, who had a horrified look on his face.

"Give me your tool, man. I'll do it." Charlie grabbed it and ran over to the grave. Another soldier joined him.

The already-churned dirt was easy to spade. When they got to the body, Charlie gently picked it up and lifted it out of the hole. Then he picked up the head and placed it onto what was left of the neck. The stench was evident, but not as bad as the bodies he investigated back at the infirmary.

He took a deep breath and sighed. "Okay, let's get this over with. Let's see what else is in this pit."

In less than five minutes they dug an additional two feet down and found a canvas tarp. When they unwrapped it, they found nine AK 47 rifles. As soon as Charlie was sure there wasn't anything else, he reached up and carefully pulled the body down, placing the head back where it belonged.

He pulled himself out of the hole, and looked back at the corpse.

"Okay, Buddy. Maybe now you can rest in peace." *Thank God the person isn't in there anymore,* he thought.

The men packed up the AK 47s and descended the hill. At the bottom, Charlie spoke with the lieutenant in private.

"I guess if it were up to me, I'd leave all the war tactics out. I've learned how to kill all right, but I'm not into the other stuff."

"I've heard stories about how soldiers react in Nam, Charlie. But I never heard about compassion. That's not supposed to be a desirable quality in a good soldier."

"Good. All I want to do is survive this shit. I don't want to have the distinction of being a good soldier."

"Will you teach me how to survive, Charlie?"

Charlie looked into the scared eyes of the lieutenant. *This guy grew up in a soldier's home,* Charlie thought, *and he's had plenty of training. But he doesn't want to be here any more than I do.*

"I'll do my best. Now we better get these men out of here."

Charlie decided to split the men up. He left the lieutenant with half of the squad to guard and cover him and the rest of the men as they crossed the rice paddies. When he got to the other side with the first group, they stood guard for the remainder of the squad.

If there was a sniper up in the village, Charlie's plan had apparently deterred him from acting, because the squad escaped without contact.

The captain was elated with the prizes the squad brought back. "Congratulations Sergeant! Intelligence is going to be happy to hear about this find."

Charlie thought about Top back at Intelligence, and couldn't imagine him ever being happy.

"Whose idea was it to dig up the graves?"

"Lieutenant Harvey, Sir," Charlie said.

"Well done, Lieutenant. You did a damn good job for a 'greenback' out here in the field. I think you and Sergeant Armfield are going to make a good team."

The captain walked away, and Tim looked sheepishly at Charlie.

"Yeah, I think we'll do all right," Charlie said smiling. "Come on, Greenback, let's go get better acquainted."

Charlie put his arm around Tim and thought about giving the new lieutenant a joint to smoke, but changed his mind. They started to walk over to the mess area for some dinner, when the captain came back.

"By the way, Sergeant, the company secretary is here. He's trying to arrange R&Rs for the men. He brought out some allocations from your battery as well. You might want to take a look at them."

"Thanks, Sir. I'll do just that."

Wow, an R&R, he thought. *Hey wait a minute. What am I thinking? I haven't even been here six months yet and I want to go on an R&R? I'd better save that for later.*

Charlie and Tim walked up to the mess sergeant and received a box of C-rations each.

"Have you eaten much of this shit, Tim?"

"Yeah, I sure have. My father used to bring it home all the time. We used to love 'em as kids."

"Well, when you have to eat it everyday, let me tell you, it gets really old. I'd do anything for real food. Shit! I think I'd even like shit on a shingle about now."

They both laughed. Together, they pulled off their packs, dropped them to the ground, and sat down to eat.

As Charlie opened up a can of hash, Specialist Drumond walked up.

"Are you men from Charlie Battery?"

"Why? Do we look like gun bunnies or something?" Charlie said sarcastically.

"No you don't, but I met most of the men out here when they came into country, and I didn't recognize you guys."

"Well, you guessed right. We came through the artillery, all right. But we haven't seen anything of those damn guns except what they spit out to save our lives," Charlie said, laughing.

He was feeling spirited, and he didn't know why. Maybe he was just showing off for the lieutenant.

"I have some R&R allocations for you to look at from Charlie Battery. They didn't give me very many of them. I guess the good ones have already been spoken for."

"Figures," Charlie said, disgusted. "They forgot about the forward personnel who are responsible for keeping them in business. We're out here getting hit, sleeping on the ground, and eating this shit," he said, pointing to the can, "while they're safe and sound back there, sleeping on cots and eating food prepared by real cooks. Then they plan vacations for themselves and leave us out here to play with the gooks."

Specialist Drumond turned red. "I'm sorry, Sergeant."

Charlie looked at the embarrassed secretary. "Hey, I'm only kidding."

Damn, he thought. *What the hell am I doing, coming on like such an asshole? This guy is in Camp Enari most of the time. He's got the best deal of anybody, except when he has to come out here for the day. Maybe I do need some R&R.*

"So what do have?"

"Well, there are three allocations," Drumond said as he sat down on the ground next to Charlie. "The first is for Hong Kong. That leaves in a month."

"No, I don't think so," Charlie said. "Will went there, and I didn't like the sound of it."

"The second is for Kuala Lumpur, and is six weeks away."

"Where the hell is that?"

"It's in Malaysia, somewhere. I had a friend who went there, and he said the women were beautiful."

"Hey, that sounds cool. Where's the third one going?"

"The third one is for Bangkok—that's in two weeks, but I'm not sure if it's spoken for or not."

"Wait a minute. Isn't Bangkok in Thailand?"

"Yeah, why?"

"Because I think that's where my brother is. Yes, I'm sure of it. My mom wrote me last week and said he's in Thailand. I'll go there."

"Well, as I said, I'm not sure I can get it. It's only two weeks away and sometimes somebody at the last minute takes them. But I'll try. Can I put you down for Kuala Lumpur for your second choice?"

"Yeah, sure. But I want Thailand, man. Try really hard, will you?"

"I'll do my best Sergeant. Sergeant Armfield, right?"

"Right, Sergeant Charles W. Armfield! Thanks a lot, man!"

"You're welcome," Drumond said as he stood up and turned to walk away.

Charlie turned toward Tim with a huge smile on his face. Tim looked white.

"What's the matter? Aren't you happy for me? I might get to go visit my brother, man. He's in the Peace Corps, serving in Thailand."

"Yeah, sure. It sounds really great," Tim said. Sweat beaded up on his forehead.

"Hey, don't worry, okay? I'll teach you everything I know in the next two weeks. I swear to God, man. You're going to be ready for anything."

Charlie stuck his hand out toward Tim, who grabbed it.

"Let's shake on it. Right on, brother! You're going to be ready for anything." Charlie let go and reached over into his pack and grabbed a tablet of paper.

"What are you doing?"

"I'd better write my mom and tell her I might be going to Thailand, so she can tell Mike. I wonder if I'll be able find him?"

Two weeks later, Charlie, Tim, and two others were hiking back to camp after two days on a short range patrol. SRP's were small patrols consisting of four men who would set up a reconnaissance site two to three miles out from the main unit. It was common practice in the Fourth Infantry Division in Vietnam.

Charlie was marching point when he saw a flash in the bush, and a shot rang out. He dove to the ground and returned four shots from his automatic weapon. All was quiet. After five minutes he stood slowly with his helmet-protected head down, and walked into the bush. He discovered a single sniper, shot four times in the left side of his chest.

He breathed in deeply and exhaled. Number 14, he said to himself.

The lieutenant walked up behind and surveyed the body. Charlie looked into his anxious eyes and shook his head. There were no words exchanged. Charlie turned and walked away.

Before reporting to the captain, Charlie slung off his pack and turned to look at a red-eyed Tim. There was mud on his cheeks. Since it was hot and dusty, Charlie knew that tears might have made the mess.

"You did good for a greenback."

Tim laughed nervously. "Thanks, Charlie. That gook shook me up though."

"Yeah, I know. Hey, if it makes you feel any better, it shook me up, too. My friend Will said I'd get used to it, but I haven't. Every time I kill another gook, I see all of the others I've killed in the new one's face. I haven't forgotten a single one of them, Tim. I even count them. That last guy was number fourteen."

Tim stared blankly into Charlie's eyes, as if touched by the words of an experienced soldier. Then he shook his head and said, "I can't believe you got him right in the heart."

"I saw the flash and shot just underneath it. Here, hold your rifle up like you're going to shoot it for a minute."

Tim grabbed his M-16 and held it up.

"See where the muzzle of your weapon is? It's right above where your heart is."

Charlie put his finger back on Tim's chest. "That is, of course, because you're right-handed. Most people are right-handed. So that's where I let him have it. If he were left-handed I might have only wounded him, and we might have been goners."

Charlie shrugged his shoulders. "Chance you have to take sometimes."

Just then Charlie heard a radio transmission. "Charlie Battery, I'll be landing in 05 minutes to pick up Sergeant Alpha-Romeo-Mike-Foxtrot-

India-Echo-Lima-Delta."

It was U.S. army policy not to repeat a man's name over the air. "I need to take him back to Enari for R&R, over."

Charlie looked at Tim with wide eyes as the reply began to be transmitted.

"He's not here. He's out with Delta Company of the 125th, over."

"Shit! Nobody told me he was a front man. He better be in camp, or he's just missed his R&R."

Charlie intercepted the call. "I'm here, fly guy. I'll be the one with the huge grin on his face, over."

"Roger that."

Charlie put the receiver down.

The battery spoke up, saying, "Have fun, Charlie."

Charlie didn't reply. He looked back at Tim who had his head down.

"Hey, man, you're going to do all right out here. Shit, you've even had your first contact already."

"Yeah, but I didn't do anything. You shot the guy, not me."

"But you would have if I didn't go first. I know you would have, man. Listen, you know it all, Tim. They'll get you an RTO and you'll carry on just like it was me by your side, you hear?"

Charlie heard the sounds of the chopper. He picked up his pack, detached the radio and handed it to Tim. He swung what was left of the pack onto his right shoulder. He watched for a moment to see where the helicopter was going to land. When it began to descend, he started running toward the LZ. Tim ran beside him, still clutching the radio. As soon as the runners of the chopper hit the ground, Charlie loaded his pack on board, and turned to yell at Tim over the slapping sounds of the blades.

"You're going to be all right!" He jumped aboard, and as the chopper lifted up he waved to Tim.

Lieutenant Harvey didn't raise his hand. He just stood there with a helpless look on his muddied face.

Come on, you damn greenback. Wave at me, man. I'm going on R&R, and you're going to be all right. Please, man. Wave at me so I know you're going to be all right.

Tim didn't move.

11

The wheels of the C-130, filled with R&R bound soldiers, touched down at the Cam Ranh Bay landing strip. While the others aboard told jokes and laughed, Charlie remained silent, lost in his thoughts. Even though it was wonderful to be out of the bush, Charlie wondered what would become of the greenback lieutenant.

Is he really going to be all right? I want to see Mike, but maybe I should have bagged the R&R and stayed with the lieutenant. Shit, how am I going to find Mike, anyway? He may not have heard from Mom that I'm coming. Maybe she didn't tell him since I wasn't sure I was going to be able to go.

It was the sight of the landing strip in Cam Rahn Bay that brought Charlie out of his funk. He looked out of the porthole of the plane, and suddenly remembered when Gage ran after him when he left for Pleiku.

Oh my God! Gage! Gage is here! When the plane landed he could hardly wait to get out. The back door opened and he ran over to the bus waiting to take the passengers to the processing center.

"Do you know Gage Saltman?" he asked, addressing the driver as he climbed the steps two at a time to get into the bus. "He's a cook. I don't know his rank anymore, but he's a cook. Do you know him?" Charlie was anxious.

"No. I know all of the cooks who work at the R&R processing center. He's probably either at the new arrival center or at the departure center."

"Departure center?"

"Yeah. That's where you'll go when your DEROS comes up. You know, the "Date you're Eligible to Return from Overseas." You should be able to find him. The centers are pretty close to each other at the camp. You won't be leaving for your R&R until tomorrow anyway."

"All right! Thanks a lot, man."

At the processing center—a small wood building with a canvas roof— the men received information for their departure flights scheduled for the next day, sheets for their bunks, and directions to the barracks and the PX, where they could shop and have a few drinks at a bar. Charlie had a few other questions.

"Where's the DEROS center?"

"Why, are you planning to sneak on a plane going home?" the specialist giving information said, chuckling.

"Not a bad idea, but no. I have a friend who's a cook somewhere around here. I think he's either there or at the arrival center."

"What's his name?"

"Gage Saltman. He's my best friend from home."

"Gage! Hell yes, I know Gage. Are you Charlie?"

Charlie's eyes widened. "That would be me."

"He talks about you all the time. He says you're a champion surfer."

"I don't feel like it—not anymore. So where is he?" Charlie was excited.

"At the DEROS center. When you walk out of here, turn left and go to the end of the road. Hang a right, and the mess area where he works is the third building on the left."

"Thanks a lot!"

Forgetting his sheets, Charlie hurried out the door, turned left and ran as fast as he could. When he got to the DEROS mess area, men were lined up outside the door.

"What's this line for?" he asked the last man.

"Dinner."

"All right! I'm starved."

The line moved slowly, adding to Charlie's impatience. *I wonder if*

Gage is here, he thought, as he walked through the door. The room was filled with tables, half of them already occupied. The men in the line edged along the wall. Up ahead Charlie could see a cook serving food. Was it Gage? The guy was wearing green fatigues and a white chef's hat, but Charlie couldn't make out the face.

With all the dinner commotion, it was hard to tell who the man was until Charlie approached the serving area. No, it wasn't Gage! He stepped out of line and walked to the end of the serving area where a private was handing out silverware.

"Excuse me, Private," Charlie said, looking down at the man, whose finely starched fatigues contrasted sharply with his own scruffy ones. "Do you happen to know Gage Saltman?"

The private glanced at Charlie's collar, at the small black pins with three slashes for buck sergeant, customarily worn at the front.

"Yes I do, Sergeant. He's on graveyard shift this week. He should be sleeping in his barracks."

"Hey, I'm a good friend of his from back home. I know he wouldn't mind if I woke him up. Can you tell me where he is, please?"

"He's in the first building behind this mess hall, upstairs, the third room on the left."

Charlie hurried out. *Holy shit! Gage has his own room and everything!*

He ran up the outside wooden stairs and hurried down the hall to the third room. Quietly, he opened the door. A man slept with his back facing the door, covered with a sheet. He tiptoed in and slowly lifted the sheet at the foot of the bed.

Boy, I sure hope this is Gage, he thought. Charlie tugged at the hair on the man's left leg. The leg jerked away. Charlie stifled a laugh. He tugged again, pulling a little harder.

Gage sat up, rubbed his eyes and tried to focus.

"Holy Shit!" Gage yelled. He dove across the bed to embrace his friend. Then, laughing, he pushed Charlie away. "What the hell are you doing here, man?"

"Oh, I just thought I'd come down and shoot the breeze with you." Charlie said. Laughing, they hugged again.

"No, really, man. What are you doing here?"

"I'm going on R&R!" Charlie yelled. Quietly he added. "I'm going to Thailand, Gage."

"Wow, you're going on R&R already? I didn't expect you'd be coming through here for quite awhile yet."

"Yeah, well, there was this allocation to Thailand. Mom wrote me and said Mike was there, so I couldn't pass it up. I don't know if I'll be able to find him. But, what the hell, at least I get to see you."

"Whoa, Charlie!" Gage said studying his friend's face. "That's a bitchin' looking mustache. I didn't recognize you at first. But then I thought, who else would be pulling my leg hair like that?"

"Don't forget. You started that shit," Charlie said, chuckling.

"Yeah, I know, I know." Gage touched Charlie's collar. "What the hell is this? Are you a sergeant?"

Charlie shrugged. "That's what they tell me. I don't know how in the hell it happened, but it did. All I do is try to get by out there, man. It's a bunch of goddamn shit. So, what's your rank now?" Charlie said, trying to change the subject.

"I'm a spec 4. You know, like a corporal without the clout. But I heard about the goddamn shit part."

"Meaning what?"

"Will was through here last month and told me all about it."

"Will! Why that sonofabitch. He didn't tell me he ran into you when he went on R&R."

He paused, remembering how they were hit right after Will returned during the fashion show. "Then again," he said lowering his head. "Maybe he just forgot."

Gage started to speak, but Charlie held up his hand, anticipating what he wanted to talk about.

"When do you have to go to work, anyway?"

"I don't have to work tonight. It's my night off."

"No way? You get a night off?"

"Yeah, I do, man." Gage laughed, and slapped Charlie on the back. "Let's head over to the PX and get drunk."

"Whoa!" Charlie said, eyes wide. "I don't know if I can do that, man. I've been in control every single minute I've arrived here. That would freak me out."

He hesitated. "Have you smoked pot over here, Gage?"

"Sometimes. Will turned me onto it."

Charlie burst out laughing. "Did he call it 'an angel in Vietnam'?"

"As a matter of fact, he did. Come on, man. I know someone who can get us some."

Charlie, dressed in his military khakis and carrying a small black military bag, started up the gangplank to board the plane that would take him to Bangkok.

Gage was there to say goodbye.

"When you get back, I'll take you to the beach."

Charlie stepped aside so the other men could pass. He leaned over the railing. "The beach?"

"Yeah, the beach!"

"You got it, man!" He shook his head wondering what in the world his friend was up to. He turned and walked into the plane.

During the forty-five minute flight, Charlie sat next to the window and gazed at the jungle below. If only he could see what was happening down there. Was the greenback all right? And Will, where was Will now? Thoughts about the war and its ugliness plagued him until the huge city of Bangkok came into view.

Wow! It's so big, he thought. *How will I ever find Mike?*

After disembarking at the United States Air Force Base in Bangkok, Charlie and the others were ushered into a big hall with rows of chairs lined up facing a podium at the front. They sat down and a staff sergeant introduced Colonel Billings. The colonel began briefing the men on civilian life in Bangkok.

"Men, you will be given a hotel coupon after this meeting, and a shuttle will transport you to various hotels. After checking in, you will be on your own to explore and enjoy the sights of Bangkok. I must warn you that you may be asked where you're from and what you are doing in Vietnam. You must only reply that you are an American advisor in the Republic of Vietnam."

"An American advisor," Charlie repeated to himself. *That's a crock of shit! We're fighting a goddamn war. An Advisor, my ass!*

The sergeant returned to the podium and handed the colonel a note. The colonel, annoyed at the interruption, looked at the note.

"Sergeant Armfield, are you in this room?"

Charlie, still fuming about being called an advisor, slowly

raised his hand.

"Are you Sergeant Armfield?"

"Yes, Sir."

"Front and center, Sergeant."

Charlie stood and approached the podium.

"It's about time you got here. We've been calling your name now for the past three days. This note is for you."

Startled and uncertain, Charlie continued to stand in the front of the room with the note in his hand.

"Unless you have something to say, Sergeant, you'd better take your seat."

The other men in the room laughed as Charlie, red faced, shrugged his shoulders and hustled back to his seat. What in the hell was going on here?

He opened the note. It was from Mike! He read, "Hey Bro, meet me in the back afterward."

Charlie's mind raced. *Meet me in the back? He's here?* Charlie turned around and peered over the other soldiers, looking to the back of the room. *Mike!*

Mike smiled, raising his eyebrows and nodding.

Charlie stared at Mike. Oh, my God! My brother found me. A joyful tear spilled down his cheek. He brushed it away before anyone noticed. He forced himself to listen to the rest of the briefing, then rushed to greet Mike.

They embraced, and then Mike pushed Charlie back. "Come on, Charlie. We have to hurry so we can catch a plane."

"A plane? What are you talking about, man? I'm not supposed to leave Bangkok."

"I got permission from the U. S. Armed Forces of Thailand to take you to Songkhla, where I live. But we need to haul ass if we're going to catch today's flight."

Together they boarded another plane, and flew to the southern peninsula of Thailand. Charlie saw the ocean from his window seat and turned to look at his brother.

"Do you have a beach by your place, Mike?" Charlie said, with anticipation.

"Yes, but before you get your hopes up, it's on the inside of the peninsula so there's no surf."

"No surf?"

"Sorry about that. But there's a beautiful sand beach that goes on forever, and the water is great for swimming. It's about eighty degrees. I have a couple of snorkel masks so we can go sightseeing in the tide pools."

Charlie grinned. "Hey, it's okay, man. I forgot my board anyway."

The expression on Mike's face changed.

"Charlie?"

"Wait a minute," Charlie said, trying to read his brother's mind. "If you're going to ask me about Nam, don't. I'm on vacation, man, and thanks to you, I get to go to a beautiful beach instead of staying in a big, crowded city."

Mike studied him for a moment. "Sure, Bro, anything you say."

"Hey, can I get flowered shirts in Songkhla? I'll be damned if I'm going to wear army clothes on this vacation."

Mike nodded and punched Charlie's shoulder. Smiling, Charlie returned the gesture, thinking this was the first time he'd been happy in a long while.

For the first three days, they swam and snorkeled. They walked for miles along the beach every evening, occasionally playing Frisbee, and watching beautiful sunsets. By the end of the fourth day, Charlie started to relax.

"Do you hear from Mom and Dad?" Charlie asked.

"Of course I do. I talked to them on the phone when they found out you might be coming to Bangkok. Mom was so happy—said they might go on a vacation to celebrate."

"Celebrate?"

"I think they're celebrating a chance to relax, Charlie."

Charlie tilted his head. *Relax?*

"They've been so nervous about you being in Vietnam, they haven't done anything since you left. They just sit around home and worry about you."

That evening, Mike stopped at a street vendor to check the available snacks.

"Charlie, I want you to try something." Mike handed him a piece of fish that had been soaked in some kind of peanut sauce. "You're going to love this, Bro."

Charlie sniffed at the fish. It smelled funny, but since Mike devoured his, Charlie popped it into his mouth and ate it.

The next morning, Charlie awakened with stomach cramps. He raised himself out of bed and rushed to the bathroom, vomiting.

Mike, hearing his brother up, hurried to Charlie.

"What's the matter? Wow, you're white as a ghost, Bro."

"I don't know, but I can hardly move. It even hurts to talk."

Mike decided to drive Charlie to the military hospital five miles out of Songkhla.

The doctor, a captain in the army, checked Charlie. "What did you eat?"

Charlie noted his brother's chagrined look. "I don't know what it was, Sir, but it sure was tasty."

"Well, I hope it was worth it, because you have food poisoning. I'm keeping you here today on intravenous fluids. If you're better by this evening, you can go home with your brother. I'll need to have a copy of your R&R orders so I can make some notations for your medical records."

Charlie felt his R&R slipping away like a perfect wave paddled for, but missed. That evening he was released from the hospital, but only because he faked feeling better. He announced that he was fine, stood up and gingerly walked out of the door. When he bent to get into the car, he let out a yelp.

"Are you sure you're all right, Charlie?"

"Yeah, sure. Let's get out of here," he said, holding his stomach while he slammed the car door shut.

By the next morning, Charlie felt well enough to get up early, slip on a pair of swim trunks, and walk alone on the beach. Later that morning he would be saying goodbye to Mike and flying back to Bangkok to report to the Armed Forces Headquarters for departure to Vietnam. He fantasized what it would be like if he didn't go back.

You know, big guy, if you just hung out here with Mike for a while, you might be able to disappear, and the army would never know what happened to you. He tried to imagine life in Songkhla, but the vision of his brother, surrounded by military police, popped up. No, that won't work. Mike had to get special permission for him to come here—signed a bunch of paperwork.

Charlie walked to the shoreline and waded in. The water felt like a warm bath as he gently immersed his weak body. Slowly he began to stroke out a ways. *Maybe a damn fishing boat will pick me up and haul me out of here,* he thought. *Take me to a deserted island where I can live without war.*

I don't want to kill anymore.

He cried out, "I don't want to kill any more!"

Mike, who was walking along the beach looking for his brother, dove into the water and swam out to him.

"I can't do that shit any more! No more! No more! I want to go home." Charlie's salty tears became one with the sea as Mike swam up.

"Charlie! Are you okay?"

Charlie was startled, and he turned around quickly.

"What the...? Yeah, yeah, I'm all right. Just taking a morning swim, Bro."

Charlie, knowing Mike had probably heard his outcry, didn't volunteer an explanation.

Later, while driving the uniformed Charlie to catch his plane, Mike spoke up.

"Charlie, about what you were saying when I reached you in the water this morning."

"Forget it, Mike. Just having a little swim and goofing off, that's all."

"But, Charlie, I heard you."

"It was nothing, okay? Whatever you heard, I was just messing around. And please, don't tell Mom and Dad anything. Promise me, man. I've got to do what I've got to do, but I don't want anybody to have extra reasons for worrying about me. Everything is just going to be fine."

At the airport, they got out of the car and embraced.

"You know, around here it's not customary to show affection in public," Mike said.

"No shit," Charlie said, not letting go. "Well, if anybody sees us they're just going to have to be appalled. I'm not letting go till I damn well feel like it."

They shared a laugh, but when Charlie let go, Mike's eyes were watering.

"Hey, man. I doubt it's okay to do that, either." He wiped his brother's tears with his hand, reached into the car for his bag, and headed toward the plane so his brother wouldn't see him cry.

Without turning back, Charlie called to Mike as he jogged to the gangplank, "See you next year."

During the flight, Charlie's apprehension about going back to Vietnam began to grow. By the time the plane landed in Bangkok, he knew he wasn't going to report back—at least not that day.

He found his way to a park and sat waiting, wondering what to do.

Later, he caught a cab and asked the driver to take him to a medium priced hotel. After he checked in, he climbed up three flights of stairs to his room and ordered dinner from room service. He stood at the window and watched the busy city while he ate. After dinner he decided to take a walk. Still wearing his khaki uniform, he hurried down the stairs of the hotel.

It was dark when he got out to the street.

"Hey, soldier," yelled a cab driver in hard to understand English. "You want girl?"

"No thanks," Charlie said, walking on. *Shit,* he thought, *maybe that's what I need. A nice girl to help me forget what I'm doing.*

He walked aimlessly for hours, mixed thoughts churning in his mind. Time flew—the temple bell chimed twelve times. *Midnight? I must be out of my mind. What am I going to do? If I go back, I have to kill. If I don't, I will be running for the rest of my life.*

A young Siamese man on a motor scooter passed by, saw Charlie, and turned around. "Hey, soldier. I got girl for you. What do you say?"

Feeling desperate, Charlie said, "Sure, why not."

"Hop on. We'll go meet her."

Charlie climbed on and the young man gave him a tour of the city he hadn't seen. As they cruised for nearly twenty minutes, along side streets and back alleys, he saw shack homes and smelled the stench of a third world city. Finally they pulled up in front of a large courtyard with several rundown stucco buildings. They got off the scooter and Charlie was led into the first structure.

Inside were close to twenty beautiful Southeast Asian girls, scantily dressed in colorful clothing, with long, well groomed dark hair, and most of them about his age or younger.

"Take your pick," said the man.

All of the courtesans began to eye Charlie.

"Choose me, GI. I make you happy," one of the girls said.

He walked around looking at the girls, and decided on a pretty, smooth-skinned girl who was sitting quietly in the corner. She wore a short yellow flowered dress that flattered her shiny legs and arms, and quietly confirmed her breasts.

"What's your name?"

She pointed to herself, acting almost surprised that he was talking to her.

"Annie."

Charlie smiled at the picking of an American name for her vocation.

"Would you like to be with me tonight, Annie?" he said, as if he was asking for permission.

She looked at the young man for translation. He was nodding affirmatively, so she did as well.

Charlie was given a choice of staying in one of the rooms available there, or going back to his hotel. He chose the latter, and a cab was arranged. He paid the young man twenty-five dollars and left with Annie.

"Do you like your work?" Charlie asked.

"I sorry, no understand very good English," she replied.

"I'm sorry, too. I thought maybe you could help me decide what to do tonight. You see I' m faced with a terrible situation. Either I go back to Nam and fight for my life, or I escape and live a life on the lam. Either way it sounds pretty lousy. I'll be damned if I know which is right."

The girl with the smooth skin looked up into Charlie's eyes and somehow, even though she didn't understand him, he felt like she knew he was troubled.

I will make you forget, her eyes said.

At the hotel they walked arm-in-arm up the stairs to the third floor. Charlie thought, *this is crazy, big guy. How is this woman, beautiful though she may be, going to help you forget anything as heavy as what you've got going?* He opened the door, and allowed her to enter first. She put her arms around his neck and kissed him. He immediately became aroused.

Then she unbuttoned his shirt and started to rub her fingers through the hair on his chest. He took off his shirt and she turned around so he could unbutton her dress. After the third button, the dress fell to the ground. She turned around to show Charlie her body. He smiled, but then frowned.

"You no like?" she said, her mouth forced into a pout.

"Oh, I like all right. But you see, I have a girlfriend back home, and all of a sudden I feel pretty uncomfortable."

He looked into her eyes, knowing she didn't understand what he was saying. Finally, she knelt down and unzipped his trousers, pulled them down, and started to fondle his genitals.

He stepped back and pulled his pants back up.

"I think I know what would help me more."

He led her over to the bed, pulled back the covers and motioned for her to get in. Then he climbed in next to her and just held her tightly in his arms. After a while she fell asleep, and Charlie tried to process his future. Finally, at five a.m., he fell asleep, and rose again at eight.

Charlie was dressed in his military khaki uniform when he greeted the waking Annie.

"Good morning, Annie. I don't know what's the matter with me," he said, gazing at her buxom figure. "I should have enjoyed you last night. Instead I used you to settle my emotions. I feel better now. You were a great pacifier. I've decided to return to Vietnam and perform my so-called duty."

He placed five dollars on the bed—more than enough money for her cab fare, he thought—grabbed his bag, and departed.

It was nearly ten o'clock when he reported in at headquarters. He thought he would be cited for being absent without leave.

The lieutenant checking him in asked, "When were you supposed to be here, Sergeant Armfield?"

"Yesterday, Sir."

"Oh, wait a minute," he said, thumbing through Charlie's orders. "You were hospitalized for food poisoning. Are you all right now, Sergeant?"

Charlie looked at the lieutenant for a moment and then stammered, "Yes...yes, Sir."

"Very good. Go ahead and check in with the flight officer. The plane will be leaving at 1300 hours."

Charlie walked away from the lieutenant feeling like he just gotten away with stealing. *Oh well,* he thought, *I'll take it.*

Gage was cutting meat and didn't notice him when Charlie got in line at the DEROS center mess hall.

When Charlie reached him, he said, "I'll have a piece off of the end, please. I like it well done, as you know."

Gage looked up. "Hey, man, where've you been? I expected you back here yesterday."

"Oh, yeah, well...that's a long story. When are we going to the beach, anyway?"

"Do you have a flight out tomorrow?" Gage asked.

"I don't know. I didn't check in, I wanted to see you first."

"I'll go with you and see if I can get you laid over here for a few days."

"How in the hell are you going to do that?"

"I know some guys over there who are pulling strings all the time. I know they'll do it for me. I'm on the swing shift tomorrow, so we'll go to the beach in the morning. You can stay with me in my room."

"That sounds great. Are there any waves at this beach?"

"Sure. They're small with a weird shape, but you can body surf them."

"All right! Let's have at it!"

The next morning, Gage checked out a jeep. The two Las Olas Surf Club members headed for the beach, with all of its glorious sand, and waves. Charlie knew that even if he hadn't been to that particular shoreline before, and even if it was in Vietnam, it was going to feel like home.

After they had been bodysurfing for nearly an hour, Charlie noticed the board riders. He wasn't sure at first, but then he saw a surfboard fly up in the air when somebody wiped out on a take off.

"Gage! Look down the beach, man. Do you see what I see?"

"What?" Gage turned to look down the beach. "Where?"

"Way down there, man. It looks like there are a couple of guys on surfboards. I can't believe what I'm seeing, Gage. Let's go!"

"Hold on, pal. You can't go down there."

"What are you talking about? There's surfing going on, and we're a surfers. Let's get on it, man."

"Charlie, listen to me, man. That is a military rehabilitation hospital down there; it's completely off limits. That is unless you're unfortunate enough to get wounded and have to stay there."

Charlie stared at the surfers. *"Unfortunate" would not be the word I would use,* he thought. *Staying on the beach instead of back in the field somewhere would definitely be my preference, especially if I got to surf for rehabilitation. Hell, I'd gladly get wounded for that kind of duty.*

"Look carefully, Charlie," Gage said while pointing down the beach and out in the water. "There is a barbed wire fence extending out into the water about two hundred feet. You can't get in there, man."

"Gage, what do you say we take a walk?"

"Oh shit, man, you're going to get me into trouble, aren't you?"

Charlie focused on getting down the beach to scope out the situation, his stride vigorous and determined. As he neared the fence, he slowed down, trying to figure out his strategy. Just short of the barbed wire, he turned to Gage.

"Listen, Gage, I'm going to take a little swim around this wire thing. If you don't want to take a chance, I'll meet you back here in a little while. Any trouble I could possibly get into would only be a welcome diversion from the hell that's waiting for me."

That said, Charlie dove into the water and started to swim out the length of the fence. When he made the turn around the wire at the end, he saw that Gage, an equally powerful swimmer, was with him. Quickly they swam back in on the other side.

When they were close to the shoreline again, they stroked into a wave and bodysurfed onto the beach. As the water receded, they stood up quickly, and casually walked down the beach.

They sat down near some other soldiers to watch the surfers. The small, roughly shaped surf was poor for board riding, but Charlie felt it calling, urging him in. *Surfing in Vietnam,* he thought. *What a wonderful thing to do in such a horrible place.*

"I'm going to give it a go, Gage."

"Charlie, those guys are patients here. They'll never let you have a board."

Charlie grinned. "Hey, man, maybe I just became a patient."

He waded out into the surf and right up to a heavy-set man lying on a board trying to paddle, a guy who apparently had never surfed before, as he kept falling off.

"Hey, Buddy, I've been sitting on the beach, waiting for a turn on one of those things. Can I have a go at it?" Charlie asked.

"Oh, I'm sorry," the man said. He rolled off and pushed the board over to Charlie. "I can't ride that damn thing, anyway. Maybe you'll have better luck."

"Thanks a lot, man. I'll give it a shot."

Charlie pulled himself on and started knee-paddling out. Meanwhile Gage, who was still sitting on the beach watching, jumped to his feet with his hands on his head. Charlie looked at his friend, laughed and waved for him to come out. While Gage waded out, Charlie paddled over to another beginner fumbling with a board.

"Hey, Buddy, that guy wading out needs a turn," he said, pointing at Gage.

The guy nodded and shoved the board through the water to Gage. The two California surf rats began to rip the Nam swells apart. Those who were still in the water joined the soldiers on the beach, and watched as if spellbound by the surfing demonstration. Despite the poor surf conditions, Charlie and Gage surfed for more than two hours. If anybody figured out what was going on, they chose not to say a word.

"Charlie, you are a trip! This is unbelievable, man. Never in a million years would I have thought you could pull this off."

"Remember that knife my grandfather gave me when we left?"

"Yeah, it had the inscription, 'Believe' scratched on it."

"Right. As soon as I saw those guys on the boards, I believed I was going surfing today."

Charlie remembered when he gave the knife to Will. "You know who has that knife now?"

"Who?"

"Will. I gave it to him before he left on his last mission. I don't know if I gave it to him so he would have good luck, or so I could believe he was going to be all right. I sure hope he's all right."

Gage studied his friend and then looked out toward the horizon. Six dolphins appeared just out from the break line.

"Charlie, look, we've got some company."

"All right!"

The dolphins glided along in the swells. *How beautiful they look,* Charlie thought, *so peaceful and happy.* He recalled the conversation about the dolphins he and Gage had with the old Hawaiian man on Oahu—the one who said dolphins were civilized, that they didn't have wars or fight among themselves like men do.

"Gage, remember that old man on Oahu?"

"I was just thinking about that. You know, one day I was talking about dolphins with one of the Vietnamese workers in my kitchen. She said that in Vietnam the dolphin is considered like a mandarin—which is high official—like royalty. When a dead dolphin is washed up onto the beach, they take it to the temple and perform a ceremonial cremation. They store the remains there in a special box."

"Why do they do all that?"

"She said that back in the eighteenth century a pod of dolphins helped the Vietnamese Navy rescue a group of sailors whose boat sank after they were attacked by Chinese invaders. That rescue by the dolphins enabled the Vietnamese to win a strategic battle, and the dolphins have been heroes ever since. She said the dolphins still help the Vietnamese people by leading them to great schools of fish and warding off sharks."

"That's a great story, Gage. Angels of the sea."

"That's what the Vietnamese call them, too. The woman told me they believe that when dolphins die, their souls automatically ascend to heaven, where they become angels of the sea in the sky."

Charlie looked at Gage. *Oh my God,* he thought, *is this a message? Are these my angels in Vietnam? I've been spoofing the idea ever since I got here. But maybe they've come to let me know they're by my side. What was that Bible verse?* "He who dwells in the shelter of the most high..." *Is that where I am right now, in my shelter, where I can learn my spiritual connection? That's what Dad said he thought my surfing was for me.* "My God, in whom I trust, for he will give his angels charge of you, to guard you in all your ways."

"Charlie? What's going on?"

"I was thinking how wonderful it is to be out here in the water with you, man. And maybe those dolphins have just issued me a special blessing for the rest of my stay here in Nam."

Gage looked at Charlie with a solemn stare.

"I certainly hope so, Charlie. Goddamn it anyway! I really hope so, man."

Charlie laughed and hit his hand against the water, splashing Gage.

"Gage, you're the best friend anybody could ever have."

12

Charlie left for Pleiku the next morning. Gage told him he thought he could get the guys over at the R&R processing to stall his departure another day, but Charlie thought it was about time to get back out in the field and check on the greenback lieutenant.

"Do you remember what you told me last time we said goodbye at this airport?" Gage asked, just before Charlie boarded the plane.

"No, man. What?"

"You said, 'Don't worry about me. Before you know it, we'll both be back on the beach.'"

Charlie smiled and hugged his best friend.

On the plane, Charlie chose the bench on the side of the C-130, next to a porthole again. He put his bag next to him. He leaned back and closed his eyes, reflecting silently.

What the hell am I doing, heading back to the goddamn war? I could be surfing with Gage today. The greenback's face hovered in the shadows of his mind. *Come on, Tim. Wave at me, man. Wave at me so I know you're all right.*

When the plane landed, he boarded a bus to Camp Enari and, once there, he was given instructions to report back to his unit. Charlie slowly walked to Battalion Headquarters, in no hurry to report—kicking rocks to see how far he could make them go. *Here I am again,* he thought. *Wonder what's going to happen next.*

When he arrived, he was amazed to see Captain Williams walking toward the mess tent. He ran to catch up.

"Excuse me, Sir," Charlie called out.

The captain turned and looked surprised to see Charlie.

"Hey, Charlie. What are you doing here?"

"Just got back from R&R, Sir. Went to Bangkok!"

"All right! I sure have missed you since you transferred out of Intelligence. You're the only guy I know from San Diego in this damn war."

"I missed you, too, Sir," Charlie said, embarrassed that he would admit to missing the captain. "How's the new guy working out?"

"Not bad, I guess. He has a college education, but sometimes I wonder from what school. He's not as quick as you were, Charlie. Don't know why I let Top talk me into trading you for him."

"But I thought..." Charlie stopped himself from saying the rest—that he thought it was the Captain's idea to trade.

"What's that, Charlie?"

"Never mind, Sir. I hope it all works out, that's all."

"Well, I'm out of here now, Charlie. I'm going home tomorrow."

"You are? Fantastic, Sir! Say hello to the ocean for me, will you?"

"I sure will. Charlie, aren't you assigned to "C" Battery as a forward observer?"

"Yes, Sir. I've been trying to forget that while I was on R&R, but I guess I better get used to the idea again."

"I guess you'll have to. They've been getting hit pretty hard out there. I'm sure they'll be glad to get you back. Your infantry company has been reunited down south, and there has been a lot of action near Cambodia."

"Yes, Sir." Charlie stared at the ground. "Have a nice trip home, Sir. Maybe I'll see you on the flip side."

He lifted his head again and started to salute, but was greeted with a handshake instead.

"I hope we do, Charlie. Good luck, man."

Charlie turned toward the main headquarters tent. *Shit! They've been getting hit pretty hard. Now I really wish I were surfing with Gage,* he thought.

The battalion first sergeant hustled over to Charlie. "Are you Sergeant Armfield?"

"Yes."

"We've been looking for you. Where have you been?"

"Just returned from R&R."

"We expected you back here a couple of days ago. Well, you're here now, and we've got to get you back out. They need you, Sergeant. Get to the supply tent on the double and get some clean fatigues. After you change, you'll be on the next chopper out of here."

Thirty minutes later, Charlie was on his way back to the front. The plan was to drop him at the battery for briefing, but when the pilot radioed that he would be landing soon with the sergeant, he was instructed to take Charlie out to the 125-Infantry's Delta Company instead.

"Roger that," said the pilot. "Did you hear that, Sergeant? There's no time to waste. You must be important for them out there."

Charlie sat in the open doorway of the chopper, thinking. *How important could I be? Shit! Three days ago I was contemplating AWOL. How can a guy who thought about running be important? This is the most peculiar...*

His thoughts were interrupted by the sounds of explosives in the distance. *Whoa, shit! Here I go again.*

The moment the chopper landed, a medic ran to the doorway and yelled to the pilot, in order to be heard over the slapping sounds of the helicopter.

"Can you take these bodies out of here?"

"Yeah, but hurry up!" the pilot shouted.

Charlie jumped out to help with the loading. The bodies, crowded together on the landing zone, were mutilated. Some were missing arms and legs. The dirty faces were so bloodstained he didn't recognize any of them—until he reached to pick up the last one. The man's eyes were still open, staring.

Lieutenant Tim Harvey's eyes, staring—at him, through him—with the same frightened look he had the last time Charlie saw him. A shaft of ice shot through Charlie's spine, paralyzing him, preventing him from touching the body—or from stepping back.

"Oh, my God!" Charlie cried. "No! It can't be."

The medic ran over to help. "He got it two days ago, Sergeant. This is the first chance we've had to get him out of here."

He bent down to help, but Charlie raised his hand.

"No, man, let me do this."

Charlie put his right arm under the lieutenant's upper back and his left under the lieutenant's knees. He lifted him, stood up and trudged toward the waiting chopper.

"Hurry up, Sergeant!" screamed the pilot. "I've got to get out of here!"

Charlie picked up his stride. Gently, he placed the body in the helicopter next to the others.

"I'm sorry. This is my fault," Charlie said, addressing the corpse.

"This is nobody's goddamn fault," the pilot yelled, pulling back the throttle and lifting the helicopter off the ground.

Yes it is, Charlie thought. *I should have been here.*

He sat down on the ground, his clean fatigues splotched with the blood of his comrade. He felt numb, frozen to the spot. He put his head down, covering his face with his hands. *I left him alone. It's my fault.*

"Hey, where the hell have you been?"

Charlie jumped at the sound of the familiar voice. He looked up and saw Will smiling down on him. Charlie leapt to his feet and clutched his friend.

Will pushed Charlie back, holding him at arm's length.

"When I got back here, I thought you were dead, Charlie. They told me to carry a radio for this new lieutenant, but didn't tell me where you were. I asked the lieutenant, but he never answered me. I thought maybe he was just in shock or something, and I thought you were dead, man."

Charlie peered into Will's eyes. "What happened to him?"

"We were on a company march. The lieutenant and I were up front with a squad and took a direct hit. Everybody was killed except him and me. I crawled around and dragged all of the bodies together. When I looked around to get orders, he was gone. Gone! The damn guy had run away, man."

"Scared shitless, I'll bet."

"Oh, yeah? Well so was I! That guy was gutless!"

Yes, he was, Charlie thought. *I hope his old man is proud. His son died in battle.*

"At least you were here."

"What do you mean by that?"

"I felt guilty when I left for R&R—when I left the guy here. I never saw such a dejected human being in all my life. At least you were here, so he was in good hands. He just wasn't meant to be here, that's all."

"And we are?"

Charlie shook his head from side to side. "No. I didn't mean that, man. None of us are supposed to be here."

The captain told Charlie that he was his main man again, and he assigned Will permanently as Charlie's radio telephone operator. There was a shortage of new lieutenants coming from stateside, and considering all the action the company was getting, the captain said he didn't want any more greenbacks for awhile.

"I need experience out in the field, Charlie, and you're as good they get."

The two surf rats were inseparable, and that suited Charlie just fine. He knew where Will was now and that was one less thing to worry about. Will had become his blood brother. And they didn't have to prick their fingers and rub them together for that distinction. The blood of the war they shared was a stronger bond.

One evening, while they were out on patrol, Charlie whispered, "You know what, man? If both of us have to be here in this shit, I'm just glad we're together."

Will grabbed Charlie's right hand with a handclasp grip and raised it up to shoulder level.

"I never felt so alone in my entire life. Then you got here, Charlie, and that's been very important to me. I think you've saved my life physically and mentally, several times." Will released Charlie's hand and turned his head to the side as if ashamed.

"What's the matter, man?"

"I've been meaning to tell you something, but I'm afraid."

"You're afraid? Of what? There are people all over the place trying to kill us, and you're afraid to tell me something?"

"I lost your grandfather's knife, man. I don't even know where. We were in and out of so many areas there for awhile, and one time I reached into my pocket—and it was gone. I feel like shit, Charlie."

Charlie studied Will for a moment and then smiled.

"Listen, man. I gave it to you for good luck. Apparently you didn't need it anymore, that's all. You're not in a goddamn body bag, are you? So it must have worked. That's all that counts as far as I'm concerned."

Will grabbed Charlie's hand again and shook it hard. "Thanks, man."

Over the next month, Charlie and Will accompanied nine different surveillance missions. Most of the time, Charlie was the highest-ranking soldier, and was in charge. Even when he wasn't the top rank, he was the forward observer, so his opinion was always accepted as final. Often he would refer to Will for his expertise, because he usually had the most time in country of anyone on the squad.

"I don't like the feel of this place, man," Charlie said. It was early afternoon on the second day of their ninth mission. "We've been out in the open in this valley too long. There's not enough coverage if we get hit. Got any ideas?"

"Let's head over to the bush on the south flank," Will said. "We might have to cut our way through for awhile, but I think it would be worth it. How many machetes do we have?"

"Looks like two. Clark and Elliot have them."

Charlie swung the nine-man squad off to the left. Twenty minutes later they were in thick vegetation. Clark and Elliot lead the group, swinging their blades from side to side to clear a passage. They were so focused on cutting a swatch, they didn't see the NVA soldier forty yards ahead. Charlie looked up just in time to make eye contact with the enemy.

Charlie fired a burst from his rifle, and saw the Vietnamese's chest explode. He dove to the ground shouting, "Hit it!"

He looked up and saw two more. *On shit!* He fired another burst and the other two fell off to the side. Seconds ticked by. Charlie decided to crawl ahead to reconnoiter. He slithered forward like a snake until he came to within thirty yards of an enemy machine gun that started blistering rounds over his head.

He raised his rifle slowly during the barrage of enemy fire, and, with one shot, hit a bull's eye. He saw a bullet hole appear between the enemy soldier's eyes. By this time, his entire squad was firing at the bush up ahead. Charlie was caught between both sides. He hugged the earth as close as he could to wait out the confrontation.

He felt a thud next to him, on his right. A grenade had landed two feet away. He shot out his right hand, grabbed it, and hurled it in the direction of the enemy. A split second after leaving his hand, it exploded in mid air, showering him with pieces of metal. Dazed, he remained still. His head felt like it was spinning out of control. He felt an excruciating pain in his right ear.

The conflict continued for fifteen minutes. Finally, the shooting stopped. Charlie touched his ear, then looked at his hand and saw blood. Somebody crawled up next to him on his right. It was Will.

Will seemed to be mouthing words, but all Charlie heard was a blaring, shrieking ring. He pointed to his ear, now dripping blood. Will investigated the wound, hopped over to the other side and shouted into Charlie's left ear.

"Can you hear me?"

Charlie nodded.

"I don't see any flesh wounds. Were you hit anywhere else?"

Charlie mentally surveyed the rest of his body. His back and legs felt scratched, but nothing hurt. He wiggled his fingers and toes—everything seemed in tact. He shook his head.

"I don't think so."

Will ordered the men to sweep the area. He turned back to Charlie. "Why don't you try to get up?"

Charlie looked into Will's eyes, saw him smile encouragement. He eased his way into a standing position, but his head was still spinning. He tried to take a step, but fell to his knees. Will knelt and grabbed him. Charlie held his right forefinger up and moved it in circles.

"You're dizzy?" Will asked.

Charlie nodded.

"Don't worry, man. I'm calling a medevac right now."

"No, man! I'll be all right." Charlie put his head in his hands to try to keep it from orbiting.

"Are you sure?"

"Yeah, let me sit here for a minute. Then I'll get up again."

"I better go check on the sweep. Will you be okay here?"

"Sure, go ahead, man."

Ten minutes later, Charlie felt like he should help with the sweep. He rolled onto his hands and knees. Slowly, he pushed up onto his feet, still bent over, holding his head. *Oh shit,* he thought. *The world is going around so fast, I can't keep on it.* He lifted his head and saw only the blur of the green bush going by.

He straightened up, took a step and tripped. He fell hard and hit his forehead on a rock, knocking himself unconscious.

When he came to, Will and Private Clark were carrying him into the open space. A chopper waited; Charlie saw a blurry-looking helicopter with Red Cross painted on the side.

"What's happening?"

"You're getting the hell out of here, man," Will shouted.

When they were less than a hundred feet from the LZ, a machine gun echoed through the basin. Private Clark dropped, taking Charlie and Will with him. Bullets whizzed over their heads.

"Come on! Better drag him the rest of the way," Will yelled.

Will started to crawl, pulling Charlie.

"Hey, man. Clark's still lying back there," Charlie said.

Will let loose and returned to Clark.

"Oh shit! He got hit!"

"Is he alive?" Charlie forgot about his revolving world for a moment.

Will felt for Clark's carotid pulse, shook his head, and returned to Charlie. He clutched Charlie's arm and dragged him toward the chopper. Charlie wanted to help, but his body was uncontrollable in his orbiting world.

The enemy machine gunner focused on his objective, seeming to miss them only by inches.

Charlie's mind began to analyze the situation. He wondered, *who is this man risking his life for my evacuation? Will has taken me into his heart, and it's as if our two lives have become one. Why doesn't he leave me, and try to save his own life? It's okay to leave me, Will,* he thought, but he knew it wasn't going to happen. *We are already in each other's body, and have created a survival mission for the one person we have become. We are spirits, interchangeable, humans of each other's beings.*

"Get him in here. On the double!" the pilot screamed as a medic pitched a stretcher onto the ground. "I radioed for a gunship. It will be here in two minutes. What about the other guy?"

"Dead!" Will shouted over the slapping sounds of the blades, as he rolled Charlie onto the stretcher. At the last moment, the medic jumped out and helped lift Charlie into the chopper.

"Then I'm out of here!" the pilot yelled.

The medevac lifted off, and took Charlie out of the battle before he could tell Will goodbye. The medic on board examined Charlie but, unable to determine the extent of his injuries, administered morphine to reduce any suffering. For Charlie, the drug put him to sleep and induced a nightmare.

Will, where are you, man? Gooks...gooks surrounding him...going to get shot! Don't get killed, Will! Where are you...don't get killed...I'm with you...still in your body, man...wherever you are...wherever I am. Will, come back...don't know these people...why are they trying to kill us? I don't want to kill them...all those people...didn't want to kill them. Come back, man.

Charlie opened his eyes as the chopper landed at a forward infirmary. "Where's Will?"

"Who?" the medic said.

Charlie barely heard the man from his left ear. He struggled to make sense of the nightmarish images crowding his mind. Slowly, it began to register what had happened, where he was. The medic leaned close, listening.

"Never mind. I was just thinking about my blood brother."

The medic shook his head, as if dismissing the delirious mutterings of just another injured soldier. Two orderlies carried Charlie into a tent and placed him on one of many examination tables, most of them bearing bloody soldiers. A doctor, wearing a baseball cap with captain's bars and a white smock, stepped to his side.

"Where are you hit, Soldier?"

Charlie turned his head to the right so his left ear was facing toward the doctor. "Come again, Sir. I can't hear out of my right ear."

"I think you just answered my question," the captain said.

He turned Charlie's head to insert a scope in his right ear, then spoke into his left ear.

"You blew your drum. Are you dizzy?"

"Yes, Sir. I can't walk without falling."

"I wouldn't doubt it. Were you hit anywhere else?"

"Only scratches, Sir."

The captain looked at Charlie's forehead. "What happened to your head?"

"Just fell trying to stay on my feet."

The captain smiled. "We have some seriously wounded here today, Sergeant. You, I'm happy to report, are not one of them. I'll be back as soon as I can."

The forward infirmary buzzed with activity. Every time it started to quiet down, more wounded arrived. Sometimes the doctors would drop everything to attend to a critical case. Each soldier was triaged, assigned a priority number for order of treatment, but could be bumped back if a more serious injury was brought in. Charlie estimated there must have been thirty or more wounded soldiers in the tent.

Two hours later, when the other tables had been cleared, the doctor returned.

"Sorry to keep you waiting, Sergeant." he said, smiling despite the fatigue in his voice. "Order of severity. You understand?"

"Yes, Sir. You can leave me here all night if you need to. I'm just glad to be alive."

"Not only alive, but you'll be healed and out of here before you know it." He looked at Charlie's dog tags. "May I call you Charles?"

"Call me Charlie. You mean I won't get to go surfing in Cam Ranh Bay?" he said wishfully.

"Surfing?"

"Just kidding, Sir. I saw some guys surfing at Cam Ranh when I went on R&R. Looked like fun."

"Well, you'll be spending a week, maybe two, here in a tent. You should heal up fine, but then I'm obligated to send you back out."

Out? Oh God, Will, Charlie thought. *Are you alive, man? I left you right in the middle of shit. Please be alive.*

"Are you all right, Sergeant?"

"I don't know, Sir. I left my buddy in the middle of crossfire. He saved my life, but I'm afraid for his."

"I'm sorry. I wish I could help, but there's no way I can find out about your friend from here."

Charlie was moved into the infirmary tent where other men, who were waiting to be airlifted to a hospital somewhere else, were resting. The one on the cot to Charlie's right was missing an arm and was drugged into unconsciousness. On the left, a man had a bandage around his head. He was mumbling out loud, and Charlie strained to hear with his good ear.

"Shit! I don't want to be blind. I'd rather be dead than blind."

"Excuse me, but I couldn't help eavesdropping, man. Do you think you're going to be blind?"

"I know I'm blind!" the guy said with a start, apparently not knowing anyone was lying next to him.

Charlie wished he could help. He hesitated, but then spoke quietly.

"When I want something really bad, I talk like I already have it, rather than talk about how I don't want it to be. You know, like saying that I know I'll be able to see again. That it's only a matter of time. That I just know my vision is intact and everything will be okay."

Charlie listened, but heard nothing. *Should I keep talking or let him rest? Oh, what the heck.*

"Do me a favor, man? Visualize all of the beautiful sights you remember from back home. None of this Nam shit, only the beautiful sights where you're from." *Did he hear me? Was he listening?* "Where are you from anyway?"

"New Jersey."

"Hey, man, do you like the beach? I'm from California, and I love the ocean. How about you?"

"I live right by the shore, at Ocean Beach."

Charlie's eyes felt like they would pop out of his head. "No shit? You're not going to believe this, man, but I'm from O.B. too. Not from the Atlantic O.B., of course, but I am from O.B. Do you surf?"

"Tried it a few times."

"Great! Then you and I can speak the same language. See yourself walking on that beach, man, checking out the surf. It's a gorgeous day—the sky's a perfect blue and the waves are glassy, man. There's a good swell pumping, and it's all you can do to keep from diving in and swimming out to catch a set. Can you dig it?"

"Yeah, sure. I guess so."

"Sometimes I think if you visualize hard enough, you can make what you want come true."

Charlie thought about his surfing victories—how he saw himself ripping the waves apart before he even hit the water to surf in his contest heats. It worked for him then. Could it work for this guy who thought he might be blind?

"Just keep seeing the things the way you've always seen them, man, and before you know it, the bandages will come off and you'll see it."

The guy from O.B., New Jersey started to cry. Charlie reached across to his cot and grabbed his shoulder.

"Hey, man, I was just trying to help. What kind of work did you do back home?"

"I'm an artist. I paint landscapes."

Then you have to see, Charlie thought. *You have to see so you can paint a sunrise coming over those eastern seas. Please, dear God, let him see again.*

The next day, the orderlies began to evacuate the patients. Eventually one came to Charlie's cot.

"Where are you going, Sergeant?"

"How about Cam Ranh Bay? I can hear the surf calling for me. Yeah, I need to go to Cam Ranh Bay."

Laughter came from the cot on the left.

The soldier with his eyes bandaged had been quiet ever since Charlie's conversation with him the day before, and Charlie didn't know if he should try again.

"Hey wait a minute," the orderly said, reading the doctor's notes on the chart at the foot of Charlie's cot. "You're staying right here, wise guy."

"Yeah, I know. Can't blame a guy for trying can you?"

Frowning, the orderly shook his head and moved to the next cot. This time he looked at the notes before speaking to the patient.

"You're going to Tokyo." He waited for a second orderly to come. Together they lifted the patient and placed him on a stretcher. They picked it up and started off.

"Wait a minute," the patient said. "Let me say something to that guy, will you?"

The orderlies stopped and walked back to Charlie's cot. "Here?"

"Hey, surf dude, is this your cot?"

"Yeah, man, it sure is."

"I've been visualizing. I can see the beach."

"Great! Don't give up, okay?"

"I'll try not to. Hope you're okay, too."

"I'll be just fine. Hey, catch a wave for me, will you?" Charlie said.

"Yeah, sure."

Charlie remained alone in the large tent among the empty cots. It was a lonely time. The orderlies would check on him occasionally, but most of the time he was left to himself. Much of the time he worried about Will. He tried to visualize, as he had recommended to the soldier with the bandaged head—visualize Will making it out of the mess.

Finally, after two weeks, his hearing began to improve. There was a loud ringing in his right ear, but he could hear out of it. His dizziness, however, did not improve as rapidly.

"I'm afraid I'll have to keep you here for a while longer, Sergeant," the captain told him. "You must have bruised your inner ear worse than I thought. I guess I should have sent you to the beach after all."

"Oh well, I would have been confined to the bed anyway, right?"

"You're right."

A week later, Charlie was moved to another infirmary. He was still experiencing some dizziness, so he was transferred on a stretcher to a helicopter. There were no other patients to be moved, and the doctor accompanied him.

"You changed your mind, right, Sir? We're going to the beach after all?"

The doctor laughed. "I wish! No, the division is moving back up north again. The forward camp is going to be in Kontum this time. They'll have an infirmary there, but I'll be further forward near Dak To."

"So where am I going, Kontum or Dak To?"

"I figured you might as well stay with me. I expect you out of here in about a week, anyway. I thought I'd just release you myself."

"Do you know what day it is, Sir?"

"It's Tuesday."

"No, I mean what day of the month is it?"

"Let's see, it's the nineteenth. Why?"

Charlie was speechless.

"Why, Charlie?" the captain asked again.

"Are your sure?"

"I'm positive. Sunday was the seventeenth, my mother's birthday."

"It was my birthday, too," Charlie said sadly.

"No shit, Charlie, I didn't know. Happy birthday! How old are you?"

"Twenty-one, Sir. My country thinks I'm a man now. They send boys off to war, but they only let men vote and drink."

"You're right about that. But I think if you come over here and put up with this shit, you become a man no matter how old you are."

Nine days later, Charlie was cleared to return to the field.

"It's been nice knowing you, Charlie," the captain said. "Most of the guys who come through here don't talk very much, because they're pretty scared."

"Tell me about it, Sir. I've never been so lonely in my entire life."

The captain smiled, "You'll be shipping out tomorrow. Meanwhile, enjoy the party in the mess hall."

"What party?"

"This is Thanksgiving Day, Charlie."

The doctor's words left Charlie in a muddled state. *There's Thanksgiving in Nam? What's there to be thankful for? People are getting killed at the front and these guys are celebrating. I'll bet there's no turkey for the grunts today.*

An orderly came in to check on him. "Happy Thanksgiving!"

"Big deal!"

"Hey, what's with you?"

"Just depressed as hell, that's all."

"You a grunt?"

"Sort of."

"Hang on for a minute. I'll be right back."

The orderly ran off and came back with a small bag. He opened it up and pulled out a joint.

"Whoa! Is this cool?" Charlie asked.

"Yeah, everyone is either getting stoned or drunk around here today. Nobody will even know what's happening because I'm the only one on duty. Just relax and enjoy.

Charlie took the joint. The orderly lit a match. Charlie leaned forward to touch it. He took a big hit and slowly blew out the smoke.

"How did you know that I smoked?"

"You said you were a grunt, didn't you?"

"Yeah, I did." He took a few more hits and passed it on to the orderly.

When it came back his way he said, "No, that's enough for me. You know you can only get so high, and then taking more is just a waste. Save it for the next time, man."

"Wow, I guess when you're at the front, you need to conserve it, don't you."

"Something like that. Thanks for sharing your girlfriend, man."

The orderly shrugged his shoulders and walked out of the tent. Charlie lay back and let his mind wander. He started to think about going home and surfing again. He visualized surfing waves at O.B. and he rode them just like when he won the championships. *Why not,* he thought. *I want to surf again more than anything else in the world. See it happening and maybe, just maybe, it will. Yes! See it happen and it will.*

He caught a few waves in his mind, and then he saw his family. His mom was doting over him and his dad had a tear in his eye. Grandpa was there, too, very proud. Charlie became frightened. *Stop it you guys. Stop it. I'm so ashamed. How can I ever face you all again?*

Then he thought about Cher, looking just as beautiful as ever. *You haven't changed, Babe. But, I'm not the same at all. How can I be with you when you're the same person and I'm not?*

13

The helicopter landed at Charlie Battery of the 402nd Artillery. Sergeant Armfield, pack secured over his right shoulder, hopped out, and headed toward headquarters and the guns up on a hill. Gun bunnies were busy, humping ammo up from the chopper pad. One of them stopped in Charlie's path.

"Hey, aren't you Charlie?"

"Yeah. Who are you?"

"I'm Al Strangemeir. We met on the chopper when I first got into country. Remember, I thought it was weird that Charlie was going to Charlie Battery to fight Charlie."

"Oh yeah. How's it going?"

"Well," Al said with a chuckle, "I'm still in Nam, but other than that, not bad."

Charlie laughed. "I know what you mean. Do you know where I can find the captain?"

"See that box up at the top of the hill?"

Charlie noted a metal shed about twenty feet square. "Yeah. Is that where those guys are when I'm talking to them on the radio?"

"That's where they are. But we have a new captain since you were here last. His name is Donaldson. Not a bad guy for a captain."

"Thanks, Al. Maybe I'll see you around sometime."

Charlie walked up and knocked on the door of the metal box. Captain Donaldson opened the door.

"Excuse me, Sir. I'm Charlie Armfield."

"Sergeant Armfield. We've been expecting you. Come in."

There were four other men in the battery command headquarters.

"Sergeant, this is Specialist Jerros, and that's Specialist Clinton."

"Nice to finally meet you Charlie," Jerros said.

"Same here," Clinton said.

Charlie smiled, recognizing their voices from previous radio conversations.

"Over there," the captain said, pointing to a soldier in the corner talking on the radio "is Private Sutherland."

They exchanged nods.

A lieutenant sat with his back to the group, working on maps. The captain walked over and put his hand on the lieutenant's shoulder.

"And this is Lieutenant Alvarez."

The lieutenant turned slowly.

Charlie dropped his pack to the floor when he saw Robby's face.

"Oh my God! You're still here, man," he said, stepping forward to hug his former FO. "I thought you'd be stateside by now."

"Well, I almost got my arm blown off out in the field, but some corporal tended to my injury so well I healed pretty fast. So here I am again."

"What are you talking about, man? All I did was stop the bleeding."

"The doctor said that if I had lost any more blood, I would have lost my arm, and probably my life."

Robby reached down into a bag, pulled out a terry cloth wrap and handed it to Charlie. "Sorry, I couldn't get all of the blood stains out," he said grinning.

"I don't believe this." Charlie grabbed it and hugged Robby again.

"Well, I see you two already know each other," the captain said. Everybody laughed. "Why don't you guys head over to the mess tent and get first in line for lunch."

Charlie and Robby sat at a table, each with a tin plate of hot food.

"This sure beats C's, doesn't it?" Robby said.

"I've been away from that shit for a month now."

"I heard. Are you okay?"

"Yeah, just got my ear blown up. There's still a lot of ringing, but at least I'm not dizzy anymore. Have you seen Will? I left him in a pretty bad situation."

"No. I just got back here yesterday."

"Damn! I've got to find out what happened. It's driving me crazy, man. He dragged me to the medevac in the middle of a firefight. I never thought I'd be saying this, but I need to get back out there to find out what happened."

"You're going to get your wish. They have a special assignment ready for you."

"A special assignment?"

"On a long range reconnaissance patrol."

"I'm going to be on an LRRP?"

"Yes. That's why I'm here, too. I was back at Camp Enari for only four days when they came up with the plan. It's a three-man patrol. They said I could pick the other two. I asked if Corporal Armfield was available. I didn't know you were promoted. I was disappointed when I heard you were medevaced. But when I got to the battery, I heard you were on your way back out, so I got permission to take you. Are you all right with that, Charlie?"

"Of course, Robby. It'll be cool working with you again. Can we take Will along, too?"

"Isn't he pretty short about now?"

"Yeah, I guess he is. God, I hope he's all right. You're pretty short, too, aren't you?"

"I was, Charlie, but I extended two extra months so I could do this assignment."

"You did what?"

"You think I'm crazy, don't you?"

"Damn right, I do. Man, oh man," Charlie said, shaking his head. "I sure do."

That afternoon, Charlie and Robby were airlifted back to Delta Company of the 125th Infantry. The chopper landed in a quiet landing zone, and the infantry captain came over to greet the men as they hopped out of the door.

"Glad to see you're all right, Lieutenant. You, too, Sergeant."

"Thank you, Sir," Robby said.

"Is Will Jamison here?" Charlie asked anxiously.

"I don't know what happened to Jamison. So many were coming and going, I couldn't keep track there for awhile."

"Sir!" Charlie shuffled nervously. Sweat beaded on his forehead. "Did he make it back from the patrol I was hurt on?"

"I'm sorry, Sergeant. I don't know the answer to that."

Charlie looked around frantically, trying to spot anyone who was on his last patrol. There were a lot of new faces. He didn't recognize anyone.

"What happened to everybody, Sir?"

"We've had quite a turnover recently. A lot of men were either medevaced or DEROSED this past month. Right now a lot of them are out on patrol. Which reminds me, I am excited about the new LRRP assignment. I assume you know about it, Sergeant."

"I heard, Sir. Excuse me for asking, but I thought we had special units in Nam that did the LRRP work. I didn't know an infantry company did that, too."

"Normally we don't, Sergeant. But we're kind of out here on our own these days, since we moved back north. You know what a LRRP is supposed to do?"

"Not really, Sir."

"Long range reconnaissance began with the French and Indian War. It was decided that the only way to fight the Indians was with other Indians. So they formed a ranger group, and learned the tactics of the natives."

"So in this case we're going to learn how to be gooks, Sir?" Charlie asked.

"That's right, Sergeant. You two have had a lot of experience out here, and we have someone else who will be a great addition."

"Who, Sir?" Robby asked.

"Sergeant Thom."

"The ARVN interpreter?" Charlie said.

"That's right." The captain smiled. "He's been in the army for about five years now, and knows this area like the back of his hand. You three will make a dandy LRRP team."

The captain explained that long range reconnaissance patrols were an important tactic for the American military in Vietnam. Patrols were able to collect valuable intelligence information by locating enemy troops, sometimes following them while remaining undiscovered. Often they were involved in harassment maneuvers with ambush sniper attacks on NVA reconnaissance. If they were discovered and received contact, the LRRP unit would counter with artillery and, if necessary, would be extracted from the area.

The new LRRP team in the Central Highlands had been out in the field for over a month without being evacuated. To keep as little weight in their packs as possible in order to be more mobile, their food and ammunition requirements were dropped by helicopter at designated locations. They were responsible for finding it. Because of the weight, they didn't even wear helmets, but donned camouflage-canvas jungle hats.

One evening, as the sun was setting, Charlie, who was walking point in the middle of a field of three foot high grass, stopped and held up his hand. Robby and Thom stopped dead in their tracks.

"What is it?" Robby asked.

"I don't know, but I feel like something isn't right."

Thom and Robby perked up their ears, and dove for the ground. Charlie followed.

What in the world? Charlie thought.

"Footsteps," Robby whispered. "And it's no animal. It's a two-legged stride, and there are at least three of them," he continued in hushed tones.

Thom nodded in agreement.

Charlie shook his head, feeling disabled by the ringing in his ears. He concentrated in an effort to see any signs of movement.

"There they are."

"Where? I can't see shit," Robby said, frantically trying to pull the grass out of his face.

Charlie pointed, but Thom and Robby shrugged their shoulders.

"About a hundred and fifty yards out at two o'clock. They don't see us. What do you want to do?"

"We can't give up our position," Robby said, still trying to find the movement. "There might be more behind. Let them go."

"Do you want to follow?" an anxious Sergeant Thom asked.

"Not yet. We'll wait to see how many there are. If it's quiet in the morning we'll head out and try to find them." Robby said. "We better hang loose right here for now."

They hiked out of the grass and made camp next to a small thicket of trees. Later they would take turns on watch, but first they shared some of the new LRPP rations they'd received with their latest drop.

"I can't believe this food," Charlie said, pulling a plastic bag filled with dehydrated food out of his pack. "How do you eat it?"

Robby shrugged his shoulders and looked at Thom.

"I see before," Thom said. "Mix with water and wait ten minute. Good. Not like C."

Robby carried a half-demolished claymore, and broke off a small piece of C-4 to heat some water. "I'll bet it's better hot, right Thom?"

Sergeant Thom smiled, and nodded his head.

"Hey you guys," Charlie said, feeling embarrassed. "Thanks for saving my butt out there."

"What are you talking about, Charlie?" Robby said.

"If you guys hadn't heard those footsteps, we could have ended up eye to eye with those gooks. You guys have incredible hearing. The goddamn ringing in my ears could've got us killed. Maybe I shouldn't walk point anymore."

"Charlie, we didn't hear anything until you sensed the danger. You're exactly the one we want walking point. And then you saw them; Thom and I never did. Right, Thom?"

Thom nodded his head. "You save our butt."

"That's right, Charlie. I think we've become quite a team out here. A team, I might add, that any Cong unit would be proud of."

Sergeant Thom looked horrified.

"He means because we're getting so good out here, Thom," Charlie said, smiling and putting his arm around the ARVN. "I thought I was failing you guys, but maybe my sight has gotten keener with my deafness."

"I'll say it has," Robby said. "And the psychic stuff is starting to freak me out. At first I thought it was coincidence. But I've been counting, and this is the third time this week you've known about something before it happened."

"I don't know about that," Charlie said shaking his head.

"Well, what the hell is it then?"

"I don't know. I think it's just that we've been out here so long I've become part of the jungle, man. When there's something that doesn't belong, I seem to feel it."

"Well, I don't know either, Charlie," Robby said smiling. "But I'm sure glad you're on my side."

"Yes." Sergeant Thom said, nodding his head in agreement. Then he smiled. "I glad you no gook."

Charlie and Robby looked at each other and laughed, slapping each other's hand.

That night, while on watch, Charlie thought about the extrasensory talent his comrades attributed to him. He did seem to sense a lot, and not just the irregularities in the jungle. He also knew when Robby was concerned about a situation, even before a word was spoken. Thom didn't speak much, but Charlie sensed that he was depressed and lonely.

Two weeks later, Charlie and Thom were standing watch overlooking a large valley where Intelligence suspected an enemy regiment might pass. Robby was out scouting.

"Hey, Thom, are you okay?"

Thom only nodded his head.

"You know, all I know about you is what the captain told us before we took off together."

"What he tell you?"

"That your name was Sergeant Ky Van Thom, and you were drafted into the military when you were eighteen. He said you served with several ARVN infantry companies, and because you knew English, were assigned to our units as a translator. How come you don't go by your first name?"

"My Vietnamese Unit calls me Sergeant Ky. We always use first name for identification. But Thom is like American name. I like because I like American. Why you ask if I okay?"

"You seem to be kind of down, that's all."

"You know many things, Charlie. I have missed family lately."

"Where is your family now?"

"In Saigon."

"Do you have brothers and sisters?"

Thom was quiet for a moment, then peered sadly at Charlie.

"I had six brothers, two sisters. Two brothers killed in army. Another brother fighting. One brother in New Zealand going to college. Other two brothers still little."

"Sorry about your brothers who were killed, Thom." Charlie was silent looking out across the dense vegetation of the basin below. *Damn! I think I have it bad. This guy's been fighting for five years, and has lost two brothers in this screwy war.*

He looked back at Thom. "What about your sisters?"

Thom looked away, struggling with the question.

"It's okay, man," Charlie said. "You don't have to answer if you don't want too."

"In my culture it is not polite with no answer. My sisters were killed in last Tet. The school was bombed. Many children die."

"Oh shit!" Charlie said, irritated at himself for asking.

"Not your fault, Charlie. This is bad war. I'm sorry you have to come. Many Vietnamese don't know why you here. They confused."

"What do you mean, they're confused? We're here trying to help them."

"I know, and I happy you here. But if you know our history…for many years we were colony of France. We get independence. Later, France tries to take again. Now Vietnamese people think Americans try to take us."

"Wait," Charlie objected, but Thom held up his hand to stop him.

"You have to understand most people not educated. They do not go to school, do not know about communist. When France left, there many problems about being communist, or not being communist. United States help because South wanted no communist. But some people still think Americans want Vietnam."

Holy shit, Charlie thought. *The people don't know what they want, or for that matter, what they have. We come over here after the French leave, and they think we're the new aggressors.*

"Do any of the Central Highlanders have an education?"

"Very few. There are not many schools, and the few schools here are weak. Kids don't have to go, so most farm in fields with families."

"So, most of the people I've seen here don't know why I'm here, do they? The *Montagnards* in that village where we dug up the graves? They didn't know why we came?"

"No," Thom said apologetically.

"Oh, man!"

"But cities are different. There schools teach students history. They know why you here. My father is teacher."

"What does he teach?"

"High grades. He went to college in New Zealand, came back to Hanoi to teach."

"Hanoi?"

"Yes. I was born there."

"Then that means you are a North Vietnamese?"

"When I was born, there only one country. When communist start taking over, my father moved family to Saigon."

"How old were you then?"

"Six years. I go to school, but drafted before I could decide on college."

"That's what happened to me, too." Charlie lowered his head, staring at his U.S. army issued jungle boots. *Right! But you didn't want to go to school, remember. You wanted to surf so bad you let yourself be drafted and brought to a country that doesn't want you. Thom doesn't want his country to become communist, so he at least has a reason to fight.*

"Thom, how long do you think it will take to win this war?"

Thom stared into Charlie's eyes without speaking. Charlie knew what he was thinking. Thom didn't think they would win the war.

Finally Thom said, "The communist live everywhere. Some teach in schools, some live next door to my family. Some even in the South Vietnamese army. We try to win war, but we will not, because enemy is everywhere. Someday, the Americans will go home, and we will become communist nation."

Charlie stared out over the valley and tried to comprehend what Thom had said. *We are fighting a no-win war? How can such a horrible thing be happening in this world? There's blood shed every day—and for what reason?*

"I sorry to give you bad report, Charlie."

"I'm sorry, too, but this is much worse for you than for me."

Suddenly, Thom rolled off to the right, raised his weapon and unlatched the safety. Charlie reacted, rolling to his left, but before he could raise his weapon, Robby came running through the bushes.

"There's a whole damn regiment coming this way," Robby panted, working to catch his breath. "About five miles north."

"Five miles north?" exclaimed Charlie. "How in the hell did you see them?"

"I must be picking up your psychic stuff. All of a sudden I sensed something. The jungle was too thick to see far, so I climbed a big tree and used my field glasses. Looked like a bunch of ants. I watched them for ten minutes and realized there were vehicles coming, too."

"Vehicles! What kind of vehicles?" Charlie asked.

"Tanks, I think."

Thom nodded. "PT-76 tanks. Light tanks. Only kind that can come in jungle."

"Holy shit!" Charlie blurted. "What's the plan?"

Robby pulled out his maps. "They're here, in this ravine," he said, pointing.

"Are you sure?" Charlie asked, surprised. "Man, that doesn't lead into this canyon. Look! There's another canyon over the ridge from here. They're going over there."

"Damn! You're right, Charlie. We're in the wrong canyon. Shit, if we have any hope of intercepting that regiment, we must get into position in the next valley."

They broke camp and hurried down the bank into the canyon. By nightfall they had crossed the opening, and were headed up the other side in the dark. There was no light because the moon hadn't risen yet. It was another mile to the top of the hogback; they had to keep going. The steep jungles intensified, and the blackness didn't help.

Charlie, walking point, could hardly see his hand in front of his face. *Just keep moving,* he told himself. *If the walking gets easy, that means we're not going up anymore.*

To keep from getting separated, Robby held onto Charlie's pack, and Thom held onto Robby's. Each time one of them stumbled, they all fell, slowing their pace. Charlie thought it must have been nearly eleven o'clock when they finally reached the top.

"We'd better stop here," Robby said breathing hard. "We'll get lost, for sure, if we keep going."

Mercifully, the waning moon poked up over the horizon, casting a pale light over the jungle..

"Thanks a lot, Mister Man-in-the-Moon. Where the hell were you when we needed a lantern?" he said quietly.

The three men chuckled.

"Yeah, well, that's the way it goes," Robby said. "At least we know which way is east. You guys get some sleep. I'll take the first watch."

Charlie's watch spanned the pre-dawn hours. Finally the sun rose, turning the gray tones of the bush verdant green. When the orange beam from the fiery sun bored into his eyes, he squinted. Then he saw it; the canyon was straight ahead. He reached over and shook Robby and Thom.

Robby sat up and gazed out into the opening. "If my calculations are correct, the gooks will be in there by mid morning."

"Then what the hell are we going to do?" Charlie asked.

Robby shrugged. "I'm not sure. We'll have to wait and see what headquarters has in mind."

The LRRPs hiked part way down the canyon's ledge, and set up an observation point above a thirty-foot cliff. They couldn't see the head of the twisting chasm from there, but it gave them the best view of the widest point. The morning dragged by. By late afternoon, there was still no sign of the regiment.

"Damn! Where could they be?" Robby said, shifting through the maps. "How can that many people disappear?"

"Maybe it take longer for tanks to get through," Thom said. "We keep waiting. They come."

Finally, at twilight, the enemy regiment arrived. It halted less than a quarter of a mile from the LRRP position. The sight of so many NVA unnerved Charlie. While he had seen the enemy several times before, this time there were nearly a thousand of them. He knew there were no other American troops within ten miles. He turned to find his lieutenant.

Robby was on the radio, speaking with the infantry captain. He was talking quietly and Charlie couldn't hear the plan, but when Robby returned to the group he knew what was going to happen.

"We're not going to get any reinforcements, are we?" Charlie said. "They sent us out here to find this goddamn regiment, and now we have to take care of 'em ourselves. I'm going to call in artillery and kill everyone in range."

"That's the plan, Charlie. It's too late in the day to land troops. Besides, that would give up our position. We'll start the howitzers at midnight when most of them are asleep. They'll never know what hit 'em. The Skyraiders will come in after, and finish them off. Those PT-76 tanks are anti-aircraft. That's why the 105's go first."

"We've filled the basin with water, and now we're pulling the plug. We're going to watch them go down the drain."

Robby nodded. "That's about the size of it."

And we'll have dirty hands for the rest of our lives, Charlie thought. He felt sick to his stomach.

When it got dark, their anxiety intensified. Realizing what was going to happen, sleep was out of the question. Charlie lay back, watching the stars. How beautiful—even peaceful—it was. But soon there would be fireworks and people would die. *We're not going to win this war,* he thought, *but we're going to kill as many as we can anyway.*

An hour before the bombing was scheduled to start, Robby grabbed Charlie's arm.

"What is it?"

"Shhh," Robby whispered. "Someone's coming."

Weapon ready, Thom assumed the prone shooting position.

"Don't shoot," Robby said. "That will give up our position."

Soon, Charlie could hear steps, too. A solo scout walked below them, next to the cliff, stepping high to keep from tripping on the jungle's undergrowth. When finally he passed, Robby exhaled, blowing his breath out hard.

Charlie sensed someone else in the bush. "Wait, there're more." He paused to get a clearer image. "He's up here, coming this way."

The man was walking toward them. They split up and hid behind bushes. The steps came closer, slowed down, and stopped.

Shit, Charlie thought. *Did we leave something out?* The moon surfaced and Charlie could see his face. *Thom? No! Looks like him—can't be— AK-47 in his hand.*

Charlie held still. The man took a slow step, then another. He skirted the bush Charlie was hiding in, but tripped over Charlie's foot.

Shit!

Charlie pounced on the man, disarming him. He threw his weapon into the bush.

The soldier wiggled away and started to get up.

Charlie sprang forward, tackling him. He slipped his arms under his captive's and jerked them up over his head into a full nelson. The gook was helpless by the time Robby and Thom came to the rescue.

"What happened?" asked Robby.

"He tripped over my foot. What do we do with him?"

"Don't let go. Come on up slowly."

Charlie kept his grip on the man, and slowly backed up onto his knees. He extended his right leg back, pushed upward and stood. He turned around slowly until moonlight shone on his prisoner's face.

Thom gasped. "Quang!"

"You know this guy?" Robby said.

"He cousin."

"Cousin!" Robby exclaimed.

"Holy shit, man," Charlie said. "What do we do?"

"We must kill," Thom said, as he pulled a knife out of his pocket, and struck toward his relative.

"No!" Charlie jerked his prisoner sideways, out of harm's way, but the knife swiped his own left arm instead. Blood oozed through his fatigue shirt, but he held fast.

"Permission to let him go, Sir!"

Robby returned Charlie's stern glare.

"Give me permission!"

"Granted!"

Charlie let him go. The man ran into the jungle.

"Nobody should have to kill their own kin, man. Nobody! This war isn't worth it."

Charlie dropped into the dirt and put his head into his hands. *Oh my God, I had one in my grasp and I let him go. I don't belong here.*

Thom sat next to Charlie, and rolled his left sleeve up. He took out a handkerchief and wiped the blood away.

"I am sorry. It was my duty to kill him."

"No! You can't kill your own cousin, man."

Thom put his head down. Charlie put his left arm around him and squeezed. When Thom looked up, Charlie saw remorse in his eyes.

"It never dawned on me that you'd have relatives fighting on the other side, but why not? The guy even looked like you, man. How horrible to fight your own kin. I just couldn't let you kill him."

Thom nodded his head in approval. "Is arm okay?"

"Yeah, sure. Just a scratch."

Thom rolled his handkerchief and tied it around Charlie's wound, a one-inch horizontal cut about an eighth-inch deep.

"I am sorry," Thom said again.

"Come on, you guys," Robby urged. "We need to start the mission before that guy gets back and warns the others."

They were able to use three artillery batteries for the bombing. Because the quadrants had been relayed earlier in the day, all Charlie had to do was tell them when to start. He contacted the main headquarters for the 402nd Artillery, and instructed them to prepare for an early mission.

Word came back that firepower was ready. Charlie looked over at Robby.

"I guess we're ready to pull the plug, Sir."

"All right then, Charlie. Let's let 'em have it!"

Charlie picked up the receiver and shook his head slowly from side to side.

"Attention all batteries," he said in a low voice. "Commence fire."

He looked over at Thom. "I hope Quang ran away, man."

The artillery blasted their targets for over an hour, followed by the Skyraider aircraft, which were converted C-130s, equipped with radar sensors, a couple of six-barreled 7.62-millimeter machine guns, a pair of six-barreled 20-millimeter cannons, and two 40-millimeter mortars that pumped out a hundred rounds per minute. Three planes took separate passes through the canyon.

With the possibility of enemy patrols still in the canyon bank, headquarters decided to evacuate the LRRPs. Charlie, Robby and Thom made their way back up to the top. Charlie broke out his machete and cleared a landing zone. When they heard the slapping sounds of their rescuer, Robby popped a red flare, and threw it in the middle of the LZ. The chopper landed on top of it.

Twenty minutes later they were back at Charlie Battery.

It was still dark when they walked up to the top of the hill to meet with the captain. Charlie looked up and saw Captain Donaldson standing at attention, surrounded by nearly forty men of the battery. While the captain exchanged salutes with Robby, the men applauded. Charlie looked at Thom, and shrugged his shoulders.

Captain Donaldson noted Charlie's gesture.

"They are applauding, Sergeant, because you men have become American heroes in the Vietnam War. Congratulations on a job well done."

Charlie looked around and saw smiling faces. He caught Al Strangemeir's eye. Al nodded approval. He nodded back.

A numb feeling began to take over his body—from his head down to his toes. What's going on? For a moment he felt like he had just won the United States Surfing Championships. But this was Vietnam. What's happening here?

The LRRPs continued their patrols until it was time for Lieutenant Alvarez to go home. He had been in Vietnam for 424 days, fifty-nine days longer than the normal tour of duty, and was going home a distinguished veteran.

Charlie and Thom were with their comrade as he boarded the helicopter to leave the field for good. Sergeant Thom stood at attention and saluted. Robby returned Thom's salute, and then shook his hand. He turned toward Charlie and opened his arms for a hug. Charlie obliged.

"You did it, Robby."

"Did what?" Robby asked, pulling away.

"You are a success. You told me that you joined the army to be successful at something. You did it, man."

Charlie looked down and spotted his pack. He pulled out a blood stained terry cloth wrap.

"Take this home with you, okay? I've tried to find a use for it, but I can't."

Robby took it out of Charlie's hand. "You bet I'll take it. Someday I'll tell my grandchildren that a guy named Charlie saved my life with it."

Robby turned and climbed aboard the helicopter.

"You guys take care of yourselves, you hear?"

"Yes, Sir," Thom said.

Charlie nodded. As he waved goodbye, he felt sad that his friend was leaving.

"Take care, man," he said quietly, knowing he wouldn't be heard over the chopper noise.

14

The captain of Delta Company, 125th Infantry, looked up as the two young men walked toward him. He had been sitting, cleaning his weapon, but immediately stood up to address Charlie and Sergeant Thom.

"I can't thank you men enough for the job you performed. You were the best LRRP patrol we've ever had out there," the captain said, admiringly.

"Sir, does that mean we're not LRRPs anymore?" Charlie asked.

"Yes, Sergeant. I wouldn't mind keeping you on, but the regular LRRP unit is in place now, and with Lieutenant Alvarez gone, we've decided to disband your patrol."

"So, what will we be doing, Sir?"

"Well, we already have a forward observer and RTO in place with Delta Company. You have been relieved of your front line duties, and will report to Charlie Battery."

"Really, Sir?"

"Absolutely, Sergeant. I spoke with Captain Donaldson of the battery, and we both felt you've had enough. You've been a valuable man with the communications team. We'll miss you out here, but you deserve the break."

"Thank you, Sir. What about Sergeant Thom?"

The captain turned and looked at the ARVN interpreter. "Sergeant Thom, you will remain here with the company, but first you have been granted leave in Saigon for two weeks. You deserve the R&R, and I believe you have family there."

"Yes, Sir."

Charlie smiled and reached his hand out to his comrade.

"All right, Thom. You get to go home, man."

"I very happy, Charlie. I miss you and I never forget."

The captain turned and walked away leaving Charlie and Thom alone.

"I won't forget you either, Thom. We were quite a team out there in the bush."

"Yes, Charlie, but you saved cousin life. I would have dishonor."

"But I thought you tried to kill him because it was your duty."

"Yes, I would have been hero to ARVN army, but not to myself. You help me to have honor. You hurt bad?"

Charlie rolled up his left sleeve to show Thom the healing red blemish on his shoulder.

"What, this little thing? No way! You know what? This scar is going to remind me of you and your family." He put his arm around the ARVN and squeezed. "Believe me, man, I will never forget you."

"What will I be doing here?" Charlie asked Captain Donaldson when he arrived at the battery.

"I'm going to give you a choice. Either you can stay with us in the box, or you can join Corporal Strangemeir on his gun. One of his men just DEROSED last week."

"No offense, Sir, but I think I'll choose the gun. You guys are a little too clean for me in the box."

The captain laughed and patted Charlie on the back.

"I thought you might go that way. Would you do me a favor and hang onto the radio until you go home? I could use your expertise on the handle if they get in trouble out there."

"No problem, Sir. Can I keep my LRRP hat, too? I'm not used to those helmets anymore." Charlie nodded, indicating the helmet on the captain's head.

"Sure, why not? I figure you've learned how to take care of yourself by now. How short are you, anyway?"

"A little over a month, Sir. I came over here on the big Fools Day."

The captain laughed. "We're going to miss you around here, Sergeant."

Charlie nodded and turned to walk over to gun number five. *I can't say that I'll miss anything I've seen and done around here,* he thought to himself.

Even though Charlie outranked Corporal Strangemeir, the corporal remained the chief of gun number five. It had been nearly a year since Charlie had trained on a 105 howitzer back in the States. He told the corporal he'd just be a gun bunny for awhile, and then go home, and that he didn't know why he was a sergeant anyway, so who the hell cared?

"Nobody's really in charge here anyway," Al said. "We all know every job and exactly what's required for performing the fire missions when the grunts need arterial support."

"All right, man. I think I'm going to fit in around here."

"You can call me Strangeman, Charlie. Everyone else around here does. I'm from Virginia Beach."

"No shit! Do you surf?"

"No, but my brother does. Do you surf?"

"Hell yes I do! I grew up in Southern California."

"Cool! Let me introduce you to the other guys."

The rest of the gun crew was sitting on a sandbag wall, looking curiously at Charlie.

"This here is Walk a Mile from Rockford, Illinois."

The tall black man remained sitting and stuck his fist out low. Charlie banged on top of it with his own.

"Glad to meet you, Walk a Mile?" Charlie said, questioning the nickname.

"Yeah, that's because my name is Jeff Miles."

"What do you do back home, Jeff?"

"I ran track in high school, and was training for the Olympics when Uncle Sam drafted my ass."

Sounds just like me, Charlie thought. "I think you should be called Sprint, not Walk a Mile."

Jeff sat up tall and smiled. "You guys hear that? From now on my name's Sprint. Anyone calls me Walk a Mile is dead meat."

Strangeman laughed and pointed toward a tall, red-headed man. "Meet Dirt Farmer. His real name is Al Moore and he's from Iowa. We started calling him Big Red at first, but he insisted that sounded like he was from Nebraska."

"Nebraska?" Charlie said.

"You never heard of the University of Nebraska Big Red before?" Dirt Farmer said, speaking up.

"I guess not. I don't know much about the Midwest. Are you a farmer?"

"Sure am. Have the best dairy cattle west of the Mississippi. Grow some sweet corn, too."

Dirt Farmer appeared friendly, but a little slow mentally.

A short, stocky Mexican stood up and walked over to Charlie. He stuck out his hand. "My name is Ernesto Lopez. I'm from California."

"No shit? Me, too. Whereabouts?"

"Don't ask me. I pick the fields when they're ready, and then move to wherever there's more ripe stuff."

The other men on the gun crew laughed, and Strangeman spoke up. "We call him Señor Fagoso. In Spanish that means 'creator of a good mood.' He never complains, and always finds a way to make us laugh."

Ernesto smiled, and looked like he was proud of that description.

Strangeman continued, introducing the last man. "This is Baloneyman. He's from Queens, New York."

"So where else is Queens?" Baloneyman said in an Italian accent. He stuck out his hand, "Tony DeAngelis is my real name."

"Are you a butcher or something?" Charlie asked.

"What are you talking about—butcher?"

"Well, I thought that, because they call you Baloneyman."

Dirt Farmer spoke up over the laughter of the men, "It's because he bullshits all the time. First we called him Tony Baloney, then Baloneyman."

"It's better than Dirt Farmer, you big goon," Tony said, shoving the large man. "Besides, what's wrong with a few stories to lighten up this shit? Someone around here's got to make this fuckin' thing interesting, you know?"

"So, Charlie," Strangeman interrupted. "What are we going to call you? I know, how about Arm?"

"Sure, why not?" Charlie said.

"Arm?" Sprint called out. "Where in the hell did that come from?"

"Let me introduce this guy," Strangeman said. This is Sergeant Charlie Armfield. You know, the guy who found that gook regiment we blew away."

Charlie put his head down, and felt uneasy remembering the incident.

"Anyway, he's going to help us out until he goes home. He's keeping his radio with him, too. We'll get to know about all the shit in the bush."

Charlie cocked his head curiously, then shrugged his shoulders.

Strangeman shrugged his shoulders back at Charlie. "We never know what's happening. We shoot into the jungles and never know why."

Al turned and ordered the men to get busy filling sandbags. Then he showed Charlie the sleeping quarters, which was a big hole in the ground with long metal planks covering it and sandbags piled on top. There were six cots in the bunker. Charlie shoved his gear under the vacant one.

"Looks pretty cozy down here."

"Yeah, I guess it beats where you've been sleeping lately."

Charlie shrugged his shoulders. "I was kind of getting used to it. It's nice seeing the stars at night."

They returned to help with the sandbags.

"How many sandbags you need around here?" Charlie asked.

"We never stop making bags," Sprint complained.

"The officers tell us to reinforce our position every chance we get," Strangeman said.

"Hey, Arm, how many gooks you killed?" Baloneyman asked.

Strangeman threw dirt on Baloneyman's back.

"Hey, don't ask the man a question like that."

Charlie held up his hand to Strangeman, indicating he didn't mind. The crew stopped to hear Charlie's answer.

"You know, I counted up to eighteen before I was medevaced. I told myself I wasn't going to count anymore, but I couldn't help it. I don't know why, but I just kept counting. I added nine more with the LRRPs. The bad part is I remember every single one of them."

"That's cool, Arm," Baloneyman said.

Strangeman threw dirt on his back again.

"Hey cut that out." Baloneyman turned and threw dirt back at Strangeman. "I wish I could have been out there with those grunts."

"I don't think it's too cool," Charlie said, his voice low. "If it were up to me, I wouldn't have killed any of them."

"You're just defending yourself, Arm," Señor Fagoso said.

"Yeah, Arm," Sprint spoke up. "You can't blame yourself for killing gooks. You're in a war, honk."

"You know," Dirt Farmer said slowly, "we kill gooks, too."

"I know, man. I ordered you guys to kill a thousand of them in that valley. And I've killed many more the same way on other recon missions. Now I'm going to detonate 105s that'll kill more. How many people can one person kill?" He shook his head.

The slapping sounds of a large double bladed helicopter changed the subject. It was a CH-47 Chinook that the army used like a truck in the air. This time it was hauling ammunition that was dangling underneath in a sling.

"Oh, shit!" Baloneyman said. "Here comes a fuckin shit-hook."

"All right you guys," Strangeman said. "Let's get down to the pad. There's going to be a lot of ammo that needs to be hauled up."

Every gun had an ammunition bunker built near the pit where the gun was, usually five to six feet deep, four feet wide and six feet long. It housed the 105 rounds and shells that were fired from the guns. Ammunition was delivered to a landing zone down the hill from where the guns were positioned. Part of the gun bunny's routine was to hump it up to the ammo bunker until it was needed for a fire mission. The rounds were fifty pounds each.

"Better just try one on each shoulder at first, Arm," Strangeman suggested.

Dirt Farmer was the biggest man on the crew and carried one round on each shoulder, balanced an additional one sideways on top, and a box of fuses that weighed forty pounds.

Humping ammo made the men strong, but they never looked forward to the Chinook's visit.

One passenger, a lieutenant, hopped out of the back of the chopper and ran up the hill to meet with Captain Donaldson. Later he went around to the guns and asked to speak to some of the men.

The crew on gun number five was resting in their bunker after hauling the ammo up from the pad.

"Is Sergeant Armfield down there?"

Curious, Charlie climbed out.

"I've been asked to talk to you about re-enlisting in the United States Army."

Charlie stared at the lieutenant. "Excuse me, Sir? Did you ask me if I was going to re-up?"

"I did, Sergeant, but I suspected you weren't going to be interested."

"You suspected correctly. When I get out of the army, it's going to be as if it never existed. Know what I mean, Sir?"

"Of course, Sergeant. You realize it's my job to ask, don't you?"

"I suppose so. It just took me by surprise. I'm sorry. See you around." Charlie started to climb back into the bunker.

"Hold on a minute, Sergeant. There is something else I have to ask you. The army has come up with this new program."

"A new program you think I'd be interested in, Sir? I don't think so!"

"Hear me out. This is actually pretty neat. The program is for soldiers going home from Nam, so they can be released from the rest of their commitment in the service."

"Really! How does that work?"

"Any soldier with less than five months left on his commitment can now be released from duty when arriving stateside."

"Well, that leaves me out. I'll have almost seven months left when I get home."

"That is, unless you extend the needed time over here to get you home with less than five months remaining."

Charlie stared at the lieutenant, silently processing what he'd heard. *Extend my time in Nam? Robby did that so he could embellish his career—maybe even make up for getting hit.*

"The army wants to keep the experienced men on board as long as they can so they won't have to send over so many new recruits," the Lieutenant said. "That's why this program was invented."

"Yeah, I'll bet they're glad to get rid of us drafted guys, too."

"That may be part of it. Drafted veterans have been known to be discipline problems from time to time after Nam."

Charlie began calculating the number of days he needed to make the program work for him.

Noting his efforts, the lieutenant smiled. "You need fifty-seven more days. You would be discharged on May 28."

"Wow! I'd be home to catch the summer swells."

"Excuse me?"

"Oh, nothing, Sir."

"I might be able to get you another R&R."

Charlie remembered his last R&R. It had been fun visiting his brother, but he feared that, given a second chance, he might not report back. Extending would get him back to the beach sooner, and he wouldn't have to put up with lifers back in the states. But fifty-seven extra days was a lot to consider.

"Can I sleep on it?"

"Yes, but I'll need your answer before I leave in the morning."

Charlie climbed back down into the bunker.

"Hey, Arm, what was that all about?" Strangeman asked.

"The guy wanted to know if I wanted to re-up."

"Re-up? Are you going to do it?"

"What do you think?" Charlie said, sarcastically.

"I say no, Arm," Dirt Farmer said.

"Then you would be absolutely correct, my friend. There's no way in hell I'd re-up. Not in a million years."

"Me either," Dirt Farmer agreed.

"May I speak to Specialist Moore?" the lieutenant called down.

Dirt Farmer climbed up and when he returned he said, "No way in hell I'm going to extend, either. My fiancée wants me home, Arm. I know she wouldn't let me do that. I'm going home April 22 when I'm supposed to, and getting married."

"What are you guys talking about?" Strangeman asked.

"Corporal Strangemeir," the lieutenant called out.

"You better go find out for yourself," Charlie said.

Strangeman looked disturbed when he returned.

"How can they ask me to decide something like this by tomorrow?" He was scheduled to go back stateside on May 6, and had a wife to consider.

Dirt Farmer had already decided he wasn't going to extend, and the other men on the gun had so much time left the lieutenant didn't even ask them if they were interested.

But Charlie and Strangeman talked all night about the issue. Strangeman questioned whether his wife would be upset. Both wondered what their parents would think. But if they didn't extend, would they be able to put up with the shit dictated by the lifers with stateside duty after Nam?

"You got a girlfriend, Arm?"

Charlie was silent, contemplating his reply.

"I don't know. With all the shit over here I've kind of forgotten about her. She writes occasionally, and she seems like everything is just the same between us. But a lot of shit has happened, man. I just don't think I'll be able to see her again."

Charlie picked up a rock and threw it as far as he could. It sailed over the perimeter of the firebase and into the bush. He wondered where it had landed, then remembered the first time he shot into the jungle. Had he killed anyone? Later, Top had laughed at him.

Charlie shook his head. "No way, man! There's no way I'm going back to the States and continue being in the army. When I go back, I have to be on the beach. So, I'm extending. It's not so bad here on the firebase, anyway."

"I think my wife might understand," Strangeman said. "If I come home and don't have to be in the army anymore, I'll be able to settle down. I have a daughter I haven't even seen yet."

"No shit? How old?"

"Ten months." Strangeman pulled out a picture. "That's Lisa, my wife. Our baby's name is Becky."

"They're beautiful, man. Too bad you didn't have that kid sooner, so you wouldn't have had to come over here."

"Yeah, I know. I heard they don't even draft guys with kids."

The next morning, Charlie signed the papers to extend. He declined the R&R, saying he didn't know where to go. That was a lie. Charlie knew that two R&R sites—Sydney, Australia, and Hawaii—had great surf. But he also knew if he got to surf again, he might never report back. The surf would have to wait for fifty-seven days. Then it would be his forever.

Strangeman signed, too. He requested R&R, and made plans to rendezvous with his wife in Hawaii in a week and, finally, to meet his daughter.

When he returned, he proudly shared Polaroid photos, and passed out cigars like he was a new father.

"Someday I want my daughter to meet you, Arm," Strangeman told Charlie one afternoon.

"Why?"

"I want my daughter to meet special people. When you have a child, you'll want them to know the very best."

"I can understand that, but what makes you think I'm such a special person?"

"You're a man with a conscience, Arm. You think about what's happening. You're concerned about the killing. I've not met anyone over here who cares as much as you do. I feel safe and blessed when you're around, that's all, and I'd like my daughter and my wife to meet you."

Charlie was touched. He looked at his friend. "I'm just another poor slob who was drafted and forced to come to Nam."

"You're more than that, Arm, you're like an angel. Good things happen when you're around, even here in Vietnam. You always know what to do. You save people's lives."

Strangeman's words embarrassed Charlie.

"You must be a good surfer," Strangeman continued, "because the good ones have some kind of rhythm that flows with the sea. You've got that rhythm, Charlie, that touch. I'll bet you learned it in the water."

Charlie smiled, and shook his head.

"Strangeman, I'll be happy to meet the ladies in your life. I'll come for a visit. Maybe I can catch some of those Virginia Beach waves while I'm there?"

"They aren't much compared to California's, but I'm sure you'll make them look good."

After Charlie decided to extend his tour, activity on the firebase was slight. While there were always defense targets to shoot in the evening, not much else went on. Charlie felt he had made the right decision—that the extra fifty-seven days wouldn't matter.

On April 1, 1969, Charlie was the first one out of the bunker as usual, doing the routine gun bunny chores of cleaning up the pit. Before Dirt Farmer showed his face, he had collected the shiny, brass shells left from the night's shooting, ready to be disposed of in a big pile down by the chopper pad. While the sun already shone brightly in the blue sky, it was not too hot yet.

"Only twenty-one more days!" Dirt Farmer yelled.

"Twenty-one days! Man, you're shorter than short," Charlie said. "Hey, that means today is the first. You're not fooling me are you?"

"Hell no!" Dirt Farmer said, not realizing Charlie was kidding about

April Fools Day. "I wouldn't joke about being this short, Arm. I can hardly wait to get home and see my fiancée. I wonder where I'll be stationed."

"Wherever it is, it's better than this toilet. But then, it hasn't been too bad around here lately."

"Yeah. Maybe I should have extended, too, huh, Arm?"

"Nah! In three weeks you're going to be out of here, man. The army will give you a vacation, and you can be with your woman before you have to report back to duty.

"Yeah, I can hardly wait."

The two early risers carried the shells down to the pad, and stopped at the mess area for their breakfast of scrambled eggs, toast, and canned orange juice.

"You know what, man?" Charlie said. "I would've been going home today." He felt homesick for the beach. "By tomorrow I'd be on leave, hanging ten and getting tubed."

"What do you mean, 'getting tubed'?"

Strangeman, Señor Fagoso and Sprint walked into the tent.

"He means he'd be getting inside the wave," Strangeman explained.

Dirt Farmer shrugged. "I still don't get it."

"Never mind," Strangeman said. "You guys about finished?"

They both nodded.

"Baloneyman's on guard," Strangeman said. "When you're done, relieve him so he can come and eat. He's all pissed off that he's the last to eat again."

"Well," Dirt Farmer said, "I'll bet he was the last up?"

"As usual," Strangeman complained.

"Figures," Dirt Farmer said, shaking his head.

After his breakfast, Baloneyman ran back to the pit with a rooster under his arm. It had been a mascot of the battery ever since a grunt had brought it back from a patrol. It roamed around the artillery hill, ate scraps from the soldier's plates, and responded to his name, which was "Cock." The men loved calling him that. Cock struggled under Baloneyman's arm, crowing frightfully.

"Hey, guys, watch this."

He put the crowing bird on the barrel of a 105 howitzer and cranked it up until it was pointing toward the sky. Cock was doodling away. Everyone on the firebase rolled with laugher, including Captain Donaldson.

Suddenly mortar rounds and gunfire exploded from every direction. The hill was getting hit from close range.

Charlie took charge, "Too close for our guns, Strangeman. Sprint, get the rifles out of the bunker."

He shouted at the top of his lungs so the other guns would follow his directions, too.

Sprint scrambled into the bunker for their rifles. He returned with lightning speed and passed them out.

"Spread out and stay low!" Charlie continued, still yelling. "Shoot in bursts and spray it all around!"

The captain crawled toward gun number five for cover. "Do you have a map of the area, Charlie?"

"Sure do. Is Bravo Battery within range?"

"No, but Alpha is. Figure out the quadrants. I'll be your RTO."

Charlie smiled. "You've got it, Sir!"

Within five minutes, Alpha Battery was shooting rounds around the Charlie Battery perimeter and, nearly as fast as it had started, the confrontation was over. A casualty count revealed that the battery had lost three men. Four were wounded. Nobody on gun number five was touched, except Cock. They found the mascot mutilated, lying near the entrance to their sleeping bunker.

As Charlie bent down to pick it up, he saw Baloneyman, huddled, scrunched up, and shivering in the corner of the bunker. Quickly, Charlie stood up and distracted the others.

"I guess this old bird has cocked his last doodle. He sure tried to warn us though. Think he should be put up for the Medal of Honor, Sir?" Charlie asked the captain.

"I think maybe I'll do just that, Sergeant. I'll put his name in there with yours."

Charlie stared at the captain. "Just did what comes naturally, Sir."

Strangeman, standing behind the captain, nodded his approval.

Oh, man, Charlie thought. *I don't want any recognition. I just want to go home. How come I'm not going home today?*

The captain shook his hand and started for the box.

"Hey, where's Baloney?" Sprint asked.

"I think he went to help with the casualties," Charlie said. "Why don't the rest of you guys go help, too? I'll stay here on guard."

When the men left, Charlie climbed into the bunker next to Baloneyman, and put his arm around him.

"It's okay, man. The shooting's over."

Baloneyman looked up, tears streaming down his face. "I'm a fuckin coward."

"Hey, you don't want to get nailed any more than the rest of us do. You make big talk, Baloney, but inside you're just another innocent guy forced into this stupid war. Hell, I knew a lieutenant who was more afraid than you are."

"Really?"

"Yeah, he was even my FO."

"What happened to him?"

Charlie frowned, remembering the greenback's fate. "Let's just say he's not frightened anymore. You better get out there and help with the casualties."

Baloneyman stood up and started to climb out. He looked back at Charlie. "Are you going to tell anybody?"

"What for?"

"Thanks, Arm."

Following that April Fools Day, the battery was hit repeatedly. Charlie wondered continually what in the hell he was still doing there. Maybe Dirt Farmer was right, getting out when he was supposed to. Late evening conversations in the bunker during quiet times made matters worse.

"Anybody want to hear how short I am?" Dirt Farmer asked.

"Hell, no!" Sprint replied, kicking dust in Dirt Farmer's direction.

"Someone light up a joint before Dirt Farmer gets us all depressed again," Señor Fagoso said.

Sprint, keeper of the stash, passed it over to Baloneyman. "I don't have any 'grettes," he said.

They didn't get C-rations very often on the firebase, so nobody had any cigarettes to empty and refill with marijuana. Baloneyman had a pipe. It had a short stem with a large bowl, and had acquired the name "Fire."

Baloneyman passed the filled pipe over to Señor Fagoso. "Come on, amigo, light my fire."

The bowl was lit and passed around the group a few times. Strangeman reached into his pack and grabbed a small battery-powered tape player. He fiddled with the reels. Everybody knew what the tape was going to be— *Sergeant Pepper's Lonely Hearts Club Band.* The only guy who didn't like it was Sprint, who preferred soul music, but even he joined in with the group singing;

> *It was twenty years ago today,*
> *Sergeant Pepper taught his band to play,*
> *They've been going in and out of style,*
> *But they're guaranteed to raise a smile.*
> *So may I introduce to you,*
> *The act you've known for all these years,*
> *Sergeant Pepper's Lonely Hearts Club Band.*
> *We're Sergeant Pepper's Lonely Hearts Club Band...*

Strangeman's wife had recorded the Beatles album and mailed it to him along with the recorder, a supply of batteries and tapes by the Doors, Proco Harem, and Ray Charles.

During the next Beatles' song, *A Little Help from My Friends*, the men ritually exchanged handclasps. Charlie was grateful to have friends.

> *What would you think if I sang out of tune?*
> *Would you stand up and walk out on me?*
> *Lend me your ears and I'll sing you a song,*
> *And I'll try not to sing out of key.*
> *I get by with a little help from my friends,*
> *I get high with a little help from my friends,*
> *Going to try with a little help from my friends...*

The next morning, Dirt Farmer was scheduled to go home. Charlie figured it would be hard to say goodbye, knowing that he, himself, could have been home by now. He still had five weeks to go. Charlie felt envious as he watched his friend pack and climb out of the bunker for the last time.

"See you guys," Dirt Farmer said.

Charlie joined the gun bunnies of number five, and lined up to shake Dirt Farmer's hand.

"Where the hell do you think you're going?" Charlie said, chuckling. "The chopper hasn't even called in yet."

"I'm going down and sit on the pad until it gets here. I don't want to take a chance on missing it."

The men laughed as Dirt Farmer walked down the hill. Charlie suggested they all take turns going down to keep him company until the chopper came.

An hour later, Charlie's radio echoed the chopper's announcement. "Coming in to pick up a DEROS and a Red Cross notice."

"Red Cross notice?" replied the specialist in the box. "For who?"

"Alfa-Romeo-Mike-Foxtrot-India-Echo-Lima-Delta."

Charlie was shocked. He looked at Strangeman. "What in the world? A Red Cross notice, for me?"

He jumped into the bunker, threw his stuff into his pack, and climbed out to run down to the pad. Specialist Clinton, from the box, was coming to tell him as he ran by.

"I got it!" Charlie yelled.

The chopper landed and a new recruit, Dirt Farmer's replacement, hopped out. Dirt Farmer climbed in as Charlie raced down the hill. He flung his pack into the helicopter, and hurdled in after it. The pilot took off.

Astonished, Dirt Farmer yelled, "What are you doing here?"

"I don't know, except they said I have a Red Cross notice." He turned to the pilot and yelled over the chopper noise, "What the hell does a Red Cross notice mean?"

"Usually, something's happened to someone you know back home. Maybe somebody died."

15

Slapping sounds echoed through the valley as the chopper made its way to Camp Enari. *Oh my God,* Charlie thought. *Is it Mom, Dad, my grandparents, Mike?* His thoughts whirled, matching the blades that propelled the chopper. He looked at Dirt Farmer, whose mood appeared dampened. He appeared to be concerned about Charlie's problem, and not excited about going home.

"I'll bet your fiancée is thrilled about you coming home, man. What the hell's her name anyway?" Charlie said, trying to take his own mind off of the situation.

Dirt Farmer smiled, "Marsha. Her name is Marsha, Arm. We're getting married on May third. She's pretty thrilled, all right."

"May third? You guys don't waste any time, do you?"

They both laughed.

"Well, I hope you guys have a wonderful life together and raise lots of boys to help you with those cows."

When the chopper landed, Charlie patted Dirt Farmer on the back.

"I have to run up to headquarters. If I don't see you again, have a great rest of your life, okay?"

"Sure will, Arm. I hope it's not bad news for you."

"Me, too."

Charlie sprinted three quarters of a mile to the Battalion Headquarters. Out of breath, he sped around the corner into camp headquarters, bumping into the first sergeant.

"Whoa, soldier, what's the rush? Hey wait a minute, aren't you Sergeant Armfield?"

"Yes. Is everything all right with my family?"

"No, not really. They're very upset with you!"

"Upset?"

"The Red Cross was contacted by your mother because she was worried about you. She says she hasn't received a letter from you for months."

Charlie was stunned, staring in disbelief. "You mean everybody's okay?"

The first sergeant nodded curtly, a disapproving frown on his forehead.

"You know the regulations, Sergeant. It is your duty to keep the family informed. I sent for you so I could watch you write a letter home."

While he was relieved to hear that his family was well, he felt humiliated and angry. He glared into the first sergeant's eyes.

"Why in hell do I have to be called in to write a letter? A simple note would suffice—'Armfield, write home.' Shit! I'm a goddamn sergeant and I still get harassed."

"Listen, Sergeant. The army gets a lot of notices like this, and it's regulation to bring in the violators. All you have to do is write a letter. There's no punishment."

"Well, I think suffering the chopper ride, thinking my parents might be dead, was definitely a punishment."

"I'm sorry if you were worried. Come into my office and I'll get you some paper. You can write home right now and get it over with."

Charlie sat down with the materials the first sergeant provided and tried to figure out how to begin.

I know you're worried and I'm sorry I haven't written. There have been several times I have gone without writing over this past year, so I'm not sure why you have contacted the Red Cross now. It's hard for me...

Charlie put the pen down. He looked up at the first sergeant.

"This is bullshit."

"What are you talking about?"

"I can't write about what's happening over here. You think they're going to worry less if I tell them?"

"Just lie about it. Tell them everything is fine and you'll see them when you get home."

"You know, that would be just great. The day after some lieutenant knocks on their door to 'regretfully report that their son has been killed in action,' they get this phony letter saying, 'Don't fret folks, everything is cool.' Truth is, I haven't been writing because I can't come up with the small talk."

"I just tell the truth when I write," the first sergeant said. "I've been in combat many times, and I just tell the truth." He turned and walked out of the room.

Charlie stared at his letter. *There's no way I can tell them what's going on.* He sighed and picked up his pen.

...to write about what is going on over here. I will probably never tell people about my experience in Vietnam, especially not the people I love. I have done some horrible things and I am very ashamed. I have five weeks to go. Please understand that this will be my last letter to you. If God is willing, I will be home soon.

Charlie stepped out of the office.

"Here's my letter. I'm going down to the chopper pad to go back out." He put his head down and started to walk away.

"Hold on a minute, Sergeant. We just received word that your firebase has been hit. Only medevacs are heading out now. Stay in the transit tent; get yourself a shower and a haircut. You'll be heading back out in the morning."

The news of the firebase getting hit didn't bother Charlie. He had been in so many firefights he didn't give it a second thought. What most disturbed him was that he was going to have to get a haircut.

The next morning, Charlie waited on the chopper pad to be airlifted back to the firebase. He hated the military haircut. Even his over-grown mustache was cut to standards. Dressed in clean clothes, he looked like a basecamp commando, except for his tattered, faded LRRP hat and scruffy jungle boots, which looked like suede and brown canvas, rather than the original shiny black leather with green canvas hightops.

One thing he knew, his decision to extend had been the right one. After Nam, he didn't think he would be able to contend with the military protocol. He'd surely end up in the stockade. All he had to do was survive five more weeks. Then he'd be home free.

The chopper pilots weren't starting their engines as scheduled. Charlie walked up to the nearest helicopter and saw the gunner sitting in the doorway.

"What's happening, man? How come we're not taking off?"

"There's still too much shit going on out there. We're not going anywhere until it settles down a bit. Have a seat, Sergeant."

Charlie sat down and noticed bullet holes in the side of the doorway. "Whoa, looks like a close call there," he said pointing at the pits.

"Yeah, a lot closer than you think."

"What do you mean?"

"Well, before yesterday my butt was sitting there." He pointed to the floor just below the holes in the doorway. "We got orders last week to change the position of the seats to the other side. I thought it was stupid, so I didn't do it. Then this lifer at camp sees that our chopper was not conforming to the regulation and I caught hell for it. I was really ticked— until yesterday when we got hit by the fire. I would have been a dead duck if I hadn't changed the seat."

"So are you thanking that lifer, or what?"

"Damn right, I am. He's my guardian angel."

Clearance to take off came in the early afternoon. Charlie hopped into the helicopter, still thinking about the "angel" story. *How many times had he thought about that—about angels protecting in Vietnam? It didn't happen for the guy in the infirmary, the one carrying the paper with the Psalm on it, the one that said to 'trust in God and He will give His angels to guard you.' But the gunner who defied the lieutenant was saved. How do the angels choose?*

When the chopper hovered over the firebase, Charlie noticed something wrong. "How many guns do you count down there?"

"Oh, you noticed. One's missing. One of the howies took a direct hit yesterday. Smashed it to smithereens. The medevacs took five guys out of that mess."

Which gun was it? They were still up so high Charlie couldn't get his bearings. By the time the chopper approached, though, he knew. Gun number five was gone.

Before the pilot put the chopper all the way down, Charlie jumped out and ran up the hill to find the captain.

"You are one lucky sonofabitch, Sergeant. While you were gone yesterday, your whole crew was wiped out."

Charlie put his hands over his mouth, staring in disbelief at the pit where gun number five had been. *Oh my God,* he thought. *Oh my God.* Tears filled his eyes. He shook his head. *My friends are dead.*

Then he remembered his mother, and gasped. "Mom?"

"What's that, Sergeant? Was your mom all right?"

"Yes, Sir. She's fine. My Angel?"

"Sergeant?"

Charlie looked at the ground. "I think that it's one lucky 'son of an Angel,' Sir." He turned and looked the captain in the eye. "You said 'sonofabitch.'"

The captain was silent. Finally he put his arm around Charlie and said, "Just pick any gun you want, Son. What the hell, just work around—wherever. You're so damn short. Just work where you're needed."

Charlie felt numb, that same numbness he'd experienced so many times in Vietnam. Strangeman, Sprint, Señor Fagoso, and Baloneyman—all gone. He hadn't been able to say goodbye to his friends. But then how could he have known? How do you say goodbye when you don't know who will be killed?

He sat down in the middle of the pit in the wreckage. *Mom, are you my guardian angel? Did you know about this? And what about the chopper gunner? Was the lifer his guardian angel? Did Dirt Farmer have a guardian angel, too, that made him go home?* Charlie thought about the new recruit who got off the chopper as he and Dirt Farmer got on. Shit! The greenback didn't even get through his first day. How can angels choose?

Charlie decided to use the same sleeping bunker. He cleaned out the loose dirt that had filled in from the explosions. All of the dead soldiers' belongings had been cleared out, but as he dug, he found Strangeman's tape player, buried in the corner. The tapes were nowhere to be found, except for the one in the player.

That night, he cleaned the player, removing the tape and shaking out the debris. Then he blew into every possible opening until it appeared to be dust free. He put the tape in, threaded it into the extra reel and turned it on. The reels moved; the music began:

> *It was twenty years ago today,*
> *Sergeant Pepper taught his band to play.*

Charlie let out a big sigh. *I was hoping for that one.*

"Hey, Sergeant," someone called. "Is that you in there?"

Charlie recognized Captain Donaldson's voice. He turned off the tape and stuck his head out of the bunker.

"Yes, Sir."

"Are you sure you want to stay in this bunker? The other men said you would be welcome to join them."

"Thanks, but no, I don't think so, Sir. I'm kind of used to this hole."

"Aren't you spooked with what happened here?"

"Not really. And I'll bet it's the safest place on the hill."

"What do you mean?"

"Well, Sir, have you ever heard of lightning striking the same spot twice?" He stared blankly up at the Captain.

The Captain shook his head. "No, I guess I haven't. Okay, it's all yours, Son. We won't be getting another gun in here for awhile." He turned to walk away.

"Captain?" Charlie called after him. "I found Corporal Strangemeir's tape player. Do you suppose I could keep it?"

The captain smiled, "I'm sure he would have wanted it that way."

Charlie went back down into the bunker, his own private retreat in the earth of Vietnam, and turned on the tape.

He listened to the rest of the album. Then the last song began:

> *I read the news today, oh boy,*
> *About a lucky man who made the grade.*
> *And though the news was rather sad,*
> *Well I just had to laugh . . .*

Charlie snapped off the player, and put his head between his hands.

I read the news today all right, about five unlucky men without angels. They blew their minds on gun five; they didn't notice the war was on. There was no crowd to see them go—shit! I should have gone with them.

His thoughts turned to Cher. *Oh, sweet baby. You will never understand any of this shit. I am not the same, you won't even recognize me. I want to see your beautiful face again, but I'm afraid that can't happen. I can't share this with you. You deserve someone better—someone who hasn't killed.*

Charlie grabbed his tablet and pen from his pack, and began a farewell message to Cher.

I am sorry I haven't written lately. It seems like there is little to say these days. I am scheduled to come home soon, but I have come to the conclusion that we can't stay together any longer. My heart is heavy with the slaughter of life, and to share it with you would drain your love for me. Sorry I didn't let you know sooner. Maybe someday you won't be angry with me.

In his remaining days, Charlie worked hard. One of the other gun bunnies said he was a blessed survivor—he could have sat around and done nothing if he wanted to, and not even the lifers would have complained. Instead, Charlie humped ammo for all of the guns and filled sandbags with a vengeance.

When the ammunition was delivered, he was the first one down to the pad, and carried loads much heavier than the rest of the men. When Captain Donaldson asked why he worked so hard, he answered with a shrug. Then he thought to himself, *I'm working for five guys who are dead, man. I've killed a lot of people and I don't get killed myself. I don't deserve to be alive. This is my punishment.*

One rainy night, Charlie was loading gun number two during a frantic fire mission. A mixture of sweat and precipitation dripped into his eyes. He grabbed a loaded shell, held the round with his left hand and the shiny brass portion with his right.

The assistant gunner opened the breech to expel the used shell and Charlie moved forward to reload. He made a fist with his right hand on the bottom of the shell so he could push the load in and keep his fingers out of the way. The shell was muddy and when he started to hoist, it slipped from his hands. He scrambled to regain control before disaster prevailed, and quickly jammed it into the barrel.

Charlie's right hand was open when the load entered, and the assistant gunner caught the side of his index finger in the breech. Charlie felt a pinch, but kept loading until one of the crew noticed blood all around the pit area.

"Holy shit, is somebody hit?"

Charlie's right index finger began to throb, and when he looked down he saw a bloody gash.

"No, I just got clipped in the hole, that's all. No big deal."

Later that night, the medic bandaged his finger, and told the captain that he wanted to send Charlie in.

"Needs stitches, Sir. I can see bone," the medic said.

"It's okay, Sir," Charlie said. "I only have a few days left. I can take it."

"Charlie, I think maybe you need to get the hell out of here anyway," the captain said. "Next chance we get, you're going in."

But the action never let up, and before long, Charlie's medevac was forgotten. The third day after the injury, Charlie asked for a roll of gauze and tape, and tended to the injury himself.

Charlie knew he was getting short, but lost track of the days with all of the action. There hadn't been a chopper on the hill for nearly a week because it was simply too dangerous to land. Supplies were getting low.

Finally, just a few hours after dawn on a late May morning, the familiar slapping sounds of a helicopter were heard again. Charlie didn't think much of it until he heard the pilot radio in to the firebase headquarters.

"I'm coming in to pick up code name Charles Armfield on the double."

The message, which broke U.S. Army policy regarding not reciting names over the air, betrayed the pilot's urgency.

"What's the big hurry, fly guy?" was the response from the box.

"He was due in basecamp five days ago for processing to DEROS. We've got to get him home in a hurry."

Charlie scooped up his belongings, and leaped out of the bunker as Captain Donaldson came running up to get him.

"Here's your radio back, Sir. I don't think I'll be needing it anymore."

The captain grinned, "No, I guess not, Son. You take it easy now."

"I'll try to, Sir. I just hope that I can."

"What do you mean by that?"

"I just don't know how I'm going to act, that's all."

Within minutes the chopper rose into the air, carrying him over the thick wastelands for the last time.

"Holy shit, Sergeant," yelled the gunner over the propeller noise. "You look like a scared recruit heading out to the front for the first time—not a short bastard going home."

"I don't know why, but I think I'm scared to go home."

"Naw, you're just afraid of this last ride in. After all the time you spent in this hell hole, wouldn't it be the shits if you got gunned down on the way in?" The gunner laughed.

Charlie shrugged his shoulders. "Yeah, maybe your right." *Maybe,* he thought, *but I don't think so.*

When the chopper landed at Camp Enari, a jeep awaited him.

"Hurry up, Sergeant," yelled the battalion first sergeant from behind the wheel.

Charlie jumped from the chopper and climbed into the waiting vehicle. "What's the rush?"

"It's important to get you processed and out of here as soon as possible. You have to be discharged by tomorrow. When the army makes a deal, they are legally bound. Every once in a while this happens. A guy can't get in from the field, and we have to get 'em out of here, or else."

"Or else, what? What's the big deal?"

"I guess they don't want you getting killed when you're not supposed to be here. Might make a big stink on the homefront. By the way, there's a ceremony about to begin, and you're part of it."

"Ceremony?"

As they pulled into Battalion Headquarters, Charlie saw all of the basecamp support soldiers standing in a formation. There appeared to be close to fifty men. At the front, the battalion colonel was talking to three officers.

"I want you to march behind me," the first sergeant said to Charlie. "I'll take you up to the front of the formation."

The first sergeant got out of the jeep, marched to the back of the formation and stopped.

"Battalion! Attention!" he commanded.

The men snapped to attention. Charlie followed the first sergeant, with his backpack on his back and his M-16 slung over his right shoulder. Everybody, except for Charlie, was dressed in clean fatigues, army baseball caps, and shiny boots. Charlie felt out of place in his dirty, bunker-worn fatigues, worn out LRRP hat, and scuffed-up boots.

Behind the colonel, three officers stood at attention—a brigadier general, flanked on either side by a captain.

"Sir!" the first sergeant announced. "I present Sergeant Charles Armfield."

Charlie stood at attention, and offered a salute with his right hand—his index finger still bandaged. The colonel sharply returned his salute.

"Sergeant Armfield, you are being commended here today for your service in the Republic of Vietnam."

Oh my God, thought Charlie. *What have I done?*

The colonel took a step sideways to his left, and the general stepped forward next to him.

"Sir," the lieutenant colonel said, "I present Sergeant Charles Armfield for decoration."

Charlie saluted. The general returned the salute.

"I understand," the general intoned, "that you are to be discharged from the army tomorrow. As commanding officer of the Fourth Infantry Division, I apologize for not getting you in from the field sooner. A proper ceremony is usually held at the division headquarters for such a decorated soldier in the United States Army."

Charlie gasped. *Decorated soldier?* He remembered the infantry captain suggesting that he might be put in for a medal, but surely that was not such a big deal that the general needed to award it. *Shit! I thought they would just hand it to me as I was leaving.*

The colonel stepped again to his left, and the two captains stepped forward next to the general. The captain on the left held a folder. He opened it and began to read.

"The Secretary of the Army, Major General Pepke, has issued an Army Commendation Medal for meritorious service while serving with the Intelligence squad of the 402nd Artillery, in the months of April and May of 1968."

The captain standing on the general's right stepped forward and pinned on a green ribbon medal above the left side of Charlie's left chest pocket. The captain stepped back and saluted Charlie, who returned the salute.

"Intelligence squad?" Charlie wondered.

The captain began again. "The Secretary of the Army also has issued three Bronze Star for Service Medals, with valor, for heroic achievement in connection with military operations against an armed enemy while serving with Charlie Battery of the 402nd Artillery. On July 21, 1968, while serving on the communication team for the battery, the then Corporal Armfield rendered assistance to an officer down during enemy fire. He then proceeded to take over the officer's duties as forward observer to protect Delta Company of the 125th Infantry.

"On October 28, 1968, Sergeant Armfield led a nine-man squad into enemy territory, and single handedly disposed of three NVA point elements. Then, without regard for his own safety, Sergeant Armfield reconnoitered ahead and disposed of an NVA machine gunner who was threatening his men. He was later medevaced, but not seriously injured. Only two of his men were KIA."

Two men? Oh, my God, Charlie thought, *who else was killed?* He only remembered Clark going down. *Will? Oh shit, Will?*

The captain continued. "And on April 1, 1969, while serving with the battery, Sergeant Armfield took command, and directed a ground counterattack to defend Charlie Battery. The artillery was without its own firepower due to the closeness of the enemy, so he acted as a forward observer by calling in support from Alpha Battery of the same battalion. His actions saved the firebase from serious carnage, as the end result was only three KIA and four WIA."

The captain on the right pinned three identical red ribbon medals to the right of Charlie's army Commendation Medal.

Wow, Charlie thought as he returned the captain's salute, *they remembered all that shit. But what had happened to Will? Who told them that story?*

"There is more, Sir," the captain on the left said. "The Secretary of the Army, on behalf of the United States Congress, also has issued a Silver Star Medal, for gallantry in action against an armed enemy while serving with the communications team for Charlie Battery of the 402nd Artillery."

Charlie felt dazed. *Oh, man! What's going on here? Just let me go home.*

"On July 26, 1968, the then Corporal Armfield led fifty men up Hill 595, and succeeded in eliminating the total NVA occupancy of the hill. His assault on the hill resulted in nine American KIA and thirteen WIA, but he emerged untouched while aiding and leading his men. There were no surviving NVA, with a body count of twenty-seven. This is for gallantry and is the third highest award in the United States Army."

The captain on the right again stepped forward and pinned a new ribbon medal next to the bronze stars. He then stepped back and saluted once again.

"Sir!" the captain on the left raised his voice, as if to command greater attention. "The Distinguished Service Cross is second only to the Medal of Honor for army personnel. The Secretary of the Army has issued, on behalf of the President of the United States of America, such a medal to Sergeant Charles Armfield."

Charlie's eyes felt like they were going to pop out of his head. His heart was pounding. *What did I do now?*

"He has once again distinguished himself, this time by extraordinary heroism in connection with military operations against an armed enemy." The captain emphasized each word as if to announce a momentous occurrence.

"Between December 1, 1968 and February 26, 1969, Sergeant Armfield volunteered to serve with a special Long Range Reconnaissance Patrol. This operation ended up helping to secure the safety of the entire Fourth Infantry Division for the '69 Tet Offensive, by eliminating an NVA Regiment on January 6, 1969."

The captain standing on the right handed the Distinguished Service Cross to the general, who stepped forward and pinned a dark blue ribbon with a bronze cross next to the Silver Medal on Charlie's chest.

The brigadier general stepped back, snapped to attention and saluted.

Tears scalded Charlie's cheeks as he lifted his right hand and touched his forehead to return the salute. *I get the cross for wiping out a thousand people,* he thought. *I don't understand this war, Sir. Please let me go home now.*

"What, no Purple Heart?" the general asked.

"I guess not, Sir," Charlie said, swabbing his face with his shirt sleeve.

"But you were medevaced?"

"Yes, Sir, but only because my ears were blown out."

The general looked down at Charlie's finger.

"Just a cut, Sir."

"Well, if you ask me, I think you deserve a Purple Heart, too."

"No, Sir."

"Sergeant?"

"What I mean, Sir, is I don't think I could stand up if you pinned another medal on my chest."

The general smiled. "Now, Sergeant Armfield, I think it's time we let you go home. There's not much time left. As soon as you check out and change into clean clothes, you will be escorted to my private plane for discharge to Cam Rahn Bay."

The formation was dismissed, and Charlie was rushed to the supply station where he turned in his backpack and weapon.

"Goodbye," he said to his M-16 as he handed it over to the supply sergeant. "I'm not sure if you were my friend or not, but I guess you did save my life a few times."

He scooped up his clean fatigues and took off for the shower. Afterward, cleaned and groomed, he returned to the supply station and handed over the old clothes with the medals still pinned on the shirt.

"Whoa! You better take this hardware with you," the sergeant said.

Charlie stared at the sergeant.

"Yeah, I guess so." Charlie looked at the shirt as the sergeant held it up; he studied the medals for the first time. The ribbons were all a little over three inches long. One was a green brass hexagon medal with white stripes. Three identical stars, with a blue stripe in the center, hung from ribbons that were mostly red. An inscription on the stars read, "Heroic Achievement." Next was a red, white, and blue striped ribbon with a star hanging like the Bronze Stars, but with a small raised silver star in the middle. The inscription read "For Gallantry in Action." The last ribbon was dark blue with red stripes at the edges. Hanging below was a bronze cross with an eagle. At the eagle's feet was a scroll bearing the words, "For Valor."

"Come on, Sergeant," the first sergeant yelled. "You need to get on that plane, pronto!"

Charlie wadded up the shirt and took it with him. Fifteen minutes later, he was in the air flying out of the Central Highlands.

16

At Cam Rahn Bay, Charlie was hurried through the DEROS processing. Within an hour after he arrived, he was ready to board a plane for the United States. The next plane, however, wasn't scheduled to leave until 6 a.m. the next morning, May 28. With the fourteen-hour time difference between the States and crossing the international dateline, the plane would land close to the same time it was scheduled to take off. That would give the army eighteen hours to debrief and clear Charlie for discharge.

"You can check into the barracks, Sergeant," the lieutenant from the processing center said. "You'll have to spend the night. Looks like you'll just make it back in time."

"Thank you, Sir. Do you know if Specialist Saltman went home already?" Charlie asked.

"I'm new here, Sergeant. I don't know very many of the men."

"That's okay, Sir. He probably went home a long time ago. That is unless he extended."

"Sorry I can't help you," the lieutenant said.

Charlie walked into the barracks and stretched out on one of the beds. *How ironic,* he thought, stretching his arms up over his head. *When I came to Nam, Gage and I were processed in a matter of hours so they could fill empty seats on a plane. Now the same thing happens going home, except there's no plane. Sometimes I think this outfit doesn't know whether it's coming or going.*

A voice from across the room interrupted his train of thought.

"Look at this," a Green Beret sergeant said to a soldier sitting on a bed next to him. "I found it on a gook near the Cambodian Border."

"Wow! That's the oldest knife I've ever seen," the soldier said.

Charlie's ears perked up. An old knife? Grandpa's? Charlie stood up quickly, and walked over to the Green Beret.

"Excuse me for eavesdropping," Charlie said. "But could I look at that knife?"

"What the hell for?"

"I had an old knife that was lost near Cambodia. It belonged to my grandfather."

"Well, you can forget it, because it's not this one."

The Green Beret stood up and faced Charlie with the knife enclosed in his left fist. His right fist was also clenched.

Charlie stared at him, and then turned his head as if he was going to walk off. Then, he shot his right hand out, grabbed the other man's right fist, twisting his arm around and pulling it up behind the Green Beret's back as he spun him around.

"Excuse me, Sergeant, but if that's my knife, I need it back. I'll tell you what. If there's a word inscribed on the knife and I can identify it, you give me the knife."

The Green Beret struggled, not responding. Charlie pulled on his arm, forcing it further up his back.

"All right, all right! There's a word all right, but you don't know what it says."

"'Believe.' The word is 'believe'."

The Green Beret opened his left fist and handed the knife to the other soldier, who took it and looked at the knife.

"Wow! He's right! It does say 'believe'."

Charlie carefully brought the Green Beret's arm down and let go while he stepped back. The man turned and glared at Charlie.

Charlie reached out toward the other soldier. "I'll take it now."

The soldier looked at the Green Beret for approval. He reluctantly nodded permission. The soldier handed the knife to Charlie.

"Thank you. My grandpa and I both thank you," Charlie said, turning slowly and walking back to his bunk.

I can't believe it, Grandpa, Charlie said to himself. *I got your knife back, man. Some gook found it when Will lost it. I'll bet he really enjoyed it—that is, until he died. Shit! Maybe the knife isn't good luck after all. At least it wasn't for the gook.*

The soldiers were instructed to fill in the rows from the back of the plane first. When Charlie walked to his row he glanced up and saw the number 5 below the overhead compartment. He stared for a moment, remembering gun number five.

"Holy shit!" Charlie said shaking his head.

"What's the matter, Sergeant?" the soldier sitting in the middle seat said. "Don't you want to sit next to a preacher?"

Charlie looked at the soldier and saw captain's bars on his left collar.

"Excuse me, Sir?" Charlie said, confused.

The captain touched his right collar indicating the cross pinned to it.

"No, it's not that, Sir," Charlie said as he stored a small bag overhead and sat down next to the minister. "I was just amazed that I ended up in row number five, that's all."

"So what's up with the number five, Sergeant?"

Charlie looked into the minister's eyes. They were a light brown color even though the man's hair was blond. His eyes had warmth to them, and appeared to reach out to Charlie with a friendly embrace. Charlie wanted to respond to the invitation they offered, but couldn't.

"I was on gun number five," he said quietly.

The minister put his hand on Charlie's left shoulder. "Did something bad happen on your gun, Son?"

Charlie nodded, and turned his head away.

As the plane started to move, the stewardess walked down the aisle, making sure everyone had their seatbelt fastened. She smiled when she approached Charlie, who was too busy staring at her to remember to fasten his seatbelt.

"Please fasten your seatbelt, Sergeant."

"Oh, sure," Charlie stammered.

He stared at her as she passed, then turned to the minister.

"Sorry, Sir, but that is a beautiful woman," Charlie said.

The minister smiled. "She certainly is."

He held out his right hand. "My name's Harry Finney."

Charlie shook his hand. "I'm Charlie Armfield. What kind of minister are you?"

"Methodist."

"No shit!" Charlie said without thinking. He put his hand over his mouth, embarrassed. Then he smiled, "My father's a Methodist minister."

"Really! Where did he attend seminary?"

"In Boston. Where did you go to school, Sir?"

"Call me Harry. I went to Iliff School of Theology in Denver. I joined the army after graduation."

Charlie frowned and shook his head. "Why did you do that?"

The minister stared at Charlie. "With your rank, I thought maybe you had joined the army, too, Charlie. Were you drafted?"

"That's right. I never would have joined in a million years."

"I never thought I would have either, but I was feeling guilty."

"Guilty?"

"Yes. A lot of my friends were getting drafted, but I was excused with a ministerial deferment. Someone I knew really well came home from Nam with his leg blown off. He was so depressed I thought he was going to kill himself. I talked with him and it helped. That's when I decided to join up."

"So you could help the soldiers?"

"That was my plan, Charlie."

Charlie remembered the guy in the infirmary with the bandaged head. He was worried he would be blind and wouldn't be able to paint again. *Shit,* he thought, *if I lost my leg I wouldn't be able to surf again. I think I'd want to kill myself, too.*

"Did it turn out the way you planned?'

"Not exactly. The men weren't very receptive. I held church services at the firebases, but hardly anyone attended. I begged for permission to go out into the field, thinking that those were the men who needed my help. But they were so preoccupied with the action that they didn't have much to say. They told me about the gory stuff, but they couldn't tell me how they felt about it."

Charlie peered deeply into the minister's eyes. "Where were you when I was trying to figure things out, pastor?"

The minister looked surprised. Smiling he said, "Where were you when I needed to help someone?"

They both laughed. Charlie held out his hand, inviting a handclasp. Harry grabbed it and squeezed.

As the plane lifted off, most of the men cheered. Charlie glanced around at the smiling faces.

Turning back to the minister, Charlie said, "I guess we're supposed to be happy about going home."

"You mean you're not?"

"I don't know what I am. I know I want to go surfing more than anything, but I don't know if I can..." Charlie paused and looked out the window.

"If you can be with the people in your life?" the minister said, continuing Charlie's sentence.

"How did you know?"

"Just a hunch, Charlie. I've been married for three years to the most beautiful woman in the world, but I'm not sure how I'm going to talk to her. I didn't see much action, but I heard stories and talked to the men in the infirmaries. My life has changed, and I fear that my wife won't understand."

Charlie thought about Cher. *I guess I'm not the only one. Thank God I'm not married. I don't know how I'm going to face my parents, but I know sooner or later I'll have to. At least I won't have to figure out how to be with Cher.*

"You know what, Harry?"

"What, Charlie?"

"I'm more scared now about seeing my parents again than I was on any contact mission."

Charlie and Harry continued to talk during the six-hour flight to Tokyo. The plane landed to refuel, and the men were allowed to get off to use the facilities and stretch their legs. But before the plane could be loaded up again, a fog settled in, engulfing the airport.

"I've never heard of this happening before," Harry said, scratching his head.

"No? It happens once in a while at the San Diego airport. You don't get much fog in Denver?"

"Low clouds sometimes, but not like this. Sometimes they close the airport because of snow."

"Wow! Snow! What's that like?"

They were confined to the airport, but permitted to walk around. The Japanese people in the terminal appeared to be fascinated with the soldiers. They stopped and stared, and a group of teenagers giggled as Charlie and Harry strolled through the terminal.

"Are they laughing at us?"

"I think they're admiring you, Sergeant."

"No way!" Charlie said, pushing Harry. "Oh shit! I guess I shouldn't be kidding around with a captain."

"Don't worry about it, Buddy. Besides, I'm getting discharged as soon as I get home."

"Hey, man, me, too. I'm out of this goddamn army! Oops! Sorry about that."

This time Harry pushed Charlie and they both chuckled.

A Caucasian man, who had been watching the two soldiers, walked up.

"Are you guys going to Nam, or coming back?" he said. He was clearly an American.

"We're heading home," Harry said.

"So I guess it's too late."

"Too late for what?" Charlie asked, looking at the man curiously.

"You've already killed innocent people who were just trying to be who they wanted to be. I'll bet you slaughtered them by the thousands."

Charlie's mouth dropped open. "What?"

"Excuse me, Sir," Harry spoke up quickly. "But the men who serve in Vietnam are working as peace officers for a country divided among itself."

"You meddled in someone else's business, that's what you did."

"Hey, I didn't want go over there!" Charlie protested. "I was drafted!"

"Well, you should have joined the Peace Corps or run away to Canada or something." The man spit at their feet, spun on his heel, and stormed away.

Charlie's gut cramped into a knot. Harry grabbed his shoulders as if to hold him back, but relaxed his grip when Charlie looked into his eyes.

"Are you okay, Charlie?"

"He's right. I never wanted to kill them, man."

"I know, Charlie."

Harry put his arm around Charlie and guided him slowly back to the gate.

"Is it going to be like this when we get home?" Charlie said, his voice hushed and hurting.

"Like what?"

"Are people going to be angry at us for going to Vietnam?"

"I don't know about that, Charlie." Harry shook his head. "I sure hope not."

When the plane approached the landing strip at McCord Air Force Base in Washington State, Harry reset his watch to Pacific Daylight Time.

"Would you believe it's one o'clock in the afternoon?"

"That means I have no more than eleven hours left."

"Left for what?"

"I have to be discharged within eleven hours, man. A deal is a deal."

The soldiers roared as the landing gear touched down, cheering as if they were at a sporting event.

Charlie remained silent. *What am I going to do now? How can I ever live a normal life? Will anybody understand? I've been to hell and back, and nobody will know what I've seen or done.*

The celebration continued until the doors opened. The men eagerly began to pile out. Charlie remained in his aisle seat, his thoughts of Nam weighing him down. The soldier sitting in the window seat stirred, anxious to get out.

Harry tapped Charlie on the shoulder. "Time to go, Charlie."

Charlie stood up, pulled his bag out of the overhead compartment, and plodded toward the door.

Then a light blue ocean wave washed through his mind, washing away the trepidation. *Surf—I'm going surfing again! I made it,* he told himself, *and I will surf again!* He walked through the doors into sunlight—not the dense clouds and dismal rain that had hung over the field when he was last there, the day he departed for Nam.

He smiled at Harry. "I'm going surfing again, man. Aaaahhhhooo!!!!!" Charlie shouted, as he bounced down the gangplank.

Then he stopped, remembering the final step with his right foot on

American soil between the bus and the gangplank, when he'd boarded the plane fourteen months earlier. He gauged his steps and, when he calculated that his left wouldn't land on the ground first, he shifted his gait. At the bottom of the steps, he planted his left foot firmly on the ground.

There, he thought, *that completes the cycle. I went over leading with my right, and I have come back to finish with my left. Thank you, dear God, for letting me come back home.*

No bus awaited the returning soldiers, but nobody seemed to mind. Some knelt down and kissed the ground. Others ran or skipped all over the runway. Together, Charlie and Harry walked the half-mile to the Air Force terminal, and waited until a transport arrived to take them to Fort Lewis.

"Charlie, when the surf's not breaking sometime, would you come out to Colorado and visit me? My parents have a neat summer place up in the Rockies at Grand Lake. It would be good for you to breathe some of that mountain air."

Charlie cocked his head at Harry. "What do you mean?"

"It's the purest air in the world, Charlie. Cleans the cobwebs out."

"What I really need right now is a good swell, but maybe after that I'll come try your mountain air," Charlie said, slapping Harry on the back.

When the processing unit at Fort Lewis realized that Charlie had very little time before he had to be released, they handled his paper work quickly. He was directed to get a new uniform at the supply station, and take it to the tailor so the proper insignia and medals could be arranged.

He was also ordered to visit the barber.

Charlie said his goodbyes to Reverend Finney, and reported to the barber.

"Just take a little off the sides, please, and leave the top. Don't touch the sideburns either."

"They'll never let you out if that's all I do, Sergeant," the barber said. "And that bushy mustache will have to be trimmed as well."

"Hey, if they don't like it, I'll be back."

When he returned wearing his new uniform, the captain in charge focused on Charlie's ribbons.

"Holy mackerel, Sergeant! That's quite a collection you have there."

Over Charlie's left shirt pocket were three rows of ribbons. Each ribbon was an inch and three eighths long and three eighths of an inch wide. The bottom row had the traditional three ribbons which everybody who served in Vietnam wore: the National Defense Service Ribbon, the

Vietnam Service Ribbon, and the Republic of Vietnam Campaign Ribbon. The next row up had Charlie's army Commendation Ribbon, the Silver Star Ribbon, and the Bronze Star Ribbon with the "three-V" insignia in the middle, indicating that he had received three such awards, all for valor. A single ribbon was pinned above them—the army Distinguished Service Cross. When the captain's eyes lit on that he seemed unconcerned with Charlie's hair. *It could be growing down to my knees,* Charlie thought, *and he wouldn't have even notice.*

Above the ribbons, Charlie wore a blue Combat Infantryman Badge with its silver rifle and wreath for serving with the 125th Infantry Company. Below the ribbons was his black Sharpshooter Badge with the silver bull's eye.

On each shoulder was the insignia for the Fourth Infantry Division. They were white, an inch and three quarters square, but were sewn on with the points straight up and down, and to the sides. Inside the squares were four Irish green stars. Below the patches were Charlie's gold sergeant stripes. On each lapel of his khaki shirt were brass pins three quarters of an inch in diameter. The one on the right had an U.S. insignia; on the left was the crossed cannons for the artillery.

By the time his uniform was ready, it was nearly ten o'clock in the evening. Because of the time constraint, he was given private debriefing sessions. At eleven o'clock, a captain ushered him into the front of a room filled with other uniformed soldiers, sitting in rows. The major, lecturing at the head of the room, appeared irritated at the interruption. The captain approached the major to explain the situation.

Charlie had been told before they entered, that this was a discharge ceremony in progress. He gazed around the room. The group had been together for the past three days at Fort Lewis, and this was the final step before release.

He glanced at each soldier, one by one. In the third row, second from the far end, he stopped. His eyes widened, popping out of his head. *Gage? Could it be? Yes!*

His friend, eyes equally wide, waved. Charlie stared, open-mouthed.

The captain returned to his side, and pointed toward the rear of the room, but Charlie didn't move. The captain cleared his throat to get his attention. Charlie, unable to keep his eyes off Gage, stumbled as he followed the captain to the back.

When the ceremony concluded the men let out a cheer and started filing out of the room. Gage ran to the back of the room and threw his arms around Charlie.

"I thought you were a goner, man," Gage said, his eyes glistening with tears.

"A goner? What the hell for?"

"I never thought you would extend in a million years, Charlie. When you didn't come through the DEROS center in late March, well I thought..."

Charlie held up his hand. "You thought wrong, man. I extended, and I see you did the same."

"Yeah, but why did you, with all the shit going on out there?"

"Hey, man, what was fifty-seven more days in hell compared to seven months more in the army? I considered the options and figured I would only get myself into a bunch of trouble if I came home and had to keep playing military games. Now I'm home free, and ready to surf, man."

Gage laughed. He pointed to the medals on Charlie's uniform. "Holy shit! What's all this?"

Charlie shook his head. "Come on, man. Let's get out of here."

Arm in arm, they left the room and walked toward the gates of the fort where taxis were waiting to take soldiers to the airport.

Charlie remembered Will. He stopped and clutched Gage's shoulder. "Did you see Will again?"

Gage saw the bandage on Charlie's finger. Charlie noticed his gaze and quickly shoved his hand into his pocket.

"No I didn't," Gage said. "But I was on R&R around the time he was due to come through the DEROS center. When did he leave the field?"

"I don't know," Charlie said.

"What do you mean, you don't know?"

"We weren't together when he left." Charlie decided not to elaborate. *Maybe someday I'll tell him the story,* he thought.

"Hey! Before we leave, let's call our parents," Gage said, pointing toward a phone booth.

Charlie froze and stared at Gage, not answering.

"What's the matter?"

Charlie shook his head.

"Come on, man. They're going to want to hear from us, no matter what time it is."

"It's not that," Charlie said, his voice low. "I'm afraid to talk to them."

"Afraid of what?"

"I don't know." Charlie didn't know what else to say.

"Listen, man. These are your parents we're talking about. If anybody in the whole world would want to talk to you, it would be your mom and dad. Let's go give them a call."

Charlie nervously deposited ten cents into the phone and dialed the operator.

"Operator. May I help you?"

I want to make a collect call to San Diego. The number is Academy 2-8277."

"Who shall I say is calling?"

"Just tell them it's their son."

Charlie started shaking, his forehead twitching, as he listened to the tone in the receiver, waiting for someone to answer. On the third ring his mom answered.

"Hello?"

"Hello, Ma'am. I have a collect call from your son. Will you accept the charges?"

"Yes, of course."

"Go ahead, Sir."

"Hi, Mom."

"Mike, is that you?"

Charlie was silent, realizing she had mistaken him for his brother. He could hear his mom trying to wake up his dad.

"John, wake up! It's Mike calling from Thailand."

"No, Mom. It's not Mike. It's me, Charlie."

There was silence for a few seconds. Then "Oh my God, Charlie!" she said, starting to cry. "John, it's Charlie!"

His dad took the phone. "Oh, Charlie. We're so glad to hear your voice."

"What's the matter with Mom?"

"She hasn't slept for the past three days, Son, worrying about you. Monday she started calling Fort Lewis to see if you'd arrived. They told her that you hadn't, and that it was unusual for someone who was discharging not to be in yet. She's been calling every day since. When did you get in?"

"This afternoon. They had trouble getting me in from the field."

"Well, thank the Lord you're home, Charlie. Your mother thought…

well, never mind. You're home now, and that's all that matters."

Charlie remained silent.

"What is it Son?"

"I did some terrible things, Daddy. I don't know how I can ever..." his voice broke.

"Don't try to talk about it now, Son. Everything's going to be all right. How soon can you get home?"

Part III

The Ignominy

17

The warmth of the midday sun was exhilarating to Charlie as he and Gage walked down the United Airline ramp at Lindberg Field in San Diego. Charlie wore his flowered shirt from Thailand, his army khaki trousers, and his scuffed-up jungle boots. Gage wore a plaid short-sleeved shirt with his khaki trousers and his polished army uniform shoes.

Their special military airline pass required them to be dressed in military attire to board the plane. Before they'd checked in their baggage, Charlie convinced Gage to carry on a different shirt.

"I'm changing my shirt when we get on board," Charlie said.

"You're doing what?"

"You heard me. I'm not in the army anymore, and I'll be damned if I'm going to walk into the airport in San Diego wearing all of these medals."

"A lot of guys would be proud to wear them, Charlie."

"Maybe so, man, but to me they represent something I want to forget as soon as I can. I might as well start right now."

"Okay, man, I can dig it. I have a spare shirt, too."

Each of them had changed in the restroom soon after the plane took off from Seattle-Tacoma Airport. Charlie had carried his boots on board, too. After changing, he wrapped his shoes in his uniform shirt and carried the wad back to his seat.

Together, Charlie and Gage followed the rest of the passengers to the door leading into the terminal.

"There's no wind, man. I wonder how the surf is," Charlie said, trying to ignore the nervousness he felt about seeing his parents. His forehead began to twitch.

Gage laughed and pushed Charlie on the arm. "Come on, man. We haven't even gotten into the terminal yet, and already you're talking about surf."

"That's what I've been wanting to do for over a year. We could be in the water in less than an hour."

"Think about it, man. Our parents might want to spend some time with us."

That's what I'm afraid of, Charlie thought. His stomach tightened and his heart beat quickened when he saw the crowd of people waiting to meet the passengers. In front was Paul Macon, advisor with the Las Olas Surf Club. *What the hell is he doing here? And other members of the club, too? Holy shit!*

Their friends mobbed them the instant Charlie and Gage walked through the door. "Welcome home!" echoed through the crowd.

As Charlie worked his way along, shaking each friend's hand, his apprehension eased.

"It's great to be back, guys. God almighty, you don't know how great it is to be home," he said, grinning from ear to ear.

His friends laughed, crowding around him and Gage.

He caught sight of his parents standing at the back with the Saltmans, patiently waiting. His smile faded—fear pierced into his mind. He stared for a moment, then walked into their embrace.

"Oh, Charlie," Louise said. "I thought you were…"

"It's okay, Mom. I'm home now."

Charlie's dad stepped back to study his son. "You look good, Charlie." John Armfield, who had always sported a mustache, smiled. "Nice looking 'stache you have there, Son."

Charlie could hear the Saltmans chattering away. He looked from one to the other of his parents, struggling for something to say.

Finally, he asked, "So how are Grandpa and Grandma?"

"They're fine," Charlie's dad said. "Grandma's a little under the weather today, or they would have been here."

"How did my friends know I was coming home?"

Before his dad could answer, a man with a camera snapped a picture of the Saltmans.

"Excuse me," the photographer said to Gage. "Are you Sergeant Armfield?"

"No Sir, I'm not," Gage said.

The reporter turned to the Armfields and took a picture. "So, you must be Sergeant Armfield. I expected such a decorated soldier to be in uniform. What was it like in Vietnam, Sergeant?"

Charlie's eyes widened. His face felt hot. "What? What's going on here?"

Charlie's dad stepped in front of the reporter. "Please leave us alone."

"Mr. Armfield, I'm sure the readers of the Union would love to hear from a San Diegan hero. It's not often that someone like Sergeant Armfield…"

Gage grabbed the reporter's arm and spun him around. "The guy hasn't seen his parents in awhile. Why don't you take off," he said, his voice rough.

"Yeah," one of the other surf club members shouted.

The reporter found himself confronted by a solid front of surf club members.

"Okay, okay." He frowned and shuffled away.

"I'm sorry, Charlie," his mom said. "Apparently there was a press release about your awards. It was in the papers over a week ago."

Over a week ago, he thought. *Everybody here knew before I did.*

"Then you know about my medals. I didn't want to tell you, Mom."

Charlie's mom hugged him tightly. "It's okay, Baby. You just did what you had to do."

Charlie's dad put his hand on Charlie's shoulder. "I'm proud of you, Son."

"For what, killing people?" Charlie snapped.

"No. For being the strong sensitive man you've become."

Charlie saw the sincerity in his father's eyes. "I'm sorry, Dad." He welcomed his dad into another family hug that lasted several minutes.

Finally, Charlie glanced up, and saw a lone figure standing in the corner of the terminal watching him intently. Charlie stared—gasped—his mouth dropped open.

"What is it, Charlie?" his mom asked, turning to follow his gaze.

Charlie pulled away from his parents and started toward the corner, his eyes fixed intently on the man. When he reached him, he just stood in front of him for a moment and gazed into his eyes.

Then he said, "Oh, my God, you're alive!"

He threw his arms around Will Jamison and started laughing. Charlie fell to his knees and pulled Will down with him.

"I thought you were dead, man."

"You thought I was dead! Shit! You're the one who extended and didn't come home when you were supposed to. I thought for sure that you were a goner, man. I was going to call your parents but I got scared."

"Scared? Scared of what?"

"Of what they might tell me."

"Then how did you find out?"

"I read about you in the papers, just like everybody else here."

Charlie's face felt hot. *Oh, God,* he thought, *how embarrassing.* Then he realized the rest of the group had congregated around them, staring curiously.

Will stood and helped Charlie to his feet. "You better say something to all your fans here, Buddy."

Charlie lowered his head. *Please everybody,* he said to himself, *just go home and leave me alone.* The crowd remained.

He struggled to compose himself. Swallowing hard, he said, "First of all, I want to know how all you surf rats knew when I was coming home?"

Everyone laughed.

Paul Macon stuck up his hand. "That would be me, Charlie. I asked your parents to let me know when they heard from you. Then I spread the word."

Charlie smiled, shaking his head and his fist at Paul. He looked around the group, and saw Gage grinning at him.

"Get your ass over here, Saltman. They came to see you, too."

The group chanted, "Gage! Gage! Gage!" and Gage stepped forward.

Charlie's eyes met Gage's. Neither one of them wanted to say anything. Finally, Charlie forced himself to begin.

"I haven't seen either of these guys for a long time. Will and I ran into each other in the bush. Gage and I got to surf together in Nam once. The waves were lousy, but we sure had a great time."

Gage burst out laughing and nodded his head.

Charlie put one arm around each of them.

"We're all glad to be home. There's not much else to say, except— thanks for rescuing me from the reporter."

Everybody laughed again.

Charlie walked over to his parents and put his arms around them. Together, they walked to the baggage area.

Will tagged along and carried Charlie's bag.

"Before we step outside, I have to warn you about something."

"What's that, man?" Charlie asked.

"Protesters are marching in front of the airport today."

"What are they protesting?"

Will cast a glance toward Charlie's parents.

"What is it? What are they protesting?" Charlie repeated.

"The war, man."

"The Vietnam War?"

"Yeah," Will said quietly. "They're crazy, man. Just ignore them and walk on by."

As they stepped outside, Charlie heard a commotion. Police, wearing helmets, were beating people with clubs, forcing them away from something burning on the ground.

"Stop the war!" Somebody yelled. "Get out of Vietnam, now!"

Some of the protesters carried signs:

THIS IS NOT OUR WAR!
STOP THE WAR IN VIETNAM!
AMERICAN SOLDIERS ARE MURDERERS!

American soldiers are murderers? Charlie swallowed hard. *This is like that guy in Tokyo. Why are they doing this? We didn't want to go there. Don't they understand?*

Charlie started toward the burning object.

"Charlie, no," his mother cried.

"I'll be right back," Charlie said.

When he realized it was the American flag, he shuddered. *They're burning our flag? What's with these people? I'm pissed at my country, too, but not enough to burn the flag.*

"Why are you burning the flag?" Charlie asked, addressing one of the protesters.

"Maybe you haven't heard," said the man, about Charlie's age. "America is killing innocent people."

Charlie stared at the man. *Yes, I've heard,* he said to himself.

As he rejoined his parents and Will, the Saltmans walked out the door.

"They're mad at our country, man," Charlie gulped. "They're mad at us, too."

"Let's get out of here, guys," Will said. "You know, the surf is up. Want to go hit it?"

Charlie perked up. "It is? You bet I do." He looked at his parents. "Do you mind?"

"Of course not, Son," Charlie's dad said. "You go with Will. We'll see you later."

Charlie spun around to look at Gage, who was studying his own parents.

"Go ahead, Gage," Mr. Saltman said.

"What about our boards?" Gage asked.

"Already got 'em," Will said, smiling. "Stopped by your houses on the way to the airport." He pointed to his car across the parking lot. Three surfboards were strapped to the racks on top.

"Got your wetsuits, too."

"Aaaaahhhhhooooo!" Charlie shouted.

At Ocean Beach, Charlie ran to the water, his board under his arm. He paddled out into the five-foot surf and was the first to catch a wave. As Gage and Will stroked over the peak he'd caught, Charlie cranked a hard bottom turn on a right-hand wave.

"Go get 'em Charlie," Will yelled.

"Aaaaahhhhhooooo!" Gage cried.

Charlie came off the bottom, cruised to the top, bounced off the lip of the wave, and cut back toward the white water. He cut a smooth turn, avoiding the turbulence as if he had been practicing. He trimmed his surfboard into the curl line, and put his weight onto his back foot to stall his board. The wave didn't look like it was going to tube, so he casually walked up toward the nose and placed his left foot over the edge, hanging five.

This is what I've been waiting for! No more Vietnam for me. I'm out of there. I don't have to kill any more gooks.

Unbidden, the bloody face of an NVA soldier with a bullet hole between his eyes, blasted into his mind—the first enemy soldier he had killed. He had been on Listening Post with Will; he'd shot his M-16 into the darkness and heard a thud and a moan. And then, that awful next morning, finding the body, its mouth wide open as if trying to cry out.

Before he could straighten out his board, the wave walled up and broke, slapping Charlie hard in the chest. He wiped out of the wave, his board tumbled in with the passing swell.

Charlie swam in slowly. He realized he had lost his concentration. *Shit! If I'd done that in Nam, I might not be here today. One false move in the surf and all I have to do is swim. But why the hell am I thinking of Nam when I'm finally in the surf again?*

He retrieved his board and paddled back out to where Will and Gage sat on their boards.

"How was that wave?" Will asked.

"Great—until I screwed it up."

"What are you talking about?" Gage said. "You were cranking on the sucker."

"Until I got inside."

"What happened?" Will asked.

"I started thinking about that first LP I was on with you, man. I don't have the slightest idea why. Maybe because I was so glad to see you today."

"What's LP mean?" Gage asked.

"You tell him, Will," Charlie said, not wanting to talk any more.

"It's when you go out into the bush at night by yourself and listen for gooks. If you hear something, you're not supposed to shoot—just signal the company with a code on the radio. We did that together the first night Charlie was up at the front. We had noise and the company blasted, but they missed one. Charlie got him before he got us."

"Wow," Gage said, shaking his head.

"Wow is right, man. Charlie saved my life that night. And it wasn't the last time either."

A set began rolling in outside, and the guys stroked into the water to get to it. Gage caught the first wave. Will turned around on the second one. Charlie stroked into the third wave, the biggest of the set. Before he got onto his feet, the white water pounded his back and knocked him off of his board.

So what's the deal now? Charlie thought. *You can't even take off without wiping out?*

Charlie started swimming in, thinking about what Will said. *I saved his life? Shit. He's the one who saved my life. My ears were blown up, and I couldn't even stand up. He carried me to the helicopter in the middle of a firefight.*

Charlie trudged in to the beach, found his board and dropped onto the wet sand. He stared out at the waves, then down at his hands. *With my own hands, I've killed. I am a killer. How am I ever going to live this down?*

He covered his face with his hands.

The tide was coming in. Soon, a small shore-break wave engulfed him. Startled, he jumped up and dragged his surfboard farther up onto the sand. As he sat down, Will walked toward him.

"Are you all right?" Will asked, sitting next to him.

"I don't know, man. I can't seem to get into it."

"What? You were always the most gung ho guy in the water. In Nam you told me how you used to get ready for contests. You're Mr. Focus, man."

"It's not the same, Will. I'm different now." Charlie looked out at the surf. *Different, all right—I've killed now.*

"Of course you're different, man. All of us who went to Nam are different."

Charlie looked at Will. "Do you feel guilty for going?"

Will turned his head away. "Why?" he asked softly.

"I'm just trying to figure this shit out, man."

"No," Will said, still looking away. "It's not my fault I had to go to Nam. I was drafted. Just like you."

They sat quietly watching the horizon. Finally Charlie broke the silence.

"I'm scared to be home, man."

Will turned and looked into Charlie's eyes. "I know what that's like, Charlie. Nobody understands. And all these anti-war creeps around don't make it any easier. No 'Welcome Home' for us. Most people sit around and watch the damn thing on TV, like it was some kind of adventure movie or something."

"What do you mean?"

"Wait till you see the news on TV, man. Every goddamn night you can see some shit happening in Nam, right in your own living room. It's the most pathetic thing I've ever seen."

Charlie shook his head, "No way in hell I'm watching that."

Will nodded approvingly. "I can't watch it, either."

Charlie studied Will for a moment. "Are we murderers, Will?"

Will shook his head and turned away without a word.

Later that night, Charlie rang his grandparents' doorbell. He glanced back at his mom and dad, looking for their approval. His dad smiled and nodded. The door opened, and Charlie turned to see his grandparents, standing in the doorway.

"Oh, Charlie," his grandmother cried. "I'm so glad you're home!"

Charlie gave her a kiss and a hug, and looked at his grandfather standing at attention. As their eyes connected, Grandpa Armfield raised his right hand to his forehead and saluted. Charlie took a deep breath, offering his hand for a shake.

His grandfather grasped it, and shook it firmly. "You've made us all proud, Son."

Charlie gazed into his grandfather's admiring eyes, unsure what to say. He didn't want to hurt his feelings.

Finally, in a quiet voice, he said, "Thanks, Grandpa. I have something for you."

He reached into his pocket and pulled out the tarnished, World War I knife.

18

San Diego Union, Friday, May 30, 1969

VIETNAM HERO RETURNS HOME

Sergeant Charles W. Armfield of the army's Fourth Infantry Division in Vietnam returned to his San Diego home yesterday. A former surf star, who was drafted before he could make his mark in the World Surfing Championships held in San Diego in '67, has become another kind of hero. He was decorated near Pleiku, Vietnam, with three Bronze Stars, a Silver Star, and a Distinguished Service Cross. He was greeted at Lindberg Field yesterday by his family and admirers.

His attire was not that of a distinguished War Hero, however. He wore a Hawaiian shirt as he shuffled into the terminal with his uniform wadded in his hand. Sergeant Armfield was not available for comment, but it was obvious that he wanted nothing to do with the army anymore. He was discharged the day before yesterday.

Meanwhile, outside of the terminal, an antiwar demonstration was apparently protesting Sergeant Armfield's arrival. Flag burning and signs greeted the war hero's homecoming.

Charlie picked up the phone in a rage and dialed. He paced back and forth, as far as the cord would allow, until someone answered his call.

"Will, it's me. Did you see the goddamn newspaper this morning?"

"The newspaper?" Will answered, still half asleep. "Shit, Charlie, it's only six o'clock in the morning. I'm not even awake."

"Sorry, man, but I couldn't sleep. Guess I'm still on Nam time."

"Jungle time, Charlie; it's going to be a long time before you sleep the whole night through again. So, what does the paper say?"

"My picture's on the front page with my parents. There's a bunch of crap written about me, too. The guy doesn't know shit about me and he's writing a story. This isn't news, man. Why in hell am I in the paper anyway?"

"Because you're a hero, man. Not often someone comes home with a cross. What did you get that for, anyway?"

Charlie sighed before answering. He spoke quietly, "I pulled the plug on a gook regiment."

Will was silent for a moment. "Sorry I asked."

"It's okay, Will. You're the only one I will ever tell. It was pretty shitty. Must have been close to a thousand of them."

"Charlie?"

"Yes."

"Did you keep counting?"

"Yeah, I couldn't help it, Will. I counted twenty-seven before they put me on the firebase." Charlie sighed. "But shit, that doesn't count all the others. That's only the ones I saw go down. There must be thousands..." Charlie choked, feeling like he wanted to cry.

"It's okay, man. Come on over. We'll check out the surf."

"I already checked it out. It's blown out. The wind came up at about two this morning."

"You've been up all night?"

"Off and on. Hey, man, what are you doing today?"

"I have to work. Got my old job back at the shipyard—eight to four-thirty. Why don't you come over when I get off? Maybe the wind'll die down and we can catch a few before dark."

"Okay. Hey, Will?"

"What?"

"Those demonstrators—they weren't protesting me, were they?"

"Of course not. Besides, they're stupid, man. They don't know what the hell's going on."

Later that afternoon, Charlie sat on the front steps of Will's apartment, his hair blowing in the persistent wind. He felt dejected knowing there wouldn't be any surfing that evening. He folded his arms over his knees and put his head down.

"No surf?" Will said, startling Charlie as he walked up the steps.

"No, the damn wind has been blowing all day."

"How about we just take a walk on the beach," Will said. "Wait here for a minute while I go get something."

Will returned and they trudged through the sand on Ocean Beach and stood at the end of the pier as the sun dropped westward, its orange reflection dancing across the choppy sea.

Will pulled out a joint, turned away from the wind, and struck a wooden match on his pant leg. He took a long drag and passed it over to Charlie. As Charlie drew the magic smoke into his lungs, his head immediately was tranquil, and his body felt warm and smooth. The sunset became mesmerizing.

"Now, that's better, man," Will said. "I should have brought this to you this morning when you were all up in arms about that article."

"I'd rather share it with you. Remember when you first turned me on to this stuff? I never would have dreamed it could make such a difference."

"It saved your life, didn't it?"

"I don't know about that." Charlie hesitated, watching colors change in the water. Then he looked up at Will and stared into his eyes. They were the eyes of his surf buddy, but more than that. Those eyes had seen the same slaughter that his had seen. They were the eyes of his blood brother. He turned back to watch the fading sunlight glisten on the Pacific.

"You okay, Charlie?"

"What's next, man? Will I ever be able to have a life again?"

"Of course you will."

Charlie passed the joint back to Will.

"My folks want me to go back to school." He shook his head and spit over the railing of the pier. "I can't handle that, man."

"How about competition? You can still kick some ass, Charlie."

Charlie shook his head "I don't think so. I just don't have the drive. Besides, you saw me surfing yesterday. I was a total spaz."

"What, on your first day back? Listen, Charlie, you're one of the best surfers in the world…"

Charlie held his hand up.

"I never got to prove that, remember? I was focused on nothing but that before Nam. Now, too much has happened, man. My mind's all over the place. I could never tune into competition again."

Will shook his head and passed the joint back to Charlie. Then a hand from behind grabbed onto Charlie's left shoulder and forced him up against the railing.

"The cops," Will gulped.

Charlie dropped the weed on the pier, and kicked it over the edge and into the water.

"All right!" the police officer yelled. "Where's the rest of it?"

"The rest of what?" Will said.

"You know what I'm talking about. Both of you—hands on your head." The officer searched them. "Nothing. I know you were smoking dope out here."

He cuffed their hands behind their backs, read them their rights, and walked them through a curious crowd to his car. It was after dark when they arrived at the police station. They were booked and placed in a cell.

"You'll be arraigned in the morning," the guard said, clanging the door shut. "Want to make a call?"

They looked at each other and shrugged their shoulders.

"No? All right then."

The guard marched away, his footsteps echoing through the hallway.

"Well, look at what we have here," a voice slurred from the corner of the cell.

Charlie looked toward the voice and saw a large black man, six and a half feet tall, unshaven, and dressed in scruffy clothing. He was grinning at them. Two other men stood next to the big man; one was black, about six feet tall, the other was Mexican and short.

"Looks like we have some kids in the jail tonight, boys." He laughed and floundered over to Charlie.

"What are you in for?"

Charlie gazed into his eyes, smelling whiskey on his breath. He wanted to say "None of your goddamn business," but thought better of it.

"Just enjoying a sunset."

The big man cocked his head back.

"Enjoying a sunset? What the fuck are you talking about?"

"Well, my friend and I were standing on the end of this pier watching the sun go down, when we were rudely interrupted."

The drunk leaned forward. "You messing with me, honky?"

Charlie looked sternly into his eyes.

"I don't ever intend to mess with anybody, but sometimes it's unavoidable."

The man reached out to grab Charlie's shirt, but stumbled as Charlie quickly stepped to the side.

"That's why we didn't drink in Nam, right Will? You're too damn clumsy when you're drunk."

The man clenched his teeth. "You calling me a drunk?"

"I call 'em as I see 'em," Charlie said. "You smell and look like you're drunk."

The man struggled to get up, his fists clenched. Charlie stepped out in front of him.

"Listen, man," Will spoke up abruptly, grabbing onto Charlie's shirt, trying to pull him back. "Nobody's calling you anything. The last thing in the world we want to do is hassle with you."

Charlie wiggled free from Will's grasp, and held out his hand to hold him back.

"Let me tell you something" Charlie said, turning toward the man. "For a year, we had to kill gooks. It was bloody, man. We didn't want to do it. We didn't want to hassle anybody, then or now."

The drunk peered at Charlie. His eyes were blurry, not entirely focusing. He looked sad, then he said, "You were in Vietnam?"

Charlie nodded, looking grave, but stern.

"My brother was killed in Vietnam last year." The man stuck out his hand. "Sorry I messed with you, man."

Charlie grasped his hand, and shook it firmly. "Sorry about your brother."

He turned and walked over to the bench attached to the side of the cell, and gestured for Will to sit next to him.

"Wow, man," Will said. "That was a close call."

Charlie looked into Will's eyes. "It's not the first time for that, is it?"

Will shook his head.

"The biggest bummer," Charlie continued, "is that the first time I get high in the States, I'm busted."

Will frowned and lowered his head. "It's not like Nam around here, man. The cops are always trying to catch you."

Charlie put his arm around Will. "You know what, man? We've been through a lot of shit together, right?"

Will looked up at Charlie. "Yeah."

"I'd say this is a piece of cake in comparison, wouldn't you?"

Will smiled, shook his head. "You're a trip, Armfield. You always find a way to make things better."

Charlie shrugged.

"After I put you on the medevac," Will continued, "I was alone. Shit flying all around. Thought for sure I was a goner. Then I remembered what you said; you said to visualize myself going home. So I pictured myself walking up the gangplank of a goddamn airplane in my uniform. Before long the guns stopped. I made my way over to the rest of the guys. We were evacuated to camp and, before I could get off the chopper, the first sergeant ran up and told me to stay on, and ride on in to basecamp so I could process for DEROS. I looked at him and said, 'Thanks, Charlie.'"

Charlie grinned.

"He thought I was talking about the gooks," Will said. "He looked at me and said, 'What the hell did you call me?'"

Charlie started laughing.

"I said," Will continued, "'Thanks, Charlie, you saved my life again.' He just looked at me like I was crazy and said, 'Good thing you're going home, Jamison.'"

Charlie and Will laughed so hard they didn't hear the guard approach their cell.

"What's going on in here?"

Charlie looked up, still smiling.

"Oh, nothing."

"What's so funny?"

"We were just reminiscing."

The guard frowned.

"Hey," Charlie said. "A few months ago, my friend and I were dodging bullets in Nam. Being here in jail is kind of a joke compared to that."

The guard stared at them for a moment. "You've got a point." He turned to walk away, stopped, and looked back. "Good luck to you guys."

Charlie looked back at Will, and saw the serious look on his face.

"You saved my life that day, Charlie."

"What day?"

"The day I put you on that chopper."

"What are you talking about? You saved *my* life that day."

"Maybe so, but you saved mine that day, too, and every other day I was in Vietnam after you got there, man. I used to wake up every morning wondering if that would be the day I was going to die. Then you came up with the cockeyed idea about visualizing surviving every battle and going home. Well, it worked, man."

Neither Charlie nor Will spoke about the arrest with their parents. They arranged for a bail bond, and were ordered to appear in court on June eighteenth. Charlie moved in with Will, with no objections from his parents.

Then the newspaper article came out.

San Diego Union, Sunday, June 1, 1969

WAR HERO ARRESTED

The highly decorated Vietnam Hero, Sergeant Charles W. Armfield, was arrested Friday night for suspicion of drug use. It was only his second day home from Vietnam, and he was allegedly arrested for smoking marijuana on the Ocean Beach Pier. He was arraigned yesterday morning and will appear in court later this month.

The use of marijuana is highly suspected among the soldiers in Vietnam. According to Major General Stremple of the 101 Airborne Division, "Marijuana is everywhere within the ranks." Evidently there is so much utilization of the drug that there is little or no penalty handed down. American soldiers coming home

will face difficulties if they continue with the substance.
Sergeant Armfield was not available for comment.

"Shit!" Charlie crumpled the paper and threw it into the trash as he stormed into the apartment. Out checking the surf early that morning, he had bought a paper to learn the tide schedule.

The phone rang.

"Hello?" Will said. "Sure, just a minute."

He held up the receiver toward Charlie. "It's your dad."

Oh, no, Charlie thought. *I hope he didn't see the paper.* Reluctantly he took the phone and sucked in a deep breath.

"Hey, Dad. What's going on?"

"Did you see the paper this morning, Charlie?"

Charlie took a deep breath and sighed. "Yeah."

"What happened, Son?"

Charlie gulped. "I...I don't..."

"Don't you think it would be a good idea if you came back home for awhile? Maybe you need some time to settle down before you're out on your own."

Charlie didn't know what to say. Going home was the last thing he wanted to do. Will was the only one who understood.

"I'm all right here, Dad. The arrest was a mistake. There's no evidence of anything. I'll be cleared when I go to court. Honest, there's nothing to worry about."

"But, Son..."

"Really, Dad, everything's all right. Tell Mom not to worry, okay?"

There was silence on the other end.

"You still there, Dad?"

"Yes, Charlie. Will you let us know if we can do anything to help you?"

"Sure."

"By the way, there was a major calling for you this morning. I gave him your phone number. Hope you don't mind."

Charlie was silent. *A major calling for me? What in the world for?*

"What did he want?"

"He said he was in Vietnam with you. You sure you're all right?"

"Yeah, Dad. Talk to you later."

Charlie hung up the phone and sat on the couch.

"So what's that all about?" Will asked, walking into the room.

"They wrote another goddamn article about me."

"No shit! What about?"

"About me getting busted. And now some major wants to talk to me. Called my house to see if I was there."

The phone rang.

"Whoa!" Will stepped aside, like the phone was diseased. "You'd better get that, man."

Charlie let it ring a few times. Finally he picked it up.

"Hello?"

"Charlie, is that you?"

"Yes, who is this?"

"Irv Williams." His voice hesitated as if he was waiting to be recognized. "You know, I was your captain in Intelligence."

"Oh, my God, Sir. How the hell are you?"

Irv Williams laughed. "I'm fine. How the hell are you?"

"Okay, I guess. Just got home a few days ago. How did you find me?"

"How did I find you? I come home on leave and you're all over the papers. First you're getting decorated; then you come home; and now you've been arrested."

Charlie was dumbfounded.

"Are you okay, Charlie?"

"Yes, Sir."

"Hey, Charlie, I didn't call to give you shit. I'm calling as a friend. Is everything all right with you?"

"Not really."

"What do you mean?"

"I'm scared, man." Charlie hesitated, gulped. "Not about getting arrested. That was a mistake. I'm scared to be home, Sir."

There was silence on the other end for a moment.

"Listen, Charlie, I know you went through a lot after you left Intelligence…"

"Yeah. And now I come home and the whole damn town knows what I did, because the newspaper printed it. I didn't want anybody to know about that shit. Now, they won't leave me alone."

"I'm sorry. You're a great guy, Charlie. I'm sure things'll settle down for you."

"Thanks. So I heard you're a major now."

"Yes."

"Well, you know what I think about that, don't you?"

"What?"

"I think you're crazy."

Irv was silent for a moment, then he laughed. "Well, maybe I am. Can't get the lifer blood out of me, I guess. I'm going back to Nam tomorrow morning."

Charlie gasped. "Oh, no!"

"It's all right, Charlie. I'll be stationed in the rear again. Probably working in Intelligence, somewhere. Well, I have to go now. You take care of yourself, will you? Maybe we can get together sometime when I get home again."

"Yeah, sure. Hey, Irv?"

"Yes, Charlie."

"Please take care of yourself, man."

19

Charlie and Will stood at ease in front of Judge Parker. They wore dark slacks, white short sleeve shirts, and loosely knotted ties, their hair still wet after early morning surfing in the biggest waves so far that summer.

I can't believe we're here, Charlie thought. *Eight-foot tubes, a hot session in the surf, and now it feels like I'm back in the damn army.*

Judge Parker read the case report. He looked up at the prosecutor, frowned and shook his head.

"Counselor," he said, "approach the bench."

Charlie looked over at Will and shrugged.

"What's going on?" Will whispered, looking concerned.

"Beats me. Maybe they saw the big surf this morning and are trying to figure a way to take the day off."

Will shook his head.

Charlie smiled. "Come on, man, what are they going to do, send us to Nam?"

The prosecutor returned and addressed the court.

"Your honor, obviously there is a lack of evidence in this case. I move that the court drop the charges against Charles Armfield and William Jamison."

"Granted," Judge Parker said.

Charlie reached over to Will for a handclasp.

"I have a few words, gentlemen," Judge Parker said. He looked sternly toward Charlie and Will.

"I've probably done a lot of the same things you young men have done, including fighting in a war. World War II was no picnic; and we drank a fair amount of alcohol to heal our emotional wounds. But, quite frankly, I'm scared to try marijuana. As far as I'm concerned, you're taking a serious risk using the drug. Due to the lack of evidence, we're going to dismiss this case. However, you had better take warning: next time, you will pay. Do you have anything you'd like to say for yourselves before I dismiss?"

A hush hung over the courtroom.

Charlie looked over at Will, who shook his head. Charlie turned to the judge.

"Excuse me, Your Honor, but may I ask you a question?"

"Go right ahead," Judge Parker said, with interest in his voice.

"Your Honor, did you volunteer to serve your country?"

"Yes, I did. I was proud to defend my country in the time of war."

"And rightfully so." Charlie spoke with enthusiasm in his voice. "Our freedom was challenged, and you stepped up in the time of need. And I thank you for that, Sir."

He lowered his voice. "Will and I were drafted, Your Honor. I know there was a draft in World War II, but the difference was that those who were drafted then must have felt that they were defending their country, as you did. We were not defending our country. Therefore, when we killed, it was not because we thought it was the right thing to do. We killed only to keep from being killed ourselves. I agonized about that, Your Honor, and it seemed the only way to keep my sanity was to smoke marijuana. Some soldiers claim it saved their lives."

Charlie glanced over at Will and then turned back to the judge.

"I'm not saying it is good to smoke, just like I wouldn't say it's good to drink. But it was wartime, Your Honor, and now I guess we are still trying to cope with the aftermath."

Charlie hesitated, not knowing if he should continue. Finally he said,

"We came home, and there were protesters condemning us, Sir."
Charlie choked, trying to resist the tears welling in his eyes. "They called
us murderers. I never wanted to kill anyone, Your Honor, and I am not proud
of what I've done."

Judge Parker looked down at Charlie from the bench.

"Thank you for that, Son. I am sorry we do not celebrate and honor
your service in Vietnam."

The judge looked from Charlie to Will, then stared into Charlie's eyes.

"I didn't want to kill anyone either, Charles." He looked stern,
but choked on his words. "After I survived Europe, I was sent to the
South Pacific. I'd had enough of the war, but there was more. And this
time it was in jungles with malaria and leeches. I think you know what that's
like, too. My clothing and skin began to rot with the unceasing rains, and all
of this with the enemy pounding into our positions."

He took a deep breath. "I came home an alcoholic and was arrested
several times before I found my way out. I want you to understand that
nobody wants to go to war. When you are in the middle of battle, you forget
that you're defending your country."

Charlie felt a rush of blood flooding into his face. How embarrassed he
felt for defending marijuana.

Finally he spoke. "May I approach the bench, Your Honor?"

The judge sat back in his chair, looking surprised. "Yes."

Charlie walked up, and paused in front of the bench.

"I have been feeling sorry for myself, Your Honor. I never dreamed…"

"It's okay, Charles. There is no such thing as an easy war. Please be
careful out there."

"I will never smoke again," Charlie whispered, turning to walk back to
stand next to Will.

Judge Parker raised his gavel and said, "Case dismissed."

He slammed the mallet down on the podium behind the bench, and
smiled at Charlie.

Charlie was solemn when he and Will exited the courtroom, but Will
was ready to hit the surf again.

"Come on, Charlie. Let's get back out there."

When they arrived at the beach, the waves were exploding nearly a quarter of a mile out at sea.

"Holy shit! Look at that," Charlie exclaimed. "The swell's picked up and it's really closing out."

Charlie pointed to a wave that broke all at once. "We wouldn't get much of a ride on that."

"You got that right, man. Let's go check out the cliffs."

They shoved their boards in Charlie's van and drove south along the coastline to Sunset Cliffs. Charlie loved the cliffs. The rocky reef bottoms managed the bigger swells better than the beach breaks, with sandy bottoms.

They drove along and checked out the local surf spots—Osprey, Bird Shit Rock, Indicator, Needles Eye, Luscombs, Rockslides. Surfers were in the water at all of them. They drove on to Garbage, where the road ended. Further on down, the surf spots were accessible only by trail, including Charlie's favorite—New Break.

"Let's take a hike, man," Will said. "New Break will be awesome."

Charlie grinned, "I'm with you, Buddy."

"And if it's too crowded there, we'll have Thirty Threes all to ourselves." Will hooted, "Aaaahhhhoooo!"

They grabbed their boards out of the back of Charlie's van and started down the trail. It was over a mile to New Break.

Out in the bush again with Will, Charlie thought. *But this time we get to hump surfboards instead of weapons.*

"I'm sure glad you're here, man," Will said.

"Where the hell else would I be?"

"For a long time, I believed you didn't make it back, that's all. Nobody knew what happened to you; so, naturally, I thought you were dead."

"I'm as alive as you are, buddy, and we're about to catch the biggest swell of the year."

They climbed down the cliff at Abs—nicknamed that because of the great abalone diving at low tide—and walked the additional quarter of a mile down the beach to New Break. A long right hand wave, New Break had become popular over the last few years.

"Holy shit! Look at that crowd," Charlie exclaimed. "Should we go for Thirty Threes?"

"I'm up for it, if you are."

Getting to Thirty Threes, another half mile down the coast, involved walking over slick reef rock and around jagged portions of the cliff. Because the tide came in higher with a large swell, Charlie and Will had to time their progress to avoid being washed up against a crag, and at the same time, walk gingerly so they wouldn't slip.

On the last projecting bluff, Will timed it perfectly, and scooted around before a crashing wave splashed against the cliff. Charlie, tailing Will by a few steps, was hurled against the jagged wall and slammed onto the slab of rock.

"You okay?" Will asked, peering back around the bluff.

"Yeah," Charlie said, standing and wiping blood from a new scratch on his right shoulder. "Just humiliated."

He quickly scanned his surfboard. "Didn't ding my board though." He sprinted around before the next wave came in.

"Hey, where did you get that scar?"

Will pointed to the blemish on Charlie's shoulder, just underneath the new abrasion.

"That doesn't look very old. Did you get cut in Nam?"

Charlie looked at his arm and remembered the altercation with the NVA soldier. What would he have done if the man hadn't been Thom's cousin? Could he have let Thom stab the man while he was holding him? He felt sick to his stomach at the thought of a man dying in his arms.

"You okay, man?" Will asked.

Charlie's recollection faded with Will's words. "Yeah, just remembered something that happened."

"How you got the scar?"

"Just an accident. Hey, that surf is calling, man. Let's get on it."

When they arrived at Thirty Threes, they paddled out into twelve foot surf. Nobody else was out.

"This is it, man," Will shouted over the roar of the breaking waves. "You couldn't ask for it to get better than this. I'm not even scared."

Charlie never thought about being scared. There had been a time when he'd had a natural fear surfing big waves. Now, after having been shot at, and feeling how fragile life was, his fear of the waves was absent.

This is why I survived Vietnam, he thought. *If something happens out here, it will be while I'm playing, not while I'm combating the enemy. For some reason, dying while surfing seemed all right.*

They surfed the colossal breakers for two and a half hours, until they could hardly paddle anymore. The pounding they took while pushing through the white water took its toll on their bodies.

"One more and I'm heading in," Will said. "That is, if I have enough strength to catch one more."

"I know what you mean, man. I must be out of shape for this big stuff."

"Yeah, me, too. Shit! Here comes a set."

Will pointed toward the horizon and started feverishly stroking out. Charlie chased behind, barely making it over the first wave of the biggest set of the day. The second wave was huge. Charlie stroked with all of his ability, but he soon realized he wasn't going to make it over. He slowed down to prepare for the white water.

Will, however, was trying to make it over. Charlie watched his friend thrash up the massive wall of water. Half way up, Will was buried with the turbulence of the breaking curl.

Charlie sucked in air and rolled over into the water, clutching his board with all his strength. The surging white water picked Charlie and his surfboard up like a log being hurled over a waterfall. He held on as tight as he could, but the board was ripped from his hands as he was tossed unmercifully in the churning water. He was held under for what seemed like an eternity.

Finally he surfaced, drew in a quick breath, and dove to the bottom to avoid the advance of the third wave. He repeated his plunge for the fourth, and the fifth; he finally surfaced to a quiet sea. His board had been washed in to shore, and he began his long tread in.

He swam until the water was almost shallow enough to touch the rocky bottom, and noticed that both his and Will's boards were perched on the rocks next to the cliff. *Where's Will?* he wondered. He swam a few more yards until he could put his feet down, and stood up to survey the area.

Will, where the hell are you, man? He scanned the cliffs, but there was no sign of him. In desperation he turned back toward the oncoming surf and saw something floating, nearly a hundred yards out.

What? Oh, no! Not...

He pushed off of the bottom and flew through the water with Olympic strength. He paused, but only to make sure he was still heading in the right direction.

Shit! That's a goddamn body out there.

Will was floating face down when Charlie reached him. Quickly he turned him over.

"Will, speak to me, man. Will!"

No reply—nothing.

Charlie threaded his left arm under Will's armpits. With his right arm stroking, his legs kicking rapidly, he made his way toward the shore.

He flashed back. Will was dragging him to the medevac. It was as though the two of them had become one person in the quest to survive the enemy attack. They shared the same heart, spirits linked. It wasn't any different now. But could he feel Will's spirit this time? *Get into my heart, man,* he pleaded. *Please.*

He pulled Will along until he could get footing on the bottom. He pushed ahead toward a flat rock jutting above the water's surface. He laid Will on top of it, rolled him onto his stomach and turned his head to the side. He pushed on Will's back until water streamed from his mouth. He flipped him over and proceeded with mouth-to-mouth resuscitation.

Come on, man! Breathe!

Still there was no response.

Charlie rolled him over and pushed on his back again, but no water came out. Again he tried mouth-to-mouth. He stopped and put his ear onto Will's chest.

Nothing—no beat, no throb.

Charlie lifted Will's head and saw blood. Will had been struck by something on the temple, perhaps his own surfboard.

No, man, you can't go now. Please, Will. Come back, man.

He pumped on Will's chest. *Beat! Goddamn it, beat!*

Desperately, he tried mouth-to-mouth again—listened to the heart—pumped on the chest—mouth-to-mouth—listened to the heart.

Will was dead.

Charlie laid on the rock next to his friend and sobbed.

No, man. Nooooo!

When he gazed up, he saw puffy white clouds whisking slowly across the sky. They began to take on forms, creating shapes. He saw a face—Will's face, he thought—in the haze. But then the eyes pulled back, took on a slant. More appeared, gooks surrounded him, firing weapons all around. He covered his head and rolled over onto Will.

Just shoot me, Motherfucker. You've already killed Will. Just shoot me, too. Get it over with, man. He stood on the rock and shouted at the top of his lungs, "Just shoot me!"

The sound of his voice cracked the illusion. He looked down and saw Will, put his head into his hands, and wept again.

A wave gently washed in, covering Charlie's feet and enveloping Will's body. Charlie knelt down and put his ear on Will's chest, seeking a pulse one last time. There was none.

Slowly, he leaned over and picked up the body, and carried his friend out of the great sea.

It was dim and foggy outside the Ocean Beach Methodist Church. The morning air was thick and cool, unusual for late June. Inside, the mood was equally solemn. The dark clad congregation lined the pews, waiting for the funeral service to begin.

There was no casket. Will had been buried in a private ceremony earlier that morning at the National Cemetery on Point Loma, less than a mile from where he'd died. He received full military honors, and was buried next to thousands of other war veterans. The only attendants at that ceremony were the members of the Jamison family, the Reverend Armfield, and Charlie.

Charlie sat next to Nate Jamison and Gage Saltman at the funeral. He looked at the numerous bouquets of flowers, and then at his father who was dressed in a black robe and holding a Bible at the front of the sanctuary.

"Dearly Beloved," Reverend Armfield began. "We are gathered here today to honor the life of Will Jamison."

Charlie put his head down as his father continued. *How can this be happening,* he thought. *I need Will. He's my only confidant in the whole world. Nobody will ever understand what's happened. Shit, Will! How can I make it without you, man?*

Music followed his father's opening statement. When the final organ note faded, Reverend Armfield gazed out into the assemblage, and made eye contact with Charlie. When he nodded, Charlie stood and made his way to the aisle. Slowly, he walked up to his father and hugged him.

"Why, Daddy, why?" Charlie whispered.

His father shrugged his shoulders, and shook his head. A single tear ran down his cheek.

Charlie turned and saw all of his surf club friends sitting at attention.

His father had asked him to speak at the service, but how to begin? He took a deep breath.

Here goes nothing, big guy. Just let the words come out.

"Most of you know that Will and I have done many things together." He shook his head. "We've been to hell and back again, man. Vietnam!"

He turned and looked at his father.

Reverend Armfield nodded, and confidence surged through Charlie's veins. He wiped a tear on the sleeve of his suit jacket, cleared his throat, and continued.

"You know, we've also been in heaven together. We've surfed in some unbelievable waves. And while surfing, we were great friends, sharing the Mother Ocean of life. While serving in the trenches of combat, we were blood brothers in the fire of death. Once before, I thought Will was gone while we served in those fires, but then I came home and he was here. Needless to say, I was overwhelmed.

"Is he gone now? No!" Charlie said, raising his voice.

"He will never be gone," he continued quietly. "A lieutenant in Nam told me that only the body dies—the person doesn't. 'We are human beings,' he said. 'The human is the body. The being is the person, and will live eternally.' He will always be with us in spirit and in memories. We will have the memories of our comrades forever. They can never be taken from us."

"Will, my friend," Charlie said, looking up, and stretching his hands toward the ceiling. "Strange how we survived all of that crap together and now you go like this. All I can say is, I'm glad it was surfing, and not that other damn way." His voice rang of hysteria. "You did it doing what you truly loved, man. I commend you for that. When I join you someday, I hope I can do it in style, just like you did. See you around, my friend."

Charlie hugged his father and turned to walk back to his seat. Family, friends, everyone wept. When he returned to his pew, Gage and Nate stood and embraced Charlie.

"That was beautiful, man," Gage said.

"Thanks, Charlie," Nate said.

After the service, Charlie met with Mr. and Mrs. Jamison.

"I'm sorry," Charlie said, shaking Mr. Jamison's hand. "I wish it could have been different."

"Thank you for speaking, Charlie," Will's mother said. "Will would have wanted it that way."

"Would you mind if I took one of the bouquets?" Charlie asked.

"Of course not," Mrs. Jamison said. "You take what you want."

Charlie took one of the white flower arrangements, walked out to his van, and drove down Sunset Cliffs Boulevard to the end. The sun began to poke out from behind the clouds, and the temperature was rising. He changed into his surfing trunks and walked all the way to Thirty Threes, his surfboard and flowers in hand.

Unlike the previous day, the surf was flat when Charlie knee paddled out, the flowers resting on the nose of his board. When he was well outside of the breaker line, he sat and contemplated.

Will, I wanted you to tough this living stuff out with me, man. I don't know if I can do it alone or not.

He reached forward, pulled a daisy out of the bunch, and flung it out onto the water.

Maybe I envy you, he thought. *You don't have to live with Nam in your veins anymore.* He pulled out a rose and smelled it, then pulled the petals off one at a time and threw them onto the water.

He continued with the rest of the bouquet, making each blossom a ceremony. Then he paddled in.

A man wearing a black suit, his trousers rolled up, was wading out into the water. At first Charlie couldn't see who it was, but when he got closer, he recognized his father.

"Want to borrow my board?" Charlie said, chuckling.

"I don't think I'd know what do to with it, Son. Are you okay?"

"No." Charlie stepped off of his surfboard. He looked into his father's eyes.

"I don't think I want to live anymore, Dad."

John Armfield put his arm around Charlie. They walked out of the water and sat on the rocks.

"I killed a lot of people, Dad," he said, weeping. "I wanted to avoid it, but I couldn't. And then it just kept happening, over and over again. Honest, Dad, I didn't want to do it."

Charlie's dad hugged him and cried, too.

"Oh, Charlie, you only did what your country asked you to do."

"But the war is wrong. It can't be won. It's a waste of time. I killed for no reason, Dad."

Charlie looked out toward the horizon. "Now, I have to live with my sins. I'm scared, Dad. I don't know what to do. And now Will's dead, too. He was the only one..."

"There are others you can talk to, Charlie. Will was special because he was there with you."

"He's the only one who knows what happened."

"Yes, that's true, but he's not the only one you can talk to. There are people who specialize in..."

"There's no way in hell I'm going to a shrink. They don't have any idea what Nam is like. I don't care what kind of training they've had."

"Son, I know a minister who has been doing some work with..."

Charlie interrupted. "Was he in Vietnam?"

"No, but..."

Charlie shook his head and turned away.

"I know this may be hard to understand now, Son, but your pain can help you to do things—great things. These hard times will pass, but you may need some help to get through them."

Charlie listened to his father, not really comprehending what was said. *Who could he talk to?*

Wait a minute. What about Harry, the Reverend Harry Finney? He was in Vietnam; he wanted me to come to Colorado.

20

Charlie's 1960 VW van labored up into the Rocky Mountains, creeping along the switchbacks of the steep grade. He thought he would never reach the top. But the sign read: Berthoud Pass—Elevation 11,314 feet. He had been driving across the country for the past two days on his way to Grand Lake, Colorado, to find the Reverend Harry Finney. Berthoud Pass was his last big obstacle.

It's all down hill from here, he thought.

It was nightfall when Charlie drove past the sign reading: Welcome to Grand Lake Village—Elevation 8,369—Population 369. Grand Avenue, the town's single main street, was five blocks long. Near its end, he parked in front of The Lariat Saloon, and stepped out to stretch his legs. The air seemed cool for summertime.

Harry had said his parents had a summer place. Charlie wondered if he'd even be there.

A glance around told him that the saloon was the only lighted business. *Oh well,* he thought, *maybe someone in there knows Harry.*

He stepped up onto the wooden boardwalk. The hand-etched sign over the saloon door read:

There is nothing which has not been contrived by man, by which so much happiness is produced, as by a good tavern or inn.
                                        —*Benjamin Franklin*

Okay, Ben, whatever you say, he thought.

Charlie walked through the bar's swinging doors. He saw men wearing cowboy hats lined up at the long bar, and immediately felt out of place in his Gordon and Smith Surfboards T-shirt, shorts and sandals. Cautiously he meandered toward the group and took a seat on a stool.

"Excuse me, Sir," Charlie said to the bartender.

"What'll you have, stranger?" The man was short, portly, with a thick handle bar mustache. He wore wire-rimmed spectacles, a white shirt, jeans with suspenders, and a red handkerchief around his neck.

Charlie smiled. He glanced around the establishment and noted it was just like in a western movie.

"Actually, I'm looking for someone who has a summer place up here."

The barkeeper frowned. "Looking for a weekender, huh? I don't know very many of those. What's his name?"

"Harry Finney. Actually he is the Reverend Harry Finney."

The barkeeper stared for a moment, then glanced toward the back corner of the room.

"I think you'll find him sitting over there. He's been here all afternoon. In fact, he's been in here every day this week. We've been kicking him out so we can close the place up at nights."

Charlie turned on the barstool and checked out the situation. Harry was leaning over the table, his head lying between his arms. An empty bottle of whiskey sat in front of him. A half-filled shot glass perched in his right hand.

"I heard he went to Vietnam," the bartender said.

Charlie nodded. "Yeah, he did."

Charlie stared for a moment wondering what he should do. Finally, he stepped over to the table and gently shook Harry's shoulder.

"Hey, Harry. Is that you, man?"

Harry grumbled, but didn't stir.

"Harry, it's me, Charlie. We were on the plane together coming home from Vietnam."

Harry lifted his head and squinted. "Charlie?"

"Yeah, man. Let me help you out of here."

Charlie took the shot glass out of Harry's hand and set it on the table. He grabbed Harry under his arm, stood him up, and helped him stagger out of the saloon. *Shit! What'll I do with him now?*

"Harry, where do you live, man?"

"Crossa lake," Harry slurred.

"Across the lake?"

Harry nodded.

"Okay, man. I'll drive you home."

Harry shook his head back and forth.

"What do you mean, no."

"No road," Harry slurred.

"How in the hell do you get home?"

"Boat."

"Boat?"

Charlie poured Harry into his van and drove down by the lake. He found a lonely rowboat tethered to the dock.

"A rowboat, Harry?"

"Row," Harry mumbled. "Row home." Harry stuck his head out of the window and heaved.

What have I gotten myself into, Charlie wondered. *He seemed like such a nice guy on the plane.*

Charlie walked gingerly around the van. He opened the door and caught Harry as he fell out. He wrestled him into the boat and shoved off into the night. The lake was quiet. A waxing moon lit the way. Charlie could see lights in several cabins on the other side, but which one was Harry's?

"Harry, which one is yours, man?"

Harry had passed out in the bottom of the boat. Charlie continued to row, looking for some kind of a sign.

"Harry?" a female voice called. "Is that you?"

Charlie saw a woman standing on a dock.

"Harry?" she repeated.

"Harry's with me, Ma'am. I'm Charlie Armfield."

"Charlie Armfield?"

Charlie continued working the oars. The shapely woman stared cautiously at the boat.

"Yes, Ma'am. I met Harry on the plane from Vietnam."

"Oh, yes. Harry told me about you. I'm Patty, his wife. Where is he?"

Charlie pulled up next to the dock and pointed to the floor of the boat. "Right here, Ma'am."

"Oh, Harry! Not again!"

The next morning, Charlie rose early, a half-hour before daybreak. Wrapped in a blanket, he sat at the end of the dock awaiting the sun's appearance over the crest of the ominous, high mountain ridges surrounding Grand Lake. As the mist dissipated, the lake water appeared to be a dark blue-black color. When light began to fill the valley, reflections of the trees appeared on the water's surface.

As he stared in fascination at the glassy, mirror-like water, his head felt clear, freed from distractions. He drew in a deep breath. *I feel so light,* he thought. *Am I even in my body now? Harry was right about this mountain air.*

He focused on the water. Soon he felt as though he was part of the water, floating freely in the shimmering liquid. A fish surfaced to snag a low-flying mosquito and disappeared. Ripples displaced from a small circle and moved outward. Slow, lapping waves pulled his eyes toward shore.

Suddenly he heard a low moan. A low, penetrating female sound, it seemed to come from the middle of the lake. Was it real? Or had he imagined it? He held still, watching the water. He heard it again, but saw nobody. He concentrated on the spot where the sound seemed to come from.

The sun rose higher in the sky, warming his face. Charlie stood and threw off the blanket—took off his shirt, challenging the sun to penetrate his skin. The sky was the deepest blue he'd ever seen. He sucked air in through his nose and exhaled loudly through his mouth.

He heard it again—the cry from the lake. *Come,* it seemed to say. And again, *Come!*

Charlie unbuckled the clasp on his shorts and when they dropped off, dove into the water. It felt smooth and refreshing as he stroked under the surface, but suddenly, it hit him. *Holy shit! It's like ice.* He kicked frantically toward the surface and gasped as he popped his head out of the water. "Wooooo!"

As he started to swim back, he saw Harry's wife walking out onto the dock. She looked different in the light—long, red hair—pretty.

"A little chilly out there, isn't it, Charlie?"

"You're telling me," Charlie shuddered. What was he going to do? Buck-naked in the middle of the coldest water he'd ever experienced, and a woman standing on the dock where his clothes were lying in a heap.

She looked down, saw the clothes, and smiled. "How long will you be visiting Colorado?"

"Excuse me?" Charlie's ears were ringing. Is she trying to make casual conversation while I'm out here freezing?

"I said, how long will you be visiting in Colorado?"

"I'm…I'm not sure."

She giggled, "Maybe you should come out of the water and get warmed up."

She turned her back to Charlie.

Charlie stroked as fast as his frozen limbs would allow, clumsily pulled himself onto the dock, and slipped into his shorts.

"It's okay now, Ma'am," he stammered, pulling his T-shirt over his head.

She turned around, picked up the blanket, and held it up, offered to wrap it around him.

"Call me, Patty."

"I, d-d-didn't know that the water would be that c-c-cold," he said, snuggling into the blanket.

She smiled, then Charlie heard footsteps on the dock.

"Patty, what's going on?"

"You have a visitor, darling."

Harry walked out and stared at Charlie, his hair soaking wet, bundled in the wrap. "Charlie?"

"H-hi-i, Harry," he said, unable to stop shivering.

"Did you swim over here, Charlie?"

Patty laughed, "No, he didn't swim over here, silly. He rowed over here last night. Don't you remember?"

Harry ran his hand through his hair. His eyes were bloodshot and he appeared to be unsteady on his feet.

"I found you in the Lariat Saloon last night, Harry," Charlie said.

Harry's face turned red as he stared, speechless.

"Hey, don't worry about it, man," Charlie said, laughing. "We all tie one on once in a while." He knelt down close to the edge of the dock and stuck his hand into the water. "Come on down here, Reverend, and stick your face into this water. It'll make you feel better."

Harry stretched out on the wooden boards and dipped his head in. "Woo! I can't believe you went swimming in this," he whooped. "You surfers must be crazy!"

Later, Charlie sat drinking coffee with Harry and Patty, a stack of pancakes in front of him.

"How did you find me, Charlie?" Harry asked.

"Just lucky. I remembered you telling me about Grand Lake, so I came here first. When I arrived, the saloon was the only place open."

Harry, looking sheepish, lowered his head.

"Is everything all right, man?" Charlie asked.

Harry looked at Patty, apparently uncertain what to say.

"It's okay, Harry. Tell him. You've been in the bar almost every night since you got home from Vietnam. Maybe Charlie can help you."

Maybe I can help him, Charlie thought to himself. *But I came here so he could help me.*

"What is it, Harry?"

Harry's eyes welled up with tears. "I can't sleep Charlie. It's like I'm afraid to close my eyes unless I'm drunk. That's the only time I don't see the faces."

A single tear began to roll down Harry's cheek.

"What faces, Harry?"

"I don't get it, Charlie. I wasn't involved with the contact like you were. But I saw many dead American soldiers, their bodies mangled, some beyond recognition. People I knew from counseling sessions and from services I'd conducted. I'd talked to them and they'd showed me pictures of their families. Some of them were short-timers. I wanted to help them. They couldn't talk...pain, Charlie...I felt their pain."

Charlie sat still, hardly believing what he was hearing. *Oh, God. He hurts as bad as I do, and he didn't even kill anyone.*

"I looked at those soldiers, Charlie, and felt God had betrayed us. Where was he? Why in the hell was he letting that happen?" Harry raised his voice. "Why, God, Why? Please tell me it's only a nightmare!" He struck the table and looked at Charlie, rage in his eyes. "But it wasn't a dream, it was real. Dead bodies everywhere, being loaded onto a chopper—so many they were sliding back out. God. You sonofabitch!"

Harry put his head down on his arms. Patty scooted next to him and put her arm around his shoulder. Charlie sat speechless.

"I'm sorry," Harry sobbed, trying to quiet himself. "I don't know what gets into me."

"It's okay, darling," Patty said. She looked at Charlie, seeking support for her husband.

Charlie sighed. "I saw those bodies, too, man." He took a deep breath. "I saw them and wondered how God could choose who should die and who should live. Nobody wanted to be there. One guy had a Bible verse with him that said something about trusting in God and he will give his angels to guard you. But even if you trusted in God, I don't think there were enough angels to guard everyone in Vietnam."

Charlie sighed. He was stoic, composed.

Harry stared into Charlie's eyes.

"I saw gooks without angels, too, Harry. I counted twenty-seven. Took their lives, without really knowing why, took them away from their families."

Now tears began to roll down Charlie's face. He could hardly mumble his words. "I didn't want them to die, man. But I had to do it, or they would have killed me."

Both Harry and Patty gawked at Charlie. He grabbed the napkin next to his plate, wiped his eyes and blew his nose.

"I killed way more than that, too—hundreds, maybe thousands—that I never saw because it was artillery that killed them. There couldn't have been enough angels, man."

Harry shook his head and smiled, "You're right, Charlie."

"About what?"

"There weren't enough angels. We all have angels, Charlie, but God knows when they need to be back in heaven. When it's time for us all to go to heaven, God calls his angels home so we can follow. All of this time, I've been mad at God. But he knows, Charlie. I never thought about it this way until you said there weren't enough angels."

Charlie sighed, shrugged his shoulders. "I don't know about all that, Harry."

"Psalm 91, verse eleven says, 'For he will give his angels charge of you, to guard you in all your ways.' Even if it's time to die, Charlie."

"That's the verse—the one the dead guy had." Charlie was looking into the light brown eyes of the sympathetic chaplain he remembered from the plane coming home. They were warm and appeared to reach out in a friendly embrace.

Charlie put his arms around Harry. Patty moved her chair behind and hugged them both.

"You guys feel like family," Charlie said quietly, thinking of his parents back home.

"We are family, Charlie," Patty replied.

They sat in silence for several moments.

Finally Harry snickered. "Charlie, what in God's name possessed you to swim in the lake?"

"I heard a voice."

"What?" Patty said, sitting back from them.

"I was really in a trance, watching the reflections in the water, and all of a sudden I heard this moan. I didn't think anything of it at first, then I heard it again. I looked around but there was nobody in sight."

"What did it sound like?" Patty asked.

"Like a woman, I think, a deep female voice that vibrated through my whole body. When I heard it again, it sounded like it was saying 'Come.' That's when I dove in."

"Just like that?" Harry questioned.

"Yeah. I don't know what got into me. It was so impulsive, I didn't take time to think." Charlie shrugged. "I just dove in."

Patty sighed, her eyes beaming with the story.

"Is there something I should know?" Charlie asked.

Patty opened her mouth, but Harry spoke first.

"There's an old tale about the lake, Charlie. Let's take a hike. We'll tell you about it later."

Charlie remained at the Grand Lake cabin for nearly a week before deciding to go home.

"I'm going back to Highway 40," he said. "Thought I'd head over to Salt Lake City and across to Frisco. There's some great cold-water surfing

just south of there around Santa Cruz. I surfed in a contest there one time."
He grinned. "Figure I'm used to cold water after being in that damn lake."

Harry laughed, "You got a surfboard in that van?"

Charlie nodded. "Of course."

"Okay, but before you go, you have to drive over Trail Ridge Road. Don't ask why, just do it. You can drive down the other side into Estes Park, and catch up with Highway 40 in Denver."

"Okay, man, whatever you say. Hey, you never did tell me the tale about Grand Lake."

Harry sighed and looked at his wife. "Patty, you know more about it. You tell him."

Patty's eyes widened. "Well, Grand Lake was named by a white man. Before that, the Indians called it Spirit Lake."

"Spirit Lake?"

"Yes, Charlie. The story is that a band of Ute Indians used to frequent this area—about a hundred warriors and more than a hundred and sixty women and children.

"For three days and nights there were storms on the lake. The Utes believed that was bad luck. They thought ghosts and goblins were born from the winds. Then the wolf began to howl. The mountain lion roared and the owl hooted—all signals of danger. When the whippoorwill sang, their leader, Chief Chekiwow, prepared the warriors for battle. Sure enough, a wild band of painted Arapahoe warriors appeared."

"Oh, no. This peaceful area was the sight of a war?" Charlie asked.

"Afraid so," Harry said. "I was hoping you didn't have to hear this story. But that's not all. Go ahead, Patty."

"The men went into battle, the women loaded the children and themselves on rafts and paddled into the middle of the lake for safety.

"The battle was vicious. Many men lost their lives until Chief Chekiwow of the Utes, and Chief Red Wolf of the Arapahoes met face to face. Both waved their hands high, signaling a cease-fire to their men. They agreed to finish the battle with single combat.

"The two leaders fought with spears until Chekiwow disarmed his foe. He would not kill an unarmed man so he, too, dropped his spear and they fought with knives to the finish, until the Ute chief became victorious.

"That should have been the end of the bloodshed, but Black Bear, second in command of the Arapahoe band, decided to revenge the death of Red Wolf. He led the Arapahoe to kill Chekiwow and all of the Utes, save one. That one slipped away into the foothills where he hid out to survey the battleground.

"That's when he witnessed the storm. Winds blew harder than ever before. Waves splashed over the rafts and canoes in the middle of the lake. One after another sank. All the women and children drowned."

Charlie listened, spellbound.

"The escapee fled to a neighboring Ute band and told of the battle. Chief Black Eagle gathered his Ute warriors and eventually defeated the Arapahoe. But the damage was done. From that day forward the Indians considered the lake to be haunted. Thus the name, Spirit Lake."

Charlie stared at the ground. *Are there wars in all of the beautiful places in the world,* he wondered.

"Charlie," Harry said. "There are people who claim to hear voices coming from the depths of the lake. That's why we were so interested when you talked about hearing strange sounds."

"Have you two heard them?"

"No," Patty said sadly. "I've spent hours out on the dock listening, but never have heard them. You must be special, Charlie."

Charlie swallowed. "Has anyone ever dived down there?"

"There have been a few attempts," Harry said. "But Grand Lake is the deepest lake in Colorado, 265 feet down. I think it's too dangerous."

Charlie sighed. "Well, I guess I'd better hit the road."

"I'll row you back," Harry said, smiling. "I think I owe you one."

Charlie hugged Patty. "Thanks for the story."

When they reached the boat, Charlie jumped in at the stern. "Do you think it's true?"

Patty nodded and waved as Harry rowed toward Grand Lake Village.

"Thanks for helping me figure out the angels," Harry said.

"What angels?"

"The angels in Vietnam. They were always with us, Charlie, even if they were leading some of us to heaven. In the heat of the battle, I forgot that God is always in charge. I can sleep in peace now, and I owe it all to you. I'm never going to drink again, my friend."

And I'm never going to smoke again, Charlie said to himself, *but I don't think I'm any closer to figuring anything out. That's why I came here, Harry. You were supposed to help me. All I learned was about another war.*

From Grand Lake to the top of Trail Ridge Road was nearly thirty miles. Charlie soon discovered why Harry wanted him to take the drive. The road wound way up—far above the tree line—to 12,183 feet above sea level. Alpine tundra, the only vegetation able to survive at that altitude, grew at a rate of one inch every hundred years. It seemed like a timeless place.

He pulled into a scenic-view area and parked. He walked out to a ledge and sat on a rock overlooking the vast mountain range, feeling as if he were on top of the world.

The world is so big, he thought, *and here I am above it all. Vietnam seems so far away. From way up here, you would never guess there's so much trouble in the world.*

Dear God, is this closer to heaven? Can I communicate with my dead friends from up here? Will, where are you, man? Strangeman, are you up here?

He thought about Al Strangemeir, his wife and their baby daughter. How old would little Becky be now? Fifteen, maybe sixteen months? He remembered Al, so proud, showing off the picture from his R&R in Hawaii.

"Someday I want my daughter to meet you, Arm. I want her to meet special people," Al had said.

"What makes you think I'm a special person?"

"You're a man of conscience, Arm. You're concerned about the killing. I feel safe and blessed when you're around. I'd like my daughter and my wife to meet you."

"I'll be happy to meet the ladies in your life, Al."

Did I say that? he thought. *You're dead now, Al— do you still want me to meet them?*

"Come."

What the hell was that? The voice from the lake?

"Come."

There it is again.

Charlie jumped down off of the rock and hurried back to his van. He inserted the keys into the ignition and jammed into first gear, heading for Virginia Beach.

21

Charlie drove east through Colorado and Kansas. He pulled into a rest area outside of Topeka and stretched out in the van's bunk. Although he was tired, he slept restlessly and dreamed about Vietnam.

He and Will were climbing Hill 595. Charlie raised his weapon, squeezed the trigger. A dead gook tumbled down the hill. He jumped out of the way to keep from getting crushed. Number eight. Robinson hurt— oh my God, Hawkins, blown up, into a million pieces. Will, in trouble, throw grenade—ka boom! Three dead, intestines hanging out, no arms or legs, no head—nine, ten, eleven—don't do that, man, no counting—no counting—no counting—no...

Charlie woke, drenched in sweat, yelling. "No counting! No counting! No...no..." He rolled over and smashed his fist against a pillow, "no counting, man!"

He checked his watch—2 a.m. He settled back, but couldn't sleep. Finally, around five o'clock, he climbed back into the driver's seat and headed east. He felt groggy; his head was spinning from the lack of restful sleep.

The sunrise cast an orange glow over the plains. *A new day dawning,* he thought. *What an incredible way to begin. If only life could begin again as easily.* The glow spread through him, warmed him, rejuvenated him.

By noon, fatigue sifted in again. Maybe I'll stop and call my parents from St. Louis, he thought. It's Thursday; his folks would be home. Tomorrow, July Fourth, they would be away, probably at his grandparents.

He followed Interstate 70 into the city until he saw the banks of the Mississippi River and Eads Bridge. *What in the world?* He pulled off the highway on Market Street, parked, and stepped out of his van, gawking at the immense steel arch. *Oh yeah, I remember reading about that thing.*

He walked into the Jefferson National Expansion Memorial park where the Gateway Arch stood, noting that Missouri's blistering heat, mixed with high humidity, felt like Vietnam. He followed museum visitors inside and learned that the massive arch, not yet four years old, stood 630 feet high and was equally as wide.

He stepped into a phone booth, dropped in a dime, and dialed the operator.

"I'd like to make a collect call to San Diego, please. Academy 2-8277. I'm Charlie."

"Hello?" his dad answered.

"Yes, I have a collect call for anyone from Charlie. Will you accept?"

"Yes, of course. Charlie?"

"Hi Dad. What's happening?"

"Not much, Son. Where are you?"

"I'm at the most amazing place, Dad. Have you ever heard of the giant arch by the Mississippi River?"

"You're in St. Louis?"

"Yeah. It's unbelievable."

"Where are you going?"

"Virginia Beach. I have to go visit someone there."

"But, Charlie, don't you think you should come home?"

"Can't, Dad. Have you ever heard of Trail Ridge Road?"

"In Colorado?"

"Yeah. Have you been up there?"

"Your mother and I went last summer when you were visiting Mike in Thailand."

Charlie hesitated, remembering his visit with Mike.

"We thought if you were on vacation, we could go, too."

"What? You guys were alone, you could go any time you wanted to."

"No, Charlie, we wouldn't have enjoyed a trip while you were in Vietnam."

"Dad, I visited a minister in Colorado."

"Who?"

"Harry Finney. He was an army chaplain in Vietnam. I met him on the plane coming home."

"Great, Charlie!"

"Yeah, but he's having a lot of trouble, too—nightmares and everything. Now I'm going to go meet the wife of one of my dead friends."

"Whoa, Charlie."

"I know, Dad. Maybe I'm crazy, but I have this feeling I'm supposed to go there."

"Then there must be a reason, Son. Sometimes you have to go with your gut feeling. Take care of yourself, okay? Your mother wants to talk to you."

Charlie reassured his mother that he was fine and would call again soon. Outside, a thick spreading maple tree offered a cooler patch of shade. He stretched out and slept.

The explosion woke him. Quickly he rolled and low-crawled behind the tree to survey the area. It was dusk. *Where had it come from? Where were the gooks?* The rising three-quarter moon shone beyond the arch. *Arch? Arch! What?*

When he realized where he was, he stood and brushed himself off. Then he heard the laughter.

A group of Shriners dressed in ceremonial caps, stood nearby holding their bellies, laughing at Charlie.

"What's going on?" Charlie said, glaring at the group.

"Just a little Independence Day fun," one of the men said.

"Fireworks? Shit! I thought it was a goddamn grenade."

They stared at Charlie. Finally, one spoke up.

"Grenade? What's the matter with you? It was just a little cherry bomb."

Charlie sighed, "I don't know…I don't know what's the matter with me."

He shook his head, turned and walked back to his van. *Shit. What is the matter with me?*

When he crossed the Mississippi River, into East St. Louis, it was dark.

He needed gas and stopped at a filling station. The sign on the pump read twenty-one cents per gallon.

The gas station attendant, a young black man, reminded him of Sprint—killed on gun number five. Wasn't he from Illinois, from Rockford?

"Where's Rockford?" Charlie asked.

"That's way up north. I thought you wanted gas."

"Yeah, yeah, fill'er up. How far is it to Louisville?"

Charlie started across the Hampton Roads Bridge and Tunnel, seventeen miles northeast of Virginia Beach. He pulled up to the north-side tollbooth and gave the man twenty-five cents. *Ah, the ocean,* he thought. *It's not the Pacific, but it is an ocean.*

He drove along the Chesapeake Bay on Shore Drive until he reached the beach, then south along Atlantic Avenue. *Not much wave action around here,* he thought, gazing at the swells.

The first main road he came to was Virginia Beach Boulevard. He turned west and pulled into a service station—went to the phone booth.

Can't be too many Strangemeirs, he thought, thumbing through the white pages of the directory. *There he is! "Albert Strangemeir." Wonder if that's Al or his father?* Al hadn't talked much about his parents. He memorized the address and walked into the station.

"Excuse me, Sir, can you tell me how to get to Twentieth Street?"

The attendant, an elderly man with gray stubble on his chin and wearing a sea captain's hat, pointed west along Virginia Beach Boulevard.

"Head that a way. Turn left on Holly. Follow 'er around, it'll run into Twentieth. Where are you from?"

"San Diego. Drove across the country to visit somebody."

"Must be someone important."

Charlie nodded. *Yeah,* he thought, *must be. Should I get wet? Nah, surf's too small. Should I call? Better not, might freak them out. I'll just drive over and see if anyone's home.*

He pulled up in front of the small, light blue home, opened the van door and stepped out. Flowering shrubs grew around the house. The front sidewalk was cracked and heaving.

Suddenly, a young woman opened the front door and screamed "Help, Mister! Help me!"

Charlie swallowed his surprise and dashed onto the porch and followed her into the house. She ran to the kitchen. A little girl—face blue, not breathing—sat in a high chair, a half-eaten hot dog was on the tray.

Charlie pulled the child out, put his arm around her waist and held her face down while he slapped her back—hard. Out popped a wad of food an inch-and-a-half in diameter. The child gasped to catch her breath, panted in and out, and started crying. Charlie turned her over and cradled her in his arms.

"It's all right now, Becky. Everything's going to be just fine." He looked at the woman and handed the child to her.

"Oh! My poor baby," she cried, embracing the child, stroking her back.

Charlie looked around the kitchen and at the dirty dishes on the table, settings for three. Where were the others?

A man about twenty-five years old walked through the front door. "What's going on?"

Charlie turned to him, "Becky was choking."

"Oh my God!" He put his arm around the woman. "Lisa, is she okay?"

"Yes. Thanks to this nice man."

The man turned toward Charlie and held out his hand.

"Jack Strangemeir. Whatever you did, I thank you."

The woman looked into Charlie's eyes, then her mouth opened. "How did you know her name?"

"Whose name?" Charlie replied.

"My daughter's name. You called her by her name."

Jack and the woman stared at Charlie.

"Al told me. I met Al in Vietnam. He told me about you and Becky. I'm sorry, Lisa. I intended to introduce myself."

Lisa put Becky down on the floor. "You knew Al?" She seemed surprised.

"Yes, Ma'am. We were good friends. I'm Charlie Armfield."

Lisa stared, shaking her head.

"You can't be. Charlie Armfield was killed with my husband. They were on the same gun."

Charlie gasped. He felt blood rushing into his face. His mouth opened, but no words came out.

"Who the hell are you, mister?" Jack demanded, lowering his eyebrows.

"I got called into basecamp before it happened," Charlie said, tears welling up in his eyes. "I could have been there, too."

"Did Al tell you about Charlie?" Jack asked Lisa, speaking as if Charlie weren't in the room.

"Yes. He thought Charlie was the greatest guy he'd ever met."

"Did Al say where Armfield was from?"

"California."

"He has California license plates on his van," Jack said.

Lisa turned toward Charlie. "Al told me Charlie had a sport."

"Yes ma'am, I'm a surfer."

"Oh my God." Lisa began to cry.

Jack stared at Charlie. "Wait a minute, Charlie Armfield, the San Diego surfer?"

"You know him?" Lisa asked, surprised.

"I saw him at the surf movie—a promotional for the World Contest."

"I never made that contest, Jack." Charlie spoke softly. "I got drafted before it happened."

Al and Betty Strangemeir, the parents of Charlie's dead friend, walked in. They had taken a stroll after dinner. Lisa and Becky had lived with them ever since their son, Al Jr., went to Vietnam. Jack, their other son, lived three blocks away on Baltic Avenue. Everyone was pleased to meet Charlie; they invited him to join them for the Fourth of July celebration that evening with their daughter, Marilyn and her family.

Marilyn and her husband, a medical doctor, had three sons, Matthew six, Luke eight, and Daniel, eleven. Their home had a large, beautifully landscaped backyard. Charlie thought most of the family treated him well. Almost as if he was their dead relative. Everyone except Marilyn, that is.

"You were on Al's gun? How ironic you didn't die, too."

"It wasn't my doing, Ma'am," Charlie said, feeling embarrassed.

"Marilyn," Betty said, shocked by her daughter's comment.

Charlie felt ashamed. *I'm thinking I would have preferred it that way,* he said to himself.

Betty made sure he had plenty to eat. There was no more mention of Vietnam. Charlie relaxed into the setting and drank a few beers with Al, Sr. *They're a real family,* he thought, realizing that he'd never given his own family a chance. *I stayed away. Why am I so scared to talk to them, my own family?*

He felt comfortable with the Srangemeirs chattering and laughing all around him. When Marilyn's oldest boy, Daniel, and his father went into the corner of the yard, Charlie didn't think much of it. When a firecracker blew, he dropped to the ground.

"Hit it!" he yelled.

More fireworks exploded. Charlie hugged the ground, sweat dripping from his underarms. He raised his head—saw the boy throwing a lighted fuse into the alley behind the yard. Ka boom!

Oh no, he thought, *not again.* He saw Betty running to the boy with her arms up in the air to stop him. Then it was quiet.

Charlie covered his face—felt the family staring down at him. *Shit,* he thought. *I feel like such a fool.*

"Are you all right, Charlie?" Lisa asked.

Charlie stood up and brushed the grass from his clothing. "Yeah, I'm…I'm sorry," he stuttered. "I don't know what got into me." He stared at the ground.

Marilyn snickered. Charlie thought she was mad at him for surviving the demise of gun number five.

Then Al, Sr. spoke up. "It's okay, Charlie. I remember when I came home. It took me a long time to relax."

Charlie gazed into his eyes—no words were necessary.

The party continued as if nothing had happened. Still embarrassed, Charlie slipped away by himself. *Damn it all, anyway. You sure made a spectacle out of yourself. Shit!*

"Charlie," Lisa said, walking up behind him.

"Hi, Lisa."

"Will you stay with us for a while? I asked my in-laws and they'd like that, too."

"Well, I don't know."

"Please. We need you to stay with us, Charlie. We hurt." her eyes were red.

Charlie reached out and she grabbed his hand willingly.

"You're the only one who knows," Lisa continued. "Someday, Charlie, we need to know from you what happened to Al."

Charlie stayed with the Strangemeirs, sleeping on the couch in the living room. Jack, Al Jr.'s surfing sibling, came every morning to take

Charlie to Seventeenth Street Beach. They surfed, visited surf shops, and met some of the top East Coast surfers in the area. Everyone remembered Charlie from the World Contest Promotional.

He spent most of his time with Lisa and Becky, grocery shopping, going to the playground—whatever Lisa's daily activities encompassed. Charlie began to feel a closeness with Becky. Once she called him Daddy.

"What did she say?" Charlie stepped back, shocked.

Lisa laughed, "She only met Al once, Charlie. I'm surprised she even knows what a daddy is."

Me, a father, Charlie thought. *He stared at the ground. I couldn't even be a husband. Shit! I can't even be a boyfriend.* He shook his head and looked up to see Lisa watching him. Admiring him? She was beautiful, with long blonde hair like Cher's, and she was a wonderful mother. Al had loved her so much. *Should I even be hanging around with her? What would Al think?*

On July twentieth, a Sunday afternoon, the three of them returned to the house, laughing and talking after a walk in the park.

"Shhh!" Betty held her finger up to her mouth. "They're walking on the moon."

Betty and Al were glued to the television set. An astronaut, dressed in a big suit with a helmet on his head, left the Apollo Eleven Space Capsule and walked on the surface of moon.

"One small step for man, one giant leap for mankind," came the scratchy voice from more than two hundred thousand miles away.

"Wow! Who is that?" Charlie asked.

"Neil Armstrong," Betty said admiringly. "He's from my home town—Wapakoneta."

"Wapa...what?" Charlie said, studying the television screen.

"Wapakoneta, Ohio," Al answered, smiling up at Charlie. "North of Dayton in Ohio. It was old Shawnee stomping grounds."

"Shhh!" Betty said. "I want to hear if he says something else."

"Good luck Mr. Gorsky," the voice on the television said.

"Mr. Gorsky?" Lisa said. "Who's that?"

"Probably one of his neighbors or something," Charlie said. "You know, from back in Wapakoneta. Probably told his wife he'd build her a new house when the boy next door walks on the moon."

Everybody laughed with Charlie. He felt like they appreciated his humor and his presence in the household. *But,* he thought, *it was time to go back home.* Lisa had been acting like she wanted to get more familiar, but he didn't know about that. He almost felt like he'd replaced Al in the Strangemeir's home, and that was a little unnerving.

At dinner that night, Charlie made his announcement. "I think I'll be heading out in the morning. I really appreciate your hospitality."

Lisa looked surprised. "Oh, Charlie! You don't have to leave so soon."

"I think I'd better, Lisa."

"Well," Betty said, "if you have to go, you have to go, but we sure have enjoyed having you, Charlie. You're always welcome." She caught her breath to keep from crying. "With you around, it's like Junior's come back home to us."

The room was quiet. Finally Lisa spoke. "Charlie, before you go will you tell us what happened?"

"You mean...?"

"Yes. All we know is that every one in his gun crew was killed."

Charlie looked around the room, made eye contact with everyone—Al, Betty, then Lisa.

"A helicopter came in and said I was being summoned into basecamp, a Red Cross emergency. One of the other guys was going home, so both of us jumped in and were transported to basecamp. Turned out my mom was worried about me because I hadn't written home. When I tried to catch a ride back, there weren't any choppers because of all the action up front. I couldn't get lifted out until the next day. We circled before landing and that's when I saw the gun was gone. I couldn't believe it—gone. Where was it? The door gunner told me it had taken a direct hit. When I landed, the captain said..." Charlie hesitated and took a deep breath, "...that everybody on the gun was dead."

Sobbing, Charlie continued, "He said I was a lucky sonofabitch."

Betty stood and walked over to Charlie. She leaned over and hugged him.

"I told him I was a lucky son of an angel."

Everybody at the table was crying—even Al, Sr.

"Why me? That's all I could think about. I stayed in our old bunker until it was time for me to go home. I found Al's tape player with the Sergeant Pepper's tape inside. I listened to that tape every night, over and over. They were my pals. Al was my best friend on the gun."

Charlie fell asleep on the couch that night. He tossed and turned. He dreamed of that fateful day for Gun Number Five. *Strangeman, where are you, man? Sprint? Señor Fagoso? Baloneyman? Why? I didn't even get to say goodbye. Why me? How do angels choose? Mommy, are you my angel? Who is Dirt Farmer's?*

Someone slid under the covers with him. "Cher? Oh sweet baby, will you ever understand?"

"Yes, Charlie. I understand."

"But I've seen so much. I've killed…"

The female body snuggled close. She caressed his back. With each stroke he felt calmer. Then, she kissed him. He kissed back—passion infused his body. He felt an erection and made love.

He woke in a daze with the first morning light. What? What happened? Nobody was with him, but, but—had he had sex? He shook his head to clear it, stood and got dressed quickly.

The house was quiet. He wrote a note.

> *Thanks very much for everything. You are all wonderful people to let me stay so long. Your son and husband, Al, Jr., will be in my memories forever—Charlie*

22

The beaches on the outer banks of North Carolina stretch for nearly a hundred miles. Charlie figured he had walked most of them over the past week, looking for any sign of a rideable wave. He had come down the coast because the surfers in Virginia Beach told him that the East Coast's best surf could be found there, but the surf was flat. He decided to wait for a swell, but that gave him what he hadn't anticipated—time to think.

That last night in Virginia Beach haunted him. The dream of the demise of Gun Number Five seemed so real, probably triggered by his having just told the story to the Strangemeir family. But then, making love to a woman? His body felt like he had, but who? Lisa? Why did she do that? Why did I? Guilt riddled his mind.

An old fisherman, clad in hip waders and casting his line out in knee-deep water, distracted his thoughts.

Charlie waded out next to him. "Any luck?"

"Pretty good so far." He pointed toward three large fish, about twelve pounds each, on the beach lying in the sand."

"All right," Charlie congratulated him. "When was the last time for big surf around here?"

"Been awhile. A tropical storm's headed this way, though. Not good for fishing, but you'll see great waves before the police close the beach."

"Why would they do that?" Charlie asked.

"You're not from around here, are ya?"

"No, sir, California."

"Gets pretty messy during hurricane season. Sometimes they even evacuate all the residents. Folks board up the windows and hightail it out of here. Try the hurricane center—back on the main road toward Hatteras. They'll have it tracked down by now."

Charlie headed south on Highway Twelve and pulled into the parking lot at the Hurricane Center. Inside he found maps and charts of past hurricanes, mounted on the wall. He read how they start in the middle of the tropical seas as small thunderstorms. Warm air rises collecting water. Cool air rushes into the gap behind the warm air, creating high winds that begin to swirl in a counter clockwise direction. The center of the swirl, the eye, is calm, but the outside becomes brutal with torrential rains and fierce winds that can travel up to two hundred miles per hour and cover six hundred miles in diameter.

"Can I help you?"

Startled, Charlie spun around to see a man dressed in a National Park Ranger's uniform.

"Just learning about hurricanes. Heard one might be coming?"

"As a matter of fact, we're following Anna, the first tropical storm of the season, right now. She should be in the area the next day or so."

"So we're going to get some big surf?"

"Yes, we're expecting very high surf out of this one. While it's classified a 'tropical storm' now, it could become a hurricane anytime. If that happens, we might evacuate the Cape. Where are you staying?"

"I'm camping at the National Seashore Campground."

"Listen to your radio for information, please."

That night, Charlie climbed into his bunk, his mind anxious with the possibility of big surf. Then, Vietnam crept into his consciousness like a low crawling NVA in the jungle. He looked out the window, scanning the area for danger. He sighed after realizing he was safe. *Shit! I'm never going to be the same. Goddamn it! Why couldn't I have been knocked off over there? If I were dead, I wouldn't have to live with myself.*

He thought of Al, dying with his crew. Then he remembered Lisa. Sorry, Al—didn't intend to do that, man.

Then he heard a loud cracking sound, almost like gunfire. Unnerved, he sat up. Then again. But this time he recognized the sound—the reverberation of the rising surf slapping down as a wave breaks. *Ah, here it comes, big guy. Here it comes!*

In the morning, the surf was ten feet high when Charlie checked the south side of Cape Hatteras. He grabbed his board and paddled out. There were no other surfers and he wondered why. The waves were nothing compared to what he'd seen in Hawaii.

The peaks were not consistent and popped up helter-skelter without warning. *Like my moods lately,* Charlie thought.

He surfed for an hour and went in, unsatisfied with his session. *Man, this is the best surf in the East?*

He walked back to his van, shoved his board in and decided to hit the road. He drove north toward Buxton and stopped at a restaurant for breakfast. He noticed stacks of plywood out front and no patrons inside.

"Hello? Anybody here?" Charlie shouted.

A man stuck his head out from the back room. "What can I do for you?"

"Hoping to get something to eat."

"Well, I guess we can help you with that," he drawled. "Might be closing up in a few hours with this storm, but for now the kitchen is still open. I'll get you a menu."

"Actually, I'll just have a short stack and three eggs over easy and a large orange juice."

"Coming up."

What's all the excitement about? Charlie wondered. The surf seemed pretty melancholy to him. Music from the radio broke, interrupted with a news broadcast. With his hearing still impaired from Vietnam, Charlie couldn't make out the announcement.

The waiter hustled out with his order. "You'll have to hurry with this," he said, putting a plate down and shoving it over to Charlie. "We're closin' up. That storm's getting closer."

The man grabbed a hammer and a bag of nails from a toolbox and rushed for the door.

"Where is it?" Charlie called after him.

"About a hundred miles out and two hundred south. If it keeps this pace we're in fer it."

Charlie wolfed down the eggs, wrapped the pancakes in a napkin, gulped the juice and ran outside.

The man was struggling with a piece of plywood.

Charlie ran to give him a hand and steadied the wood by holding it at the bottom edge.

"Thanks," the man said. "You'd better be headin' on outta here, now. We'll all be evacuated soon. Go north—road's closed to the south."

Charlie nodded. "Okay."

Curious to see the surf before leaving, Charlie drove to the lighthouse, which was perched up on a bank, right off the shore. It had large black and white stripes painted on it—swirled up from the bottom, around the tower to the top where a light flashed. He parked and walked up the slope to see the water.

"Holy shit!"

The surf bounded in close to twenty feet high. Charlie studied it for a moment. The wind swirled on the bank, but the water looked amazingly smooth. *The cape to the south must be blocking it,* he thought. *I'm going out.* He ran back to the van, climbed in the driver's seat and started putting on his trunks.

A black jeep pulled up with "Beach Patrol" written in large white letters on the side. A policeman climbed out and walked over to him.

"Hello. You're going to have to vacate. This storm is getting close."

Charlie sighed, slapped his steering wheel.

"Sorry, I have orders. It should blow out in a few days."

"Okay, thank you, Officer."

The man climbed back in his vehicle and drove up the beach.

Shit! Charlie sat for a moment. *What the hell do I care? Life sucks anyway. I can't think of a better way to go, can you, Will?*

He looked up the beach and turned around in his seat to see if anyone was behind. *It's all clear, big guy. Go for it!* He jumped out, grabbed his board and ran for the shoreline. The waves pounded into the beach, and Charlie began to work on a plan to get through the white water with his surfboard.

He spotted a riptide to the north about a hundred yards—water rushed out to sea, absent of swell. He sprinted as fast as he could and dove into the rip, and paddled with all his might. The speed of the current flowed like a river. In minutes, Charlie made it outside and moved into the line-up of continuous set waves.

He lay on his board and paddled over the swells, trying to get an idea of their action. He had surfed a lot of big waves before, but these were rough. Most of the surfers in Virginia Beach, who had spoken about hurricane surfing, considered it too dangerous.

After twenty minutes of cautious observation, it was time to take off. *This may be your first and last, big guy. Make it a good one.* A likely peak emerged. He paddled toward it and turned around. He saw Will's head in the water, bloody, surrounded with flower pedals.

"I'm coming, Will!" he shouted. "Make room for me, man!"

He stroked into the monstrous surge, stood up and raced down its crest. Wind blasted his eyes. Nearly reaching the bottom, he leaned forward and turned slowly into the massive reservoir in motion. The curl looked more than three times his size—the barrier unforgiving. *Just a matter of time,* he thought.

Moments seemed like hours, but he remained on the board. The wave started to collapse. Charlie straightened his board toward shore, lay down and held onto the surfboard with all his might—white water hammered down.

Charlie felt weightless, like a helpless microscopic organism in a turbulent bath. Suddenly a hand reached down and grabbed him—grabbed him out of his body.

What's happening? Where am I? Then he realized that he was above looking down—saw his body in the tremendous explosion of water. He felt so calm, peaceful, at one with the Universe. *Am I dead? I feel wonderful; full of love. It's like I am the whole, no longer just a part.*

He watched the churning soup of the ruptured swell ebb toward the beach. Then he heard a voice.

"It's not time for you, Son," the voice said, a voice that sounded like his father's.

"Not yet time for what? Dad, is that you?"

"Your time has not yet come."

"What'll I do?"

"You must create."

"Create? Create what?"

"Life, Charlie. Your time has not yet come."

Charlie looked down at the body in the turbulent water.

"You can do it, Charlie."

"Okay, big guy," Charlie said, directed toward the body in the wave. "I guess we're supposed to create life out of this mess."

He murmured, "Come on Charlie. You can do it. Hold it—don't breathe in. See yourself making it, man. Like Nam. See yourself arriving home."

He felt himself slipping back into his body. *I'm coming home. I'm coming home.* Charlie popped out ahead of the white water like a hot kernel of corn—gasping for air repeatedly.

"I made it!" he shouted. "I made it!"

When the wave finally deposited him on shore, he rolled off of his surfboard onto his back. He was totally exhausted, but euphoric. His body tingled, and he laughed out loud. *I feel phenomenal,* he thought. *What had happened? Like I was with God or something.*

"Dad!" he shouted. "Daddy! I have created life, with God."

He stood up and saw a uniformed policeman running toward him.

Charlie's mother answered the phone. "Hello?"

"I have a collect call for anyone from Charlie. Will you accept the call?" the operator said.

"Yes. Charlie?"

"Hi, Mom. I just wanted let you know that I'm on my way home."

"Where are you?"

"I'm in North Carolina. Should be home in less than a week. Just surfed a hurricane swell. The waves were huge."

"Oh, my Lord. Isn't that dangerous?"

"That's what the beach patrol said, but I had to try it. Mom, I had the most incredible experience of my life. I only caught one wave, but it was worth it."

"Did you get in trouble?"

"Nah. A policeman did escort me out of the area, though. I think he was afraid I might go back out."

"Oh, Charlie. I do worry about you."

"Is Dad home?"

"Yes, but he's not feeling very well; been dizzy a lot. This morning he had really bad indigestion. He's been sleeping for the last few hours."

"That's okay. Tell him I hope that he's feeling better soon. And, Mom, tell him that I think I'm ready to talk about Vietnam now. I want to talk to him about it."

"That's wonderful, Charlie. I'm sure he'll be pleased."

"Mom," Charlie hesitated. "I have a question for you."

"What is it?"

"Why did you call the Red Cross?"

Silence on the end of the line. "Mom?"

"I'm here, Son. I had a dream that you were in danger. That happened many times during the year you were away, but that time it seemed so real. I saw you dying, Charlie. An angel appeared and said you were in great danger. She begged me to help you. The next morning I told John about the dream, and he said I should make a call to the Red Cross. I didn't want to embarrass you, honey."

Charlie was silent—remembering not seeing his gun from the helicopter.

"Charlie, are you okay?"

"Your call saved my life."

"What? What happened?"

"Everyone was killed, Mom. Everyone, except me, because I wasn't there. I was in basecamp writing you a letter."

Ten days later, Charlie pulled his van into his parents' driveway in San Diego. Although it was a beautiful day, the drapes were drawn. Hope somebody's home, he thought. He bounded up to the front door, tried to open it, but it was locked. He rang the bell and waited impatiently.

Mike opened the door. "Charlie!" He reached out and hugged Charlie and wouldn't let go.

"Whoa, Brother, not so hard."

"Glad to see you," Mike said. "When it took you so long to get home, I thought maybe you were caught in Hurricane Camille."

"Hurricane Camille?"

"Yeah, 258 dead in Mississippi and Louisiana."

"My radio went out," Charlie said. "Haven't checked the news lately. I hit hard rains when I was driving down south. Had to stop because the highway was barricaded, but I found an old country road that was open. Hey, what are you doing here anyway? I thought you were in Thailand for another year."

Mike looked deeply into Charlie's eyes.

"Dad died, Charlie."

Charlie stood still, not believing what he just heard. *No. Please, God. He couldn't have said what I thought he said. Please.*

Tears rolled down Mike's face. Their mom and another woman walked into the front room.

"Oh, Charlie. Thank God, you're home." She rushed to hug him. "We thought maybe something happened to you, too."

"Mom, tell me it's not true." Charlie cried. "Tell me Dad's just taking a nap in the bedroom."

"After I talked with you last week, I went in to check on him. I thought he was asleep, but then noticed he wasn't breathing. Your father had a heart attack, Charlie."

Charlie fell to his knees, put his hands on his head and wailed, "No, no! How can this be happening?"

He buried his face in his hands and leaned forward onto the floor. His brother and mother knelt next to him, their hands on his shoulders.

After a while, he rose onto his knees and wiped the tears from his face. Then he saw her. The other woman in the room was Cher. He stared quietly. It was the first time he'd seen her since the night in the cave, the night before he'd departed for Vietnam.

"How's your ankle?"

She smiled. "It's been better for over a year now. Good to see you."

Charlie nodded. "Nice to see you, too."

"Cher has been like a daughter to us," his mother said. "Ever since you and Mike went overseas."

"I didn't know that," Charlie said, still looking at Cher. "Thank you for being here. I haven't been much of a son lately."

After supper, Charlie and Cher walked on the beach. Neither of them spoke for awhile

"It seems like my world is collapsing around me. Just when I think I've figured things out, something happens. I'm losing the people I care about and need. First Will dies and now Dad." Charlie's voice was soft. He sat down in the sand, and motioned for Cher to join him.

"I don't have anybody to talk to," Charlie said.

"You can talk to me," Cher said.

He shook his head and grabbed a handful of sand, threw it to the side. *Oh sweet Baby,* he thought, *if only I could. But how can I tell you what it's like to kill people? Twenty-seven people.*

He sighed and with only the light of the crescent moon, he looked into her eyes and saw their beautiful blue color. They were eager, anxiously awaiting a response. Charlie stared, not knowing what he could say to Cher.

Later that night, Charlie phoned Gage.

"Hey, Buddy. It's been a long time," Charlie said.

"I'll say. Where the hell have you been?"

"Traveling. Surfed a hurricane swell off of Cape Hatteras."

"You crazy sonofa…"

"Angel," Charlie piped in.

"Yeah. Sorry to hear about your dad, man."

"Thanks, Gage. Hey, I think I'm taking off again. Down Mexico way. How about coming along? Like old times."

"I can't, Charlie. I've got a really great job now at a new restaurant in La Jolla. Besides, there's something else I haven't told you yet."

"What's that?"

"I met this girl, Charlie. Her name is Darlene. I like her a lot, man. Might ask her to marry me."

"Will you let me know where you are, Charlie?" his mother asked on the eve of his departure to Mexico.

"Sure, Mom. But…" Charlie was hesitant, unsure of what else to say.

"What is it, Son?"

"I'm afraid, Mom. Afraid of losing you, now."

She put her right arm around Charlie and kissed his cheek.

"I have something for you." She handed him a bound book.

He opened it to the first page. It read: *John W. Armfield—Journal—1943.*

"Dad's Journal?"

"Yes, I know he would have wanted you to have it. He wrote in it while he was in seminary, before he met me. It goes on for several years and talks about World War II."

"But, Mom…" He shook his head. "How can I read this? Is he going to tell me how bad it is to fight in a war? Thou shalt not kill."

"Take it with you. You don't have to read it right away. Wait till you're ready."

"When I'm ready? But how will I..."

"You'll know, Son."

23

The waves at Matachen Bay curled for nearly a mile along the jagged coastline. The beaches were backed by thick jungles, of banana trees and coconut palms. Charlie stroked into the swell at the outside point and rode for ten minutes before the wave finally petered out inside.

"Aaaahhhhoooo!" he hooted.

He waded into the beach and decided to trek back to the point. Paddling would take thirty minutes or more. Immediately, sweat beaded on his forehead from Nayarit's heat and humidity. He needed a drink, but finding potable water was difficult. He stopped at a little cabana owned by a family that served bottled drinks and food to the beach public. He laid his board up against a palm tree.

"*Una cerveza, por favor*," Charlie said, panting.

"*Si, Señor. Corona o Pacifico?*" an elderly Mexican man asked.

"*Pacifico, por favor.*"

The man grabbed a brown bottle with a yellow label from an ice chest, popped the top off, and handed it to Charlie.

"*Ah, gracias. Es mucho frio*," Charlie said.

"*Si, de nada.*"

Charlie pulled out some coins he had in the button-down pocket of his surf trunks.

"*Cuantos por la cuenta?*"

"*Dos Cenquenta.*"

He handed the man three pesos. The man dug in his money pouch for centavos.

"*No, gracias. Quedese con la vuelta,*" Charlie said, putting up his hand, gesturing for the proprietor to keep the change. He had just paid twenty-five cents for the beer.

"*Gracias, Señor,*" the Mexican said, smiling at the unexpected tip.

"*De nada.*"

A few lopsided wooden tables and chairs faced the ocean. An American couple, looking to be in their thirties, sat at the next table. They smiled at Charlie and he smiled back.

"Nice wave," the man said.

"Thanks," Charlie said.

"How long have you been surfing here?"

"Just pulled in this morning. Are the waves always this good?"

"We've been here for a week. This is the first day it's been like this. Before, the surfers were only riding small waves for short distances. Now, with the bigger swells, the rides look incredible."

"Don't you guys surf?"

They both chuckled. "No," he said, "we're sailors."

Charlie studied them. He appeared tall, strong and tan. His beard and hair were sun-bleached; his hair grown over his ears. Since Charlie hadn't shaved since he'd left, they looked somewhat alike.

She was short, shapely but muscular. Her hair was long and strawberry-blonde. They looked like surfers.

"We're on our way around the world," she said.

"Wow! Where's your boat?" Charlie asked.

"Anchored in San Blas harbor," the woman answered. "We needed a break. Our next stop is Costa Rica. Then we'll head out into the Pacific toward Australia."

"Cool!" Charlie said. "How long will you be hanging out here?"

"We don't know," he said. "We just play it by ear and go with the wind. How about you?"

"I just play it by ear, too, except I don't know where I'm going."

"What do you mean?" the woman asked.

Charlie lowered his head. "I left San Diego nearly three months ago in my van. I'm just looking for surf."

"Would you care to join us?" the woman said, pointing to an empty chair at their table.

"Sure, why not?"

Charlie sat down and the woman held out her hand. "I'm Jacque. This is my husband Rick. We're from San Francisco."

"Nice to meet you," Charlie said, shaking Jacque's hand. "I'm Charlie." He turned and shook Rick's hand.

"You speak good Spanish," Jacque said admiringly.

"Not really. All I can do is order food and beer. If anyone starts talking to me, I'm lost. That's when I say '*lo siento, no comprende.*'"

"What does that mean?" Rick asked.

"That means, I'm sorry, but I must have ditched high school Spanish that day to go surfing."

They all laughed.

"Where have you been so far?" Rick asked.

"All the way down Baja, then yesterday I caught the ferry over to Mazatlan. There was no surf, so I started driving south till I got here."

"You spent three months surfing in Baja?" Rick asked. "It looks like desert along there."

"That's right. A thousand miles of nothing but desert, but I found some great surfing spots. My favorites were Puntas Abreojos and Pequeña. Roads are bad around there, but I'm pretty good with a map."

"Weren't you afraid to be alone?" Jacque asked.

Charlie looked into her eyes. They appeared to be trusting. "That's the way I want it, Ma'am. I need to be by myself for awhile."

He took a long drink of his beer and set the bottle down on the table. "Well, guess I'll head back out and catch some more of this swell. Thanks for the conversation."

He surfed until the sun began to set, then returned to his van. His stomach growled. *Man, I'm hungry. Wonder how far it is to San Blas.* He started along and noticed Rick and Jacque walking alongside the road.

He pulled up next to them.

"You guys need a lift?"

"That'd be great. It's about three miles to town," Rick said. They climbed into the front seat, Jacque in the middle.

"Would you join us for dinner, Charlie?" Jacque asked.

Charlie ate fresh fish tacos with his new friends at a San Blas Resturante. After dinner, his new friends invited him to see their boat. They squeezed into the small rubber raft tethered to a rock on the harbor shore and Rick rowed them to a forty-five foot sloop. *Jacqueline* was written on the stern in cursive.

"This is really cool. How long did it take you guys to sail down from Frisco?"

"Forty-one days," Rick said, appearing to be embarrassed. "I've been sailing all of my life, but never on a trip like this. It took us some time to get a routine going and we did do a lot of stopping along the way. We hope to get to Costa Rica in less than three weeks."

"Then it's out into the big waters," Jacque said, looking uncertain.

"That's right," Rick said. "But we're going to do just fine." He put his arm around her.

They spent the rest of the evening sharing stories of their adventures down the coastline. It was late when Rick rowed Charlie back to the shore.

"Charlie, we could use another hand on the boat."

"What do you mean?"

"Sailing is hard work. Jacque does pretty well, but another man on board would probably make both of us more comfortable. I hear there's good surfing in Australia."

Charlie stared wide-eyed at Rick, surprised by the offer. Sailing down under? That would be incredible, but...

"Think about it," Rick said, bumping the raft onto the rocky shore. "We probably won't be leaving for a few days. Hell, if you want to come, we'll wait until the surf dies down."

Overwhelmed by the offer, Charlie mumbled his farewell, and drove back to Matachen Bay. He parked and climbed into the back. He lay in his bunk with notions grabbing at his mind. *Australia? Good surf down there. Shit! The world champion, Colin Robins, surfs there.*

During the night, tiny sea gnats swarmed over his body. He slapped at them, but they persisted. He turned on the light. Where the hell are they?

There was nothing to see, but the biting continued. He grabbed a blanket, wrapped himself up as tightly as he could and sweated through a sleepless night.

Still bothered by the bugs at the crack of dawn, Charlie grabbed his surfboard, ran to the ocean and dove in. He paddled furiously until the throng of gnats diminished. Relieved, he moved toward the line-up of waves. The swell was still pumping. He stroked into a perfect wall and was immersed in his love for the sea.

Later that morning, he sat in a small restaurant in San Blas with a plate of eggs, a large glass of orange juice, and a basket of tortillas in front of him. Shirtless, he wore sandals and his surf trunks, still damp from the morning session. He felt worn out, not only from the surfing, but from the restless night as well.

Rick and Jacque walked by the restaurant, saw Charlie, and joined him. "You look exhausted, Charlie," Jacque said pulling up a chair.

"Must have been some mighty surf this morning," Rick said, smiling.

"Yeah, it was unreal. But I'm tired mostly from the lack of sleep. Damn bugs kept me up all night."

"*Jejenes*!" Jacque exclaimed.

"Hey, what?" Charlie questioned, squinting his eyes.

"We call them no-see-ums," Rick said. "The Mexicans say *Jejenes*."

"You sure can't see them," Charlie said. "Damn near ate me alive."

Rick and Jacque laughed, and Charlie joined in.

"I guess we forgot to warn you about that one," Rick said.

"Yeah, you did. Thanks a lot, man," Charlie said, giving Rick a light shove. "I wasn't going to sleep much anyway. My head was jammed thinking about what..." Charlie paused, looking at Rick. He wondered if Rick had told Jacque that he asked him to sail with them.

Rick smiled, nodded his head. "I'll bet. So what do you think? Are you up for a trip across the ocean in our little craft?"

Charlie looked from one to the other. They seemed anxious for his reply. "I don't know. That's a long time out at sea. I don't know if I could..."

"Do you think it's too dangerous?" Jacque interrupted.

She seemed concerned, maybe for herself. Danger wasn't Charlie's problem, however. The sea could never pose a pitfall for him. What did concern him was the concept of abandoning his life to an unknown future. While he didn't know where he was going now, he was close to home and could always turn around.

But what kind of future did he have anyway? The nightmares wouldn't stop and death kept following him—Will, then his father. *Shit! I'm even haunted by Al. I should have given up in that hurricane swell. Why couldn't I have died when I had a chance?*

"Charlie? Are you all right?" Jacque asked.

"Yeah, yeah, just thinking." He looked outside at his van.

Rick followed his gaze. "Maybe you could sell it to one of the Mexicans. All they drive around here are older vehicles; probably find a buyer if you wanted to."

Three days later, Charlie climbed aboard the sloop, a grocery bag filled with clothes under his left arm. Rick passed him his surfboard, which was dripping water after being towed behind the dinghy. Charlie looked toward shore and waved to Pablo who stood next to his old van.

Pablo was only able to scrounge up twelve hundred pesos, a hundred U.S. dollars, but had a cousin who made sails. He had offered to trade for the rest with sails and some canned food. Charlie had shrugged his shoulders and made the deal.

He laid his surfboard on deck and climbed down the ladder into the cabin with his other possessions.

"You can store your stuff in this bend," Jacque said, pointing to a cabinet near the bulkhead.

As he poured his belongings into the space, his father's journal dropped to the floor. Jacque bent over and picked up the book.

"What's this, Charlie?"

"My father's diary from when he was about my age. My mom gave it to me after he died."

"I'll bet it's pretty interesting."

"I don't know; haven't read it yet."

"With all that time you've had alone?"

"I'm kind of afraid to, I guess."

Jacque lowered her brow, appearing to be concerned for Charlie. "Why are you so sad, Charlie?"

He didn't answer, just shrugged his shoulders and went up on deck.

It was December 1, 1969, when Charlie finally wrote a letter to his mom.

> *I hope you are well. I've been catching some really good waves so far on my trip. First, I drove all the way down Baja and ferried over to the mainland. Then I met a really nice couple who are sailing around the world. They invited me to go along. As I write we're on our way down the coast to Central America. It should take us a couple of weeks, then who knows how long to Australia.*
>
> *You must think you have a crazy son. Sorry I can't be home with you, but I just need to be traveling right now. Would you please tell Gage my plans? Wish he could go with me. Maybe you could tell Cher, too. I'll be mailing this letter from Costa Rica and I don't know when there will be a chance to post another. I hope you won't worry about me.*

The second day out from a Costa Rican port, Charlie lay prone on the bow, daydreaming. As he watched waves splash against the hull, eight bottle-nosed dolphins appeared, leaping in and out of the water as if leading the boat.

Charlie yelled to Rick and Jacque, "Look at this!"

Rick was busy at the helm, so Jacque came up to join Charlie. She lay down next to him and marveled at the sight.

"Beautiful, aren't they?" she said, smiling.

"They sure are, and smart, too. The Vietnamese call them 'angels of the sea.'"

Jacque looked curiously at Charlie, then continued watching the dolphins. They bounced up and down as if synchronizing their efforts in dance for their admirers.

When the dolphins swam off, Charlie let out a deep sigh. "Goodbye, my friends." He turned and looked at Jacque. "There's something special about those creatures, Jacque. And they're civilized, too. They don't have wars."

Jacque studied him, her eyes searching for answers. "Were you in Vietnam, Charlie?"

His eyes felt like a well when the water is pumped to the surface. A tear leaked from the corner of his left eye. He nodded, unable to speak. She held out her arms. He stared for a moment, then sobbed into her embrace. She held him tightly until, finally, he nudged her away.

They stared into each other's eyes. He felt relieved—felt that Jacque could understand, could be trusted. He wished he could have felt that way with Cher.

Later that night, Charlie told his story to Rick and Jacque. The couple sat quietly and listened until he got to the part about being sent to the front as a forward observer.

"No wonder you found your way around Baja so well," Rick said. "I heard those roads are impossible to follow."

Charlie laughed, "Hey, I didn't need to be a forward observer to find waves. I can smell 'em miles away."

"I sensed you were a man of deep feeling and experience," Rick said. "That's why I wanted to get to know you. When you accepted our invitation to sail, I felt like we were going to be safe on our journey. You have a survival feel about you, Charlie. Maybe you have a guardian angel or something."

Charlie's eyes widened—he was surprised.

"We're very happy to have you with us," Jacque said.

Charlie lowered his head and thought to himself, *what if my angel gets called home? What if I've lost my survival feel? Maybe it's finally going to be my turn to die—then I can escape.*

On Christmas Day, Charlie forgot all about wanting to escape. Something happened in his travels. He was excited and wrote another letter to his mom.

Merry Christmas!

You won't believe this, but I'm in the Galapagos Islands. This is the most incredible place. I've never seen so many fish and birds. Apparently the water is really cold here before December. The Humboldt Current flows from Antarctica and all of the southern species come up, including penguins. But then the warm

El Niño currents arrive and the northern species come down. Sometimes the two breed together and new species, only found in the Galapagos, originate.

I went snorkeling for five hours this morning. Forgot all about breakfast. When I started back for the boat, a pair of dolphins swam with me. I think this is like heaven, Mom. I wonder if Dad would agree.

We got to Costa Rica in fifteen days. Rick and Jacque, the couple I'm traveling with, couldn't believe how fast we made it. Docked in Quepos for three days. I got some incredible surfing in. There's a National Park nearby called Manuel Antonio, and a trail goes down the coast through thick jungle. It felt like Nam except nobody was trying to shoot me. There were only tropical birds with unbelievable colors and playful monkeys swinging in the trees.

Then we sailed down here in six days. Had a great twenty-knot wind almost every day, so we put up a spinnaker sail, kind of like a big kite, to pull us along. One time I even jumped in the water with my board and a towrope and skied along in the wake of the boat.

When we crossed the equator, we took down all the sails and dove overboard to celebrate. The water felt like a warm bath. Traditionally, sailors shave their heads when crossing the equator for the first time. Rick and I wanted to do it, but Jacque, the best cook on board, said no more gourmets if we did. Needless to say, we kept the hair.

You may be surprised to hear from me again so soon. I know I didn't write much from Nam, but I'm so happy now that I want to share it with you. We'll leave by the end of the month and head for the Marquesas Islands, nearly 3,000 miles away. That's nautical miles, which are longer than regular miles. Could take a month. It all depends on the wind.

24

Charlie learned much about sailing and navigating the *Jacquelyn*. He watched Rick operate compasses and the sextant and transfer data, using protractors and charts to establish the latitude meridian of their position. Then, using a chronometer set on Greenwich Time, Rick measured longitude meridians by acquiring local hour angles with the present position of the sun.

Charlie was intrigued, recognizing that it was far more complicated than what Robby had taught him in the jungle. But then, there weren't any landmarks for them to follow in the middle of the Pacific Ocean.

Until he developed calluses, Charlie's hands were blood-blistered and painful from working the halyards and sheets to hoist and trim the sails against the wind. He never let on to Rick and Jacque, but labored with the same intensity he had during his final days on the firebase with the artillery battery.

Charlie enjoyed studying the winds to achieve maximum speed, tacking the boat. He experimented with positioning the sails to guide the sloop without using the steering mechanism.

"What the hell are you doing?" Rick asked.

"Just leaning this sucker in and out of the tack. Feels like I'm surfing. And look. As I go from a port to a starboard tack, I can turn left and right if I keep the trim constant," Charlie said.

"How did you figure that out? It took me five years to learn how to turn by sail."

Charlie shrugged. "It's just balance, man."

Each of them took two-hour shifts at the helm, giving each of them a four-hour break. Charlie spent a lot of his spare time on deck daydreaming or reading, dipping into Jacque's box of fiction rather than reading his dad's journal. He often fell asleep under the stars.

Once, Charlie was at the helm when he spotted something through the binoculars that looked like a water fountain, two miles or so to the northwest. Then a splash appeared as a giant beast surfaced.

"Holy shit!"

"What is it?" Rick yelled from the cabin.

"I don't know, but it's the biggest damn thing I've ever seen."

Rick and Jacque quickly climbed up on deck. Rick grabbed the lenses.

"Holy shit, is right! It's a whale. Jacque, take a look at this."

Jacque, the resident expert based on her having memorized a book on seafaring species, said, "I think it's a blue whale. Yes, I'm sure of it. It has a tiny dorsal fin, three-quarters of the way back from its head. That's the biggest living creature on earth."

She handed the binoculars back to Charlie but when he looked, the whale was gone. They continued to gaze and, five minutes later, it appeared again, this time about a mile and a half out.

"Beautiful!" Jacque said. "See, it's blue and has kind of a white pattern on its back."

Charlie stared through the binoculars, staggered by the vastness of the whale. "How big is that sucker? Fifty, maybe seventy feet?"

Again it dropped from sight. When it resurfaced, it was only three-quarters of a mile away.

"Wow!" Charlie said, looking through the binoculars until it disappeared again. He shot his arms up in the air, nearly dropping the lenses, and hooted, "Aaaahhhhoooo!"

Three minutes later, Charlie felt a rush, a feeling of danger, like when he sensed the enemy in the bush. But there were no gooks in the ocean.

Then it hit him—the whale! It's the whale!

He seized the main sheets, released them so that the sail went limp.

"What the hell are you doing?" Rick demanded.

"Let the jib out! Quick!" Charlie yelled the order.

Rick reacted fast, and the boat lagged off its forward progress. It continued to drift slowly. He turned to question Charlie. Charlie took a deep breath.

The boat rocked back from bow to stern, then forward as an immense head rose out of the water a hundred feet in front. Charlie thought its large eye appeared just as startled as he felt.

The whale's body lifted out of the water, nearly ninety feet of blue flesh, easily twice the length of the sailing vessel. It crashed down before the tail breached the water, flooding the deck.

The sloop tottered like a toy in a bathtub. Jacque screamed and fell to the floor. Rick grabbed onto the lifeline attached to the starboard railing. Charlie held onto the helm for dear life, thinking it was just a matter of time before they would capsize. But the waves eased as the gigantic creature lay still on the surface of the water.

The whale blew a straight, slender column of water nearly thirty feet high out of the top of his head, and seemed to peer at the boat.

Now what? Charlie thought, standing in ankle deep water. "What are you thinking, big fella?"

The blue whale remained motionless. It could tip the boat over with a swoosh of its tail.

"Hey, man." Charlie continued talking as if the whale understood. "You've got to be the biggest surf rider I've ever seen, and the sleekest. Not even a hurricane swell would give you a thrill. But, hey, I think you're more into making waves than riding them."

The whale continued to blow out of its spout about every fifteen seconds, seemingly not wanting to move. Then it let out a loud, low-pitched moan.

"Well, okay, man." Charlie continued. "I can dig that. By the way, do you happen to know the way to Australia? Heard it's over yonder a ways. I've got a date to do some tube riding down there—if you see fit to let us be on our way. I think you look kind of peaceful, but we'll just hang out here until you make up your mind."

After a few minutes, the whale moaned, ducked his head under water, and slowly immersed his entire body, creating a draft. The sloop moved with the motion until the wakes moved outward from the hole left in the sea by the whale's departure.

"Goodbye my friend," Charlie said. "It was a pleasure to meet you. Maybe we'll see you around sometime."

Rick helped Jacque up off the deck. Her knees were bruised, but she was fine. She reached out to hug, and both Rick and Charlie obliged.

"You did it, Charlie," Jacque exclaimed.

"Did what?" Charlie slipped out of the hug.

"You sweet talked that whale into leaving us alone."

Then the boat began to rock.

"Wha…wha…what's that?" Jacque stuttered.

"Shit!" said Rick. "Is the whale coming back?"

"I don't think so," Charlie said "I don't feel his energy anymore. Look, there's another swell coming from the west. We better trim these sails and get a move on."

Charlie got back onto a port tack and started taking on the swells, heading right for them, and then, at the last moment, turning to go over them at thirty degrees. The maneuver created less of a backlash on the other side of the surge, and allowed the *Jacquelyn* to keep up its speed. The rolling waves came at three-minute intervals. The warm winds gusted at twenty-five knots.

"What do you think is happening, Rick?" Charlie called, raising his voice over the action. "It's getting harder to trim. Sometimes I think we have too much sail and then, all of a sudden, it's fine."

"You're right about that, but for now we'll leave the sails be. We're heading into a tropical depression."

"A tropical depression? But it's sunny. And look, we can see forever. It's clear blue sky as far as the eye can see."

"That's because it's about 200 nautical miles out. I've been checking the barometer." Rick held up a small instrument. "It's been dropping steadily. I'm correlating the readings with the Tables for Diurnal Variation."

He glanced at a book in his other hand. "Unless it turns away, we're in for some thunderstorms before daybreak tomorrow. We're going to stay with this wind though, and veer off the storm's direction, to the south."

Charlie remembered his visit to the hurricane center on Cape Hatteras. *Wow, could this be the start of a hurricane? Thunderstorms, warm air*

rising, collecting water. Cool air rushing in, creating high swirling winds.
Well, I've been on the outskirts of a storm before. Maybe now I'll see how
the whole thing gets started. He felt tense, but his head was clear. Rick
didn't seem too upset. *Shit! Couldn't be worse than Nam, he thought.*

Charlie decided to tie down his surfboard along the starboard railing.
By nightfall the sky looked threatening. The wind direction changed
sporadically and, within an hour, rain started to fall. Then the lightning
began. Jacque stayed below and the two men worked through the night
maneuvering through the changing conditions, allowing the sloop to veer in
a southwesterly direction.

They knew storms swirled clockwise south of the equator. While it was
hard to tell, Rick speculated that it was traveling northeast. When the light
appeared, the rains were letting up. They directed their position toward the
north, trying to keep within the draft of the storm. But, by noon, the
weather was clear and beautiful, the wind was virtually gone.

"Guess I was right about the direction," Rick said. "We made it around
all right, but now we're on the back side of it all and we have no wind."

"That's all right with me," Jacque said. She looked relieved. "After all
of that bouncing around, I'm ready for a quiet sea."

They laughed. Rick gave her a hug.

"Well," Rick said, "it could be like this for awhile. I guess we'll have a
chance to relax."

Two days went by with just a trace of forward progression. Charlie took
the fishing pole Rick kept stored behind the fore bulkhead, and paddled out
a ways on his surfboard to do some fishing. Within minutes the pole bent.
Charlie jerked it to secure whatever he had on the hook, then reeled in a
fifteen-pound denizen of the deep.

"Looks like a Dorado to me," Charlie yelled, holding up his catch.

"A what?" Rick asked, baffled by Charlie's identification.

"Well, that's what the Mexicans call it."

"It's a Mahi Mahi," Jacque said. "Bring it back here to clean, Charlie.
We don't want you attracting any sharks out there."

That night they ate a fresh fish dinner, and stretched out on the deck to
enjoy the stars glistening in the new-moon sky. Without any distracting
glare, it seemed there were more stars than black sky. Charlie studied the

different configurations of the Southern Hemisphere. *Not even Nam has some of these stars*, he thought.

Late that night, a large swell rocked the boat, waking Charlie. Rick and Jacque, snuggled against the stern pulpit, sat up.

"What's that?" Charlie called back.

"Beats me," Rick replied. Suddenly, it happened again. The wind picked up. Rick pulled out his barometer and took a reading. "It's dropping again."

"Another storm?" Charlie asked.

"Either that or a re-curvature of the last one."

"Re-curvature?"

"Yeah, they slow down for a while, regroup, and then move in different directions. Sometimes they loop back and cross their previous track. When that happens it's usually worse than the first time around."

"Oh great!" Jacque said. "What do we do now?"

"Well, for now we can use this wind to start sailing again. I'll keep an eye on the barometer," Rick said.

By the next nightfall the storm had caught up with the *Jacquelyn*. It appeared to be traveling due east. Rick maneuvered the sloop in a southerly direction to try and outrun the vicious, boomeranging storm, but they were still in heavy seas.

It's worse than before, Charlie admitted to himself.

When dawn should have arrived, the sky remained nearly as dark as night, like an ominous force determined to hold the small sailboat captive. Waves twenty feet high and steeper by far, were difficult to plan for. Water poured over the deck, spilling into the cabin. The mighty wind prevented using the main sail. Soon, Rick ordered Charlie to lower the jib as well.

"How are we going to maintain speed to take on these waves?" Charlie shouted over the water's roar, as he worked up by the mast with the ousted main sail.

"We can't just drift through these billows. We'll get slaughtered."

"I know." Rick leaned over and lifted the lid of a storage seat in the cockpit molding. He pulled out a small, heavy looking sail.

"This is a trysail." He hurled it up to Charlie, slipped on the wet floor and fell onto the open storage lid. Blood spurted from a cut on his leg.

"Are you okay, man?" Charlie shouted.

"Yeah, no big deal." Rick stood up, grabbed the helm and steered over a mammoth breaker.

White water doused Charlie, slamming him flat onto the deck. He grabbed onto the mast with his right arm to keep from being washed overboard, keeping the trysail securely tucked under his left arm. Working his way up onto his knees, he looked at Rick, wondering about the captain's abilities.

Rick looked weary to Charlie. Jacque was busy bailing water, seemingly withdrawn from the danger as she labored.

"What do I do with this thing?" Charlie said, holding up the trysail.

"Jury rig it to the mast. Leave the boom free, I'll sheet it to a winch," Rick said, trying to yell but shaking badly.

"Charlie, I'm not sure how to take on these kind of waves. Any ideas?"

"I can't tell you how to do it, man. I'll finish up here and take over."

Charlie rigged the trysail, and took over at the helm. Waves like mountain crests broke helter-skelter in the vastness of the sea. He traversed across the wind to pick up speed before an oncoming surge, then cut directly toward the curl. The abrupt turn stalled the vessel, forcing the bow down and forward as the wave broke over.

"Hold on tight!" Charlie bellowed.

The crashing peak slid over the craft, barely slowing their progress.

"Holy shit!" Rick yelled, looking revitalized with the maneuver. "You're incredible! How did you know what to do?"

"It's just like surfing," Charlie admitted.

"Oh, my God! Rick! What happened?" Jacque screamed, seeing Rick's leg for the first time.

His leg bled profusely from a deep cut just above his kneecap. Blood smeared down his bare leg and onto the floor.

Charlie noted Rick's eyes appeared bleary. He seemed faint from the loss of blood. Charlie grabbed the collar on his own T-shirt, tugged until it ripped.

"Lay down, Rick. Jacque, hold his leg up here so I can pressure bandage it."

Charlie wrapped his torn T-shirt around the wounded thigh while he became mesmerized with the duty. Memories of his lieutenant's arm blasted into his mind.

"You're going to be all right, man," Charlie yelled. "I'll take care of the gooks."

Charlie read the oncoming swell, called for the artillery battery. He yelled out quadrants. He turned the sloop into the breaker, sucked in a deep breath. He looked at Rick but saw Robby's face.

"Hang on, man. Please! A chopper will be here for you in a minute—that is, if I do everything right."

The wave peaked. It slapped over the bow. The boat slithered under perfectly. By the time the water ebbed toward the stern, it had mostly dissipated off port.

"How are you doing, Robby?"

The couple stared, "Charlie, are you okay? Charlie?" Jacque asked.

"Wh…what?" He snapped out of his hallucination. "Yeah…yeah."

Charlie turned away, trying to act like nothing had happened.

Two waves raced at them from different directions. Charlie chose the closest one, maneuvered and got sideswiped by the second. The boat capsized, rolling over to port, the mast still above water. Rick and Jacque held on to the starboard lifelines. Charlie smacked into the cockpit molding. He sat on the port-side storage seat, neck deep in water.

Underwater currents ripped at the keel beneath the sloop and bounced it upright, catapulting Jacque overboard. Rick lunged forward to reach over the rail, but he couldn't grab her. He threw open the starboard storage seat and grabbed a red-and-white life buoy by the line.

In desperation, he pitched it out to Jacque. She grabbed, but when Rick pulled she slipped off. Frantically he hauled in the line and threw again, but she had washed out beyond reach.

Charlie jumped onto the deck untying his surfboard, hurled himself over the side onto the board and paddled swiftly toward Jacque.

"Keep your head up," he yelled. His mind flashed back: Will was floating face down in the water. "Keep your head up!"

Charlie paddled as fast as he could. Then he remembered Will dragging him through enemy fire like they were joined, spirits linked, sharing the same heart. *I was in your heart man, now it's your turn to get into mine.*

He stroked up next to Jacque. She bobbed in the water, almost out of breath. "Grab onto my heart!"

She grabbed onto his shoulders, struggled to pull herself onto his back. Charlie felt the spirit of his charge.

"I've gotcha, man. This time I've really got you."

He paddled feverishly, looking for the boat. Then he saw it five hundred yards out, bounding up a wave, heading in a different direction. Rick stood at the helm, struggling in the high seas, trying to circle back.

Okay, big guy, Charlie said to himself. *You have to make it. You are two spirits sharing one life. See yourself back on board.*

On February 5, 1970, Charlie wrote to his mom.

We were almost to the Marquesas but got into a little storm that blew us off course. I am writing you from Tahiti. We pulled into Papeete three days ago. Rick isn't feeling well, so I'm off on my own for a few days. Yesterday, I met a local fisherman who took me out to some of the remote islands. He had a little skiff and we found some incredible tubes, and I do mean incredible—some of the fastest waves I've ever seen. The swells break out a mile or so from land on coral reefs that stick up out of nowhere.

A few days later we set sail again on the Jacquelyn *for New Zealand. I heard there's some good surfing there, too. It's about 2,500 nautical miles from Tahiti. We hope to sail it in three weeks. I'll mail another letter from there.*

25

Tahiti was eight days back when Rick's health took a turn for the worse. When they had left the island, he thought he only had the flu and was feeling better. Then he became weak, his joints stiffened, his head ached, and his fever jumped to 104. Restless and unable to sleep, his body became so rigid he could hardly move.

Charlie spent most of the time at the helm, while Jacque tried to nurse Rick back to health. The winds were steady at fifteen knots, the sailing smooth. When the sun began to set, Jacque came up on deck to relieve Charlie.

"How's he doing?"

"I'm scared, Charlie. His vitals are getting weak. I don't know how he's surviving. He won't die out at sea, will he?"

Charlie froze. The thought of Rick dying had never crossed his mind.

"Charlie?"

"I hope not, Jacque. God, I hope not."

Charlie went down below and sat next to Rick. "How's it going?

Rick's blood-tinged eyes lacked life. "I'm not going to make it, Charlie," he said, his voice barely audible.

"Hey, don't talk like that, man. You're going to be all right. You'll be feeling better in no time."

"Listen, Charlie," he gasped for breath to speak. "Take care of Jacque for me. She didn't want to come on this trip. I talked her into it. She's a good sailor, but she needs moral support."

"What are you talking about? You're going to be here to help her out. You've got to talk positive, Rick. See yourself getting better, man. Like when I was in Nam. I visualized myself getting on the plane to go home."

Rick shook his head. "It's too late, Charlie."

Later that night, Charlie steered into a starboard tack when he heard Jacque's thin, wailing sound from down in the cabin. He knew that Rick was gone.

He locked the wheel in place, and went down to comfort Jacque. She held Rick in her arms, his eyes still open. Charlie bent down on one knee and, with his forefinger, gently closed Rick's eyes. He kissed Jacque on the forehead, then held out his arms. Jacque leaned forward and relinquished Rick's body to Charlie.

Charlie laid the body in a bunk and covered it with a sheet. He gathered up a blanket from his bunk, held Jacque's hand and helped her up the cabin ladder.

"You'll sleep better up here tonight," he said.

She looked at him, her eyes bloodshot. "Oh, Charlie. What am I going to do now? Rick is all I've got."

Charlie was silent. He thought about Nam, the bodies in the infirmary and the kind words from the lieutenant.

"You still have him, Jacque. His body is gone, but his being is still around. Nobody can take that away from you. Nobody can ever do that."

The next morning, the orange light from the sunrise reflected on the smooth, glassy ocean. It was bright to Charlie's tired eyes. He hadn't slept much that night, his mind riddled with thoughts of another death. *Why couldn't it have been me?* he thought?

Jacque stirred under her blanket, stared over at Charlie. "I want to bury Rick at sea."

"Are you sure?"

"Yes. I thought about it all night. Rick would want it that way."

"I'll take care of it," Charlie said.

Charlie went below and carried Rick's body up on deck. He laid it down on the starboard side and joined Jacque in prayer.

"Dear God," she began. "I give you my husband. I...I..." She grabbed Charlie's arm, unable to continue.

Charlie held her tightly for several minutes. Finally he said. "Dear God, maybe some day I'll understand how the angels chose. There were many times they could've taken me home, but they didn't do it. So how do they choose?"

He shook his head. "Rick is a good man. I'm sure he is well now—in heaven. Introduce him to Will and Al for me...and...and to my daddy," Charlie said.

With tears streaming down his cheeks, Charlie sat on the edge of the sloop and lowered his surfboard into the water, holding onto it with his foot. Then he eased Rick's body down onto the board and pushed it off.

"Take him away," he said to his faithful surfboard. "Find a proper place for him to rest."

As they sailed away, they continued to watch the board and body, until even through the binocular lenses, it disappeared.

Jacque kept to herself for the next twenty-four hours. She didn't even eat, and Charlie heard her weeping down in the cabin. Finally she came to Charlie.

"You're amazing, Charlie. I can't believe you gave up your surfboard for Rick."

"It was the least I could do, Jacque."

"Well, if he knew that you gave him your beloved surfboard, he would feel deeply honored." She looked longingly into his eyes.

He wanted to hug her but thought it wouldn't be respectful to Rick. Jacque always seemed to understand him.

"Jacque, have you thought about what you want to do?"

"I've decided to sell the boat in New Zealand. I just hope you aren't disappointed, Charlie."

Charlie was startled, then sighed. "Hey, you know me. I'm just along for the ride."

"No really, Charlie."

"If there's surf in New Zealand, I'll find it, Jacque."

Jacque's eyes watered. "I don't know what you've been through,

Charlie, but you're a special person."

Charlie felt an ache in the pit of his stomach. *Why is everybody always saying that to me? I've killed people. Lots of them. God, how can I be special with all that I've done?*

"I never thanked you for saving my life," Jacque continued.

"What do you mean?"

"You know what I mean. Not once, but twice."

"Twice?"

"The first time is when you sweet-talked that blue whale into leaving us alone."

Charlie shrugged his shoulders.

"Charlie, there's something I have to ask you. What did you mean when you said 'Grab onto my heart'?"

"What?"

"When you saved me in the water. You said, 'Grab onto my heart.'"

Charlie remembered trying to save Will.

"My friend saved my life in Vietnam. He carried me through sniper fire to a medevac. I felt that at that moment that we became one person. Our spirits joined at the heart for survival. Then, later, I tried to save his life while we were surfing."

His eyes watered. "I couldn't feel his spirit, Jacque. He couldn't grab onto my heart."

Jacque wiped the tears that trickled down Charlie's cheek. "I was in your heart, Charlie." She smiled and held out her arms.

Charlie fell into the warmth of her hug, still sobbing.

"It's okay, Charlie. It's okay," she said.

Ten days later, Charlie steered the *Jacquelyn* around North Cape, New Zealand, and into the Tasman Sea. The countryside looked beautiful, so green. They traveled offshore along a deserted beach for what seemed like a hundred miles. A huge forest loomed ahead with some of the biggest trees he'd ever seen. They followed 250 miles of coastline, and pulled into Manukau Harbour, Auckland.

"What will you do?" Jacque asked.

Charlie shrugged his shoulders. "First, I guess, I'll get a new surfboard."

"I'm sorry we're not going to Australia."

"Don't worry about it, Jacque. I'll find my way around here. I'll bet I find tubes just as good as they are in Australia."

"Do you have any money, Charlie?"

"Some. I spent most of my money the army paid me, but I sold my van, remember?"

"That's not very much."

"You have enough to worry about. I'll get along," he said.

"You can probably stay at the Youth Hostel for awhile, until you figure out where you want to go."

Charlie smiled. Jacque was beginning to sound like his mother. He tugged on his overgrown beard. "Do you think they might frown on me there?"

She smiled and ran her fingers through his shoulder length hair. "I think you look great."

He leaned forward and kissed her on the forehead.

Charlie checked into the Youth Hostel at the corner of City Road and Liverpool Street in the middle of downtown Auckland. A week's rent would cost $3.00, but he had to exchange his U.S. currency at the bank before they would take his money. He received sixteen New Zealand dollars for every twenty he gave.

"I only get sixteen back?"

"Sorry, mate," the bank teller said. "That's the exchange rate these days."

He walked back to the hostel shaking his head, his assets even less than before. *Oh well,* he thought, *at least I only have to pay three dollars for the room.*

That night he slept uninterrupted and rose early the next morning. He pulled on his shorts, sandals and long-sleeved T-shirt and stepped outside. He shivered at the brisk weather. It felt like a fall morning in San Diego.

"Excuse me, Sir, can you tell me what day it is?" Charlie addressed an older man selling newspapers.

"It's Wednesday, mate."

"I mean the date."

"Pardon?"

"The day of the month?"

"Oh, the bloody calendar count." He looked on the front page of one of his newspapers and chuckled.

"Had to look for meself, mate. It's March 4." He smiled, "Do you need the year as well?"

"Is it still 1970?" Charlie said, returning the joke.

"You're right as rain, mate."

"Sure is chilly around here."

"She'll be fall in a few weeks."

"Fall?"

"You must be from the northern hemi. We're heading for winter by the time June comes around."

Charlie shook his head. *Damn, I forgot all about the seasons being reversed.*

"Sorry about that, man. I've been out at sea for awhile. My brain's a little rusty." He slapped the old man on the back and walked up the street. *Wonder where the surf is?*

Charlie walked into a store—picked up a bottle of milk and a carton of yogurt. He put them on the checkout counter and looked up to see a young female clerk.

"That'll be fourdeen," she said.

Charlie smiled at the girl, cute with short black hair, and reached into his pocket. He pulled out a small wad of colorful bills. Each bill was a different color. He handed her a one-dollar bill.

She reached into a cash box and handed him back eighty-six cents. He looked curiously into his hand.

"Is everything right?" the clerk asked.

"I think you gave me too much change. Didn't you say forty cents?"

"No, luv. I said fourdeen. The milk is four, the culture is ten. Didn't I give ya eighty-six?"

"Yes. Four cents for milk?"

"That's the government price, four cents for a pint."

Charlie looked at the bottle; it seemed bigger than a pint. "This is a pint?"

"That's a bloody Imperial pint, luv. It's twenty ounces."

Charlie grinned. He liked the girl calling him 'luv.'

"Well, that's a heck of a deal, Ma'am. I think I'm going to be drinking a lot of milk around here."

"Where are you from?"

"Ever heard of California?"

"You're from California? Bloody oath?"

"Swear to God."

"I've met some Yanks before, but you're the first from California."

Charlie smiled. "You don't happen to know where the best surf is around here, do you?"

"That'd be Piha. On the western beach. Are you a board rider?"

"I sure am. How do I get to Piha?"

"Listen, mate, I'll be off in about twenty minutes. Would you like me to take you there?"

"Would you? That would be great!"

She held out her hand. "My name's Melinda."

They drove up the coast in her little car—a Holden that was like a European vintage, with the steering wheel on the right side to accommodate New Zealand's left-hand road driving. They parked high up on a cliff overlooking a long, deserted beach. Rocks jutted out of the water. Waves pealed off them in each direction.

Charlie got out of the car and threw back his head. "Aaaahhhhoooo!"

Melinda smiled. "Been awhile since you've seen the ocean?"

Charlie laughed. "Not really, but it's been awhile since I've seen rideable tubes. Where's the nearest surf shop where I can get a surfboard?"

"There's a board shop up the road. Would you like to go and get a board, luv?"

"You bet I would."

Charlie bought a seven-foot surfboard, the longest in the shop, and headed back to Piha with Melinda. The board was smaller than he was used to and difficult to ride at first, but soon he was ripping the waves apart. When he paddled in, Melinda ran up to greet him.

"Good job, mate. There's nobody that surfs like ya around here."

When she dropped Charlie back at the hostel, they arranged to meet later.

Charlie decided to write home before going out that night.

Made it to New Zealand. The Jacquelyn *will be sold in Auckland so I guess I'll travel around here for awhile. Bought a rucksack and might try hitchhiking. I have already ridden some pretty good waves and met a nice friend who's showing me around.*

This country is made up of two islands and together they are about the size of California. The West Coast is on the Tasman Sea and the East Coast is on the Pacific. I like sunsets over the water so I guess I'll head down the West Side first. I'll write more later.

Before leaving his room that night, Charlie stashed all but a few dollars in his new pack. He and Melinda went to a hotel pub—the only pubs that allowed women—to have a few drinks. Charlie ordered beer, which was served in large, liter-size bottles.

He poured his brew into a tall glass and took a swig. It felt smooth going down, but he immediately noticed a buzz.

"Whoa! This is quite a beer."

A man sitting next to them spoke up. "It sure is, Yank. Your choice is the best on the North Island. Seven percent—not like your weak American piss."

He laughed and whistled in the direction of the dartboard. "Hey, mates. We got a new Yank in town."

Four men broke up their game of darts and sauntered over.

"Why don't you leave us alone," Melinda pleaded.

"Now, now, Lassie. We're just going to get acquainted with the Yankee here."

"It's all right, Melinda." Charlie said, patting her arm. He turned to address the man. "I'm Charlie Armfield from California." He stuck out his hand to the man doing the talking.

The man, tall and brawny, scrutinized Charlie. Charlie held his ground.

Finally one of the other men extended his hand. "I'm Trevor. This here is Ian, Reggie and Connor."

Charlie stood, shook all of their hands and turned back toward the first man. "What's your name, mate?"

The other men were quiet. Finally the man spoke up. "Gavin." He seemed reluctant to continue at first, then stuck out his hand. "Gavin Blankenship."

There was a sigh of relief from the group as Gavin shook Charlie's hand. "Where are ya staying, Yank?"

"At the hostel. Don't know for how long, though. I intend to head down the coast to find some surf."

"Where in California are ya from?" Trevor asked.

"San Diego."

"Is it good for board riding there?"

"Sure is. I'd say some of the best in the world. Well, not as good as Hawaii, but there're a lot of good breaks."

Gavin shook his head. "Sounds like you haven't surfed Aussie yet."

"You mean Australia?"

"That's right. Met the world champ in this very bar last month. He says the best is in Queensland."

Charlie's eyes felt like they were going to pop out of his head. "Colin Robins was here?"

"So you know him, do ya?" Gavin spoke curtly.

"Heard of him, is all."

"Listen up, Yank. How about a game of darts?" Gavin said, gritting his teeth.

Melinda shook her head, "No!"

"Come on, Yank. It's just a friendly game," Gavin challenged.

"Why not?" Charlie said. "Never played before, but it sounds like fun."

They lined up across from the board and Gavin held out six darts, three with red feathers and three with white. Charlie chose the red darts. Gavin put his hand out toward the target, indicating Charlie should go first.

"Shoot the numbers down in order," Gavin said. "If you get through that, you get to go for the bull's eye."

Charlie took aim and nailed numbers one and two with his second and third shot. With his turn, Gavin got one, two and three. They continued neck and neck, tied when it was time for the bull's eye. Gavin shot first and missed with all three darts.

Charlie missed on his first two—one dart left. He looked at the other men. All smiled and appeared to be cheering him on—except Gavin, who looked nervous. Melinda appeared nervous, too.

Charlie turned back toward the target. He saw the gook, machine gun in his hand. *Oh my God.* Charlie raised his M-16, took aim, and squeezed the trigger. A bullet hole appeared between the gunner's eyes.

Dazed, Charlie stared blankly. Had he killed, or not? Then he saw the red-plumed dart, stuck into the bull's eye. The crowd was cheering.

Melinda threw her arms around him and kissed his mouth. "You did it!" she yelled. "I can't believe you beat the pub master."

Trevor congratulated Charlie. "Good shooting, mate. You must have been puttin' us on with your experience."

"What do you mean?" Charlie asked.

"Darts, mate. How long have you been shootin'?"

Charlie lowered his head. *Darts,* he thought. *I've never shot darts before—only gooks.*

The men anteed up to buy the victor a round and saluted Charlie. All except Gavin, that is, who had disappeared.

After drinking up, Charlie suggested he and Melinda find a private table. They talked into the night, Melinda moving closer and closer until her arm moved around his shoulder.

"You're quite a bloke, Charlie Armfield. What do you say we walk back to your flat?"

They walked arm in arm to the hostel and when they arrived, Charlie noticed immediately that the door to his room was ajar. He dashed in and found his clothes spread all about, his money and surfboard gone. He darted out of the room, surveyed the hallway, then sprinted to the street. Nobody. Nobody in sight. He talked with the clerk, but no information was available. He returned to his room, dejected, and sat on the bed, and put his head into his hands.

Melinda sat next to him and put her arms around his waist. "No worries, luv. The authorities will find the thief in the morning. Besides, we still have each other for the night."

Charlie looked her in the eye and shook his head. "I don't think so, Melinda. I don't think I'm up for having each other for the night."

Part IV

The Renaissance

26

Charlie stayed awake, contemplating his fate. He was alone in a strange country, no money, not even a surfboard. He paced around the room, stared out the window. A man slept on the sidewalk in front of the hostel. He shook his head, ripped the shirt off his back and threw it across the room. He stewed until the early morning hours, and finally fell into a fitful sleep.

The jungle pressed in on him. Two men swinging machetes to clear passage didn't notice the gooks. Charlie looked up just in time to make eye contact with an NVA soldier, forty yards out. He squeezed the trigger of his M-16 and a burst headed toward the enemy. Charlie dove to the ground, yelling for his men to follow. Then he saw two more and fired. They fell off to the side. He slithered forward to reconnoiter. Enemy machine gun rounds blistered over his head. He took his last red feathered dart out and threw for the bull's eye—got him right between the eyes.

When the sun peered into his room, he woke with a start and gasped for a breath. *Oh, no! Not again—not again! When will it ever end?* He rolled over and pulled the sheet up over his head.

The facts of his situation crowded in—no money, no surfboard. *Shit!*

I have no life. What's the damn point? I've got to get out of this body. Please dear God, get me out of this body.

Charlie dressed quickly and ran out into the street. He stuck his thumb out, and a car with a surfboard on top pulled over.

"Where are ya headed, mate?" the driver asked.

"I don't know. Piha, I guess. Yeah, Piha. Are you headed that way?"

"Could be, mate. I'm just out lookin' for a swell this morning. Piha could be the place. Get in."

Charlie opened the passenger door and hopped into the seat. "Thanks, Mister."

The man put his car into gear and started up the road. "You just land in New Zealand?"

"A couple of days ago."

"You know, mate, most people don't take kindly to the thumb gesture."

Charlie looked curiously at the man. "The thumb gesture?"

"Around here, the thumb is the same as the middle finger in your country."

Charlie was surprised. "Really? How do you hitchhike around here?"

"Just point with your index."

Charlie held up his finger.

"Right, mate, but point it in the direction that you're hitchin."

Charlie laughed at himself. "Guess I could have gotten myself into a heap of trouble."

The man chuckled. "Sure could have."

"That's all I need." He sighed and watched for the water as they pulled out of the city.

"Everything all right, mate?"

Charlie shrugged his shoulder, remembered Rick floating away—dead on his surfboard. *Why couldn't that be me? Falling off the cliff at Piha might work.*

When they pulled up at Piha he was ready to hurl himself off of the cliff, when the man spoke up. "You ever ride before?"

"Ride? Ride what?"

"The waves—ever ride the waves before?"

"Yeah. I've tried it a bit."

"Listen, mate. I'm going to stretch out on the beach a bit before hittin' it. Why don't you take me board and catch a few?"

Charlie studied the man; he was probably in his fifties. He sat tall, sported a bushy mustache and shoulder length brown hair, a bit longer than his own. Wrinkles creased his forehead. His pale blue eyes returned Charlie's gaze, as though he recognized the dark thoughts roiling in his mind.

"Are you sure?"

"Couldn't be more sure, mate. There's a spare swimmer in the boot. Wetsuit, too, if you like."

"Thanks." Charlie smiled and held out his hand. "My name's Charlie Armfield."

The man gripped Charlie's hand. "James Richards."

Charlie looked in the trunk and found the bathing suit and wet suit top. He changed in the back seat of the car. Then he worked the straps to loosen the surfboard and ran with it to the shoreline. The man followed behind and settled into the granular silica.

The surfboard, longer and with a wider nose, felt better to Charlie than the one he had purchased. He took off on his first wave, faded left on his knees, stood up and cranked a hard smooth turn to the right. He stalled to allow the nose to perk up and walked forward, hanging five, then ten toes over. The wave, nearly five feet high, began to curl over Charlie. He crouched down sliding his right foot back, his left still perched on the nose. The wave peeled over his back, placing him in the tube for nearly two seconds. Then he stood up and back peddled, cut several turns and kicked out of the wave.

He rode for the next half-hour, then came in with the shore break to return the board. James took it, smiled, and paddled out. Charlie lay in the warm sand watching the ocean. After the water's chill, the morning sun felt good.

He watched James move through the water, his style fluent and intentional; he was certainly more agile than Charlie expected. Who was this man?

When James came in, they walked together back to the car.

"You're pretty good on the board, mate," James said, smiling at Charlie.

"You're not so bad, yourself. How long've you been surfing?"

"Started as a wee tot. Me family used to travel a lot. Went to Hawaii once and they let me bring a board back. People around here never saw one before, so I was the only bloke in the water, until the late fifties. Now it's pretty common. You're a champion, eh, mate?"

Charlie stared for a moment. "Used to be. Then my life got screwed up. Now it's gone all the way down the drain."

James looked away, then back into Charlie's eyes. "Things are never as bad as they seem, Charlie. Just when you think that it's the worst, something happens to make it better. And it's all inside of you, mate. The good and the bad—it's all inside of you."

Charlie cocked his head and looked at James. *It's all inside of me?*

"Why, I'll bet," James continued, "at this very moment something is happening to make your life better."

Charlie shrugged his shoulders. "I don't know how." Charlie contemplated—something happening?

"Do you live around here?"

"Nah, I'm from New Plymouth, mate. Just up to Auckland for some business. The city life is a bit much for me."

James drove Charlie back to the hostel. "Thanks for the surf, James."

"Pleasure was mine, Charlie. Maybe you'll come down to New Plymouth in your travels?"

What travels, Charlie thought to himself.

James continued, "You know, when things take a turn for the better, eh, mate?"

"Yeah, sure. Thanks again, man."

Charlie trudged into the hostel. He saw Jacque sitting in the lobby.

"Hi Charlie," Jacque said, extending her arms for a hug. "I've been waiting for you."

They embraced and she held him tight. "I'm leaving for California this afternoon and I wanted to see you again before I left," she said. "I have something for you."

"Something for me?"

"Yes." She looked around at the people in the lobby. "Is there some place we can talk in private, Charlie?"

"Do you mind coming to my room?"

"Charlie, we traveled together for three months. We shared the same bedroom on the boat, remember?"

Charlie laughed, "Okay, follow me."

They walked into his room and sat next to each other on the bed. Charlie looked at her.

"Charlie, I want you to have this." She reached into a bag she carried over her shoulder and pulled out an envelope.

Charlie stared, puzzled.

"Take it, Charlie."

He reached out and took the bulging white envelop. He peeled open the flap and money spilled out. He gasped and looked into Jacque's eyes.

"It's for you, Charlie. I sold the boat and thought you deserved half. It's the least I can do."

"But…you don't need to do this, Jacque."

"Oh, yes, I do. I owe you my life. Besides, without you I think I would still be out in the middle of the Pacific somewhere."

"I doubt it. You're a great sailor, Jacque."

"I was great with you and Rick around." She smiled affectionately at Charlie.

Her beautiful long hair draped over her shoulders, framing her small, sturdy frame. Charlie wanted to kiss her, then a glimpse of Lisa Strangemeir flashed into his mind. *No, man, you can't do that again,* he thought.

"What are you thinking, Charlie?"

"Oh nothing, I…I…mean, thanks for the money, Jacque."

"Now you can go to Australia," she said.

"Yeah. Maybe I'll do just that."

He remembered James, how he said that something was happening to make his life better. "I think I need to go to New Plymouth first."

"New Plymouth?"

"Yeah, I don't know why, but all of a sudden I need to go there. I don't even know where that is, Jacque. Somewhere here in New Zealand, I think."

The coolness of the foggy morning caressed Charlie's face as he walked up Hobson Street toward the Auckland-Hamilton Motorway. The backpack on his shoulders was filled with new clothing suitable for a New Zealand winter: a sweater, rain jacket, jeans, and a wetsuit. It also contained a sleeping bag and a small pup tent. Under his right arm he held a new surfboard. Curious stares glanced off him as he wove his way through the early workforce of Auckland City.

"Where ya headed, mate?" shouted a young schoolboy, clad in his neatly pressed uniform, carrying a brown satchel.

"New Plymouth."

"Taranaki Peninsula, eh? Best surfing on the North Island."

Charlie stopped to talk to the lad. "Really?"

The boy laughed, "First trek south, mate?"

"Yes. Don't know much about the area."

"When you see the mount, you'll know you're almost there."

"Mount?"

"Mount Egmont, mate. She's right in the middle of the Peninsula. Second most perfect mountain in the world, next to Fuji."

"Sounds beautiful. Do you get down there much?"

The boy grimaced. "No, me older brother surfs down there a bit. Says there's surfing all along the hundred kilos of Peninsula and every spot has a peak of the mount. Has snow on it most of the year, mate."

"Thanks for the info, man. Hope you get to go surfin' down there sometime."

The boy grinned. "Next summer, mate. Me brother promised to drag me along."

"All right! Maybe I'll see you down there."

They waved goodbye and Charlie continued his hike, a spring to his step despite his weighty load. *Sounds like I'm going to like New Plymouth,* he thought.

At the main highway, he laid his pack on the left hand side of the road, balanced his surfboard on top and stuck out his index finger.

Cars sped by, small New Zealand cars. Very few had racks on top. He wondered if the drivers were put off by all of his stuff. He picked up his surfboard and put it in the ditch by the side of the road and returned to his luggage.

He put his finger out again and a car pulled up. "Where ya headed, mate?"

"New Plymouth."

"I'm off as far as Hamilton. Will that do ya?"

"Great! Do you mind if I load my surfboard in your trunk?" He pointed into the furrow.

"In me what?"

Charlie hesitated, then remembered James calling it a boot. "In your boot. I have some rope."

"Give it a try, mate."

Charlie put his gear into the back of the car. The surfboard stuck out nearly five feet. He retrieved a red T-shirt out of his pack to tie onto the tail, and used a tent rope to secure the load.

"Blimey. I didn't think you were going to get that done."

Charlie smiled as he got into the car and stuck out his hand. "Charlie Armfield, from California, U.S.A."

"Grayson Edgerton, mate. Welcome to New Zealand."

When they arrived in Hamilton, Grayson offered to drive Charlie down to Raglan. "Me day's wasted anyway, mate, and they say Raglan's good for board riding. It's only fifty kilometers out of me way. I wouldn't mind watching a California rider."

Raglan, a long left-handed point break, was bursting with an eight foot swell when they arrived. Charlie rode seven waves, each ride lasting nearly five minutes. After each one he walked back to the point, stumbling over the rocky shoreline. Grayson walked along with him.

"Good on ya, mate. You're riding way better than any of the Kiwi's out there."

"Kiwis?" Charlie questioned.

"That's the jargon for a local New Zealander, mate. It's also the national bird. Useless fowl, can't even fly."

Grayson took Charlie home that afternoon to meet his wife. "Will you be staying for tea, Charlie?" she asked.

"Of course he'll be staying for tea, Maggie. Pull out that lamb and we'll have it when we get back from the pub."

"But we were saving that for Sunday tea with mother."

"Christ, Maggie. There's twenty bloody sheep per person in this country. We'll get another one. Come on, Charlie. Let's get you acquainted with some New Zealand grog."

Charlie shrugged his shoulders toward Maggie before following Grayson out the door. *Sorry, Ma'am,* he thought. *Didn't mean to inconvenience you.*

Charlie drank beer with Grayson and his friends. Later they returned to the house for dinner, both of them tipsy. After the meal, Charlie offered to help with the dishes. Maggie looked shocked. Grayson ignored the gesture and dragged Charlie to the dartboard.

The guest bed, a wire mesh, springy contraption with a feather mattress on top, did little to invite sleep. Despite his fatigue and the grog he'd drunk,

Charlie couldn't get comfortable. His buttocks sank six inches lower than the rest of him. By the middle of the night his back ached. He tossed in and out of sleep. When he did doze...

We followed this regiment into the valley and, now, I'm going to call in artillery and kill everyone? No, man! I don't want to do it. We're not going to win the war anyway. I think we should get out of here. It's like we filled the basin with water and now we're pulling the plug. We'll never get to wash our hands—dirty hands forever.

The next morning, Grayson questioned Charlie as he drove him out to the main road. "What was all that about dirty hands, mate?"

"Wh...what?"

"I could hear ya in your sleep. You said something about dirty hands."

Charlie shook his head, and shrugged his shoulders. "Sorry, Grayson, must have been dreaming."

Charlie unloaded his gear and waved goodbye to Grayson.

He sat on his pack, making no attempt to conceal his surfboard. He was angry with himself. Angry because of the dreams that just wouldn't go away. Cars whizzed by. He failed to stick out his finger. *It's the pain, big guy. It's the goddamn pain. Why won't it leave me alone? I don't want anymore pain.* He spread his legs and beat his fist against his pack.

Then a car drove up and screeched to a stop.

Charlie didn't look up until he heard James' voice. "G'day, mate. You be headed my way?"

Startled, Charlie stood up quickly. "Oh hi, James. I...I guess I am."

He loaded his gear in the car and climbed into the passenger seat. As James drove on, he stared out the window.

Finally James said, "Pardon me, mate, but every time I pick you up you seem to be down."

Charlie turned toward James, looked into the eyes of a wise man. A man to entrust his woes to?

"I've done some horrible things, man. My country made me kill people." He sighed heavily. "And now I'm paying for it."

"So what is it that you feel, Charlie?"

"Pain, man." Charlie felt agitated by the question. "I can't get rid of it. It's bad, man, really bad. Sometimes I want to die."

James remained silent until Charlie settled down. "First of all, mate, where is it going?"

"What do you mean?"

"If you went through a heavy trauma, do you think you will ever forget the experience?"

"Never! I will never forget that shit."

"Right. I wouldn't think you should. So consequently, you will always have the pain, as well."

Charlie felt confused. *What's he saying?*

"Don't get me wrong, mate. I believe that you can understand your pain and it won't hurt so badly. But it has nowhere to go. Now I have to ask you: why is it so bad?"

Charlie raised his voice, "Because it hurts me. I feel like I have a dagger in my chest."

"If you did all the horrible things you say, shouldn't you feel wounded?"

Charlie was stunned. *What's this guy trying to prove?*

"Hang with me, mate, before you tear me head off. I'm saying, if you did horrible things and you didn't have the pain, something's amiss. Pain is good, Charlie; and that's good with a capital G, mate. In your life, have you had any exciting things happen to you that made you feel elated?"

Charlie shrugged his shoulders. "Sure."

"When was that?"

"Whenever I won a surf contest. Those were the greatest moments ever, because it meant I surfed good."

"Would you say the emotions you felt were natural?"

"Of course."

"Then horrible things happening should have natural emotional reactions, as well. They don't feel very good, but they're as natural as rain coming from a cloud. Like the tears you cry, mate."

"But I don't like the goddamn tears."

"What's wrong with them?"

"I feel like such a fool." With that said, he began to cry. "They come all the time, man. I get flashbacks and I can't stop crying."

"They're good tears, Charlie, and they are for you. You mustn't worry. Those tears are angelic droplets that you are blessed with, to clean your soul. Without them you would be destroyed from the build-up of torrential waters, which would only block your responses to the world. The dam is breaking, mate, and you are being set free."

"It's good to cry?" he asked, wiping his face.

"It's great!"

Charlie turned his head to look out the window. *Angelic tears? Angels are trying to help me? Are they the same angels from Vietnam?* He leaned his head on the glass, exhausted from the conversation and from lack of sleep. In moments, he fell asleep.

Angels appeared in his dreams. *Yes, Charlie, we were with you in Vietnam and are still with you today. Throughout all of your experiences, we are here to help you laugh and cry. Both are good, Charlie. Both are expressions of love.*

When Charlie woke, James tapped his finger on the windshield. "Look, mate, there's Mount Taranaki."

Charlie looked ahead and saw the perfect mountain peak. "Is that the same mountain they call Egmont?"

"Yes, mate, but the Maoris call it Taranaki. They're the original people of New Zealand; been here since about 800 AD. They call us *Pakeha*, white people, and we've only been here since the late 1700s. I reckon we had no business changing the name."

"Sounds reasonable to me, James." He looked at his driver, awed by James' knowledge and presence of mind.

"I want to thank you for the help, man. I feel a lot better."

James looked over at Charlie and smiled. "You were ready, mate."

Charlie stared at James. *Who is this guy?*

"I have a farm out on the peninsula, mate. Would you honor me wife and meself with a visit? The peninsula has some great surf beaches."

27

As James drove along the coast, through the town of New Plymouth, and south around the peninsula to his farm, Charlie rode in silence. The scenery was beautiful. The rolling hills were the greenest he had ever seen. They pulled off on a dirt road and headed east, up into the grasslands, and stopped in front of an old vacant house.

"I think you should stay here, mate. It's the closest to the surf on me property. We call it the beach house," James chuckled.

"You'll be alone, but you can walk to the water any time you wish. It's a bit more than a kilometer. The main house is up and away a few more. Get settled and I'll send someone down to get ya at tea time."

"What time is that?" Charlie asked.

James smiled. "That's dinner time in your country, mate. About six o'clock. You've got plenty of time for a surf. Wear footgear though, there's sticker bush in the grass."

Charlie moved into the beach house—one small bedroom with a kitchen-dining room combination. He located a shower outside, and an outhouse. *Cool,* he thought.

He changed into his wetsuit, slipped into his sandals and walked fifteen minutes down to the shore.

He paddled out into a five-foot swell. The waves broke hard onto a rocky bottom, and it took him ten minutes to make it to the outside. He was panting as he looked around.

The sun shone brightly where he sat on his board, but a rain cloud hovered near the grassy hills. A perfect double rainbow emerged, with faint signs of a third form arching above the snow capped Mount Taranaki.

"Wow!" He spoke out loud, even though no one was around. A chill drove up through Charlie's spine. *Oh my god,* he thought. *I've never seen anything so beautiful in my whole life.*

Passing on several waves, Charlie sat quietly, viewing the rainbows before they faded. Feeling rejuvenated, he surfed hard for an hour before returning to the house to clean up for dinner.

The shower, he discovered, supplied cold water only. He washed quickly, jumping up and down to warm himself. Then he saw the old pickup truck driving up to the house. He hurried to get the soap out of his hair, whipped a towel around his waist and rushed for the backdoor. Too late—a girl stood in the front entrance as he popped in.

"Excuse me," she said. "Sorry."

"It's okay," Charlie said, ducking into the bedroom.

He dressed in jeans and a sweater and came out. "Who are you?"

"I'm Gwen. Dr. Jim sent me to get you for dinner."

Charlie studied the girl; she was gorgeous, about five-foot-five, and had shoulder-length dark hair. About his age, he thought.

"Dinner?"

She smiled. "Yes."

"You sound American."

Gwen cocked her head as if to tease him. "I do?"

Charlie looked at her, frowning. "Yes, you do." Then he smiled. "I'm Charlie. Where are you from, Gwen?"

"Cleveland. How about you?"

"San Diego. Did you say Dr. Jim sent you?"

"Yes."

"You mean James is a doctor?"

"Yes."

"He never told me. I thought he was a farmer."

Gwen chuckled.

"He's a doctor all right, a special kind of doctor. People come from all around to see him. He works on their spines, but he has many gifts."

"He works on their spines?"

Gwen laughed. "Yes, he's a doctor of chiropractic, but he's a lot more than that. Dr. Jim is a special man."

Charlie remembered his conversation about pain with James, and how good he felt afterward.

"I think he already did some healing on me."

"He would say that he only enticed the healer within you, Charlie. Dr. Jim says that all things good and bad are within."

Charlie hesitated, remembering James' words in Auckland.

"I think he already told me that, too. What are you doing here, Gwen?"

She smiled. "I used to ask myself that question all the time. Dr. Jim says that wherever we are, that's where we're supposed to be. I traveled to India, where I met him."

"He was in India?"

"We studied yoga together with B.K.S. Iyengar. Dr. Jim invited me to come to New Zealand and work in his practice. I've been here for over a year now. Do you like it here?"

"I sure do," Charlie said, remembering the rainbow framing the mountain. Was Gwen married to James? He hoped not.

"We'd better get going. Dinner will be served shortly," Gwen said.

As they drove to the main house, he noticed several small dwellings off to the side, and people walking along the road. Gwen stopped several times and the pedestrians climbed into the back of the truck.

"Who are they?" Charlie questioned.

"They've come to stay at the sanitarium. Folks come from all around to be with Dr. Jim."

"That must be expensive."

"There's no charge to come here, Charlie, although many people leave donations. Some work on the farm and help with the chores or with the construction of new houses. It's like a commune, except most people come and go. They come to rejuvenate their health—sometimes their lives."

Gwen parked next to a large barn. She motioned Charlie to follow her into the structure. To Charlie's surprise, he found polished hardwood covering the floor. Large glass chandeliers dangled from beams. Colorful tapestries decorated the paneled walls. In the center was a large round table set for fifty or more. People congregated near the table; some looked sick, others were spirited and laughing.

James walked into the barn, holding hands with a pleasant looking woman.

"G'day, everyone."

"G'day," the group replied in unison, as they joined hands in a circle.

Gwen grabbed Charlie's hand and joined the group.

"We are gathered here," James said, eyes closed, "to honor the omnipresence of the universe—the one supremacy that is within and throughout all things, including all of us here. We give thanks for our pleasures in life. We give thanks for our pains in life." He hesitated.

Charlie felt a shivering wave surge through his body. Gwen squeezed his hand.

"For we know," James continued, "that all has been given to us as essential blessings for our experience in this life."

His voice seemed to change; it sounded like Charlie's father.

"Grant us knowledge and understanding, so that we might become relaxed within to embellish our wholeness with thee."

James opened his eyes and looked at Charlie.

"We have a guest with us today. His name is Charlie Armfield."

Everybody turned toward Charlie.

"If you get a chance," James said, "watch him in the waves. He's a master."

James broke the circle, still holding hands with the woman he'd arrived with. She was short, with long graying hair.

"Charlie, this is me wife. She goes by Kate."

She held out her hand. "Thanks for joining us, Charlie."

"Let's get on with tea," James said, motioning Charlie and Gwen to join him at the table.

Platters with vegetables, rice, and fish were brought to the table, and were circulated by the guests.

"This is an incredible place," Charlie said.

"Thanks, mate," James replied. "This farm used to belong to me granddad. Still have sheep and milk cows. When he died, I moved me practice here, and the retreat just sort of happened. We have to keep building flats to keep up with the demand. Spread 'em out though, so we don't look like a bloody city. How's your accommodation?"

Charlie grinned. "It's fantastic, man."

After dinner, the floor in the barn was cleared, and James led the group with yoga postures and meditation. The session concluded with chanting. Gwen's beautiful soprano voice began the mantra.

> *There is on-ly love,*
> *There is on-ly love,*
> *There is o-o-only,*
> *o-o-only- looove.*

The group joined Gwen. Music vibrated through the barn. *There is on-ly love.*

Charlie sang, mesmerized by the pitch. Suddenly, an image of a bloodied face appeared in his mind. He stopped singing. *There is only love? He asked himself. What about war, what about killing? There's no way that is love.*

The early morning glow over Mount Taranaki reflected on the ocean. The water glimmered with orange as Charlie sat on his surfboard, waiting for the first set of the day. His mind thrashed endlessly, still trying to process the message in the song. *How can everything be love?* Anger boiled through him. *War is not love!*

He surfed for two hours, until he spotted a feminine figure on the beach. He paddled in to see who it was.

"Hi, Gwen. How long have you been sitting here?"

"About two hours. I saw you leaving the house while on my morning walk. You don't waste any time in the morning, do you?"

"An old habit, I guess. The waves are better before the wind picks up. And, back home I can avoid the crowds if I go early."

Gwen laughed, "I don't think you have to worry about crowds around here. The only other person I've ever seen surfing here is Dr. Jim."

She looked into Charlie's eyes. "Are you all right?"

"Yeah, I'm just tired. I didn't sleep very well."

"I thought you would sleep like a baby. I'm out cold after a session like we had last night."

"It felt good, but then I had nightmares."

She studied him. "What about, Charlie?"

"I…I can't say."

"It's okay." She put her arm around Charlie. "We all have a story."

Charlie shook his head. "Not like mine."

Gwen peered at Charlie. "I'm the oldest of ten children. My parents are alcoholics. We didn't have much money. Twelve of us lived in a two bedroom house. Mom couldn't manage very well, so I had to take care of my brothers and sisters. I never felt much love in the household, Charlie. A schoolteacher persuaded me to have sex, and I became pregnant at seventeen. My parents were ashamed of me and sent me away to live with my aunt until the baby was born. I lost a full scholarship to Ohio State."

Charlie noticed that Gwen's eyes appeared clear and focused; there were no tears.

"When the baby was born, I gave it up for adoption. I felt like I didn't have a choice. I had no money, no future. I did not want my child to be raised in the same household I was. I went to work in a factory, but I felt so guilty for giving up my daughter to strangers."

Charlie's heart pounded. He shook his head.

"Most of the people at work were men. I was harassed until I couldn't take it anymore, so I quit my job and started traveling. I went to England, and met a man I fell in love with. He promised to marry me. Then I caught him with another woman. I went to France and met somebody else. But I couldn't trust him, either. I couldn't trust anyone. I traveled across the continent into Asia and ended up in India."

"Where you met Dr. Jim?"

"That's right. He's been a great teacher for me. Without him I don't know where I might have ended up. I'm okay with my past now, Charlie. I love what I do here."

"Gwen, what about your daughter?"

"Enough about me. What about you, Charlie?"

Charlie felt a warm flush spread across his face; his forehead twitched.

"I was drafted," he said, lowering his head. "I went to Vietnam."

Gwen studied him for several minutes without speaking. Finally she said, "Sit in front of me, Charlie."

"What?"

"Sit in front of me and lean back against me."

Charlie felt puzzled as he moved into position as she directed.

"Now, look out at that beautiful ocean. Let yourself become quiet inside."

"Quiet inside? How?"

"Relax, Charlie. Watch the surf."

He looked at the sea, drew a deep breath and let it out. Gwen sat still behind him, supporting him, allowing him to recline against her. Gradually calmness spread through him.

Then, Gwen said softly, "I want you to think about Vietnam, Charlie. Slowly, not too fast, move your consciousness into Southeast Asia. Think about what you saw, what you did."

Charlie's mind raced. *What? She wants me to go to Vietnam?*

Gwen repeated her direction; her voice was so filled with love Charlie felt moved to follow her instruction.

He saw Sergeant Payne and heard the order to go to the infirmary to report on the casualties, then smelled the stench as he opened the first body bag. Oh, my god! He grabbed his nose, even though he was still sitting in the fresh air by the ocean.

He saw the face of a young man, his chest open—blood everywhere. Then Bill MaGuire came into his vision, his face unrecognizable, a green jade ring on his hand. Then Top laughed.

"Stop laughing, you asshole! I didn't want to come over here. It's your fault. It's your fault."

"Whose fault is it, Charlie?" Gwen whispered.

"Sergeant Payne. He drafted me," Charlie said. "Well—I guess he didn't really draft me. But...but..."

"People like him drafted you?"

"Yeah, people in my government. They drafted me and made me go. I didn't want to go, Gwen. I wanted to stay home and surf. I wanted to surf in the World Contest. They wouldn't let me do it. I was so close."

"Close to what?"

"I don't know. I guess I was so close to being the best surfer in the world."

Charlie realized what he'd said. "No, it wasn't that. I wanted to become close with the ocean, Gwen. Like a dolphin. I figured that if I could be like a dolphin, the world contest would be mine. I would be connected. I was almost there," he raged. "Then my goddamn country grabbed me. Before I could…"

"What are you feeling right now? What emotion?"

"Anger! I feel anger! I'm mad as hell!" Charlie shouted, hysterically.

Gwen wrapped her arms around him and held him tightly as he wailed.

"You can still do it, Charlie."

"Do what?"

"Be the best surfer in the world."

"I will never surf competitively again." He felt irritated.

"Maybe not, but you could learn how to surf like a dolphin."

Charlie shook his head. "The drive's gone, Gwen. For awhile I even thought about taking my own life."

"Why didn't you?"

"I'm not sure." He remembered his discussion about pain with James.

"I guess because I met James. He helped me to understand pain." Charlie shrugged his shoulders and turned toward Gwen. "What happened to me?"

"You experienced a healing, so now you can deal with the pain. You can deal with the anger, too."

Charlie lowered his brows. "I don't think so. My country…"

Gwen held up her hand. "Listen for a moment."

He nodded, agreeing to listen.

"There are no mistakes in a lifetime. Everything that happens has a reason."

"What? How can that be?"

"You promised to listen," she said, squeezing his shoulders, looking him straight in the eye.

"In the Universe, there is a rule. Everything happens because of a natural flow. There are plans for you, Charlie, big plans. Maybe surfing is not a part of them."

"But surfing is my whole life."

"Exactly. So I guess the Universe had to do something drastic to get your attention."

"Like making me go to war and kill people?"

"I know it's hard to believe, but nothing happens outside of the plan. Surfing was your whole life, and there wasn't room for anything else. Perhaps Vietnam was the only thing that could help you see there was more in life than the waves you so passionately love." She giggled. "How else was the Universe going to get you off of the beach?"

"But where am I now? I'm still surfing."

"I'd be willing to bet you'll always be surfing, Charlie. But now you're out seeing the world and learning the mysteries of the creation. You're supposed to be doing this, too. What you master on your journey will help you to become a great person."

"So what am I learning?"

"Whoa! Let's back up. How did you get to New Zealand?"

"On a sailboat. I met this couple when I was surfing in Mexico and they…"

"Invited you along?" Gwen said.

Charlie nodded. "I'd never sailed before, and they taught me. I learned how to navigate."

"Wow, Charlie that's something few people can do. You must have had an unbelievable experience with one of the greatest teacher's of all."

She pointed out toward the water. "If it weren't for Vietnam, you never would have been persuaded to take such a journey."

Charlie grabbed a handful of sand and threw it to the side.

"Look at me, Charlie. I believe the knowledge of the Universe comes from our hearts. It's all there in each of us, and our job in a lifetime is to experience it. There are many avenues to gain information, but there are no mistakes. Some pathways are easier than others, depending on whether we're able to listen to our hearts. When you understand this, Charlie, you will no longer be angry at your country."

The cool afternoon breeze was not enough to keep Charlie from sweating as he climbed down a shaky ladder from the roof of a house under construction. He jumped past the last three rungs, wiped his brow and started jogging down the road. Time for surf.

"Charlie," a voice shouted.

He stopped and turned to see Gwen walking toward him.

"Where have you been, Charlie? I haven't seen you all week."

"Just hanging out here working on that new place," he said, pointing toward the construction. "I've been learning how to build a house from those guys."

He pointed toward the skeletal framework and the two men working on the roof.

"Nice guys."

"But you're not at dinner."

"I work early and surf late. By the time I get out, dinner is over."

"Do you eat?"

Charlie smiled, "Of course I eat. I couldn't pound nails and ride waves without eating. I hitched into town and bought some supplies."

Charlie felt calmness radiating from her eyes. He had been avoiding her since their talk on the beach. At first he was angry with her, then with himself. He knew he needed time to think. With the hard work and solitude, he had processed her statements about anger.

One night, he'd dreamed that he never got drafted. He was the world champ, but he was getting older and the surfboard companies declined to support him anymore. Cher appeared and he wanted to marry her, but she wasn't interested. He had no money, no job, and no interests, except surfing.

He'd awakened with a start, depressed. He walked up to a construction site and started helping with wall construction.

"You do good work, mate," Dr. Jim had said as he toured the project.

"Thanks. Not so sure I'm cut out for this, though."

"Let me see your hands." Charlie held out his hands.

Dr. Jim held them so he could study his palms.

"No, you're not cut out for this, mate. You're going to work with people. I think you have the makings to be a doctor. And, look at this life line."

He traced a long line wrapping around Charlie's thumb. "You're going to be around for awhile. You could help a lot of people on this earth."

Charlie looked at his palm, remembering the conversation with Dr. Jim. He reached for Gwen's hand.

"I don't want to grow old as a surfer. I want to do something to help mankind."

Gwen smiled and threw her arms around Charlie. "You can still surf, you know."

"I'll never give up surfing, Gwen. But I want to do a lot more than that."

He held her tight; he felt her heart beating against his chest.

"I don't believe in war," Charlie said. "Never would I have chosen to go. But if Nam was necessary to get me to New Zealand, I guess I had to go." He paused, took a breath. A tear ran down his cheek.

"I'll never figure out what happened to me over there, though."

She held him with one arm as she wiped his tear with her sleeve. "We'll just see about that, Charlie Armfield."

28

Charlie's surfboard seemed heavier than usual one evening as he trod alone up the hill toward the beach house. His shadow, long and droopy in the setting sun, matched his mood. What was wrong? The surf had been tremendous; waves were larger than usual. Dr. Jim had joined him for awhile. They'd talked briefly between sets.

"You're not frightened out here, are ya, mate?" Dr. Jim had asked.

Charlie couldn't respond. The last time he'd talked about fear and surfing was with Will, the day he was killed. "This is it, man," Will had told him. "You can't ask for it to get any better than this. I'm not even scared."

Charlie stopped walking. He looked up at Mt. Taranaki. Then he turned around and saw the last remnants of the crimson sun disappear below the horizon. Everything turned dark. He shivered, feeling a panic rise in his chest, overcoming him. He tried to take a step, but couldn't. What was happening? He tried again and fell forward, his board slamming down next to him on the road.

He lay in confusion—fright permeated his flesh, then his bones.

"What's going on?" he cried. He covered his head with his hands and shrieked with pain.

He heard the roar of an engine, and saw headlights bearing down on him. He grabbed his surfboard and low crawled toward the furrow at the side of the road. A truck narrowly missed him as he slithered out of the way.

Brakes screeched. A door opened and someone ran to him.

"Did I hit you? Are you all right? Oh my, did I hit you?"

Charlie looked up, and saw Gwen.

"Charlie, is that you? Are you all right?"

"You didn't hit me."

Gwen lay down next to him, and put her arm around his shoulders.

"I came to find you, Charlie. Dr. Jim said I should check on you."

Charlie looked at Gwen. "Why?"

"He felt a strange energy from you out in the water. With the big surf, he wanted to make sure you made it in okay."

"I don't know what happened to me, Gwen," Charlie said, his voice shaky. "I don't know what's going on."

Gwen stood and held out her hand. She helped Charlie up, picked up his board and put her free hand under his arm. Slowly they walked to the truck.

Back at the beach house, she turned off the motor and looked into his eyes.

"We're going to meditate together, Charlie."

Charlie swallowed. "Like on the beach?"

"Yes. We're going to investigate fear."

"But…"

"But, what? You don't think you're afraid of anything?" Gwen said.

"Well…"

"Were you afraid in Vietnam?"

"Yes—I think so."

"When, Charlie? When were you afraid?"

"Well…"

Was I afraid, he wondered? *Yes, I had to be scared.* Then he remembered when he and Gage were riding on the bus, on their way to McCord Air Force Base to catch the plane to Vietnam.

"Once, on the bus. Then again, when I was on the plane. Yeah, I was scared shitless."

"How about in combat, Charlie. Were you scared?"

"Of course. I had to be."

"When?"

Charlie gazed out the window. *When? I don't know when.*

The sound of a helicopter roared in his mind. He heard a voice saying, "You'll be going farther forward to be on a communication team."

"Communication, Sir? What exactly does that mean?"

"That means you'll be with our liaison officer with Delta Company of the 125th Infantry," the voice said. "You'll be a forward observer operating a radio for Lieutenant Alvarez."

He looked over at Gwen.

"When I was on the helicopter heading out to the front. There was smoke in the bush, and explosives. I was never so scared in all my life."

Gwen put her hand on Charlie's shoulder. "Then what?"

"They told me to jump."

"Were you scared then?"

"I don't know. I just jumped, and started low crawling."

"Let's go inside, Charlie."

Gwen grabbed a bag and helped him into the house. She instructed him to sit on the floor. Then she removed a stick of incense, a candle, and a match from the bag and handed them to Charlie.

"Light these. I'll be right back."

Gwen returned with a blanket from the bedroom, and wrapped it around Charlie. She retrieved a tape player from her bag and turned it on. Music—gentle flute sounds from India—filled the air.

She sat down in front of him.

"Charlie, I don't think you were ever afraid in Vietnam. Oh yes, when you were traveling to and from assignments, but not when you were in the thick of it."

"How can that be?"

"Look into my eyes. Now, I want you to go back in time, back to Vietnam."

"But, Gwen..." Charlie whined.

She stared into his eyes. He saw beautiful blues and greens in her irises. He began to feel light-headed, like he was floating in space, maybe in another dimension.

"Close your eyes, Charlie. You're in Vietnam."

He closed his eyes. Instant images fired through his mind. There was movement in the bush, an explosion nearby, a flash in the distance.

Hit it! Open fire! A dead face, blood, a lifeless body lay in front of him. I shot someone's son—younger than me. This is wrong, goddamn it. Wrong! Call in artillery. Trapped in cross fire. Evacuate. Choppers, sweeping, bodies pinned—dead.

No! I don't want any more. Have to take the hill. The medic—stepped on a mine—body parts flying.

"Watch out, Will!" Bodies, blood everywhere, parts missing. Counting—counting—don't you be counting, man. Sniper fire.

Hit it!'New lieutenant, bloody face, not meant to be here. Nobody meant to be here. Gooks in the bush, crawling ahead, machine gunfire blasting overhead. Fire. Bull's eye.

Will, where are you, man? Don't get killed! Still in your body—come back, man. LRRPs, intelligence information, harassment, ambush.

Can't kill your own cousin. No!

Attention all batteries, killed an entire regiment, hundreds of people killed. I killed them all. Loading howitzers, more fire missions, more dead. A gun missing. Blown to bits.

Al, where was your angel, man? How can they choose? Don't want to go home. Afraid, afraid.

Afraid to go home? Charlie's eyes popped wide open. "I'm afraid, I'm afraid…"

"What, Charlie, is somebody shooting at you?"

Startled, he looked at Gwen. "No, no, I'm afraid to go home," he sobbed. "I'm afraid to go home."

Gwen wrapped her arms around Charlie and held him tight.

"What about the combat? Were you afraid?"

Confused, Charlie pushed away from her. "How long was I gone?"

"Over an hour. You shook, screamed, and cried. I know you were fighting in a war."

He bent forward and covered his face with his hands. "I killed a lot of people. More people than I know. I was afraid to go home, and now I'm afraid to live with my sins."

He looked up. Her eyes met his. She looked so beautiful, rosy cheeks, dark hair glistening in the candlelight, lips sweet and inviting like fruit. He felt embarrassed that he would be attracted to her when she was trying to help him. Charlie cleared his throat.

"Dr. Jim says I can be a doctor, that I can help a lot of people."

"That's wonderful, Charlie."

"But, how can I help people when I've killed people? Many, many people."

Gwen placed her hands onto his shoulders.

"Because all things happen within the scope of the big plan, Charlie. Remember, the Universe has a plan for you, and if you're supposed to do something, you will do it. You were supposed to go to Vietnam, and you did it with class, no matter if that's what you wanted to do or not."

"But look at me. I'm all screwed up."

"You are a very compassionate person, and you feel the effects of war. If you are supposed to help people, you will be great at doing that. Dr. Jim is a very wise man, Charlie. He seems to know things before they happen."

"But Gwen, I'm afraid…"

"If you become a doctor, your energy will be focused. You will not be afraid. Just like in the war."

Charlie stared at Gwen. "What do you mean?"

"I don't think you were afraid in Vietnam, Charlie. There was no time for fear. There are no mistakes, Charlie. The Universe needed you to come back home. Maybe your guardian angel helped you stay poised when it was important for you to be so."

Charlie gasped.

"Don't you believe in angels, Charlie?"

"I…I'm not sure. Mom saw one in a dream and contacted the Red Cross. Her call saved my life."

"Maybe that was the only way the angel could help you that time. Most of the time the angel was right by your side."

"And when God wants a person to die, he calls the angel back to heaven?"

"When it's time to go through the transition, the angel guides the soul home."

"But how does God decide who…?"

"We don't always know when it's our time," Gwen interrupted.

"Remember that nothing happens outside of the Universal plan. You went to Vietnam to get off of the beach. And you came home because you are needed. Maybe Dr. Jim is right. You are needed to work with people."

Charlie wondered how. "But…"

"Charlie, I'll bet you were even needed to help people in Vietnam."

"No way!" Charlie said, horrified at the idea.

Gwen smiled, "You have a spirit about you, Charlie. I can imagine it was a great comfort for the other soldiers to have you around. Kind of like a morale boost. The Universe not only needed you over there, but probably kept you there as long as possible. I feel that you helped them, even though they might have died in the end."

Charlie cocked his head, surprised she'd figured these things out. "I…"

"You probably came home a hero, too. Not that you wanted to be, but you had no choice. You're a natural when it comes to helping people. Besides, you had to save your own life so you could come home. You created life for yourself."

"Created life? Gwen, I did that surfing once. I thought I had died in a hurricane in North Carolina, but a voice said it wasn't my time. It was my Dad. Oh my God…" Charlie stopped.

He took a deep breath. *When I almost drowned, Dad was already on the other side.*

"The Universe seems to have a special communication with you, Charlie. My guess is that Vietnam was given to you as a gift."

Charlie shook his head. "No, Gwen."

"I know it may be hard to believe, but I think you can find some good in your experience in the war."

What? Charlie thought. *Who is this person? Now she wants me to find good in Vietnam?*

"I have an exercise that can help you find it."

"An exercise?"

"Yes. It's a writing technique Dr. Jim showed me."

"Do we have to do it tonight?"

Gwen chuckled, "No, we sure don't, Charlie. I don't think you're quite ready for it, anyway."

"So what do we do now?"

She smiled and put her arms around him again.

"I think we should just relax. Cuddle for awhile."

Charlie woke early the next morning. He was rolled in a blanket, lying on the floor in the main room.

What happened last night? Charlie wondered. *Fear?* No, he wasn't afraid of anything, except himself, and what he'd become. But now he felt different.

Gwen said he was needed in Vietnam. He would have to think about that for awhile. Maybe for Will. Charlie remembered what Will said when they first ran into each other in Vietnam: "Let me tell you something, man. Seeing you right now is the most important thing that has ever happened to me in my entire life."

But that was just because he knew me from back home, wasn't it?

He heard footsteps in the other room. *Gwen?* The last thing he remembered about last night was holding her in his arms. He'd wanted to make love, but what had happened?

"So, are you going to miss the best waves of the day?" Gwen asked, yawning as she walked into the room. "It might get crowded if you wait any longer."

Charlie struggled out of the blanket. "What happened last night?"

"You fell asleep, lover boy."

Charlie felt embarrassed. Had she wanted to get sexual, too?

"S...sorry, Gwen," he stuttered. "I must have been exhausted with the meditation."

"So how do you feel this morning?"

Charlie shrugged. "I think I feel great; slept like a baby."

"You worked out a big part of Vietnam last night, Charlie."

"I really did, didn't I?"

Gwen smiled and nodded.

"I never would have guessed that fear was an issue for me."

"Well it was, just like pain and anger."

"So, is 'good' the next issue?"

"Good?"

"You said I can find some good from Nam."

"Oh, yes. Well, maybe. We'll have to wait and see."

"Why do we have to wait?"

She moved close to Charlie and put her arm around him.

"Everything has its time. When you're ready, it will happen."

"Like us, Gwen?" Charlie said sheepishly.

"I think we're already there."

She put her other arm around him and kissed him.

Gwen stayed at the beach house for the next two weeks—a passionate time, filled with lovemaking and desire. They took long walks on the beach, and shared stories of their travels. Charlie was happy and should have felt content, but something else was happening, too. He was dreaming at night, dreams that confused and disturbed him—dreams he didn't mention to Gwen.

One morning, Charlie awoke with a stomachache.

"I think I'd better stay in bed today." He grimaced, holding his abdomen, the pain so bad he could hardly stand up.

"No," Gwen said. "I'm taking you to see Dr. Jim."

Despite Charlie's protests, Gwen had him dressed and in Dr. Jim's office by the time the doctor arrived.

"Have you ever been adjusted, mate?"

"What's that mean?"

"A chiropractic adjustment," Gwen said. "A realignment of the vertebrae in your spine. When they become subluxated, it puts pressure onto your nervous system."

"Subluxated?"

"That's when the segments of your spine get out of their normal juxtaposition." Dr. Jim said. "Let's give you a check."

"But I'm fine. It's just something I ate."

"Mind if I check your posture, mate?"

"I guess not."

Dr. Jim positioned Charlie in front of a full-length mirror. "What do think of your shoulders? Are they even?"

"No, my right one looks higher."

Dr. Jim knelt behind, put his forefingers on Charlie's hips. "What about your pelvis, here?"

"The left one is higher."

"Now look at your ears, mate."

"Oh, man, the left ear is higher, too. Am I all screwed up?"

Gwen grinned. "No, Charlie, you're just out of alignment. The muscles are not even, because they are adapting to your subluxations. Dr. Jim can fix you."

"But how does that relate to my stomachache?"

Dr. Jim led him over to his adjusting table.

"Lay on your stomach, mate." He palpated Charlie's spine and stopped in the middle. "Sore here?"

"Ouch."

With a gentle thrust, Dr. Jim adjusted the middle of Charlie's spine, and a bone seemed to pop.

"That ought to fix that gut of yours."

He continued working, adjusting several other vertebrae. "Sit up now, mate."

Charlie sat up and took a deep breath. To his surprise, his stomach felt better.

"What happened?"

Dr. Jim smiled, "Just took a hard bone off a soft nerve, mate. We don't do very well with nerve interference."

He walked over and turned the light switch off. "The light can't burn without juice either."

"Was my stomach wire turned off?"

Dr. Jim smiled, "Not entirely, just partially. Has there been a lot on your mind lately, mate?"

Charlie shrugged. "Like what?"

"Charlie," Gwen spoke up. "What about your dreams?"

Charlie looked at her, startled.

Gwen smiled. "Seems to me like you're working something out in your dreams."

"W…Well I have been having some strange…" He stopped, shook his head. "I don't understand. Can dreams make my vertebrae go out?"

"Our thoughts can change body function, mate," Dr. Jim said, putting his arm around Charlie.

"Emotion, subluxation, gut ache. For most people who come here, it's a lot worse. Gwen," he put his other arm around her, "I think you need to take this bloke outside and do some dream work."

Charlie felt the ocean breeze as they sat silently on a grassy knoll. *How do I begin,* he wondered. The dreams seemed so real. People were talking to him, even though some of them were dead. Ghosts?

He peered into Gwen's eyes.

"I told Will that we should visualize ourselves surviving every battle and going home. He said that one time he thought he would die, then he remembered what I'd told him."

Charlie looked up at the sky as he spoke. "'You saved my life many times, Charlie.' That's what he told me in my dream. But that was his ghost talking, because Will's dead."

"Will died in Vietnam?"

"No, afterward. He drowned surfing. I tried to get to him, but he was already dead. In the dream, he told me it wasn't my fault; he was supposed to go home."

"That's beautiful, Charlie."

"Yeah, I guess so, but he wasn't the only dead guy who appeared. Lieutenant Harvey and Strangeman showed up, too."

"What did they say?"

"They said, 'Thanks!' I said, 'Thanks for what? You guys died when I was gone. Maybe if I had stayed around, you'd be alive today. Or, at least I would have died with you. I deserted you in your time of need.'"

"Did they reply, Charlie?"

"They laughed and said something about 'time for everything.'"

Gwen put her arms around his shoulders. "You couldn't give them life."

She placed her hands around his head, pulled his forehead toward hers. "But you did give them something special, and they came back to thank you." She kissed him.

Charlie pulled away.

"There were others, too. Richard Robinson was injured when we were taking a hill over. He said, 'I saw myself in a nice comfortable hospital bed like you said. I was okay.' Then the man in the forward hospital, one who had a bandage around his eyes, said, 'I saw my home beach like you told me.' And Baloneyman appeared, too."

Charlie smiled and shook his head. "'I was a fuckin' coward and you helped me keep face, Arm,' he said."

"Did he really talk like that?"

"Yeah, he always talked like that. He hid out when we were getting hit on the artillery hill."

"Who else appeared?"

"Robby. He was my forward observer. He said, 'You're some corporal, tending to my injury. I healed so fast we had to go into long range recognizance duty together. Then, that psychic stuff saved our asses more than once.'"

Gwen perked up. "Psychic stuff?"

"Yeah, I lost most of my hearing, yet I still seemed to be able to sense stuff. I could feel the gooks in the bush before Robby and Sergeant Thom could even hear them. Thom was in a dream, too. He said he was glad I wasn't a gook." Charlie laughed.

Gwen cocked her head.

"Thom was a South Vietnamese soldier," Charlie explained. "So it sounded funny coming from him. And he thanked me for saving his cousin Quang's life."

Charlie shivered, remembering the incident with Quang.

"Charlie, did all of this happen in one dream?"

"No, it's been different every night, ever since that last meditation. When you said something about being needed in Vietnam, I couldn't believe it. Then the dreams started. Last night was with my best friend, Gage. We went to Vietnam together, but he got to stay in a safe place and be a cook. I'll never forget the look on his face when I left for the war. He was more scared than I was, and I got angry with him. 'Don't worry about me,' I told him. 'Before you know it we'll both be back on the beach. Just keep cool, man.'"

"Then you woke up with a stomachache. That's because you were so overwhelmed with the gratitude from others that you couldn't accept."

"I think you're right, Gwen," Charlie said, shaking his head and smiling.

"And I don't think I understood until Dr. Jim explained why we need spinal adjustments."

29

White foam from Dawson Falls spilled over moss covered rocks. Mesmerized by the beauty, Charlie breathed deeply and sighed. The mountain air, even though Taranaki was close to the ocean, reminded him of his visit to Grand Lake.

"Have you ever been to Colorado, Gwen?"

"No, but I've heard it's beautiful. Have you?"

"It was the first place I traveled to after Nam."

Charlie remembered finding Harry drunk in the Lariat Saloon. Harry had said, "I wasn't involved with the contact like you were. But I saw many dead soldiers, their bodies mangled, some beyond recognition. I looked at them and felt God had betrayed us. Where was he? Why in the hell was he letting this happen? Why, God, Why?"

"Because the angels left," Charlie said out loud, forgetting he was on the side of Mount Taranaki.

"What?" Gwen asked.

"Nothing." He nodded toward a trail leading up through the trees. "Let's take a hike."

They trekked along the winding trail, Gwen leading the way. Charlie stayed back a few paces, his eyes glued to the ground, his mind lost in a field of dead bodies—blood, guts hanging out of abdominal cavities, some headless, some without limbs.

Gwen stopped abruptly, and Charlie slammed into her.

"Gwen, are you all right? Sorry, I wasn't paying attention."

"I'm okay. I just wanted you to see the trees in this forest."

Charlie looked at the trees. "Oh, no!" He let go of Gwen and put his hands over his eyes. "No!"

Gwen grabbed Charlie around the waist. "What is it?"

"Don't look—it's my fault." He burst into tears. His body trembled.

Gwen pulled Charlie close and held him tightly.

"It's okay, Charlie. You didn't do anything wrong."

"I killed those people!"

He looked again and gasped. *Trees? Only trees? But...*

He walked off the trail and into the woods. These are no ordinary trees, he thought. They're all deformed. What kind of trees are these anyway? Embarrassed, he shook his head and touched a limb.

Gwen walked up and held his hand.

"I'm going crazy, Gwen, looney as they come. I thought these trees were bodies."

"Flashbacks can happen to anyone," Gwen said, running her fingers through his hair. "You're not crazy, Charlie. They call this the Goblin Forest because these misshapen trees *do* look like bodies."

"Yeah, but..." He gazed at the timber and shook his head. "My mind was seeing bodies before we came upon these trees."

Charlie sat down in the dirt and put his head into his hands. "You've helped me so much, but I still see the crap. How can I learn about what good could have happened in Nam, if I'm still seeing the crap?"

"It's guilt." Gwen sat beside him and held him close. "Before you can find the good, I think you need to deal with the guilt."

Tears erupted from the corners of his eyes. He wiped them with his hands, which were soiled from the earth, leaving mud streaks on his face.

"I killed..."

"I know, Charlie."

He held his hands up, clenched them into fists, and shook them in the air.

"Gwen," he sobbed, "I killed twenty-seven people with my own hands. I saw them, dead. But I killed more, too—hundreds, maybe thousands. I killed with artillery guns and never knew how many died. I took all of those people away from their families."

"But Charlie…"

Charlie pulled back. "I know, I know. Everything happens for a reason. But I can't get over this. I still see their faces, victims of my marksmanship. I never wanted to kill anyone."

Charlie raised his voice. "People say I'm a goddamn hero, but I'm not proud of anything. I feel like I've committed a crime. I murdered, and I am guilty. I can never be the same."

Gwen reached for him, cuddled him.

"You were forced to go to war. You did not want to go. You didn't personally kill the enemy."

"But I did! I raised my weapon. I pulled the trigger. I saw them fall and I saw their bodies, Gwen—what was left of them."

"Listen, Charlie. The armies were at war. The army that drafted you was at war. You were shoved into battle and you performed to stay alive. You had to kill to keep from getting killed."

That's right, he thought, *I never would have pulled the trigger if I hadn't thought they were trying to shoot me. Were they trying to shoot the U.S. army or me? Okay, maybe the army. But that still doesn't forgive my crime does it? Dad taught me the commandments. Thou shalt not kill.*

"Gwen, I was taught that I shouldn't kill. Just because I was in the army when I killed, doesn't forgive what I did. Does it?"

"Who's supposed to forgive you?"

Charlie shrugged his shoulders. "God? No…me. How do I forgive myself?"

"Charlie, try to look at it this way. Let's suppose that we choose our situations on earth."

"Hey, no way I chose to go to Nam. You know I didn't want to go."

"You didn't want to go. But perhaps your soul needed to go."

"What?"

"Your body and your conscious mind are where your soul lives while you're here on earth. When you die, your soul is set free to become one with the Universal energy again."

Charlie remembered the conversation with the lieutenant in the infirmary. "The body is dead, but the person isn't," the lieutenant had said. "The person is the being part of a human being. The human will go home now and rot in the ground somewhere, but the being part is still alive and will always be around in spirit."

Gwen turned Charlie's chin toward her till their eyes met.

"Perhaps your soul, for some reason, needed to go to Vietnam. It chose to undergo all it did and then come home again. With all of those close calls you had over there, you were still destined to survive."

"Wouldn't any soul want that?"

"Maybe not. Your soul must have had other plans. Perhaps it wanted to experience humanity in its worst form, so it could be more compassionate later, and partake in life as a healer. Your soul has an agenda, Charlie. Those twenty-seven Vietnamese also needed to go to war. But their particular experience was meant to end with death."

"Why would a soul choose to die?"

"Everyone has to die sometime, but it's the agenda that determines when. You are not responsible for anyone's experience, even though you may have been a part of it."

"I was a part of it all right. I killed them."

"You were an important part of their agenda, Charlie. There are no accidents. Everything that happens is supposed to happen; and the maturity and wisdom we gain is intended, even if it means the end of a lifetime."

Charlie shook his head. "Oh, Gwen, I don't know."

He stood and walked among the disfigured trees. *They sure do look like bodies,* he thought. *Like evil goblins? Maybe this is where I belong—living amongst the goblins.*

He shinnied up a trunk and grabbed onto the first branch to pull himself up. Perched in a squatting position, he stared at the forest.

Then, before his eyes, a flash of light, and the forest instantly transformed into a battlefield.

The sweep was on. He and Will stepped out from the LP and saw number one. Charlie stood over the NVA soldier looking at his bloody face, a bullet hole right between his eyes, his mouth wide open like it was crying out with pain. He wore green fatigue clothing, his pantlegs rolled up to just below his knees. He wore leather thong sandals and a small backpack on his back. A strap around his neck was attached to the fatigue hat, which lay next to his head. A small bag was tied around his waist. Charlie knelt down to touch it. It was full of rice.

Charlie put his head in his hands and started mumbling to himself.

"Oh, my God. I killed you, man, and I don't know why. I didn't want you to die."

Will had said, "I remember my first one. I was shook up for over a week. But after awhile over here, you start to get numb to this shit. I don't know how many I've killed by now. It's like I've become a hardass, because it doesn't faze me much anymore."

"I don't want to get like that," Charlie had said, shaking his head. "I just killed this guy, man. I took him away from his family. Damn it, his parents are going to be devastated."

He stared back at the corpse. *I murdered you, man. I feel like a criminal.*

The bloodied form began to blur, seemed to seep into the earth like evaporating liquid. Charlie rubbed his eyes. The body was gone. But then a phantom appeared. It looked like the NVA, but with no blood on his face, no bullet hole between his eyes. He stood before Charlie, his eyes open, his face serene.

"Do not weep, my American friend. I am not any different now than before. I am one with the Buddha, always, which is all things. Buddha is not one phenomenon, one event, one body, one being. Buddha is everything— life, death and beyond.

"My country has been at war for many years. All of my forefathers have been killed with this fighting. I have chosen to be among them, as perhaps my son will do also, if the skirmish continues. This life is all we have known, and it is the lesson we yearn for.

"Buddha experiences all things through the encounters of life on earth, and that is what balances the Universe. What we think of as good and bad is only balance for what is. And what is, is love. There is only love."

Charlie rubbed his eyes, but the image continued.

"Even in war, there is love, for all the souls have a timetable to encounter knowledge for the omnipresence. We are all the Buddha, and Buddha is all there is.

"Now you may be enlightened, for this is no ordinary perception that you realize. This is a vision from the Universe to help you understand your soul's plan; to experience the balance of love in the Universe."

The figure disappeared. Charlie remained in the tree, awed—afraid to believe. But then, he felt an incredible uplifting sensation.

There is only love, he thought. *I chose Vietnam to encounter knowledge. I killed to keep from getting killed. I survived with the help of an angel because there is more for me to do on earth.*

He jumped down out of the tree and ran to Gwen, threw his arms around her shoulders and hugged her without speaking.

Finally he said, "This is a magical forest."

Walking back down the trail, Charlie broke into song:

> *There is on-ly love,*
> *There is on-ly love,*
> *There is o-o-on-ly,*
> *o-o-on-ly – looove.*

Fatigue from the pounding surf weighed heavy on Charlie as he trudged up the road to the beach house. *Man, I ought to talk Dr. Jim into building a place down by the water, he thought.*

When he arrived at the house he leaned his surfboard on the front porch. He took in the aroma of fresh baked bread as he walked inside.

"What's going on?" Charlie asked, wrapping his arms around Gwen's waist as she leaned over the oven.

"Watch it, surferboy, or you'll make me drop the pastry."

She placed a sheet of sweet rolls on a hot pad and kissed Charlie. "How were the waves?"

"Fantastic!"

"I figured they must be. You've been gone a long time."

She put a frying pan on the burner and started cracking eggs. "I guess I don't have to ask if you're hungry, right?"

"Famished! I can't believe you made these rolls."

He tore one off gingerly, trying not to burn his fingers as he juggled it across the room.

She handed him a plate, then reached into the icebox. "Here, try some of this."

Charlie grabbed the dish and stuck his finger in the creamy substance. "Butter?"

"Made it myself. I went up to the main house while you were surfing. Someone brought in a bucket of milk, fresh from the cow. I scraped the cream off the top and churned it for us."

Charlie's mouth watered as he spread the butter.

After breakfast, Gwen went into the bedroom and came back with a piece of cardboard, three-feet square. She laid it and a pencil on the floor.

"I want you to write something for me."

"Is this that 'good' exercise?"

"Maybe, but first I want you to write what you learned in the Goblin Forest."

Charlie cocked his head and smiled. He thought for a moment, knelt down on the floor and wrote across the top of the cardboard:

Everything that happens is supposed to happen, and the maturity and wisdom we incur is intended, even if it means the end of this lifetime.

Gwen read what Charlie had written, then crawled onto his back and squeezed his shoulders.

"You're ready!"

Charlie bucked her off and rolled on the floor next to her. He kissed her, and moved his hand along her curves.

"Hey, loverboy, not now."

"You said I was ready."

Gwen giggled, "Yeah, you're always ready for that. But right now I have something else for you to do."

"Oh, all right." Charlie sat up smiling. "What?"

"Draw three columns on the board."

He drew two parallel lines.

"Now write the word 'Good' in the center section."

Charlie glanced at Gwen. *Is she going to ask me to write the good from Vietnam? How do I know what was good?*

He wrote the word, apprehensive of what would come next.

"Now write 'Bad' in the left column."

Charlie's mouth dropped open.

"Go on. Write it down."

She placed her arm around his shoulder when he finished. "Now, my friend, I want you to write all the bad things you associate with Vietnam."

"Gwen..." Charlie whined. "You've got to be kidding."

"I'm serious, Charlie. Write all you can, and if you run out of room we'll turn the board over."

"But I thought…"

"First things first."

Charlie frowned and pinched the pencil. He began scribbling with rapid fire. Gwen went into the bedroom and returned with a box of Kleenex. Charlie was already crying.

Thirty minutes later, the raving continued onto the back of the board.

"Okay, Charlie, that's enough of that."

He put the pencil down and rolled away from the board. He covered his face and, trembling, curled into the fetal position. Gwen cuddled up behind him.

When the shaking subsided, she said, "Back to the board. Now the fun starts."

Charlie picked up the pencil. "Am I going to write the good now? How?"

"Did you meet any good people over there, Charlie? Make friends with any? What was the scenery like? Did you get pleasure from anything?"

Charlie nodded, getting the idea. Images charged into his mind like an advancing wild fire. Before he knew it, the good items on the board equaled the bad. He laughed and cried as he wrote, but this time they were tears of joy.

When he finished, he stood up and stretched.

"Aaaaahhhhhooooo!"

"That felt good?" Gwen asked.

Charlie walked over and kissed her.

"Incredible. I did it. I discovered the good in Vietnam."

"There's more, Charlie."

"What?"

She pulled him back to the cardboard.

"In the last column, write all the good that can come from all the bad that occurred in Vietnam."

Charlie frowned and shook his head.

"You thought the last assignment was impossible, too. You can do this. What's the first thing you wrote in the 'Bad' list?"

"I got drafted and taken away from the World Contest."

"Okay, then, what have you learned about that?"

Later that evening, Charlie and Gwen sat by the beach, watching the sunset. After he'd completed the exercise, he'd walked alone in the grassy hills for the rest of the day, ending up down by the water, where Gwen joined him to watch the sun disappear.

"Can I tell you some of the good things that happened in Nam?"

"Of course, Charlie. I would love that."

"You were right. I made a lot of friends over there. Some of those guys are the closest friends I've ever had. Maybe it's because of all the shit flying around. We shared that stuff and nobody will ever know what it was like, except me and my friends. I have never been so close to human beings in my life, and…" Charlie took a deep breath, "it was worth it."

Gwen looked deeply into his eyes.

"I know that was hard for you to say."

He wiped a tear before it rolled down his cheek.

"The scenery was incredible, too. Different than here, even though there were mountains around. They were covered with the thickest jungle. Sometimes you couldn't see anything in front of you. That made it dangerous, but it was beautiful. If that war ever gets over, I could guide you into a tropical paradise with waterfalls and great swimming holes."

"What about the wildlife, Charlie?"

He shrugged. "I saw a few water buffalo. Don't remember much more. Too much shooting going on, I guess. But that couldn't chase away the stars. Except for on the sailboat in the middle of the Pacific, I have never seen so many clusters. When there was a new moon, the sky would dance with joy. That made me happy."

He sat quietly for a few moments.

"And I don't know if this is good or not, Gwen, but I think my soul was able to leave my body over there."

"Charlie, that's a meditation technique I learned in yoga."

"Well, I don't know how I learned it. I could be on patrol and see myself humping through the jungle, struggling with a pack. Damn things were heavy, but not when I was out of the body. Sometimes I just went surfing while the rest of me fought in the stupid war."

Gwen laughed. "Anything else?"

Charlie hesitated. "I got a lot of good letters, especially from my folks. They were very supportive. I didn't write them nearly enough, but they kept me informed about their lives and what was happening at home."

"Who else?"

"Who else what?"

"Who else wrote you letters?"

"My girlfriend." Charlie felt embarrassed. "Her letters were good sometimes, but after a while, I couldn't read them any more."

"How come?"

"Gwen, I don't want to talk to you about her. Besides, we broke up."

"Why did you break up?"

"Because she couldn't understand."

"Did you give her a chance?"

Annoyed, Charlie said, "Listen, Gwen, nobody has ever understood me like you do."

Gwen looked surprised.

"You have helped me more than anybody. Gwen, I want to spend the rest of my life with you."

Gwen looked deeply into his eyes.

"Charlie, you know that everything happens for a reason, right?"

Charlie nodded.

"We were supposed to meet, but you're not going to be able to spend the rest of your life with me."

30

Rainwater beat onto the roof, dripped off the sides, and splattered into the puddles on the ground. Not even the ringing in Charlie's ears could keep him from hearing every sound of the dreary day, feeling the heaviness in his heart. Gwen lay in the next room, weakened from illness.

Dr. Jim opened Gwen's door and walked over to Charlie.

Charlie looked up anxiously.

"How is she?" he asked, afraid of the answer.

"I think she's nearing her transition."

"Transition? You mean she's going to die now?"

"Yes, Charlie."

"But…how can this be happening so fast?"

It had only been three weeks since Gwen had told him they couldn't spend the rest of his life with her.

"What do you mean?" he'd asked.

"I have a disease, Charlie."

"What kind of disease?"

"Dr. Jim thinks it's something I picked up in India. Probably from the water."

"But he's a miracle worker. Can't he figure out how to cure you?"

"We've tried everything, but it continues to progress."

Charlie snapped back to the present. Dr. Jim's eyes seemed to radiate into his body.

"She's okay with this, Charlie."

"Yeah, but I'm not okay with it. I can't bear losing her, Dr. Jim."

Dr. Jim put his arm around Charlie's shoulders.

The rain seemed to intensify Charlie's sadness. *More death! Everybody I get close to dies. I don't want this to happen anymore. Please, dear God, don't take her from me.*

Dr. Jim pulled away.

"You've never grieved, have ya, mate?"

"What do you mean?"

"The people in your life who have passed away—you've never grieved them. I think you've built yourself a wall, mate."

"A wall?"

"When something sad happens, we usually are upset for a while and then, with time, we slowly get used to the idea and feel better. It's like this rain outside. It puddles up and slowly runs down the hill. Eventually it runs into the stream and merges with the great sea, where it becomes one with every other drop that has ever fallen from the sky.

"We need to let the grief become one with the rest of our lives, mate. You've built yourself a dam, and the reservoir needs to burst over the bloody falls. You're drowning behind the wall of grief."

Charlie shook his head. "How do I break down the wall?"

"Come with me."

He led Charlie into Gwen's room. "Gwen, luv, do you feel up for an exercise with Charlie, here?"

Gwen smiled and nodded.

Charlie thought her eyes seemed at peace, not concerned with her ultimate fate.

"Are you sure, Gwen? Maybe you need…"

"I'm fine, surferboy."

"Have a seat, mate," Dr. Jim said, pointing to a chair beside the bed. "Hold her hand."

Charlie reached out and Gwen put her hand in his. More than anything, he wanted to say that he loved her.

"Now let's say that," Dr. Jim began, "for the point of this exercise, Gwen here has already gone through the transition."

Charlie felt like a dagger pierced his heart.

"What?"

"It's okay, Charlie," Gwen said. "This is important for you."

Charlie scanned her pale face.

"It's good for me, too," she said.

"I want you to tell Gwen why you are sad about her leaving, mate."

Weeping, Charlie whispered, "I feel so selfish."

"Why, Charlie?" Gwen asked.

"Because you're so important to me. You've helped me so much. I'm sad because you won't be here with me—for me—anymore."

"So, what's wrong with that?" Gwen said.

"It's that...I'm thinking only of myself."

"Isn't that the way we all think of it?" Dr. Jim said. "We can't be sad for Gwen here. She's moving into the realm of the infinite soul. We're not sad for her, but for ourselves, because we know we'll miss her."

Charlie shook his head. "I can't believe we're doing this."

"Tell me, Charlie," Gwen continued. "Why will you miss me?"

"I really thought we would get married, Gwen. You're so beautiful. Not just your physical beauty, but inside, too. I love everything about you," Charlie cried. "Why do you have to leave me?"

"Now we're getting somewhere," Dr. Jim interjected. "Tell Gwen why you're angry at her for leaving."

"I'm not angry." Charlie scowled at Dr. Jim and thought for a moment. "Well, okay, maybe I am."

He turned back to Gwen. "Damn it, Gwen, why are you leaving me? Everybody leaves me."

"Who else has left you, mate?" Dr. Jim asked.

"All the guys on the gun—they left me all alone. Al Strangemeir, one of my best friends, was killed when I was away. Then Will, after we got back. Nobody else knew about the shit like Will did. But..." Charlie put his head in his hands.

Gwen handed Charlie a Kleenex.

"But what, Charlie?" Dr. Jim said.

"But why did he leave me? I needed him."

Dr. Jim blurred and resolved into Will, sitting on the side of the bed.

"Goddamn it, Will. You saved my life. Why in the hell didn't you let me save yours? You were all I had! You were all I had…"

Charlie shook his head. Then Will faded and reappeared as his father.

"Daddy? Why? I finally was ready to talk and you…" Charlie gasped. "You, you did talk to me—when I almost died in the hurricane. You said I wasn't ready, that I had to survive. But I needed you to tell me more. Why didn't you tell me more? I was ready for you."

Charlie's dad faded.

"You sound angry, mate."

"I guess I am angry. But now I really feel selfish."

"Things change whether we're ready or not," Gwen said. "Like when you were drafted. Remember how angry you were?"

Charlie nodded.

"But then you learned that there are no mistakes," Gwen said. "At first you will be sad and mad when change occurs, but then you must remember that everything has a reason. Nothing happens without it being a part of the natural flow within the Universe."

Charlie felt a gentle assurance seep into his body.

"There's a lot of change headed your way, mate," Dr. Jim said. "Other people you know will die, too."

"They already have," Charlie said. "Rick died on the sailboat. I guess I'm mad at him, too. He kept death happening in my life. Now you, Gwen."

"Very good, mate," Dr. Jim said.

"Now I want you to imagine that you are Gwen. You've gone through the transition, and you are telling Charlie how you feel."

Charlie thought for a moment, then took a deep breath and exhaled.

"I chose to have certain experiences in this lifetime. I needed to give birth to a child I couldn't raise, and to travel the world. I was supposed to meet Dr. Jim and learn from him. And I needed to meet you and help with your Vietnam emotions."

Charlie sighed. "But I had to leave because it was my time." He lowered his head.

"Okay, mate, now the others."

"What others?" He looked over toward Dr. Jim.

"Al, I believe…and Will. Your father and Rick need to talk to Charlie, too."

Charlie nodded.

"Okay, Charlie, this is Al. I didn't get to go into basecamp with you because my agenda was different than yours. I'm sorry you had to stay in the gun pit by yourself after we all died, but I needed to move on. Thanks for going to Virginia Beach to meet my wife."

Charlie was surprised he'd voiced that last comment.

Dr. Jim nodded, encouraging Charlie to continue.

"This is Will, man. I couldn't believe that you came to be with me in Vietnam. We saved each other's lives several times. I needed to experience war in my lifetime, and I needed to be there for you when you got home. But then I had to go. The waves had to take me. Thanks for trying to save me that last time, but it wasn't supposed to be."

Charlie looked at Dr. Jim.

"Will wasn't afraid of the big surf."

"Then he wasn't afraid when he died," Dr. Jim said. "Now, what about your father?"

Charlie continued, this time as his father.

"I wasn't afraid either, Son. I felt so bad for you when Will died. You know I wanted to talk, but you weren't ready. I'm sorry I wasn't available when you finally came around. I guess I chose a body with a weak heart. We almost went together during that hurricane, but you weren't meant to join me yet."

Charlie paused, then became Rick.

"Thanks for taking over the helm when I died. We struggled through the heavy storm together and I appreciated your help. And thanks also for saving Jacque's life and then navigating to New Zealand. I'm sorry we couldn't all continue sailing around the world together."

Charlie ran his fingers through his hair. "Wow!"

"Now, one more thing," Dr. Jim said. "I want you to be a third party."

"What do you mean?"

"Look at Gwen as herself, but look at me as though I'm Charlie. Analyze the situation between these two people."

"Well, I guess they…"

"No, talk to us personally, as if we're Gwen and Charlie."

"Okay. Listen, Charlie. It's all right to be sad when Gwen dies…" He paused, noticing that the rain had stopped. "But don't build a dam. You're going to flood out Dr. Jim's farm if you do that."

Gwen looked puzzled.

"You know, if the rain doesn't drain we're going to have a swamp around here."

Dr. Jim smiled.

"Be sad, and be mad if you need to," Charlie continued as the third party, "but no walls. That's what you've been doing with everybody else's death, isn't it? It's time to pull your thumb out of that dam and let the water flow. Besides, man," he said, as if he were talking to Charlie, "you understand now that you had to experience Vietnam. You needed everything you got out of that ordeal. Someday you'll know why. You'll look at yourself in a mirror and you will thank God for Vietnam. Sounds hard to believe now, but someday you'll understand."

Charlie could hardly believe what he was saying, but Dr. Jim nodded, and Gwen smiled.

He continued speaking to Dr. Jim, as though he were talking to Charlie.

"Now about this sadness stuff. When it's time for someone's agenda to go through transition, it's time. Remember all those times you thought you were having close calls with death? Well, you weren't. You will not die until it's time for you to die. You couldn't have died in that hurricane swell because it wasn't time. Your dad was right. You weren't ready to go then, just like you weren't ready when you were in Vietnam. The Vietnamese you killed were ready. So was Al, and everyone else on the gun who died, because each one had completed his agenda.

"We all have a timetable. Knowing that, why should you be sad? If something is supposed to happen, let it. Why be sad about something as wonderful as the natural flow of life?"

"Because we have emotions," Gwen interrupted. "That's the human aspect in our lives on earth that we also need to experience."

"That's true," Charlie agreed, speaking as the third party. "But think of it," he said addressing Gwen. "If we truly understand how this Universe works, even when we are alive as human beings, then grieving doesn't have to happen. Charlie here doesn't have to grieve your death or anyone else's. You can go into the eternity, and he can live happily with the memories of your time together."

Charlie stopped short, nearly out of breath. *How was he able to say all of this? Did he believe it?*

"That is our final quest," Dr. Jim said. "And surely the hardest of all for every human being. I think if we do truly understand how the Universe works, then we no longer need to live lives on earth. That is why we come here—so we can educate our souls with adventures. We learn while living so we understand all that is. Once we comprehend, we don't need to come back."

"I think I'll be coming back for a while," Charlie said.

"Me, too," Gwen said, smiling at Charlie.

For the first time in his life, Charlie felt as if he could mourn the death of a special person. He was a learning human being, so he would feel sad when Gwen died, but it seemed to him now that her passing was with purpose. He believed she was supposed to share precious time with him, then move on to another experience. This time there would be no dam. The water would flow down to the sea.

On her deathbed, she spoke to Charlie.

"You've come a long way from the angry surferboy on the beach."

"I sure have, Gwen. If it wasn't for you…"

Gwen held up her hand. "If it wasn't for you, too. And if it wasn't for the way things were supposed to happen, I suppose it wouldn't have."

Charlie smiled at his friend. What a lovely person she was.

"I wish I could marry you and live happily ever after."

"We will be happily ever after. Just not as a married couple. Like you said, you will always have me in your memories. Nothing will take away our time together."

She looked into his eyes. "It won't be me you marry, Charlie, but you will marry and be very happy. Maybe even that ex-girlfriend who you never let understand you." She smiled, "And you'll win another surfing contest, too."

"What?"

"There's one more in you, I just know there is."

"But…"

"You can do it. I'll help you."

Charlie smiled. "You're crazy, you know that?"

"I know that." Gwen stared into his eyes and never looked away.

When the life was gone from her gaze, Charlie closed her eyelids with his finger, kissed her forehead, and knelt to pray.

"Dear God, your experience through Gwen's body is now finished.

Thank you so much for allowing our choices to be together. May the angels guide her into the next realm."

Her body was buried on a grassy knoll overlooking the sea. Dr. Jim held his arm around Charlie's shoulders as he gave the benediction.

"Dearly Beloved," he began. "We are gathered here today to honor the life of our dear friend, Gwen."

Surprised, Charlie looked at Dr. Jim. He sounded just like Charlie's father.

Afterward, Dr. Jim and Charlie walked into the meadow to collect flowers. Half of them were spread over the grave. The other half they carried out into the water on their surfboards.

"Well, Dear God, we meet again." Charlie said. "Seems like I have given you a lot of the people in my life. I know we're all a part of you anyway, and you are everything—life, death, and beyond. Gwen is not any different now than before but, as a human being, I will miss her."

They threw the flowers into the water and proceeded to surf the waves.

Afterward, Dr. Jim and Charlie waded out of the water and sat on the beach.

"Thanks for the service," Charlie said.

"And thank you for the great surf session, mate. Gwen would be happy we got good waves today."

"Yeah, she would. Dr. Jim, could I build a house on the property?"

"Sure, mate. Where?"

"Right up on the hill." He pointed up onto the grassy bluff.

"There. That other beach house is too damn far from the water, and besides, I'd like to build it there in memory of Gwen."

31

It was mid winter in New Zealand, July, 1970, when Charlie wrote home again.

I'm so sorry I haven't written. A lot has happened in the last five months. I'm living on a farm near New Plymouth, New Zealand, owned by Dr. James Richards who operates a sanitarium here. Don't worry, my health is fine. As a matter of fact, I'm feeling better than I have in a long time.

I've been helping construct houses for the sanitarium. Now, I'm building a house that overlooks the ocean. I sleep in my tent next to the project. Everyday, experienced builders give me pointers and then I do all the labor by myself. It's gratifying to see it all come together. There's a lot of time for thinking. With all the solitude, my emotions have settled down.

It may take me three or four months to build this house, even though it's not very big. I'm not very fast, but Dr. Jim says I'm doing a great job. The framework of the walls is nearly finished. Next I start on the trusses for the roof. When it's finished there will be a bedroom, kitchen, living room, and indoor bathroom. In the attic there will be a meditation room with a bay window overlooking the water—a great place for watching the sunset.

Please say Hi to Gage; and Cher, too, if you still see her.

In late September, Charlie stood admiring the red, yellow and violet spring flowers that polka-dotted the green grass around the house. Their brilliance seemed appropriate for his monument to Gwen.

One of his final tasks was to build a front porch. A perfect place to check out the surf, Charlie thought, as he braced two-by-sixes for the joists on the ground next to the front door.

When he'd first started building, he'd hit the surf every evening. But then he became so engrossed with the project that he worked until dark. Each evening he told himself, tomorrow I will surf. But when the next nightfall came, he was still dry.

This evening I'm surfing for sure, he pledged, whether I finish this porch or not!

The sound of a motorcar caught his attention. An Australian-made Holden, with surfboards strapped onto the roof-rack, pulled up to the house. Two young men, with long, sun-bleached blonde hair, got out.

"G'day, mate," the taller one said. "We're looking for a bloke named Charlie."

"You found him. How can I help you?"

"Dr. Jim said we could rack out with ya for a few days, if you don't mind."

Charlie's stomach felt like it turned upside down. Strangers? Staying here in Gwen's house?

"Well, I…I'm not quite finished with it yet."

"No worries, mate. We plan to give ya a hand. Beautiful place you've put together here."

"Thanks." Charlie looked over his project. *Shit*, he thought. "Well, I guess it wouldn't hurt if you helped with the porch."

"Good on ya, mate. Let us get some footgear and we'll be right on it."

The taller one did the talking.

Charlie noticed the thongs on their feet, as they went to their car. They also wore nylon surf trunks and T-shirts advertising Barry Bennett Surfboards.

"My name is Kevin," the taller one said when they returned, now wearing tennis shoes. "This here is Colin. We're from Brisbane, Queensland."

Charlie cocked his head. "Queensland?"

"That's in Australia, mate. Where are you from?"

"San Diego, California."

"Blimey, he's a bloody yank, Col," Kevin said, smiling. "We've been in San Diego before."

"Really? When was that?" Charlie said

"Nearly three years ago."

"No shit! Did you get some good waves?"

"I'll say. Especially Col, here. So what's next with the deck, mate?"

Charlie gave them building instructions, and soon the three were working as a team. Kevin measured and marked the boards, Colin sawed and Charlie nailed the structure together.

So they're from Australia, Charlie thought. *In San Diego nearly three years ago. When the World Contest was held?*

"Did you guys go to San Diego for the World Contest?

"Bloody oath, mate. We went to give it a try," Kevin said. "Colin here did pretty well. Surprised you haven't heard of him."

"If his name is Colin Robbins, I have."

"That would be his name," Kevin said, smiling.

Charlie was stunned. Finally he stuck out his hand.

"Congratulations, Colin."

Colin frowned as he shook Charlie's hand.

"It's been a while since the victory, mate."

Charlie shrugged his shoulders. "It sure has…"

And if I hadn't been drafted, he wanted to say. "I…I've just never met a world champion before."

"Have you been getting any good surf here at Dr. Jim's?" Kevin asked.

"Not lately. Been working too hard. But the break is pretty consistent. How did you meet Dr. Jim?"

"Col here, met him a few years back at Noosa Heads."

"Noosa Heads?"

"North of Brisbane," Colin said. "Some of the best surf in Aussie."

"All right! Hope to get over there sometime," Charlie said.

By early afternoon they'd finished the porch. Kevin leaned over the handrail and looked out toward the water.

"Charlie, what do you say the three of us do a little ridin'?"

"I'm a little rusty," Charlie said, hesitantly. He caught Colin's questioning glare. "But, what the heck, I did promise myself a surf this evening."

"Then let's have at 'em, mate," Kevin yelled, slapping Charlie on the back.

Charlie led the way down to the beach, but dawdled to watch Kevin and Colin surf, before paddling out himself. He wondered why he felt so nervous. *It's not like a contest or anything. It's just a session with a couple of new friends. I don't have to surf better than the world champ, do I?*

Even so, he took time to visualize surfing a couple of waves before paddling out. As he stroked through the swell, both Colin and Kevin rode waves in, leaving Charlie alone for an outside take-off.

He moved his board toward a great peak. After taking off, he faded into the curl and aggressively cut around in front of it. He walked to the nose and crouched down, getting completely covered up inside the tube for almost two seconds. When he popped out, he saw Colin paddling out—his mouth wide open.

Kevin, paddling behind Colin, yelled, "Whoooo! Good on ya, mate!"

Charlie ripped through the waves until darkness called a halt to their session. He joined the two Aussies waiting for him on the beach. All the way back up to the house Kevin talked about how Charlie surfed.

The famished surfers were joined by Dr. Jim; they all sat on the living room floor to dine on a large platter of fresh fish and bread. The room was silent.

"It must have been a mighty surf," Dr. Jim said, smiling at the others.

"That it was, mate," Kevin said. "You didn't tell us Charlie, here, was so smooth in the waves. He took them all apart."

Colin frowned, studying Charlie.

"He's a beaut out there, isn't he?" Dr. Jim said. "He's some sort of a champ himself, back in the States."

Finally, Colin said, "You never told us your last name, Charlie."

Charlie hesitated. "Armfield," he said, softly.

Colin nodded.

"Armfield? Hey, Col!" Kevin said. "Wasn't Charlie Armfield the bloke who was drafted into the army before the contest? The bloody U.S. Champ everyone talked about?"

Charlie focused on buttering his bread.

Colin nodded again.

"The bloke everyone said would have won."

Embarrassed, Charlie shrugged.

Dr. Jim smiled. "Well, what do you know?"

Charlie glanced sideways at Dr. Jim. Did he know about this? *Why you shifty...*

"Just thought it was time you two met, that's all, mate," Dr. Jim said to Charlie. "I reckon the best should always meet."

Charlie smiled and shook his head. "Yeah, but that's not me anymore."

"Don't know about that, mate," Kevin interjected. "The way you surfed out there this evening, you've still got it."

He looked over at Colin. "And the bloke said he was bloody rusty, too."

Colin and Charlie eyed each other for a moment in silence. Charlie felt almost apologetic toward Colin.

Finally, Colin spoke. "Say, mate, there's a contest over in New Plymouth this weekend..."

"No way!" Charlie interrupted. "I'm not doing that anymore."

Colin held up his hand. "Hear me out, mate. I'm only inviting ya to help out with the judging. I'm not even ridin' in this one, only refereeing."

The Taranaki Surfing Championships were held at Fitzroy Beach, New Plymouth, under clear skies in the warmth of a new season. A five-foot swell blessed the weekend with a consistent light wind blowing offshore from the south, keeping the surf up and smooth throughout the event.

Sunday afternoon, after the final heat, the contest emcee introduced the judges to the crowd.

"We have been honored this weekend to have an international judging panel. First, I would like to introduce a long-time favorite to this area, former Taranaki Champion, Dr. James Richards."

Dr. Jim stood up on the judge's platform to the crowd's applause. Charlie looked over at Dr. Jim, shaking his head.

"Champion? You never told me that," Charlie said, smiling.

"You never asked, mate. Besides, it was a long time ago."

The announcer continued. "We also have the honor of South African Champions, Mark Young and Shaun Hansen." They stood to acknowledge the gathering.

"From the United States, Charlie Armfield." Charlie stood briefly and waved his hand.

"And from Australia, Kevin Gates; and former World Champion, Colin Robbins."

The crowd cheered. Colin stood, folded his hands together, and raised them over his head. The ovation grew louder with Colin's gesture.

Charlie clapped quietly, trying to be polite. But he felt sad, sorry for himself. *That could have been me,* he thought. *No, it* would *have been me.*

"Now," the announcer began again, "I would like to invite the panel of judges to honor the people of New Plymouth with an exhibition meet."

Colin nodded approval, and the others conjoined—all except Charlie.

"You guys go ahead. I don't feel comfortable with this."

"Come on, mate," Colin pleaded.

"You knew this was going to happen, didn't you?" Charlie asked.

"Listen, mate," Kevin interjected. "Colin, here, has been speculating what would have happened for the past three years now. It's the least you…"

Charlie shook his head. "I'm just not into it, man."

"It's for fun, mate," Dr. Jim interrupted. "I'm going to give it a go."

But you guys don't understand, Charlie said to himself. *I just can't compete anymore. I just can't.*

He shuffled off the judge's platform.

The others paddled out for a forty-five minute match. Charlie sat by himself in the sand, staring at the water. It was a beautiful day. He really wanted to surf, but not competitively—never again, competitively.

He thought of Will, then thought he heard Will's voice, "You're one of the best surfers in the world, Charlie. You said you never got a chance to prove it. Well, here's your chance."

Will, is that you, man? I'm just not that competitive guy anymore. I can't get into the preparation that's needed.

There was no answer from Will, but rather a female voice whispered instead, *Come.* It was like the voice he'd heard at Grand Lake. *Come.*

Come? It almost sounded like Gwen. *Gwen, is that you?*

A dolphin appeared beyond the break.

Come.

Mesmerized, Charlie stood—and went for his board. He paddled out past the other surfers, searching for the dolphin.

Surf like a dolphin, Charlie. A smooth gray form surfaced, chattering in a high pitched sound, mixed intermittently with Gwen's voice.

Oh, Gwen, it is you.

You can do one more surf contest. I'll help you.

But, Gwen...

Okay, don't think of it as a contest. Just become close with the ocean, like a dolphin. You can be connected like you always wanted to be, Charlie. Just surf like me.

With a flip of its tail, the dolphin was gone.

Okay, Gwen, I'll do it, but not to win anything. I'll do it to surf like you.

Charlie paddled into the line-up with twenty minutes left in the heat.

"Glad you decided to join us, mate," Dr. Jim said.

"Me, too," Charlie said, stroking into the set of the day.

He dropped into a six-foot swell and cut unruffled squiggling turns that made colossal wakes into the face of the wave. Then, with a strong deliberate move, he came around on a right turn and swept back up the wave to a feathering section at the height of the surge. Charlie bounced off the lip and side-slipped on the rail of his board; the surfboard's fin was completely out of the water. He felt suspended, weightless on the wave.

Then, applying pressure with his back foot, he dug the skeg into the water and moved up into the slot, as the curl created his disappearing act. He was tubed in the tunnel for nearly five seconds before shooting out. He stalled his board to nearly a standstill within the action of the swell, then walked to the nose and hung ten, as his board sped across the wall. After a lengthy nose ride, he turned around, placed his heels over the nose, and walked back to the center of his board. He turned around again and glided up and out of the wave, standing easily on his plank as if it were a dock extending out from the beach.

Instead of his customary hoot after such a wave, he spoke quietly.

"Thank you, Gwen. That was the best wave of my life—like a dolphin would have had."

No trophies were awarded for the exhibition heat. No winner was announced. But when the emcee reintroduced each surfing judge as he emerged from the water, the crowd's loudest ovation was for Charlie. He was by far the best surfer of the day, and he knew it.

"Congratulations, mate," Colin said, holding out his hand.

"I didn't win anything, Colin."

"No, but the crowd indicated who gave the finest performance. I always wanted to prove to myself that I could have beaten you in San Diego. But, I guess I wouldn't have been able to do it."

"That question isn't meant to be answered." Charlie put his arm around Colin's shoulder. "You're the world champ because your victory was inevitable. My agenda wasn't in San Diego for the World Contest. I had other plans, Colin, and that doesn't take anything away from your success."

32

Charlie paced anxiously in Dr. Jim's outer office, impatient for his turn with the doctor. The house was finished. *What was next?* With Gwen gone and the memorial completed, he felt like he needed to move on. But where should he go? Colin and Kevin invited him to go to Australia with them and it sounded great, but...

"G'day, mate. Thought I might be seeing you this morning. Come on in to the adjusting room."

"I don't know if I need an adjustment today, but my mind needs some work."

Dr. Jim smiled, shutting the door behind them. He pointed toward the table.

"Have a seat, mate, and let me be the judge of that." He felt Charlie's neck and set the fifth cervical vertebra. "Lay on your right side."

Charlie lay on his side while Dr. Jim conformed the headpiece to accommodate Charlie's shoulders. The doctor stood by the side of the table and put the outer edge of his right palm on Charlie's first cervical vertebrae with a torque in the clockwise direction. He placed his left hand on top of his right.

Charlie lay quietly with his eyes shut, completely confident. Then a swift force impacted his neck. It didn't hurt, but it left him dazed. Slowly a light began to fill his cranium and stream down his spinal column. He opened his eyes and saw Dr. Jim smiling at him.

"Sit up, mate."

"Wow!" Charlie said. He sat up, shaking his head. "Feels like you just flipped on a toggle switch in my body. I feel like a new person."

"Right on, mate. Now what is it you wanted to talk to me about?"

"I…I was wondering if I should move on," Charlie stuttered. "But now I don't think so."

"No, I don't think so either. Seems like you have something else you need to do before you go."

"So, what is it?"

"Can't be sure, Charlie, but you brought it with you."

"I brought it with me?"

Dr. Jim nodded his head and opened the door. "You'll find it."

Charlie shook his head and shrugged his shoulders as he walked out. *Find what?* He turned back to question Dr. Jim, but the door was already shut. *What?*

Charlie shook his head as he walked down the road to the new house and sat on the porch looking at the surf. The waves were small, but maybe a session would help him figure out what it was that he needed to find.

Inside, he rummaged through his clothes piled in a box. Where the hell are my surf trunks? Then he remembered he'd hung them outside. *But I have an extra pair,* he thought. *Where are they?* Charlie spotted his pack. He opened it, grabbed at the spare suit, and saw his dad's journal.

He gasped. *Oh my God! Dad's journal?* He fidgeted with the cover until finally, he pulled the journal out.

Is this what I'm supposed to do? Read Dad's diary?

Charlie carried the book down to the beach. He plunked himself down into the granular silica and turned to the first page.

July 16, 1942

One of my professors suggested I keep a diary, a daily record of the things that happen and the thoughts connected with my work and studies. He thinks that the experience I am getting and the knowledge obtained will be invaluable to me in my life ministry. He says, "Put things down. Don't let them go a day or you'll forget them."

I have been working with social services during my summer breaks while attending seminary. The work is challenging, helping society deal with abuse. The problem is helping each man into a right relationship with God. It is a tremendous task. I shudder to think of attempting to do it alone; but when I think of doing it with God, it doesn't seem quite so formidable or hopeless.

A sound philosophy of life is essential for maintaining a smooth equilibrium, individually and as a nation in this time of war. How we use our understandings is critical for each one of us. When the world is at its worst, we all must be at our best. But how can I best serve?

My thoughts are torn between continuing school after seminary to obtain a Ph.D., and beginning my ministry. But how can I begin even that notion? With a church filled with worried parishioners? Or join the forces to serve as a chaplain? Or, it might be best to become a missionary and contribute to the elusive concept of world peace.

Oh dear God, please help that I might best hear my duties call.

I am not the only one facing difficulty. At supper this evening I sat with an ensign who is stationed in Boston for training. He has been in the Navy only two weeks. As he arose to leave, he remarked that, just as I was going to my quarters to study spiritual truths, he was going to his quarters to study the most effective ways of killing men.

He said he could not join the army because he could not aim a rifle at a man and snipe him off. A big gun on a boat is less personal. He will not feel quite so responsible. He couldn't and *wouldn't be a conscientious objector; but the whole idea of war sickens him and goes against all of his ideals and ideas about religion and metaphysics.*

I admire the ensign in some strange way, for he has been able to choose his direction; but I feel that he will still experience great pains. To be drafted and forced onto the battlefront would be worse, of course. Killing of any kind will be hard. I even feel the pains with just my country being involved.

The day is ended now. Darkness has closed in on this gray city. To some, darkness brings fear; to others, it brings protection. To some it means torment, to others coziness, while to others it means rest from labor. For some it means loneliness, for some revelry, and for others friendship close and dear, the intimacies of love and family. Greed, lust, and hate have taken their toll. The war presides over the earthly kingdom of finite men. The scourge of conflict among nations is hacking away at the roots of culture and civilization.

Dear God, guide us through this black night with its terror to the dawn of the day when night will no longer be fearful, but friendly.

Charlie closed the journal on his lap and lay back in the sand. The crystal blue sky was splotched with puffy white clouds. He saw his father's image and cried.

Oh Dad, how could I have been so afraid to read this? You understand; you always have. Maybe I wasn't ready. Maybe I needed to learn about pain first—about anger, fear, guilt, good, and grieving. Now I'm ready to read your diary, Daddy. I'm thinking that I'm really ready. You have been so important in helping me form my ideals. I'm so honored to have had you for my father.

He sat up and continued to read.

Heredity is important in the building of a man or character. Environment is important also, but the will is greater than both together. It seems you cannot predict how anyone will come out of a particular situation without a clear understanding of the person's volition.

Whoa! Charlie sat back and looked into the sky.

I'm not only reading this, I am talking with you, too, aren't I? Well then, how about you speak to me about pain? You told me, after Will died, that it could help me accomplish great things. I thought you were nuts when you said that, because I hated the pain.

He opened the journal at random and began to read again.

Suffering seems to be an essential and integral part of progress and also part of happiness. Little can be accomplished without sacrificing one experience in favor of another. Sometimes we don't understand why we choose the way that we do, especially when we must suffer; but it all seems to have some sort of order. Understanding the self seems to come about as we struggle through pain.

Charlie's heart pounded. He felt as if he were conversing directly with his father.

You know, Dad, I don't think we're supposed to kill each other, even in the time of war, but I just didn't know what to do. Now, after the fact, I'm trying to understand myself. It's so hard.

I just returned from seeing the motion picture, Mrs. Miniver. *It left me distressed, mentally and emotionally. The picture was excellent, portraying a portion of the life of one family in a small English village during the early part of their war. But now it is our war, as well. Seeing this picture upsets one's apple cart of emotion; spills them all out on the sidewalk. Just when one's intellect gets them picked up and in the cart again, another disturbance occurs. Once more, the order becomes chaotic. Multiplicity, self-contradiction, conflicting feelings and thoughts replace the precarious unity, which was balanced on top of the heap.*

What will be my role in the war? I've heard all the arguments, but

I'm restless. I suppose these feelings are nothing compared to feelings experienced by those who end up doing the fighting in the war.

"This above all—to thine own self be true, and it follows as surely doth the night and the day, that thou canst not be false to any man."

Oh Lord, please help me to understand the workings of man in his wars; and most of all, help those who have to participate to feel secure with their homecoming.

You know I didn't get a homecoming, Dad. You saw those demonstrators. I didn't want to do what I did, and then I found out some of my own countrymen didn't even want me to do it, either. What is the deal with war, anyway? I know you were hoping that World War II would be the last, but it just keeps happening over and over again. Why can't we learn?

Today I read from one of my favorite mentors, E. Stanley Jones, on the competitive system and the sins it causes men to commit. One of these sins is war, which results in and includes within it a multitude of other sins. Stanley condemns and repudiates war and all that he says about it is true.

But when man continues to have different attitudes without practicing diversity, there can only be conflict. Then when threatening aggression is announced, there leaves little choice except to fight within the present situation.

That's it! Countries don't respect each other for their differences. And the South Vietnamese must be the most confused of all. They didn't seem to have a clue about what was happening. The NVA told them the Americans were trying to take over, and the Americans said the NVA was trying to take over.

Charlie shook his head. He closed his dad's journal and walked back to the house.

Later that night, he sat on the floor and thought about what he wanted to ask his father.

You know, Dad, ever since I went to Vietnam, I seem to have lost track of the time. I never knew what day it was over there, and now I'm traveling around and it goes so fast. Things have been happening for me, though, and it seems it's all according to my being ready for it to happen.

The newsreel in the movie this evening placed time as the most important and precious thing there is when the nation is at war. On the battlefront, life becomes bizarre and cheap. Seconds determine life and death. Even in a non-war period, time is important.

But how to use it wisely is determined by what we're ready to use it for. We can try to allocate time for this and for that, but until we are ready, we rarely have accomplishments. But when I am ready, I know I will make effective use of it so as to build solidly a plus sign for God.

Yeah, a plus sign for God. That's what I want to do, too. But I want to do it differently. You tried to bring the church into my life, Dad, but I found it hard to stay directed. Christianity seems so restrictive. I don't know if my recent discoveries could have been accomplished within its structure. But, can I work with God without being a minister?

This particular morning I have been using E. Stanley Jones' Abundant Living *as my devotional guide. He wrote, "Higher than the mists of midnight, Augustine found his sky again and higher than the mists of midnight built the city of God with towers that touch the stars."*

We seem to have lost our sky in this civilization of ours and as the artist said to Jones, "I can paint good pictures if I can get the sky right."

It is natural to have a God who gives purpose to the Universe and to us. It is in harmony with the nature of the Universe to live moral lives. Human beings have lost their sky and have become out of harmony with the natural order, with or without Christianity. We are trying to solve the problem and ease our predicament by substituting chaos for chaos.

God is the unifying principle and purpose, which must run through our own lives and through the world, regardless of religious affiliation. It is the duty of every human being in this Universe to be with God in their work. He is the one unifying and consistent aspect that can neutralize the chaos.

That's what Dr. Jim does. He is truly a disciple of God, and he's a chiropractor. Sometimes I even hear your voice when he speaks, Daddy. He's helping with the chaos. And Gwen was, too.

Charlie thought about Gwen. What a beautiful angel she had been.

Without Gwen and Dr. Jim, I would still be a mess, Dad. Now, they think I would be a good doctor. I would like to help people. Did I go to Vietnam in order to witness the worst, so that later on I could help people bring out the best within themselves?

The tide of purpose is running through my life giving it unity, even though I do not always recognize it. Sometimes I feel as if I am jarred out of emotional and intellectual distress by some Universal force, in order to keep within the realm of my intentions. I think all events have some sort of reasoning behind them. The directions we choose help us with the purpose we need to fulfill within our lives.

Okay, I can accept that now. But you didn't go to war. I have a minister friend who went because he wanted to help the soldiers. Why did you decide not to go?

I heard the news over the radio of the bombing of Pearl Harbor and the official start of U.S. participation in the war. For me it seems a short time in which much has happened, but I wonder what it seems for some who have had drastic changes, separations, and suffering. I saw Andrew Griffith go forth to war. I saw him return a year later with his body shot up. Perhaps I can do a job that a chaplain cannot, but at times I desire to get into the chaplaincy.

Was I wrong not to pursue the Navy further? Should I try the army? It would be the path of least resistance—that is certain. "No," comes rebounding back as the answer, but I am not sure that even now, swamped as I am, I am functioning to the best of my ability in the most important services I can render. Should I stay and try to raise the consciousness of the glory of God and the advancement of His kingdom? "Yes," is the answer that comes.

I thought the Vietnam War was the worst thing that could have ever happened to me. How could I get involved with such mayhem? Now I believe everything happens within a natural order of what has to happen.

This is one of those beautiful mornings. There is a blue sky with the sun shining brightly. I have had a good night's sleep and now it seems for the moment that "God is in His heaven and all's right with the world." Now I know that God is in his heaven and his earth, but all is not right with the world.

If I should stop and intellectually examine all the logical contradictions in my beliefs and actions, it would astound me! All is not right in a world of war. Therefore, there is a principle of evil. When I pray to God in my public prayers, I often use the expression "Infinite God." Yet, it seems God must be limited.

The limitation is either external or internal of God. If it is external, why doesn't God remove the evil? God's moral character is called into question if there is said evil and if God can remove it and doesn't. This applies whether the evil is in the form of a person known as the devil or some other type of limitation or principle. The question still remains; "Why doesn't God kill the devil?" If God is a moral and just God, the reason there is said evil is because he can't prevent it. Then God is limited. However, any logic we use is within the limitations of our human intellects and bodies.

Is it possible that additional data exists, which we have not yet discovered or cannot discover because of our limitations? Perhaps there is no such thing as evil. Could it be that everyday occurrences, be they seemingly good or evil, happen with design and with purpose? Sometimes it seems impossible, and it might be true. God is good, he is moral, and he is great. While we cannot know God's purposes, we can presume his goals are moral and good.

Wow, Dad! That was incredible. I think love is the key to the Universe. Not just personal love, but love for everything that exists. But sometimes it is so hard. How can I love war? I want to think that there is only love, but then I remember shooting somebody in the face. Maybe I'm not as changed as I think.

A few minutes with E. Stanley Jones this morning has given me an amazing new, or rather, different insight. He states in a unique way certain truths that I long to express in words, but more than in words—in life itself. "Throw your will on the side of outgoing love, and all the healing resources of the universe will be behind you."

Since coming to love Louise, I have come to appreciate the meaning of love. Therefore I can appreciate more fully the sorrow of those whose loved ones go astray or are taken from them. Likewise, I can appreciate God's love toward us more fully. If God is love, then we must cause him considerable distress by our erring ways. I feel, like Augustine, that the life of God pursued me until I began to reciprocate a little bit.

"O Thou who art always reaching out after me in love and awakening me, help me this day to do the same. Help me to quicken and awaken some life by the touch of my friendliness and love. Here is something I need not be afraid of—I cannot be too loving. Help me. Amen."

Last night I led a prayer meeting. The brief message which I delivered, was very vital to me. Religion will not go further until it goes deeper. The Holy Spirit must not only be with us, but also within us. Many have queered this concept for us, so we have stayed clear of it. But Christianity, or any religion or conceptual interpretation of Universal Life, becomes a mere set of moral and ethical principles without it. God is within and throughout all things. God is love.

Charlie put the journal down and walked out onto the porch. The night was crisp, the sky clustered with stars. The brightness of the full moon made his eyes squint.

There is only love, Dad. You knew it all of the time. I wonder why we never talked about it while you were alive. Charlie shook his head and stared at the stars.

We've sure had a great conversation now, though. One of the most revealing I've ever had with you. How strange, too, that your diary ends before I was born. Do you think everything we say or do is in the Universal experience forever, and can be retrieved for review at any time? Does everything have purpose? I know your writings were primarily for you, but could the Universe also have had them in mind for me as well?

Charlie sensed the answer: *Yes, yes, and yes, my son.*

"Hello?" A warm sensation filled Charlie's body when he heard his mom's voice on the phone.

"Hi, Mom."

"Charlie, is that you?"

"Yes, it's me, all right. I'm in the Auckland Airport. I'm flying home, Mom."

"Oh, darling, that's wonderful. When are you arriving?"

Charlie laughed. "According to my itinerary, I should be home already. New Zealand is nineteen hours ahead of San Diego. Anyway, I guess by your time, I'll be home tomorrow morning at eleven."

"I'm so looking forward to seeing you, Son."

"Mom, I finally had that talk with Dad."

"What do you mean?"

"It was finally time for me to read the journal."

After Charlie said goodbye to his mom, he and Dr. Jim strolled through the airport toward his gate.

"How can I thank you enough for everything?" Charlie asked.

"You just go home and do what you have to do, mate, whatever that is. You'll be great and that's all I could ever ask for."

They walked by a young girl listening to a transistor radio.

"Hey, mate, listen to that song."

Charlie perked up his ears to hear part of a verse.

...And a time to every purpose under heaven.

He looked over at Dr. Jim.

"Have a seat, mate and let's listen. It's by the Byrds."

> *A time to be born, a time to die*
> *A time to plant, a time to reap*
> *A time to kill, a time to heal*
> *A time to laugh, a time to weep*
> *To everything, turn, turn, turn,*
> *There is a season, turn, turn, turn,*
> *And a time to every purpose under heaven.*

Charlie thought about his experience in New Zealand. When he'd first arrived, he was ready to hurl himself off of the cliff at Piha. Then, with the help from Dr. Jim and Gwen, he discovered that there was a time to heal. He discovered that pain was okay, and then came to understand his anger. He learned why he was never afraid in combat. After working through his guilt, he actually found some good in his war experience. Then, finally, he learned how to grieve and understand that all people have agendas, and those agendas have their own time for a transition with death.

> *A time of love, a time of hate*
> *A time of war, a time of peace*

Everything happens because of a natural flow, Charlie thought. *That includes a war that erupts between people that don't understand each other. And also, it includes the reason why non-interested people get drafted to fight for an unknown cause. Everything has purpose—reason.*

> *To everything, turn, turn, turn,*
> *There is a season, turn, turn, turn,*
> *And a time to every purpose under heaven.'*

Charlie thought about his blood brother, Will. He saw the bloodied face of Bill MaGuire and the greenback lieutenant. Al Strangemeir and all the soldiers on gun number five came to him next. He heard his daddy telling him it wasn't his time yet and saw Rick's body floating out to sea on his surfboard. Then, he saw the twenty-seven NVA soldiers that he had killed. He still didn't understand how God chose who should die when, but did understand that there were "Angels in Vietnam," and his were not yet ready to take him home.

A time for peace, I swear it's not too late.

Thank you God for letting me find my way out of the hell I knew as Vietnam. Charlie sighed. *Thank you also, for my experience in Vietnam.*

About the Author

John Wesley Fisher was born in Boston, 1947, and raised in San Diego. He graduated from Point Loma High School, 1965, and was drafted into the Army in 1967. He served with the Fourth Infantry Division, 1968-1969, and later traveled extensively around the world. Upon his return and after pre-medical studies, he entered Palmer College of Chiropractic in Davenport, Iowa, graduated magna cum laude in 1977, and founded the Foothills Chiropractic Health Center in Golden, Colorado. *Angels in Vietnam* is his first novel.

Unlike the rapid rehabilitation of Charlie (main character) the author spent many years trying to understand his role in war. He worked with many techniques and received help from several professionals and friends along the way. He gives thanks to all involved and hopes that his understandings have been demonstrated comprehensively in this book. Pain, anger, fear, guilt, understanding purpose, finding good, and grieving are viable concepts that are suffered with post traumatic stress disorder (PTSD.) They may never go away, but they can be understood and neutralized so that the negative implications cease.

Special regards to the One Foundation and the technique it supports with research, Neuro Emotional Technique. The author is an advocate of the technique and utilizes it at his health center to treat PTSD and other health concerns. The author also wishes to recognize Dr. Ed Tick, author of *War and the Soul* and director of Soldier's Heart and Charles Wesley Fisher, his father.

LaVergne, TN USA
07 May 2010
181863LV00004B/1/P